THE
JOURNEY HOMEWARD

Prabhu, the new maharajah of the mountain state of Jashimpur, has just returned home with his wife and two young sons after a long stay in England. He means to rule well, and raise his people from their economic and moral degradation by a system of up-to-date reforms. Unfortunately his ideas have little appeal or meaning for a people formed by a past which has left them passive, sceptical, cowardly and vastly amused by their own shortcomings. Unfortunately also, Prabhu, like his wife Lila and his brother Prem, have acquired, along with their Western notions, the habit of drink as a refuge from unwelcome reality : Lila in particular, who, feeling herself English, hates her brown skin yet cannot square her life either with her Christian upbringing or her love affair with an English soldier. But if Prabhu fails, so does his chief adversary, Hassan, because he too was formed by the West—in his case America—and though he mocks at Prabhu's idealism and will settle for nothing less than revolution by violence, the people, by nature, fearful of violence, in turn mock at him. Only Hari Lal, shrewdly rooted in the ancient Indian instinct for self-denial, seems able to point the way towards which power must lead . . .

Gerald Hanley

THE JOURNEY HOMEWARD

COLLINS
ST JAMES'S PLACE, LONDON
1961

© GERALD HANLEY, 1961
PRINTED IN GREAT BRITAIN
COLLINS CLEAR-TYPE PRESS: LONDON AND GLASGOW

To
Pyara Lal Aggarwal
with love

" Tir mharbh tir gan tighearna "
A land without a lord is a dead land
(an old saying)

Chapter One

Jashimpur had been invaded so often in the past that a long period of peaceful semi-slavery, even in steadily increasing poverty, had been welcomed by the Jashimpuri people, until the cold winds of reason began to blow into the valleys after the first world war. That war, which broke the ageing back of the old world, brought the first agitators from India. These were swiftly arrested, locked up, documented, and then sent back into the world of Gandhi in British India, and a policed peace descended again on Jashimpur. But what the agitators had said was remembered. They said there was no need for men to suffer in poverty and hunger in a land of plenty, and that men who grew fruit and vegetables for sale so that they could pay their taxes, and lived in rags, on a little rice themselves, were slaves. " This is a police-country," they said, " and it is your own fault for bearing it. How long will you go on carrying the name of timorous creatures ? You are famed for your docility and your cowardice." This was still being discussed when the second world war began.

The Jashimpuris had been enslaved by one invader or another for about three hundred years. The worst time, still spoken of in story, was the occupation by the tribesmen from the north. That period was known as " The Time of the Sore Back." In that time the tribesmen had looted Jashimpur down to its skin, and the tribesmen had walked the streets of the city and the villages, proud with swords and daggers, and if a tribesman felt tired he simply leaped on to the back of the nearest Jashimpuri and said, "The master is tired.

Carry him home, slave." This had gone on for years, and the story-tellers would describe how the streets were full of Jashimpuris carrying tribesmen on their backs. " It is different now, of course," the old story-tellers would say. " Now we are still ridden, but from afar, by the tax-collector, the invisible rider with the ledger in the office, but our heaviest rider is ourselves, our loving sorrow in our slavery about which we do nothing, for Gandhi's strangers were right. We love our slavery." It became custom for the story-tellers to work in words about the slavery of the people to-day, and it had its effect. The young men who still had patience to listen to the story-tellers would become heated and would object strongly to the acceptant note, and the story-teller would nod and say, in the Jashimpuri way, " Yes, I know how you feel. It is a humiliating thing to be a slave. But you will get used to it."

The only hero of the people in the time of the tribesmen's occupation was one Hussein Beg, a coolie of great strength. One day Hussein Beg was going about his business as a conquered slave and was walking at the time near the precipice on the edge of Jashimpur town along which the motor road to India was built two centuries later. Tradition said that " on that day, walking in that place, he was ready for his death, being very weary of his slavery, but he had no weapons, for no Jashimpuri was allowed even to carry a stick." A tired master, a tribesman, happened to be nearby as Hussein Beg was passing and he leaped on to the big coolie's back and said, " The Master is tired, slave. Carry him home." Here, the story-teller usually looked round his circle of listeners and would say, " Hussein Beg had all the virtues so well thought of by a master, even to-day, the ready cheerful smile and the willing heart, and he said, ' Master, we shall go home together and Hussein Beg shall carry you there, into hell,' and instead of trotting along the road into the city he galloped towards the precipice." All the passers-by, most of them Jashimpuris with conquerors on their backs, stood in their tracks when they heard the wild screams of Hussein Beg's rider, who was struggling to free himself from the powerful arms of Hussein which gripped his legs like iron clamps.

"Free me. Free me and I'll give you a house and a sword and honour," the terrified rider was screaming, but Hussein Beg, who was ready that day, shouted, "No, we shall go home, Master," and leaped. They went sailing over the precipice, slave and rider, and that was how Hussein Beg became a hero, for riders were very few after that, except in the streets of the city, which were without precipices.

To-day, Hassan, the leader of the movement for freedom, was trying to discourage the telling of this story, for he said it had helped to begin the Jashimpuri pride in being able to bear any indignity, and that it was a defeatist and shameful act to hold in pride. He gave fifty rupees to a poet to write a song about the shaking off of chains and the picking up of a sword. "We must arise out of the mud and filth of our sickening history," he told the people. "And the people must cease sneering and laughing at themselves, for it is this kind of laughter which is our greatest enemy." The people had a humour of their own in which they belittled themselves with a kind of clowning irony, an exaggeration of all the failings and vices which were claimed for them by those who were not of them, for even as far south as Ceylon you could find a man who would tell you that the Jashimpuris were cowardly, dirty, lazy, lying, but never were they called stupid. It was said that they were almost as subtle as Kashmiris.

Jashimpur was as beautiful as Kashmir, though smaller, and like Kashmir it was ringed with high mountains where the bright sun blazed on enormous snowfields and set up a quivering pearly light which the Brahmins called "Lord Shiva's Crown." The Mohammedans made up the majority and they never sought to deny that that wonderful light from the snowfields was Lord Shiva's crown. Hate between Hindus and Mohammedans had never arisen in Jashimpur, and what

bigotry there was showed itself in irony and comedy. For
instance, a Hindu Pandit, clever or not, and they were usually
clever, was always called, because of his pride, "God's mistaken
clerk" by the Mohammedans, and a Mohammedan *Mullah*
went by the name of " The Teacher of Illiteracy " among the
Hindus, for hardly any of the *Mullahs* could read the Koran
in Arabic, in which sacred language God's revelations to
Mohammed were happiest. It was no use trying to raise a
religious riot by ringing a bell outside a Mohammedan mosque,
or reciting a *sura* from the Koran on the steps of a Hindu
temple, for the onlookers would have clapped, and shouted
a well-known Jashimpuri saying, " God is deaf to-day for
the unworthy are at prayer."

It was said that a Jashimpuri would sell his mother for a
chillum full of tobacco for his *hukkah*, which was a libel, for
the family feeling of the people was so deep that if a peasant
was emigrating to India a farewell party of sorrow was held
for him, a wake for his lost person, and prayer was offered up
monthly for his return from the blazing oven of India's plains.
They seldom returned. They were consumed in the Indian
fire, lost to Jashimpur.

It was true that they were all slaves of tobacco, and they
worked in the fields with a little boy nearby to attend to the
hukkahs with their water-bulbs and short bamboo mouth-
pieces. They smoked fiercely, as if each smoke were their last,
for they were often hungry and there is no pacifier for the
whining belly like a chestful of tobacco smoke, on which all
are agreed. Each being had as his body-image a skeleton, a
starved man who had hunted down and stolen the final lost
grain of rice from the rat and then, after nibbling it, sat still
and resigned to die, for famine was a kind of weather which
might come at unexpected times, yet was always expected.
Death by disease, and, less often now, by hunger, was always
sitting waiting in the mind of the Jashimpuri peasant and was
known as " Our Thin Brother." When the earth-tremors

came and the population ran, unthinkingly and screeching, into the open at the first tremor, they always said it was "Thin Brother" who in his impatience, without famine and cholera to feed him, was hurrying things.

Beneath the grave faces of the Jashimpuris lay ready and electric hysteria, for they were trained children of the earthquake zones whose awareness is never unaware and for whom earth can never be solid and firm. They all had a great reverence for health and good looks and fortune, knowing that God wanted all men to do well, but created a continual mystery of why so many never did well and were spent, young and unwilling but resigned. There was some curse on the Jashimpuri race, it was said. The word from Hassan and the young men these days was that there was only one curse on Jashimpur and this was the established order who had lived on the people's blood and sweat and who did not know that their time was coming to an end, and soon. Terrifying sort of talk, for the one thing the Jashimpuris wanted was what Hassan promised them; freedom, but their fear was that he and the young men would make them fight for it, and all the Jashimpuris hated and feared trouble. Trouble was when a man was singled out by an official, in front of everyone, and asked, "Did you say *this*? Did you say you are not contented?" Police spies were everywhere. Your own brother might be drawing ten rupees a month for reporting on thoughts spoken aloud in the village during the month. The police knew all about Hassan and the young men. The gaols were full of the new kind of young men, the young men in Western trousers and shirts, and usually wearing the new horn-rimmed spectacles, blinded as they were with their reading of the papers and documents and books of revolt and sedition.

After the famous book, *With Bible and Notebook through the Filth of Jashimpur*, by Colonel Harry Wugg, an attack on everything Jashimpuri, which came out in 1892, the Maharajah had discouraged foreign visitors in Jashimpur. Colonel Wugg, a happy and sinful diehard gone religious and liberal, with a mania about dirt and sloth, had intended to write a heart-rending and touching picture of a people steeped in super-stition and misery, a people whom he had tried to like, but his heart and his training overcame him in the writing and he produced the raving attack on the Jashimpuris which became famous in its day. After the second war Hassan had most of it printed in Urdu and distributed in Jashimpur, with a fore-word of his own saying, " Read about yourselves. Can we deny it ? Have we changed ? It is 1945 and we are the same slaves as described by the mad but observant Sahib." The police hunted the villages of Jashimpur and burned every copy they seized, mainly because of what Colonel Wugg had had to say about the ruling family as well as for statements such as, " It would be better to commit suicide rather than live as a Jashimpuri, though they have not the courage even for this. During my time among this vile and characterless people I thanked God again and again for being an English-man. To be born a Jashimpuri is some form of punishment. There is a curse on the race." Many pages dealt with what the colonel called " the nameless vices which maim an already sickened spirit," and " one feels among them the presence of the devil himself." Through the work ran a kind of puzzled and grudging admiration for the stoicism of the Jashimpuris, but which enraged the colonel as well, for, as he said, " If you strike one of them, he kneels down and cries. What is one to do with such people ? " The real reason for this colonel's bitterness was that, having gone into Jashimpur to preach during a famine, he got what he wanted, converts, by the thousand. Whole villages had claimed to accept the new religion, on the orders of the chief *Mullah*, until the colonel's rice stocks had given out. He had spent thousands of pounds of his own private fortune on importing rice from India. When the famine was over he found there were no more

Christians. He had had no religious training but was a sincere man who had discovered religion late in life and had gone a little mad with it. He came away from Jashimpur embittered and sickened, for they had used him cynically, and he could not know that he was remembered in the folklore as " the Sahib whose blood we ate in starvation time in God's name," for they did have a deep sense of shame but had learned not to show it. Life was a battle without mercy and a man took what he could, especially from a fool.

The reprinting in Urdu of the Englishman's ravings had had an immediate effect in the villages, where it was read out by the rare literates. The response was one of anger not quite as well hidden by ironic comment as usual, for all were stung by some of the deadly truths written in the past by the Colonel Sahib. The younger men went about snarling and denying and threatening, and found Hassan's recruiting agents ready to sign them up as revolutionaries, which was as exciting as it was terrifying, but the underground movement swelled.

In nearly all the villages men were enlisted for " the day of trial." When Hassan was arrested and locked deep in an underground cell of the prison in Jashimpur, city men went about in the villages bewailing the loss of the leader, but most of them were deeply relieved. There was a firm hope that in some magic way freedom could come of itself, without requiring struggle or " trouble," but Hassan's lieutenants killed this hope with their sneers. All Jashimpuris understood each other. In the end, as usual, they laughed and jeered at their own cowardice. " The Maharajahs cannot be blamed for trampling on us," they told each other, " for we are a rotten lot, just as that Sahib said of us. We do not deserve freedom." They wanted to hide and find freedom ready for them when they came out again.

" But you are going to fight for it all the same," the grim educated young men told them. " When the time comes we shall deal with the cowards once and for all."

When the Maharajah's son, Prem, came back from the war people passed on the news that he looked like one of themselves, gaunt, pale, hungry. And he was a bottle-lover with a shaky hand. " He will never rule," it was said. " And there is only the other one who ran off and married one not of his kind and who is eating beef openly in London." To eat beef openly was to be a part of the freedom one day to be obtained for them by the young men in the horn-rimmed glasses. Mohammedan and Hindu ate beef secretly, for the killing of the cow, sacred to Hindus, had been punished by death, but now in more enlightened days the punishment was only five years' imprisonment. The young men liked to go to a cow and slap it on the back and say to it, " One day, friend, you will be just so much steak walking about as in other lands and we will eat you openly," and the villagers would laugh and say, " By God, yes ! That time will come, cow, when Mohammedan and Hindu will be hypocrites no more."

When the old Maharajah died the rich Hindus made great ceremonial as for a lost friend, for he had not been a cruel man, only a frightened and distracted one. He had never been unfaithful to the landowners, had never been softened by his fear and pandered to the spirit of irreverence and avarice which had grown among the poor. The landowners had wanted Prem, soft and pliable and shattered by the Japanese prison camp and whisky, as their new ruler. He had hardly been sober since his return. He had returned in uniform, drunk, and had lain in his bed staring at the ceiling for over a month. He would have been perfect as a ruler, the wise landowners said, but the old Maharajah's dying wish was that Prabhu should come from London to rule, " for Prem will die soon," he said. And Prem refused to rule anyway.

Whoever ruled, it was known to all that the new India would never allow the good old days to continue, that Sardar Vallabhai Patel, a power in far Delhi, would have his way about the 592 princely states, of which Jashimpur was one of the smallest and most backward. From every direction the freezing winds of change were blowing.

As soon as the old Maharajah died the revolution began, quietly and, like a squirrel peeping nervously out of a tree, began to gain courage.

"No more taxes to be paid. No more free labour to be given. No more rice to be surrendered," the young men ordered the villages. It was the order and the frightened police began to lash out all about them, but the peasants were stubborn, hopeful that a miracle would soon come so that they would not have to face the storm.

When the news was carried from village to village across the country that the new Maharajah from London would free Hassan from prison, the people were stunned, and then they celebrated. The young men said the Maharajah would free Hassan out of fear, but it was obvious from other tales that this young Maharajah was strange enough to have done it without fear. The only secrets, it had always been said in Jashimpur, are to be found in the occasional grave, and it was soon known that the landowners hated their new Maharajah, for he wanted to punish them for their riches. He was mad, and the people pitied him from afar, for there was nothing so sad as a rich man who gave his substance away in madness. Better to have it taken by force than to give it, to be the fool of distorted senses of right and wrong. An eccentric was always safe in Jashimpur, and as the stories about the new Maharajah leaked from the palace and were carried, swelling on the way, across Jashimpur, the people warmed to him and the young men preached more desperately against all Maharajahs. The intellectual young men knew that what Hassan said was true, that the peasants, if they were given justice and the giver was a Maharajah, would be happy, for they could not deny their ancient longing to give loyalty to a ruling family, especially if they could love it. They were traditionalists to their marrow, even in starvation. "So fight," Hassan told his

B

young men. He was wise, Hassan, knowing that enormous numbers of peasants could not feel as he did, and that they had an ancient longing for a just king, if such a being existed.

Arms were being secretly supplied to the new militia squads who were drilling in the countryside near the villages. The arms were few but more were promised. The dagger would be a better weapon for it would require the timid peasants to go close to their enemies and make a true gesture of courage and hatred. Many arguments went on among the young men about the meaning of courage and cowardice, for these young men were as nervous as the illiterates but were buoyed up by borrowed fragments of reasoning and philosophy.

The landowners were sniffing the air and could scent the new atmosphere. They began to admonish, to warn, and to flog. Many got into their big cars and drove to Jashimpur City, where they could discuss the new dangers with their fellows and try and solve the problem of this maniac who had become the new Maharajah.

Chapter Two

Miss Bullen would never have come to Jashimpur at all had
it not been for the the failure of a love affair. Not *her* failure.
Not *her* love affair. But a man had loved her and because of
that her life had become almost impossible at the mission
down on the plains of India. Her superior, who distrusted
love in the young, caused her to break off all contact with
the young cavalry officer who had begun to take an unusual
interest, for a soldier, in the life of an Indian mission. Rather
relieved, but resentful, Miss Bullen had accepted her transfer
to far away Jashimpur. For information she read *With Bible
and Notebook through the Filth of Jashimpur* by Colonel Harry
Wugg, and saw that where she was going was the greatest
test she and her missionary faith could find.

That was nearly forty years ago, but she still wondered
what had happened to that young officer. What kind of
woman had he married, what children had he fathered, what
would her own children have been like had she had them by
that young officer, and had God truly intended her narrow
superior to cause her to go to Jashimpur and to forget the
curious stirrings which the young man's interest in her had
awakened ?

Now, at sixty-seven, unable to read the Bible any more
with the burning joy she had always felt, she thought perhaps
it might be old age which more and more turned her thoughts
into bitter, self-pitying scenes of drama. Had she, she wondered, wasted her life ?

When you reach the end of the Salak road out of Jashimpur

you have travelled just over one hundred miles from the
capital. From there pony tracks lead into the mountains, the
most worn of them, and the safest, leading to the little town
of Kangla, where the Mongol eyes appear and where the
Tibetan traders shout " *Julli* " in happy greeting to each other
after the ordeal of the high passes with overburdened mules.
It was at Kangla that Miss Bullen opened her mission outpost
as a girl of twenty-eight, a small, determined, intelligent,
God-loving girl who knew that she had been chosen to bring
the light of her Christ among these poor heathens of the
Jashimpuri mountains.

In nearly forty years she had made three converts. Only
prayer helped her to bear this pain, this particular pain of
what seemed to be a wasted life. Yet better those three converts given up so grudgingly by the otherwise unyielding
Jashimpuri world of sloth and narrowness, than three thousand
rice Christians baptised in an Indian river far south in one
day in the name of Christ, instead of in the name of the Belly.
For she knew how great a master was the Belly. She had
trained her own belly to be quiet on one meal a day, but
lately she found she could not live on this meagre diet which
had so sustained her energies during forty years in the mountains. She had begun to smoke, too, though in the greatest
secrecy, using a fan in her right hand to agitate the air in her
room, all the windows open, and in the tensest state lest she
be discovered. Not that the Jashimpuris would mind. They
would laugh and be pleased to hear that she was like them,
weak, two-faced, pathetic, which was why they must never
know. Her tastes in reading and music had changed too.
Guiltily, she enjoyed the vulgar comedians and singers on the
radio. Also, she had begun to lose her faith, and it was this
which brought her to her knees each night in supplication to
God, who was slipping from her, withdrawing from her
view, assuring her that He did not exist and that she did not
believe in Him.

What had done this? What had weakened her will? What had opened this chasm before her eyes, a chasm of loneliness which made her afraid of death for the first time in her life? Old age? No, it was not that. Old age had been hurried by the curious frightening process of her loss of faith. Or had she always doubted her religion but never listened to herself? Was that it? Had she been intended for mission work, or had it all been a mistake, a mistake which could never be put right, for her life was nearly over and she could never have it again. There was no one to whom she could talk. There was only Lila, to whom she had written so many of her thoughts and who had now come back from England as Maharani of Jashimpur. It was in explaining to Lila so often in her letters, in reply to ironical questions about God, that she had watched herself penning answers to her own doubts, had understood that her faith was trying to die in her.

She had many enemies all about her in this isolated place. There were the old *Mullahs* of the Muslim community near the mission who had fought a long, tireless battle with her. Agreed there was Jesus, and there was Mary, and there was the Angel Gabriel; Mohammed the prophet had said there were those. Agreed there was Adam and there was Eve. Agreed they, the *Mullahs*, and she, Miss Sahib Bullen, were what she liked to call "People of The Book," and, as she often said, "We are all children of Adam. Why then not accept the religion of Christ?" Agreed that Christ was a prophet (" But a minor mistaken one," they always whispered under their breaths) but that did not mean, none of that meant, that she had the right to ensnare Muslims into her fold. She was a good woman in many ways and had a fine medicine chest, spoke good Urdu and fair Jashimpuri, and they had no objection to her living her strange life up here in these hills, so long as she left the souls of the Muslims to their rightful owner, God, whose prophet was Mohammed (*not* Christ, they meant, and whispered under their breaths).

It was the *Mullahs* who, in a time of starvation and flood disaster and knowing that she had a real influence over the people, had forbidden them to take the dried milk-powder from Miss Bullen, the milk-powder she had worked so hard to get from Indian mission friends a thousand miles south of Jashimpur. " It is the dried milk of pigs," the *Mullahs* told the people. " Dried by Christians and sent up here disguised as cow's milk, and intended to break your religion. Once you have eaten that foul *haran* milk you are sold to the Christians for ever. Cast it away from you. God will provide."

They had found a hundred ways to make her life difficult, at times unbearable, and she had suffered it all for God, but she was convinced that one day these people would accept Christianity which would change their whole miserable life.

A fanatic herself, from childhood in Belfast, she could understand their dour determined will to fight her religion. All her life she had fought Papacy in her mind, in her reading, in her daily life, for the grip of the Pope was the thing to be feared above all else, as each year in childhood the savage throbbing Lambeg drums of Northern Orange Ireland had reminded. Since her ancestors had kicked James's crown into the Boyne there had been each year a grim, happy savage celebration of the wreck of the Papist plans for the chaining up of the sturdy Protestant soul for ever. The fanaticism of the *Mullahs* reminded her of her own, a fanaticism now strangely melting into doubts and fears and worries. There was no way of knowing what had begun this itch of doubt, or when it had begun, yet she felt it had been with her always, since childhood. One night she had been sitting on a creepie near the fire on her uncle's farm out in the country, listening to the men talking about "Home Rule" and " Rome Rule," and laughing, and she could remember even then thinking it strange and useless that men should hate other men because they had a different religion. But she had found later that it was all tied up with the ownership of land, as well as of God, and up here the *Mullahs* feared that Christians might one day own all Jashimpur if Miss Bullen had her way.

To pray for guidance each night was one solace. To hear nothing in her heart, no reply, no voice, no scriptural certainty ringing in her thoughts, was a kind of pain which she would talk to no one about.

She knew she was taking a sinful, unChristian, grim satisfaction in seeing what was happening in India now that British rule had withdrawn, for Miss Bullen loved India as much as she hated it, just as much as so many Indians love-hated the British, the British who were completely indigestible, sealed for so long in the unmeltable capsules of their clubs and their snobberies. This grim pleasure she found in seeing the proof of the hatreds and fears underlying Indian life hurt her as well as cheered her, for she was two women ; one woman racially proud and arrogant for whom Britain had never done wrong to a single soul, and another woman humble before God who had tried to believe that all men and women were her brothers and sisters, regardless of colour, race or religion, which was a lie, and which hurt her even now to think about. It was *impossible* to pretend that Papists and heathens were as good as herself, because they were not. But before God they *must* be, and nightly she would brood about this puzzle which God had set her when He first laid His searingly painful mark of choice on her.

After a lifetime spent with the Jashimpuri people she was left with the suspicion that they would never change, that five hundred years after she was dead they would still be lying, and laughing about their lies, still suffering in penury and dirt, still squandering their beautiful patient women in poverty, still smarting silently, and raging behind masks of meekness at their inability to change their world, the world which they loved and in which they suffered. A kind of hate always convulsed her when she thought of her hopeless struggle to put into them that small unquenchable fire of anger with their lot, anger cooled by love of God, the real, true, only God, the British God who had survived so many popes and so many Jesuits. It was this God in which she was now having such difficulty to believe. There had been a time, incredible now to remember, when she had believed firmly that in heaven everyone would speak English. That heaven had been a kind of stately English home surrounded by green cool fields, all of it administered by people like the Viceroy. There had been no harm in believing in that heaven, but she suffered to remember such innocence, such arrogance, such harmless nationality of soul. God now for her was real mystery at last, almost out of reach, belonging to no tongue or skin or flag. She had to fight to believe in Him, this timeless, raceless God who was withdrawing from her and from her incantations which had held Him close to her for so long. She suspected that prolonged loneliness had damaged her.

Her greatest problem had been deciding what to do when the British power withdrew from India, British India, which had always been a symbol for her of that masterful power of which she was so proud to be a part, but which was being attacked now in so many places. Why? Why that hatred? Because God had been a British prisoner for years, a God brought up in a public school, as a sneering article she had read recently in a magazine had inferred? She still felt pride in herself, in who she was, Miss Amabel Bullen of the British race, missionary and ambassadress for righteousness and order and cleanliness, enemy of dirt and of moral backsliding, slayer of lies and stupid cruelty, and undying opponent of the *Mullahs*, of the Pope, and of the million mindless mumbling Hindu gods who had dragged the Indian soul down into the mire of the swamp. It was Hinduism which frightened her most, for it could wait, red-eyed in the darkness, for a million years. For her it had red, drugged eyes and smelled of blood and sex.

Although Miss Bullen did not know it, or even suspect it, the Jashimpuris of the mountains had a deep affection for her, but dumbly, silently, carefully, suspiciously. And the *Mullahs* watched the people, the *Mullahs* so ignorant and so venal, that had Mohammed come to earth again he would have had them all slain in the name of God. Yet they were not bad men. They were men who worked with what they had been allowed to keep when all else had been taken and scattered. They had kept their belief in God, twisted and sorrowful though it was, and they had kept their pride, and their belief that one day a Jashimpuri of their persuasion would arise who would sweep clear the load of dead years which lay on the once fiery, leaping soul of Jashimpur. Jashimpur, which had produced poets and soldiers and thinkers, so long ago, and which now was a prison of labour and taxes, a slavery which had become voluntary and from which there was no escape save death.

It was the same with the Hindus. They, too, had been degraded and tied down to the wheel which could produce money in the shape of taxes and labour, the brightest and most cunning of them one day becoming tax-collectors, above the ragged Muslims, who seemed doomed to stand puzzled in the soft clay of the fields, hoe in hand, sullen with God and His world of misery.

They, too, loved Miss Bullen, but were sorrier for her than were the Muslims, because they knew that in this world such striving, such cleansing and scrubbing and shouting and toiling, was all a waste, trapped as they all were on the great wheel which turned continually from light into darkness and back, measuring whole eras as moments, each being a poor scrap of the world-soul which knew no Heaven or Hell, the cloud of nothingness itself into which all were finally drawn, bodiless, the useless flesh consumed in the cremation-fire and scattered to the racing waters of the world. There was comedy in the endless planning of the Christians, in their set of scales for weighing this kind of work called good, against that other work called bad, both parts of the whole but held apart by the Christians, in a comical effort to make them good and evil, as if separate things. There was comedy, too, in the toiling of the Muslims around and about the prophecies, in their hand-made heaven to come, and in their refusal to believe that their time as a religious force was gone. For this was the *Kali Yug* we lived in, the time of iron, the age of darkness and destruction, which would last for thousands of years until the frame of the world as it had been known for so long was shattered. The cleverest and most thoughtful of them knew that history had been strangled by legend, that religion had been poisoned by superstition and terror, which was always the price of decay. There were many secrets hugged in their breasts of which Miss Bullen and her world could know nothing, for they had decided, the Europeans, long ago, that Indians must cast away all their past and become imitation Europeans, but even Miss Bullen was known to have her doubts nowadays. Doubts about whether her message was completely right and all others wrong, and it was known among the cleverest and most thoughtful that their two tremendous wars had broken the Europeans, and this was both sad and right.

It was only the meanest of them who gloated to hear of the end of the British Raj in India. Be glad, yes, but it was childish and small to gloat, yet many gloated, especially those who had suffered insult from people far less imaginative and kind than Miss Bullen. They had struggled quietly to bring Miss Bullen down, to wear her out, to take the sharp edge off her evangelism and her good-natured contempt for their ways. Perhaps they had begun to succeed at last for she made a curious speech when she sent for some of them, Hindu and Muslim, to come and see her at the mission.

She announced to them that the British Government had gone away from India. " The Government has gone," she said, " because you are now ready and fit to rule yourselves.

(' You are not ! You are not ! ') It has taken the Government
a long time to prepare you for this, and the time has come at
last and now India will rule herself." The cleverest felt sorry
for her when she said that, for there was pathos in it. She
must know that the British Government had gone because
India would have no more of it, and that had Britain been
able to go on ruling India she would never have left. They
knew better than she how close to a great explosion of rage
India had been in 1946, and how British officers, many of
them, worriedly knew that they might have to fight to stay,
and would lose, for that will to shoot down and crush in the
final extremity was gone out of them for ever. Civilisation
had caught up with the sahibs as much as with the Indians.
That was what was said and was known among those who
listened to the world about them. So they felt sorry for the
Miss Sahib, feeling her pain in this momentous time when
that which had signified power and prestige and a kind of
firstness among the people of the world, was gone and
finished. They sat about her in a circle and listened to her
speaking quietly out of her pain, out of her secret wounded
pride, of what she wanted them to think had happened. The
oldest of them, Pandit Krishan, knew how she must be suffering, for she had always been so proud, in a way childishly
and touchingly proud of what she thought British India had
signified for the world, but most of all what it had signified
for her.

She was a small, thin, bright-eyed woman dressed in a
white cotton sari, locally-made heavy sandals on her feet, her
clear grey innocent eyes sombre now as she talked half to
herself, half to the attentive and courteous audience around
her where she sat in a cane chair in the centre of the mission
compound.

"And that is what has happened," she said. "Now you
are all *free*." It was not irony which underlined her use of
that word, but a taste of bitterness, they knowing she con-

sidered them quite unfit and unready to be free. They had
no intention of changing their ways, for her, or for a dozen
Viceroys or Maharajahs, and they knew she knew it and that
it had all but broken her courageous spirit over the years.

"It is sad," Pandit Krishan said. "But it is the way of
things to move and change. Kings are born and they die,
and men collect taxes and others pay them, and all die. It is
sad for you on this day to give us this news. You will not
leave us, though? You will not go now when we are in
danger from the tribesmen in the north? Can you not ask
the British to send a few soldiers, just a few, in case these
savage tribesmen should attack us, and then we can all live
on in peace again?"

She sighed and looked at the old dark, handsome face with
its two black eyes fixed on her, reading into her, watching
her closely. These eyes all about her which had watched her
like that for a lifetime. What had they discovered of her?
What did they know of her by now? She had hidden herself
from them. She knew herself better than anyone, bitterly
she knew herself, how weak, how mean, how unspiritual she
was. Although she had begun to believe that she had had no
right to come here and tell these people they were wrong,
mistaken, uselessly idle and backward, she still had her doubts.
In her heart she considered herself far better than all of them,
and nothing, she knew, was going to change that. Not much
humility there, she knew, but a truth was a truth, but not to
be spoken always aloud.

She smoothed her thick grey hair, her eyes looking at
something far off. She patted her bun to make sure it was
not straggling on to her neck while she thought of what to
say to Pandit Krishan. She wanted to say something kind,
yet something venomous, so that he should know now, in
his fear, that what he and his brethren had struggled so
silently to drive out, the bayonets which had kept him safe
in his bed at night, were not available. But she had read too

much Indian history, pre and post British rule, to speak venomously with a free heart. She felt, depressedly, that the mighty and unbending force of India would soon begin to roll over the brief hard passage of European ways and culture now that the walls which had protected it were gone. She knew that a couple of hundred years were nothing in the slow, steady tide of this ancient world, a world of which she was so much a part now that she could not leave it, pined no more for grey skies or trimmed hedges, or warbling birds after soft rain, the sights and sounds of her own kind of world eight thousand miles from this hot, bright, hard world of Jashimpur. She felt herself almost one of these people.

"The Jashimpuri soldiers will fight the tribesmen if they attack us," she said, and sat expressionless while they all laughed unrestrainedly, Hindu and Muslim together, as if they thought she had made one of her dry jokes. The Jashimpuri soldiers defending them? They nudged and pushed each other and laughed.

"Haven't you any shame at all?" she said quietly. "Haven't I been able to give you any sense of shame after all these years among you? How can you laugh at yourselves like that? How can you sit there and laugh like that about your own soldiers, your own men?" It was something about them which she had never been able to accept calmly, their ironic, shameless humour in their own shortcomings, in their defeatedness, yet it had a power, she knew that too. That irony made them capable of bearing enormous burdens of insult and labour, as if they were confident that one day, a thousand years from now, or a million, all this would end, not by bloodshed, but by the collapse of their masters, who could drive them no more. For years she had fought to make them eat tomatoes and apples and peaches which they grew in abundance, which they tended so carefully for sale in a far Jashimpur town. These things, tomatoes, apples and peaches and all forms of fruit, were the food of the rich, and were grown for sale so as to pay taxes and buy cloth to cover nakedness and to pay interest to the moneylenders who were among the most powerful links which chained them to their serfdom. She often thought, too, of the contradiction in her message. Man must help himself, must have courage, must have dignity, must *work*, must remember that God created men and expected them to make the best of their surroundings and to live in dignity and honesty. Yet were the Jashimpuris to follow that message they would have to rise in revolt and shake off their tyrants, in fact tear down the established order of their serfdom. That meant violence. In a way their meekness, their cowardice, their gentleness, even though it masked boiling rivers of hate, was what Gandhi asked men to emulate. Let the brutal policeman strike you down, and then stand up and let him strike you down again, until he was ashamed of himself and crept away, defeated. They laughed at that too, the Jashimpuris, knowing so well that the more you took the more you were used, and they stood in this trap like men caught fast in mud.

She had always lived alone here, for alone was to be without one of your own kind. She had never felt alone, had never minded this loneliness, but to-day, knowing that the Indian world belonged no more to Britain, she felt cast down into utter loneliness, as if suddenly Jashimpur and India, the whole great sub-continent, were strange and hostile territory in which she would get no more unthinking respect for what she had always felt she represented. She could have cried, sitting there before the men ringed about her chair on the hard, yellowish earth of the compound. For this had been her home, had always been her home; now it was no longer hers, but after forty years she could not leave it. She could see in their watching eyes that there was sympathy for her, and understanding, and she could not bear it. She got up and said in a low voice, " Thank you all. You can go now." Then she hurried away to her room, went into it, closed the door and stood there and wept silently with her teeth clenched, amused at herself as well in a small watching way. But the tears relieved her and she was able to think, "I came here and I've worked here, and I'll die here. It's only the poor, frightened, miserable flesh that's crying. I'll get over this feeling of misery. After all, the poor cowardly Jashimpuris never cry, unless they are really desperate."

Chapter Three

The Jashimpur that Miss Bullen had journeyed to through burning sands and over high mountains forty years before had not changed very much except along the few roads which had been built for motor traffic, and in Jashimpur town, where the tourists from India came to find pleasure and to be disgusted by the Jashimpuris, by their sloth, their cunning, their cynicism, their meekness when shouted at even by the meanest of men. Yet these Jashimpuris won you over in the end, especially when they said during a bargaining, " Be careful of me, Sahib. Remember I am a Jashimpuri, and you know what you think of Jashimpuris." The tourist laughed, feeling underneath the laugh the hard, thin barb of the mind behind those sad, cynical eyes of the Jashimpuri. All kinds of brilliance and cynicism lived quietly amidst the poverty and sloth and dirt. Life had come almost to a stop here some generations ago.

For three years after she had arrived, Miss Bullen had lived in a rage, in a state of unquenchable anger, but remembering always that she must be charitable, patient and kind, even when the most barefaced lies and trickery were tried on her in order to see what she would do.

She had been very fond of the mountain mutton in those days, and on one occasion when she ordered her cook to buy a sheep, which would keep for two days in the cold air of the mountain autumn, she had looked forward to eating the ribs of the sheep baked in the local manner. She received only four ribs, and when later she asked for the rest her cook said in surprise, "But you are in Jashimpur now, Miss Sahib. Don't you know about the mountain sheep in Jashimpur? Don't you know that they are famous, not only for their succulence, but for the fact that they have only four ribs? Why, every traveller knows that, surely?" She had nodded at once, saying, "Yes, of course, I forgot. I'm sorry." How innocent she had been then. How the Jashimpuris laughed at her. They still prized the lying skill of that cook of long ago who had thought of the four-ribbed Jashimpuri sheep after having eaten most of the sheep himself. She never quite forgave them for many such lies, for many playful hours they had had with her.

They would not come near her dispensary for two years, not even when men broke their bones or gashed their flesh in mountain falls. The old men forbade it, determined to freeze her out of the mountain by a refusal to ask her aid, for they knew it was their souls she wanted.

One day, in her fourth year among them, she went into a village, quivering with anger and with a will to have God's message told, come what may. Let them crucify her if they wanted, she was willing to die. She preached in Urdu for an hour to a silent throng of wretched, dirty, ragged, mud-stained men and women, half-naked children fingering her European clothes as she spoke. When she was finished she asked for questions. The whole crowd of them turned silently away and went into their small, crumbling mud houses and stayed there until she went. They seemed to her like battered, soggy clay, a ruined, broken, dejected, Godless people.

She was the first, though, to need attention in illness. She broke her ankle in a fall from a mountain track where she had gone to sketch. Two of the silent, muddy, ragged men found her and carried her down to the mission house she had rented, a mean dwelling of clay in those days like their own. These two men sat by her bed, did her bidding, brought her food, soothed her, laughed at her and at themselves, bathed her

c

ankle and bound it each day, and then went away when she was well. At last an opening, a sign, a hint. When she was well she went to their village to preach. Every human being in the village went into the houses and shut them up until she had gone. Rebuffed, hurt, she had withdrawn into months of silent work in and about her house, building, making a garden—sullen and depressed.

Forty years had passed and she had made three converts, all men, all venal, untrustworthy, shifty, unhappy, hated and despised by the others, who curried favour with the *Mullahs* by hating the converts. She knew the people looked on her as one of God's chosen made ones, to be tolerated, and helped in her final phase which must come with age, death. They now used her dispensary, paid her with rice or fruit or labour, but stood impassive and dumb when she spoke of God. What *did* they feel about God? They prayed in their own fashion, but did they believe in God? It was not possible. But she knew they had a deep and touching faith in God. If only she could have fired them with her will to work and to change the world, the hard Protestant drive to better the world, to make more money, to go on and on and on. But they were still the same sodden, heavy, beaten clay as forty years ago. They were friendly to her, but suspiciously, carefully.

When she had finished weeping as she stood by that closed door, following her speech on India's freedom, she could hear the elders moving away from the compound to their village. She felt then very close to them, treasuring the sympathy she had seen in their eyes. They knew she was wounded, was sorrowful because somehow she had lost power, face, caste, place. It was stupid of her, and she knew it, and she knew they knew it too. They would laugh about it in that cruel way they had, the cruel way that had that bitter tenderness beneath it always. The knowledge was in them that the world was not good, that it was mean and cruel to them, and that they were conquered here by a history of tyranny and that it would never change for them.

A few of the young men of the new generation in the villages had torn and wrenched some kind of schooling out of the world at last, were restless and anxious to do something, to have a part in the doing of the kind of adventure they knew was being lived down in India during the struggle to end British rule. They wanted to feel that they were taking part in the history and the doings of this world. They muttered and they talked and they planned, under their breaths to each other, as if frightened of what they knew and sensed in their own minds. But there had been one who was bolder than the others. He was a youth of almost nineteen, son of a labourer on the estates of a rich Hindu some miles away. One day he had come to her and introduced himself. His name was Hassan. He was a tall, powerfully-built man, lean and hard and sad-faced, but with shining, bright, intelligent eyes. " Miss Sahib," he said, " I can speak English. I can write a little too. Please employ me in some way. I want to study and to get ready."

And where was he now ? Agitating and preaching revolt in Jashimpur city. She knew she still loved him. She could admit it. But she could not forgive him. He had wanted to get ready.

To get ready ? Ready for what ? She had been curious and gave him a cup of Jashimpuri tea with cardamoms in it, and while he drank it he told her that he was getting ready for the day when they were all free. " Ah," she had said. " Tell me about that." She had never thought to meet a Jashimpuri peasant who wanted to be free and who thought others of his people were going to be free too. She was excited, for while she taught the people that their rulers were good men who were up against many difficulties, she despised them too, as tyrants, even though so many of them were her friends. They were wrong and mean and cruel, while not meaning to be, some of them, but all of them feared the silent, crushed and unknown peasantry.

Hassan had worked for her for two years, and at times they would talk and she would see the hatred he carried in him, the steely will to bear no more as a helot in this rich, poverty-stricken land which he thought of as *his*, his own. " You will hang," she had told him jokingly one day when he said he would live to see a Jashimpur free of the masters. His eyes had become hard and shining, and he said, " I would hang proudly." Then he went away to Jashimpur City and later to India, and she heard nothing further of him until the rumours about him had begun. He had gone to America. He had come back from India. He was the leader of the coming revolt. He was in gaol.

When a letter came from the small society in London which until now had sponsored her mission, she knew before she opened it what it would tell her. It told her what she had known for some time, that the mission could not expect to be supported any longer and that in the new circumstances it would be as well to close it. She would be welcomed at her old mission in Delhi, where teachers were needed. The letter praised her faithful work and regretted that circumstances should require the closing of the mission.

She crushed the letter in her hand, relieved, and bitter as well. Not with the Society. They had always done what they could for her. No, bitter with the hard rock of refusal which she had reached years after finding her way through the mud and clay of the Jashimpuri world, the rock of bigotry and fanaticism, of Islam which had been great and would never forget it. Then she laughed, knowing that perhaps after all it was a trial of her, her whole wasted life a trial. While God had shifted from her in some way she had to believe in Him. He was a fact for her, the same power as always. It was only that her religion did not satisfy her any more. God did, but not the narrowness she had cherished. Her pity was too great for her to hate the Jashimpuris who had so long resisted her. She was tired of reading the Bible. She wished she could capture again the wonderful happy sense of dedication she had known in her early years as a missionary. She could not place what was the matter with her. She was too unhappy to do anything but fret. Prayer did not appease this unhappiness as once it had done. Her suspicion that she was sick to her heart with the Jashimpuris might be correct, a weariness of the people and of being cut off from her own kind.

That night she sat down and wrote a letter to the Maharani, and, after explaining that her mission must close down, asked if there was any teaching post in the new girls' school in Jashimpur City in which she would be useful. If she could obtain a post in Jashimpur City she would be very happy. If not, she must seek a post in India, but she did not wish to leave Jashimpur if a post could be found there. She tore three letters up and wrote a fourth which satisfied her. She sent the letter off by a trade truck and when it was gone she felt she had at last made a start in changing the soured routine of her life. She had difficulty in believing she was as old as she was. Physically she was as sound as ever she had been, but her spirit was rusted and hardened with disappointment, and she knew it was her pride which was still her greatest enemy. But without it she would have given up to complete bitterness long ago. So she could put up with her pride. She was glad she was proud.

Chapter Four

The palace was high up on the side of the hill overlooking Jashimpur City. It was a long, low, yellow building, more like a fortress than a palace. It had been built in the eighteenth century by a ruler who had awaited assassination all his life, a great joke to the Jashimpuris, who talked lightly of assassination but feared all forms of violence. High sandstone walls ran round the palace and enclosed carefully tended lawns which were green for most of the year. The palace itself was gloomy and Lila was depressed as soon as she had entered it on her arrival from England with Prabhu and the twins.

" I hate this place," she said when they were alone after the tiresome welcoming ceremony of the garlands and speeches, of the eyes watching them both and studying all their gestures and movements.

" Now give it a bloody chance, Lila," Prabhu said irritably. She looked into his dark glasses and said, " It's gloomy and I hate it. I may as well say it as think it. Why ? Do you find it cheerful ? " They were sitting in their bedroom having a drink. Prabhu had begun to drink with her again on the ship and she still did not know what to make of it. She knew he still hunted in her room for bottles she had hidden and was as obsessed as ever about her secret drinking, which was never discussed ; but his drinking with her again was strange, and it puzzled her. He had sworn off drinking two years ago in an odd fit of puritanical sternness, but had begun again aboard ship on the journey out from England. Of course she could not ask him about it. He would have looked at her with his dark glasses and said coldly, " Why ? Do you mind ? Any objections ? " The dark glasses were new too. He only took them off when he went to sleep.

" All right, it's gloomy," he said. " I hate it too. Are you happy now ? "

" You snappy brute, Prab," she said quietly, but placatingly. " Why are you so cross ? Aren't you glad to be back ? Don't you like being Maharajah after all ? They treat you like a little tin god."

" You know quite well why I wanted to be Maharajah," he said. " I have a few things to do, that's all. As for the rest, I hate it. I feel depressed. Seeing that gang out there this afternoon made me feel sick, even if half of them *are* my relatives." She sighed and lay back in her chair and waited for him to start about the poverty and dirt of the Jashimpuri people, and about the rich who did not give one damn for anything but their own pockets. And it came out of him as usual, in a flood, like one of those orators they used to listen to with such pleasure in Hyde Park on Sunday mornings. God, but she was weary of politics and " the people " and " the little man " and the rest of it. At thirty-three Prabhu should be waking up out of his British socialist fever, but there was no sign. He would go through with his fantastic plans for Jashimpur, she knew it. Where would it all end ? That crowd out there to-day, the big, fat wealthy men with their quiet, subdued and watchful wives were not going to stand by and let Prabhu tear their world to pieces. She interrupted him just as he was describing how many calories a Jashimpuri peasant needed in winter and in summer, not just to exist as he had to now, but to *live* and feel healthy.

" Prabhu," she said, her enormous black eyes grave and appealing, unflinching before his suspicious gaze. He liked to think she was a born actress.

" Yes ? "

" Give up your plan, darling. Please give it up. You know yourself it won't work. It can't work. They won't let it work. You saw them all there to-day. The landowners. They'll only hate you for it. Give it up, darling."

" Lila ! " he said sharply, " I've told you a million times, I *care*. I mean what I say. I actually mean what I say. There's no question of me backing out. You heard their speeches to-day, full of hints and warnings about unrest and trouble. These landowners know it's coming. I'm simply going to prevent a revolution by starting reforms, that's all. You heard the speeches. They're scared, and they're right. The human clod, the Jashimpuri peasant has had enough. And of course, it's nineteen forty-seven as well. So don't nag me any more, please, Lila. I'm going to do what I said I'd do."

" All right," she said, as if resigned. But he knew her better. She would be at it again to-morrow. She could not leave it alone. True-blue to the core, but she had never realised it, imagining she was simply an agnostic Indian Christian who hated India, but when he listened to her he heard the authentic voice of traditional conservative India saying, " Change nothing. All is well and for the best. It's all gone on for a long time now." But she did not wait until to-morrow. She started again after two minutes.

" Prabhu," she said softly.

" Yes ? " He was suspicious, his whisky in his hand as he turned his dark glasses on her. He was slim and almost tall, well built, loose and limber in his white silk shirt and tan Palm Beach trousers. What was extraordinary always when she thought of it was that such a maniac about calories and labour and land reform as he had become could remain such a splendid lover, as splendid and devoted as before he had gone mad under the first days of British socialism. She remembered his exultant face as he listened to the radio in London announcing each new grey, cunning blow to what he called " the bloody, stifling, established order." He had come back from the war full of it, bursting with the Atlantic Charter and the rights of this and that, and the ten thousand freedoms, and it had lasted, right into this gloomy palace.

"One last word, darling," she said. "That's all. Please don't get annoyed."

"Oh, God Almighty, Lila, you're going to go on about it again. I know all the signs now. *Please* leave me to decide what's best. After all it's *my* bloody country, Jashimpur. I rule the place now. Why don't you leave it alone, Lila? Why?" He knew that seeing them all out there to-day, the Old Gang, had frightened her.

She drank her whisky down in one quick lift of the glass, remembering that they were drinking together, and that sanctified everything, made her drinking all right, and she could have another and another. She began to talk while she poured herself another one, hoping he was not noticing, but he was noticing. He noticed everything, even in his sleep. When she drank alone she always thought of him thinking of her drinking alone, knowing about her. She was full of him, right up to the top, full of Prabhu's eyes and mind, and after the long war years without him she had found it hard to get used to again.

"All I want to say," she said, the whisky safe in her hand and unchallenged, uncommented on, "is that you haven't the right. You can't do these things with other people's land. You can't become a dictator. It's not right. And *why* must you do it? You'll make life unbearable here, Prabhu. This isn't England. It's not ready for these things."

"Lila," he said. "For God's sake will you shut up?"

"All right," she was suddenly meek, knowing how he hated it, how it made him feel a bully.

"Now don't be cross with me," he implored her.

"Have your way."

"Lila."

"I'm just a bloody woman. All right."

" Lila ! " He shouted her name in a mock but serious anger.

She drank the whisky down quickly again, remembering that she could have another, for they were drinking together. In silence he watched her splash the whisky into the glass.

" You're drinking it fast, Lila," he said in a low voice, a fine barb of disapproval in it.

" Why don't you say, ' That's three you've had in ten minutes ' ? " she snapped at him.

" Fourteen minutes," he said.

" Oh, God ! " She stared at the ceiling. She *had* been rushing it, over-excited by the suggestion of freedom in his drinking with her.

" Pour one for me, too, there's a darling." He gave her his glass. She saw he was smiling his affectionate smile at her, and she could imagine his ironical eyes behind the dark glasses.

" Oh, Prabhu ! " she cried in a strangled, tragic tone. She went to him with a soft fruffing sound of sari in her glide and knelt to embrace him. " I hate to quarrel with you. I hate it so much." His mind was on her back and her breasts, idly, as he caressed her and thought of how much power he had with her, and of how he never got tired of her physically, and of how sometimes he wanted to scream aloud when she let her simple, ordinary mind trot about in front of him like a toy horse. She was so *good*, so simple. But was she ? He ran his electric fingers over the tight silk of her black *choli*, which was like a small, short waistcoat revealing far too much slender golden waist. She would have to dress more soberly for Jashimpur. He would have to mention it to her, and he knew it would take her a year to think it curious that one so revolutionary about other people's acres and power could be narrow for the sake of Jashimpuri good form about her waist. He felt love and pity for her. " Drink up your whisky, and have another, darling," he said into her small ear. When she sat down again he said, " Don't you worry, Lila. Everything'll go well. You always see the dark side of everything, remember. It won't be as bad as you think." With all the travelling of the last weeks they had been practically celibate and it had made him irritable and peevish, and he thought, " She's wonderful, but she's ruined me. A week without her and I'm hammering the walls. That's not right. And I resent her secret boozing, which is unreasonable, I suppose, considering I'm unable to do without her. Though that's different. Yes, quite different. All the same, though, it's a craving, just as much as her boozing. Though it's not very secret. She knows about it." He laughed aloud and she looked at him knowing it was no use asking him what he was laughing at. He always lied to her if she asked him about his sudden fits of laughter.

" D'you know what I'm laughing at, Lila ? " He was playful and warm, smiling at her.

" No."

" I was thinking that I'm going mad for you already. Darling, I can't do without you. Isn't it curious after years of being with you ? I had to laugh, thinking about it."

" That's not what you were laughing about," she said.

" It is." But she would not believe him.

" That's not a laughing subject to you, Prab," she said. " What were you really laughing at ? "

" I've told you," he said, becoming snappish again. She refused to believe him and he was so incensed he swore at her and said he would never tell her anything again. While he spoke she poured herself an extra large whisky, certain he had not noticed the size of it. She was so excited she could hardly wait to get it to her mouth. His words had reminded her of night and she could feel the tingling approach of longing for him deep down in her body, in the dark well where the lightning lived. There was a deep furrow of a bullet wound above his right breast which he had brought back from Burma, and she liked to kiss it with a curious sort of worshipful sorrow in her heart, for somehow his body had a sacred feeling for her, and the Japanese had marred it, and sometimes it made her feel she would cry. Thinking of the warm, velvety feel of his flesh under her mouth upset her and she almost said, " All right. Now. We've got a couple of hours before dinner. Now." But no. Night was the time, the time of deep silence and mystery. Yes. Patience. A little more soda in the whisky which was so strong it was almost flexing itself in the glass.

He picked up *Time* and began to read it. He missed all his weekly papers which would take some weeks to catch up with him here in Jashimpur. He read everything he could get, Fascist, Communist, Socialist, True-Blue, and what he called " Off-Beat Stuff." He lived in a perpetual state of world-crisis. The crisis of the world had become his hobby. He knew the names of all the fat little dictators of South America, how much rice was grown in Viet-Nam, the names of the Icelandic cabinet, who had been torn to pieces last year by a mob in Arabia and who had replaced him, and the horse-power of the latest American bomber. He loved reading about air-crashes, which he claimed was why he read *Time*. He was terrified of air travel and admitted it, even boasted of it, and as usual with his weaknesses, made such fun of it that people enjoyed it and did not believe him.

" Doesn't Prem look terrible ? " Lila said. " I can't get over it. He looks as if he's dying. He's like a skeleton. And his eyes ! I've never seen such sad eyes. What did they do to him ? "

Prabhu dropped *Time* to the blue carpet. She had never grown tired of watching how he dropped things to the floor when he had had enough of them. Even during the time in London, when they had had no servants, he had gone on doing it and she had fought it sullenly, and lost. She watched him closely. The mention of his brother, Prem, had tightened up his face. There was some grief in it. He loved his brother.

" He wouldn't play ball with the Japs," said Prabhu. " So they gave him the full treatment. In a way he was a fool. Poor Prem ! "

" The full treatment ? " She had never been able to properly understand the new Anglo-American idiom which had grown up in the war and had come to stay among the young. When Prabhu came back from the war he had spoken a new language, a casual shorthand and she had never let herself fall into it, attractive though it was. (" Couldn't care less." " Yes. But yes. I mean *yes*," and " Bang on," and——)

" They starved him, worked him, beat him, and all that— you've read about it. In a way it was his own fault. As an Indian he had no need to wave the flag, but he did, so the Japs gave him the full treatment. They said he was a traitor to Asia and all that kind of thing. I don't think he'll ever be right again. And he's drinking like a maniac as well. I asked him. I said, ' Prem, what made you stick your neck out like that ? Why did you play the white man and get yourself smashed up like that ? As an Indian you could have got away with it. Imprisonment was bad enough surely, in those jungles. Why did you provoke the Japs ? ' D'you know what he said ? "

" What ? " She had poured herself another whisky. There was as much excitement in drinking in front of Prabhu as drinking hidden from him. He would never approve of her drinking ; never. She had nearly filled her glass with whisky, and Prabhu had not noticed it. He was too taken up with talking about Prem.

" He said, ' We never fought in action, our battalion. I was trained to fight and I wanted to fight, and the humiliation of being captured almost straight off the ship was too much for me. The Japs laughed at us. I started a sabotage group in the camp and they caught me. After that it was a contest, but they never broke me.' But they broke him all right. You've seen his eyes. God, I've never seen such a change in a man. I didn't recognise him. And all for nothing. What use was it? Beaten and starved and worked like a coolie. And now it's all over and who cares? He's thirty-one and he looks like a man of sixty. He's not bitter, though. Give him enough Scotch and he's quite happy. Poor Prem." She saw by the set of his head that Prabhu was staring back through his dark glasses at other Prems, other Prabhus, at childhood.

"Poor Prem," she said. She remembered when he had stayed with them in London before the war. They had had a wonderful time introducing Prem into the pub world of London, and he had not wanted to leave it and go back to the other shut-off world of Jashimpur. He had been vital then, furiously alive, unsoldiered, unbroken. The Japanese had discovered his spring and had cut it off, blocked it.

There was a knock on the door and Prabhu shouted, "Come in."

Prem came in with a handful of newspapers. "India's going up in smoke," he said. "They're cutting each others' throats all over the Punjab. Oh, that looks nice. Can I have one too?" He nodded at the whisky.

"Sit down and have one," Prabhu said. Prem threw the bundle of newspapers on the table beside the siphons and then sat down. He was not as tall as Prabhu and his emaciated face was yellowish grey. He was still handsome but he had lost several of his good teeth and the gaps in the row of white teeth looked strange and gave him a curiously debauched look when he smiled. His eyes were almost without expression, as if dead. He reminded Lila of a man who had seen a great deal and had decided that life had been over-rated and must be endured as pleasantly as possible, being resigned, kind, gentle, and with too much understanding. She could imagine him defending the most brutal murderer by saying, "How do we know anything about it? How do we know what causes *anything*? We can't go around judging people the way we've been doing for centuries." He had actually said that to her during their first conversation. "There's been too much judging done," he had said, rather excitedly for him, who had such a quiet crushed manner. "Nobody knows anything about human beings. But we judge them. There's so much I hate and loathe in this world." He was like Prabhu in that, in his vehemence and burning intensity when aroused.

Now he took a letter from his pocket and said with a look of torture in his eyes, " Lila, I hope you'll forgive me. I've had this letter in my pocket for four days to give you and I've forgotten it. My memory's very bad, I'm afraid. It came in on a trade truck and was given to me to deliver to you by a merchant in the town. I'm terribly sorry. My memory's . . ."

" It's all right, Prem," she said affectionately. She was feeling light and happy and ready to get drunk. She laughed at his woeful eyes. " It's only a letter. We all forget." She knew she would be always trying to make Prem feel more comfortable, a little more happy, less agonised. It could be pretty wearing in the end. Prem was alive with corners and prickles and edges. But she liked him, and for her that meant he would have her friendship always. Her idea of friendship was that if you went out and did something terrible to-morrow, something inexplicable, like robbing a bank, it would make no difference to your friends, who loved you for what you had always been, for what they had found in you, and who, therefore, could not hate or despise you for what you might suddenly become. Friendship was forgiveness. Otherwise it was a lie.

The letter was from her faithful correspondent, Miss Bullen, the incredible old woman who had written to her for so long. Although it was about fifteen years since she had seen the old woman she could remember her perfectly.

She had first met Miss Bullen when her father, a man who had spent his life swaying in a spiritual agony between his ancestral Hinduism and the Christianity he had accepted as a young man, had taken her to Kangla, where he had spent a week in argument with Miss Bullen. " She is like the rest of them," her father had said of Miss Bullen, with his particular bitter sadness, after that trip to Kangla. " She thinks God is an Englishman and all you have to do is play the game and God will love you. How I envy her. How I envy them all that easy and trusting Christianity they have, these English people." Her father thought that once you had decided who God was and what He was you must give up everything, everything, and spend your life in adoration. What he had really always wanted was to escape from his family. She dreaded meeting him again. He was now in yet another phase of his life. He was a *sanyassi* now somewhere up near Amarnath in Kashmir, forcing himself, probably, into the cracked Hindu mould which his family had left in his youth. He wore grey ash and long coiled hair and a rag to cover him. This news had come to her from a friend in Kashmir. Her father wrote to her every year, a letter of duty, as if to say he was still alive and she was not to mourn yet. And he was lovable. He was like all men in that he demanded admiration without asking for it, but you knew he wanted it, and he did not deserve it, yet she felt something for him akin to admiration, which was pity, but that particular female kind of pity which the male could do with and imagine to be admiration. It meant being silent during, and after, long monologues, and knowing how to cook, how to use the yes. She loved him and hated him for not deserving this love. She did not miss him. If he died she would not miss him, but she would always feel this intimate pity for him, which was her love for him who had begat her, and without whom she would not be herself. It was impossible to hate a father who had begotten you, and of whom you carried a part alive in your being, with all his stupidities and mistaken passions. She began to whistle softly as she opened Miss Bullen's letter, Prem watching her and wondering if she drank as much as he did, and why she drank so much. Prabhu was reading *Time* again.

"Do you know a Miss Bullen at the mission up at Kangla, Prem?" Lila asked when she had finished reading the letter.

"I've heard of her," he said. "I've never met her, though." He had thrown his first whisky down his throat in one gulp and now he poured himself another. She watched the way he removed the cork with the thumb and forefinger of his right hand while holding the bottle in the same hand by the neck. He poured the whisky in one swift movement and corked the bottle again without using his other hand. He watched her watching him with a quick flicker of his eyes. "I wonder why we feel so guilty about drinking?" Lila thought. "Prem's like me. Furtive and worried. I wonder if he knows why he drinks. I wonder if it's just his war experiences, or something particularly horrible that happened to him? I can't get over the change in him. He looks like a skeleton. And those eyes. Prabhu wouldn't suffer like that, not about anything. If I died to-night Prabhu would eat a good dinner and read *Time*, even though I know he loves me. He'd read *Time* and go on living. That's why I always want to fight with Prabhu. I've always known I'm not absolutely necessary to him, that he can do without me, and I just wish I'd never found that out. I mean I've no proof but I *know*. I know." She often imagined certain situations involving herself and Prabhu. Prabhu finding out that she loved another man. Prabhu would kill her, at once, in a passion of rage and jealousy. Or Prabhu hearing from someone that during the war she had gone to strange wild parties with American soldiers and had been drunk enough to let them fondle and kiss her, and had liked it. Or Prabhu hearing her tell him that she had just been told she had an incurable cancer. In that scene Prabhu would look at her, put *Time* down and pour himself a drink and say, "Good Christ, is that a fact? Are you sure? I wouldn't have said you were a cancer type, Lila."

D

She knew it was half true, and yet she knew for sure that he would get over it quickly, read *Time* weekly as her death receded, and forget her. He would never get another woman like her, though, and he knew it, but even so she was not vital to him. He was too confident about her, too sure of her, almost casual, and it was her own fault. She had spoiled him. And she was jealous of him but he had never found this out. To him she had never betrayed that special poisoned ache in her. She knew he had had other women and sometimes she wanted to kill him for that.

Poor old Miss Bullen wanted a job. Her mission was closing. The old woman had written, " Perhaps all my time up here has been a waste. I wonder if I will ever know ? But it feels like a waste to me." She wanted to know if Lila knew of anyone who wanted a governess or a tutor. She would prefer to do some such work in Jashimpur rather than go down to India. She was too old now for the heat of the plains, and anyway Jashimpur had become her home. There was the usual amount about God and this part Lila read with the care she had begun to use during the last two years or so. Once she had always skipped the God part of the old woman's letters but now she read them with some understanding of the faith and wonder involved in the writing of them, but she could not believe in God. She understood, though, why the old woman believed in Him. It must be fine to believe in God, very restful and soothing. There was a God, there could be no doubt of that, but she could not believe in Him. Strange.

" Just the thing," she said aloud, but in the voice she always used when she wanted Prabhu to look up and take notice, which he did now.

" Just the thing for what, Lila ? " he asked.

" Governess for the twins," she said. " Miss Bullen. I've just had a letter from her. She sends you regards and welcomes us both back to Jashimpur. She wants a job."

" They say she's a good teacher," Prem said. " I've never met her but I believe she's very nice. But a bit cracked. You know, vague. She's been up there at Kangla too long. But as I'm cracked myself perhaps I shouldn't talk." He tittered in a curiously private way he had.

" She's a missionary, so you can forget the governess idea, Lila," Prabhu said. He turned his dark glasses on her and smiled. " It's not a good idea," he went on. " We can get a real governess instead, without any proselytising."

" I want her and I'm going to have her ! " Lila shrieked at him in such a way that Prabhu's mouth opened in astonishment. Prem sat up and stared at her as if she had gone mad. Her eyes were fixed on Prabhu with such a burning and intense look of hate in them that for some reason Prabhu snatched off his dark glasses and revealed his astounded eyes. After her fierce shriek the room was uncomfortably silent until Lila made a small sound like a sob, but she had not moved. Then she shook her long hair with one quick jerk of her head and said in her usual low, pleasant voice, " I want her and I'm going to have her."

" Have you gone out of your mind ? " Prabhu asked her in a cold, hard voice. " What are you screaming about ? What's the matter with you ? "

" There's nothing the matter with me."

" Oh, yes there is. What's the screaming about ? Did you hear yourself ? "

She nodded in a dumb, numb sort of way that was sad to Prem, who was watching her intently.

" Clear off, Prem." Prabhu jerked his thumb at the door. " If you don't mind."

" No. Stay, Prem. Stay where you are," Lila said. " There's nothing private to happen."

" Clear off, Prem." Prabhu jumped to his feet and put on his dark glasses. " She's just having one of her turns. She's never had a screaming one until now, but anyway—if you don't mind, Prem." He put his hands on his hips and watched Prem rise from his chair and stand there, slightly hunched, smiling doubtfully and looking from Lila to Prabhu and back. " Well, what do I do, please ? " Prem asked. " Go or stay ? Don't fight, please. I can't stand people fighting. I can't bear it. Please don't. It does nothing good for anyone."

" Sit down, Prem," Lila said wearily, " and pour me a drink, please." She turned to Prabhu and looked at him with her big, angry, black eyes and said, " If you don't mind, Prab, that is. I want Prem to stay. And I want to go on in an ordinary way arranging to have Miss Bullen as a governess for my children. That's my department. The children." It was the way she had said " my children " that made her defiant now. " They're mine," she added, " and I want to decide who's governess. You run everything, *everything*. But I won't be run over the governess. I want Miss Bullen." She was controlling her voice but she could not hide the shining anger in her eyes. Prabhu was looking at her but his eyes were unreadable again behind their black screens of glass. Prem sat down slowly and carefully, like a man sneaking along the edge of a crowded room. He sighed when he sat down and at once began to pour whisky into the three glasses.

" I refuse to have a row with you, Lila," Prabhu said in his cold voice. " I never row. And I'm not going to now. But I won't have a missionary, Christian, Buddhist or any other damn religion, as governess to my children. And that's that. And don't scream like that at me ever again." He was curious again. " What made you scream like that, Lila ? Please tell me. And what's the look for. The tigerish look ? Can I be told ? "

" Yes, you can be told. I'm sick of being run, of being organised, of being hammered down." Her voice began to rise again. " I won't be bullied about the governess. It was my idea, and I want Miss Bullen."

" Don't drink any more whisky," Prabhu said tenderly.
" You're drunk, darling."

She began to look ill, the golden bronze of her face taking
on an olive green pallor. She trembled and burst into tears,
her eyes tightly closed, the glass of whisky clutched in her
right hand. Prem covered his face with his hands and let out
a deep, mournful sigh. Prabhu walked out of the room and
slammed the door behind him.

" Prem, I'm sorry," she was sobbing quietly. " Don't be
so upset. I'm sorry I shouted. I couldn't help it. I'm drunk.
He's right. He's always right. God, I'm so tired of him
being right."

" I never thought you'd come back here, Lila," Prem said,
ignoring her tears. " Do you still hate it all ? Are you unhappy
because you're back ? I didn't think Prabhu would want to
come back. *I* wouldn't have come back if I'd been living in
London. That's where I want to live. London. There a
man is lost. No one cares about him. Is life expensive in
London now ? Are you sorry you're back, Lila ? "

She did not know. She opened her wet eyes and stared at
the enormous ugly Victorian painting on the wall opposite
her. That must come down, and soon too. It showed several
tired stags staring from a glen and was called *Silent Denizens
of the Wood*. The palace was full of such paintings. Prabhu
had not noticed them at all, and would not notice their disap-
pearance. They were not political in any way. She did not
know if she was unhappy to be back in Jashimpur. Places
no longer caused her unhappiness. There was only one place,
one country, and that was inside the flesh where the mind
never stopped its promptings and designings of fears and
sorrows. She would have to speak to Prabhu eventually,
have to unburden herself, but not yet, not while he was in
the throes of his mania about " the people."

" No, I'm all right," she told Prem. " Just a little over-
tired after the long journey from England, I suppose, and I've

had too much whisky." She smiled and then turned her eyes on him and looked at his worn, tired face.

"Well, even if you're over-tired," he said gently, "you're looking more beautiful than ever you've looked. I hope you're going to be happy here. Do you think you'll always hate India, Lila?" He was smiling at her indulgently, as if she were not mature in her feelings about India but that he understood her and did not mind.

"I've thought about it a lot since that night we all took our hair down about India, that night in the flat in Kensington. No, I don't feel it quite so badly now that India's independent," she said. "I think my real feeling has always been one of contempt for us, as a people. We loved being under the British, really, I think. No people need be ruled by another people for long unless it likes it. We're inferior people. But I don't hate India as much as I did."

"So you resent India having been ruled by the British?" Prem said it with a kindly malice. "You love the British but you resent them having ruled here for so long. That's it, isn't it?"

"Yes, that's it," she said. "I love the British and I'm ashamed of it, because you're not supposed to love them." She raised her voice in a sudden fit of irritation brought on by the clash of the two old dilemmas in her and said, "I don't know what I feel. How do I know what I feel? In London I used to forget I was an Indian, forget I had a brown skin which cut me off from many things. I *feel* like a European. No, I'm not unhappy to be back here, Prem."

"What's the matter then?" he asked. "Why are you unhappy?"

She got up from her chair and said, "I must go and see the children now. Don't forget that to-night we have God knows how many guests coming for dinner." She pointed at the whisky bottle and said, "You won't, will you?" Prem smiled and shook his head.

" I never reel about or fall down, Lila," he said. " Never."

" Fine," she said. " I don't know any of the guests and I'll need all the help I can get. I'm depending on you for introductions and hints and so on."

" Don't you worry, Lila," he said. " I'm not drunk." He tittered and began to pour another drink as Lila left the room.

Chapter Five

So it was to be good-bye. A letter had freed her. She told
Abednigo and the news got about that this little mission in
the wilderness was to close its doors. It had been a failure
and had only been kept going because Miss Bullen had been
willing to work without pay and to live on the small income
she had from her father's will. Every peasant in the villages
knew that.

" I could have done this years ago," she thought bitterly.
" I've just wasted a lifetime. Why did I do it ? Yet I did
believe. I did love the work. I did want to hand on Christ's
message, and I did work hard to make these sad creatures all
round me see a way to love God. And I got three converts,
who are despised, hated, unhappy, and for all I know, liars,
rice-Christians."

She wrote to Lila and thanked her and said she would
accept the post, and that she would arrive in Jashimpur City
in a week's time. When she had posted the letter she felt she
could have cried, for two reasons. One, for happiness in
freeing herself at last from this lonely and thankless existence
up here at Kangla, and two, because she was forty years late
in what she was doing. She found herself crying inter-
mittently throughout the sleepless night, while knowing she
was as hard as a rock. " What mysteries we are," she thought.
" What curious things we do. And we never know why."
One puzzle of her life which had wound itself right through
her being like a long thread of cotton tangled in a machine,

was why none of her hard and often exasperating work had been given an answer, for her three converts she could not count as success. After forty years her work deserved a thousand, ten thousand converts. She had been patient, devoted, courageous, for forty years, and here they all were still, the people, dirty, ragged, lying and despondent sinners. She felt love and hatred for them. They had stood by in their muck and misery and watched her get old and still they denied Christ without even saying a word. What kind of a Christ was it who let this happen ? That was the lifelong puzzle and she felt it in her now, like a bullet wound deep in her being, apparently incurable. Christ did not want a successful mission up here and she should have accepted that fact years ago. But He might have given her a hint, not just left her here, a failure. She believed firmly in the greatness of Christ, and in the splendour and truth of His message, which would endure for ever, but she doubted God's ability to keep an eye on all the bitter corners of this world, and to-night Kangla felt a bitter place to her, a graveyard in which she had mistakenly cast her years. Why should she deny that she had wanted success, a band of liberated, happy, hard-working Christians free of superstition and of that dark, burdened, frightened look, for their world for them as they were to-day was a place of threat and menace ? Why should she deny it ? Why pretend that the master had been trying her, had given her a cross to carry for forty years ? Why not admit that her life had been a waste ?

" A stupid waste ! " she corrected herself aloud in the dark, turning her head on the pillow to look out of the window on to the fiercely moonlit countryside which stretched dimly to the mountains. Now that she had written to Lila to say she would work for her, she suddenly hated Kangla and felt a hard and painful resentment for the people come up in her. And she cried again, thinking about being nearly seventy, one who had lived in loneliness for a Christ who would not even raise the spark of himself in fifty peasants to bless her labours. She had often known anger with Christ, with His peace-plan. Often she had wanted to take a whip, given the power, and flog a whole village into acceptance of her will. One generation and their descendants would be happy Christians. But no. She knew it to be merely poor human rage with unanswered work.

A pack of cowards they were, to take what they had taken for generations, for centuries, from their masters, many of whom were her friends.

Already she was composing in her mind her farewell message to them. She would assemble her enemies, the *Mullahs*, and bid them a bitter good-bye, would admit her defeat. But would remind them that they were not worth saving, that at last she had seen they were not worth her labours. She would flay them with her words, quietly, but scornfully, humorously but woundingly, for some things must be said, however hurtful. She felt better as the speech took shape in her mind. She would make a farewell to the *Mullahs* and the Pandits that would go into the folklore. She had never spoken her mind, having to curb herself for the greater cause of Christ's deathless message. And for nothing too. But an end had come and she would tell them what had smouldered in her heart during forty years of useless toil among them. Her rage gave her strength. It would be a moment worth living, the moment when she flayed them.

The next morning she sent Abednigo to call the *Mullahs* and Pandits to her. " Tell them it's important," she said.

At midday they came, the bearded men in their turbans and fezzes, their old clothes swinging drably about them, the *Mullahs* with their ancient faces of a greater Islam now sunk in ignorance, yet still carrying a kind of sullied dignity. The Hindu Pandits had never changed in five thousand years. They were intelligent and supple, watchful and grave, yet sensitive and cunning, some swinging rosaries of *rudhra* berries, others with long staffs. Together, the established order of the two great religions mired down here in the wilderness of outer Jashimpur, yet feebly alive and militant, faced her and greeted her. The oldest spokesman, Pandit Krishan, said, "Greetings, Miss Sahib. We have come to hear you. What can we do for you? What request have you to make of us? We trust we find you well and happy." She stared at these men who had outwitted her down the years.

As if they knew what was afoot, many villagers had come to stare and listen. After forty years with them Miss Bullen could half believe that their eyes had watched Lila write her letter, and had watched her answer Lila, and that they knew all. Nothing stayed secret in India, though better than anywhere was the impression created that none knew your secret. That was the real mystery of the East. That there was no mystery at all.

The scent of human excrement was coming into the compound, borne on the warm flower-fragrant breeze. To-day, she hated it again, noticing it in disgust as she had not done in years. That was because she was going. That was because her mind was awake again to the world as it was, a paradise peopled with scavengers who cast their filth about them haphazardly, they too far gone in dirt to remember any more that they lived in one of the most beautiful countries on the globe. Twenty years ago she had lectured the villages on sanitation, and had shown them how to build privies. They had been horrified that men should go again and again to the same chosen spot, into a small house in fact, and there cherish up a mountain of their filth. They had refused to have anything to do with it. Five years after that, cooler then, after almost stifling rage, she had bought a dozen *kurpas*, trowels, and had shown them how a human being could go out into the fields, make his ghastly little mess, and then bury it, and thus help to let the rioting flowers of Jashimpur have the air to themselves to sweeten. They refused that too, and to-day the country stank as when she had first seen it. This reminder of old battles against dirt, borne to her on the breeze, made up her mind for her and she spoke from her wounded heart.

"I have called you to tell you that I am leaving you," she began. "To tell you that at last I give up my labours to change your ways, and to tell you that you have your victory, that sloth and dirt and despair have won." She thought to pause as she saw incredulity, surprise, disbelief coming into their dark, cautious, watching eyes, but she was too moved to stop. She let the words come in a harsh unChristian tirade and poured her disappointment, and her gladness to be leaving them, over them and into them and all about them. She saw villagers running off to give the news. The Miss Sahib was going. The Miss Sahib had had enough of them at last.

She described her labours of the past forty years, in heat, in snow and freezing cold, in rain, in times of epidemic and famine. She described how she had hoped that she might light a faith and endeavour in these people, and how she, alone, had not been able to win. Had they, the *Mullahs* and Pandits, responded to her teachings? Never. Leave the matter of religion aside for a moment. Had they done anything about the filth and the needless disease? No. Nothing. She would tell them to their faces that they had done nothing but thwart and oppose her. So she was leaving them, and she was sorry to say she was not sorry, for her life here had been a difficult one, beset by opposition and an ignorance which did not wish to see itself dispelled. There. She had finished.

She could see that she had amazed them, that she had staggered them. They broke into Jashimpuri to each other, excitedly and nervously, and Pandit Krishan turned to her with a look of sorrow and reproach in his eyes and said, "Miss Sahib. It can't be true. You cannot leave us. You must not leave us. You are angry with us. We have hurt you in some way. Tell us what we have done and forgive us. But please do not leave us. Without you nothing could ever be the same again."

Astonished, she saw that he meant what he said, that they all meant what he said. She could see it in their faces. They were grieved and disturbed. She felt some triumph, like a thin temporary balm on her wounds. But she punished them again, for they could never be punished enough, these sly and sickening hypocrites who had, with slow and unhurried cunning, placed traps and snares in her way for forty years, beaming when they saw her defeated, but grave and stolid to her face. Oh, yes, she could not deny that she detested them. Why should she? They were detestable and she had been silent so long.

"Look at my three converts," she cried shrilly. "Look at the hell you have made of their life for them." The *Mullahs* and Pandits were all smiling, laughing, sniggering. She was enraged. "You think it amusing?" she demanded.

"Miss Sahib," the oldest of the *Mullahs* said when he had straightened his face to address her. "These are not converts, these three. It is time you knew. They are lowly men. They were sent to you as converts to give you a little happiness. That is all. It was when they fell in love with your food and ways that we grew angry with them. But they are not Christians. They are only there because we did not want you to feel your way on the road was without hope, for we love you like a mother, and it is pain for us to hear your words to-day. You must not leave us."

"They are not Christians?" she asked in a whisper.

All shook their heads gravely, understandingly, conscious of the pain in this particular moment for this old woman in her white sari. They stood before each other in a deep silence, tears in the woman's eyes.

"Miss Sahib," the oldest *Mullah* said with measure and

dignity, " God chose, for his reasons, to give strength to the English Christian arm for a time and to rule over Hindustan. And now God, for his own reasons, has removed the strength from that arm——"

" How *dare* you ! " she snapped at him.

" Am I to be silent then ? " he asked, suddenly Jashimpuri, coy, almost playful, yet the darkness of far-off anger behind the words, his head to one side, the cynical peasant again ready to kneel down in ironic surrender. When you have to kneel down in surrender, why not have fun as well ? Oh, she knew them.

" No. Speak on," she said, interested. It was a time for some open speaking. " But I won't be insulted."

" It is not my intention to hurt you, Miss Sahib," the *Mullah* said. " It is my intention to explain certain of our feelings which you do not understand."

" All right. Speak on." She was on her mettle. If they wanted plain talk, very well they could have it. She was ready.

" Now God has his ways," the *Mullah* said silkily. " You have not tasted defeat. You have not had the victorious stranger come to you in your defeat and tell you you should change your religion and that your ways are no good."

" And *are* your ways good ? " she asked, sarcastically Jashimpuri. The crowd burst into laughter. Oh, it was not possible to hate them. They *knew* but they were stubborn. They were even proud, though God knows what about.

" They are our own ways," the old *Mullah* said, dogged and patient, a smile in his eyes. " You have much fire in you, Miss Sahib. You are only a woman and yet you have shown yourself to us to have the heart of a dozen men. We respect you for that. You are like a brave mother. We know your hopes of the past. And you have not found one among us to come forward and eat the Christian rice in cowardice, in the turning from his own poor life to the one you could offer.

Will you not grant that you would be proud if you and yours were to do this, too, in a time of poverty and defeat? Do you admire the traitor?"

"You know my religion is the true religion," she said. "But you fight it. It is not a question of being a traitor. That is a wicked thing to say."

"God has taken the strength from your people's arm," the *Mullah* said. "Not because He does not favour you, but because He has his reasons. Why must you leave us, Miss Sahib? Stay with us. We know we are bad and wicked, but do not leave us. You are our friend, and you are like one of us now. Must you let God stand between us? God is not for that."

"God is not between us. God is above us."

"Ah, Miss Sahib, but you pull God down daily from above and place Him between us," the *Mullah* said slyly. "And you say He is *your* God. Do you not despise the poor man who is weak and spineless and comes forward and claims to be a Christian so that he shall eat and feel above his people? Do you not yourself treat the three converts we sent you as lesser men than us? Do you not despise them? But if the *rich* and *learned* one comes forward and says he will be a Christian, then men must look up and nudge each other and say, 'Here, what is this we see?' But the hungry whining one is no sign. What does it matter if we will not be Christians? We love you as our mother. You cannot go away from us now. You are one of us. We beg you to stay."

The oldest of the Hindus spoke now. "Miss Sahib," he said, "once, years ago, you gave a sermon in the village of Nadik. I was there listening. You said then that life is like a bird passing by, that it is brief. But Miss Sahib, it is only brief when you are enjoying it. For the poor man it is not brief. It feels like a thousand years for him. In Jashimpur the Muslims and the Hindus are not cutting each other's throats as they are doing in India to-day, but in the past we slew and tormented each other in the name of God. We were fools then. We shall never allow that again. You know how loaded down we are with sorrows, and with failings. God will not alter that for us. We must alter it ourselves. When we are free we shall be better men and more able to listen to you. It gives us shame and sorrow that you are angry with us and will not stay with us, that you are going to leave us because we have not become Christians. Will you not change your mind ? "

It was amazing for her to hear a Hindu Pandit speak such thoughts, and it was a sign of trust. She was ashamed. Yes, that was why she was angry with them, because they would not become Christians. It was wrong but she could not blame herself for that anger. She had wasted her life.

Because they had made her ashamed she now attacked them, wanting them to have shame as well as she, who did not deserve it so much as they. " When the people were starving I went to great trouble and expense to get dried milk from India, especially for the hungry children. And what did you do ? You told the people it was pig's milk which I was using to destroy their religion, to make them unclean. Do you think such a lie was fair to me ? None knew better than you that never would I do such a thing as you accused me of." She had never forgiven their fanaticism in that particular matter, and she never would.

The *Mullahs* were not ashamed. Their spokesman shook his head and smiled, a cynical but kindly smile. " Admit, Miss Sahib," he said, " that you always *hope*, that you always *wish* that the eater of the food you have given will feel a proper gratitude and join your religion. Will you not admit that to your old friends ? "

There was something maddening in the knowing way he had said it, and he knew it, and he watched her flush. They all stood in discreet and respectful silence and watched her face turn pink. She could feel the heat of it and she thought she could weep with anger and despair, for what he had said was true. Of course she always hoped, but had she given charity in the hope of a conversion from gratitude, or had she hoped her Christian example would move their hearts? She did not want to think about it. It was something to which she could never give an answer that would satisfy her scrupulous conscience.

"That is an insult," she said, falling back on injured innocence, but the next moment she laughed, angrily and ashamedly, throwing her head back in embarrassment as she listened to the old *Mullah's* reply.

"Nevertheless, Miss Sahib," he said, "we know you used to hope, while we never doubted your kindness. We had to fight for our own, for our weakest members, for although we are wicked and sinful people we are children of Islam, and well you know us and our religion. Even the murderer is a child of God."

"You will not go, Miss Sahib?" the Hindu said. A large crowd of villagers had gathered in the compound now. She had begun to enjoy this, the sensation she had caused, the strangely hurtful pleasure she got from their wish to keep her, and her old vanity which had never died was warmed that they wished her so well after all, and they wanted her to stay. What did she want to do? Did she really want to go? Had it all been such a waste? How did she know what seeds she had planted here and which might be nourished in secret places.

"Miss Sahib, when the revolution comes we will build you a school with our own hands and you can teach us in it," a young man cried from the crowd. "*Inquilab Zindabad!*" other young men screamed suddenly and frighteningly in the peace of the compound. It was the voice of the bloody and vengeful heart and she recognised it with tremulous fear.

The *Mullahs* and Pandits looked at her, broodingly, con-

E

sideringly, and one of them, when she showed her surprise at the revolutionary slogan shouted by the young man, said, " Yes, Miss Sahib. Revolution is about to start. The young men are going to tear down the government at last. Stay with us here, where you belong." No, she told them. She must go now.

Chapter Six

Hassan Mohamed had used the prison, as he had used other prisons, as a place in which to think and plan. He never fretted or tore at the bars of his cell door as most other prisoners did. He could wait. Nothing would stop revolution now. He was confident that a mob would come to the gaol for him one of these days. The manners of the guards, and even of the prison governor had begun to change towards him and they had joined the Party, secretly, of course. They knew he was the coming man. This gave Hassan more pleasure than anything during the year except the death of the old Maharajah. He hated all Maharajahs and landowners and merchants. He hated them almost as much as he hated the moneylenders, who were the real owners of Jashimpur.

This was the first time he had been imprisoned in a gaol in his native Jashimpur, and it would be the last. The prison governor had spoken roughly to him after he had been brought into the prison and had started to lecture him about the disruptive forces his teaching had awakened in Jashimpur.

"There will come a time when you will be as meek as a dove in my presence," he had told the prison governor. "So ingratiate yourself now while you have the chance. Believe me it will pay you." No prisoner had ever spoken like that to the governor. He had Hassan cruelly treated afterwards, but now he was tenderness itself, difficult though it was for him to undo the training in brutality which he had given his prison guards.

This morning when the iron door of the cell was suddenly opened, Hassan could hear sounds of consternation and confusion outside, with voices shouting, " Can't you see it's the Maharajah, fool ? Move out of the way," and " Let the guards in first, Maharaj Sahib. The prisoner is dangerous."

A young man in a snow-white tee-shirt and blue jeans stood in the opened doorway of the cell. He wore black glasses and in his white teeth he clenched a long yellow cigarette-holder with a cigarette smoking in it. A guard carrying a sub-machine-gun pushed his way dramatically past the Maharajah into the cell and began to menace Hassan, snarling, " Stand back there for the Maharajah." The man in the black glasses seized hold of the guard's sub-machine-gun and snatched it from his hands. Then he grabbed the guard by the collar and flung him out of the cell, saying contemptuously through his teeth in English, " Get *out*, you silly little bastard." He removed the loaded magazine from the gun and then flung both into the corridor after the sprawling guard. The prison governor was standing in the corridor, fearful and worried.

" You can go back to your office," Prabhu said to him. " I want to speak to the prisoner on his own. Leave a guard in the corridor." When the prison governor hesitated, Prabhu shouted, " Did you hear me ? " and was at once obeyed. Prabhu pushed the cell door to and then turned to the prisoner and stared at him through his dark glasses.

" So you're Hassan Mohamed," he said. " I'm the new Maharajah."

Hassan said nothing. He gave no sign of greeting, or of respect, or of nervousness. His face was quite impassive as he stood there and returned the opaque stare of Prabhu's dark glasses.

" You *do* speak English, don't you ? " Prabhu said, a little impatiently.

" Yes," said Hassan.

" I imagine it would be against your principles to show politeness to a Maharajah," Prabhu said acidly. Although he believed in socialism he did not like the prisoner's unruffled calmness and his silent unwillingness to recognise rank or title. He was a *British* socialist. There was something formidable about Hassan's calm, his air of confident insolence, which was perhaps not insolent, but was certainly confident.

" What would you like me to do ? " Hassan asked him seriously. The fellow had what sounded like a slight American accent.

" It's not a question of what I'd like you to do," Prabhu shouted, nettled after all his planning to show this man that his new Maharajah was as progressive as any agitator.

" Then what is it ? " Hassan asked him. " Why are you upset with me ? You seem very angry."

" Sit down," Prabhu said. " I've got to keep cool," he thought.

" No. I prefer to stand," said the prisoner with a hint of impatience in his voice. " What do you want ? "

" What do I *want* ? " Prabhu said incredulously. " It's not a question of what I want."

" Then what is it ? " Hassan asked with a provoking weariness of tone. " What do you want with me ? "

" That attitude's not going to help you," Prabhu warned him, almost stammering with rage. " You'll have to change your attitude."

" I'm sorry," Hassan said, shrugging his shoulders. " You come in here to my cell and start shouting at me. What's the matter ? What do you want ? Can't you control yourself and explain what's the matter ? "

Prabhu's face had swollen with blood and he looked as if he were about to fling himself upon the young man facing him. He got control of his temper and said harshly, " I suppose I can take it that you're a little surprised to be visited

by the Maharajah ? I'm not in the habit of visiting prisons."
He felt a fool after he had spoken these words, but he had
been thrown off balance and flustered.

"All right. What am I expected to do ? Kneel down and
show a proper respect ? " The man never changed his tone
of voice. He was cool and unperturbed, the most difficult
personality Prabhu had ever come across.

"I'm not going to stand for any impudence," Prabhu
blustered. "You can cut that impudence right out." Hassan
laughed, without mirth, a short hard laugh. Then he looked
at Prabhu ironically and smiled.

"What do you want ? " he said. "I'm busy."

"Busy ? " Prabhu spoke ironically. "You're busy, are
you ? Am I in your way, then ? Just say, if I'm in your
way."

Hassan sighed and looked up with weary eyes into the
corner of his cell. He said nothing. He was about Prabhu's
age, a tall well-built man with big, sharp, black eyes and a
short pointed black beard, his moustache not hiding his full
red lips. He was prison pale, almost ivory coloured, but he
looked fit and limber.

"I didn't come here to quarrel," Prabhu said. "I came to
discuss certain things with you. I want no quarrelling."

"Then don't quarrel," Hassan said. "Say what you want
to say. I'm a reasonable man. I'll listen."

The prison governor had warned Prabhu that Hassan was
a difficult man to deal with and Prabhu had ignored his
warning. He saw now that the prison governor had used
understatement. Once more he controlled himself. He had
come down here into the prison, full of idealism and goodwill,
a man with the good of the people at heart, anxious to win
Hassan over, to show him that they were men with a similar
outlook even though they were of such sharply differing
background.

"Listen," Hassan said, "I think I know what you're here

for. Apart from wanting to surprise me by showing how unusual and unorthodox a Maharajah you are by actually coming into my cell, you're going to tell me you're a reformer, that you're going to start changes in Jashimpur. I've had reports on you from London. You're a socialist and so on. Very interesting. But you're not a peasant and that makes a difference. You're a Maharajah and that makes a bigger difference. I'm not interested in your socialism. Now do you still want to talk to me?"

"We're not going to get on if you're going to take this attitude," was all Prabhu could think of to say, his fists clenched at his sides. He was wounded by Hassan's correct and cruel guess as to the reasons for his visit to Hassan in his prison. And he had come to the cell meaning well and was insulted and rebuffed.

"I don't want to get on with you," Hassan replied. "It's you who want to get on. It's you who need *us*. We don't need *you*. It's necessary for you to understand that clearly. You have nothing to offer us that we need. It's too late for all that kind of soft soap. You may even be sincere, but it makes no difference. It won't stop the revolution. It's not going to be an English socialist milk-and-water thing. This isn't England. This is a human mess made by your family and others like them. When we've finished here there'll be no need for any more Maharajahs." He spread his hands. "I'm sorry," he went on, "but we've had enough now. The people can't stand any more of the old life. You've come back to a different Jashimpur from the one you knew as a boy. It's a pity you came back. But it's as well you came to see me and heard what I have to say. It can save a lot of trouble for everyone."

"That's enough," Prabhu said. He was cut to the heart.

"You see, you can't drop your training, can you? Shouting's no good. Shouting means nothing to a man like me. I'm not one of your slaves. An ex-slave, yes. But if you want to live in this country then you'll have to stop shouting. We won't stand for it. It's out of date. Don't make an enemy of me. You'll regret it later."

Why go on with this situation? Prabhu sucked at his cigarette-holder, trembling with anger and with a longing to humiliate this arrogant, quiet man whose infuriating voice went on to say, "We'll give you a pension if you like. You can live in London. That's where you belong. You can live there in peace with your family."

"Are you threatening me?" Prabhu cried.

"No. But there's no place for you here. Parasitism is finished in Jashimpur. There's no room for parasites in the Jashimpur we're going to make."

"Are you calling me a parasite? Just say."

"You're a socialist, it's said. Are you going to deny that a Maharajah is a parasite? Is he necessary? What use is a Maharajah? Tell me what use he is."

He was no use. Prabhu could think of no use for a Maharajah. Except for a progressive Maharajah like himself.

"I came down here to offer you your freedom," he said. "But I was wrong." He was going to go on to give Hassan a sermon about how he now saw what kind of a man Hassan was, but the prisoner interrupted.

"I don't want you to free me," he said quietly. "Unless you want to free me. But whether I'm free or not won't make any difference to the revolution now. I'll be freed when I'm necessary, to rule the country. I'm in no hurry."

"So you're going to rule the country?" Prabhu's exasperation was so great that he made a step towards Hassan as if he might strike him. Hassan held up his hand and said, "No violence, please. If you attack me I'll kill you. We either discuss these things in a quiet and rational way or you must go. I'm not in the mood for a quarrel. You'd better tell me what it is you want."

" Oh ! So I'm allowed to speak now, am I ? Are you quite sure you've had your say and I can speak ? "

" Please ! " said Hassan disgustedly. He sat down now on his narrow bed and laid his hands on his knees and inspected them. " All right," he said. " I'll listen. But make it to the point." He looked up at Prabhu with his intense, staring eyes and added, " And no soft soap, please. Be brutally frank if you like. I prefer it. If you've come to bargain with me you're wasting——"

" Will you shut up and let me speak ? " Prabhu shouted at him. The guard opened the door and looked in with his big, soft, frightened eyes. Hassan picked up a sandal and flung it at him and the guard's face vanished.

" Go on," he said to Prabhu. " Sit down. Do, please."

The cell was about fifteen feet by ten, whitewashed walls completely bare of ornament, cool and stale smelling, Hassan's home in which he seemed quite at home and even happy. Already Prabhu admired and envied him, but he was unable to control a growing hatred for him. Without much effort Hassan was formidable and completely assured, and he was wary and astute, as when he suddenly said to Prabhu, " Don't be put off your socialism by my attitude to you. You may be sincere but we can't afford to deal with you. Patronage means nothing now. Your family are finished here now. But don't hate the people for that. It's your own fault. Don't be bitter."

" Bitter ? You've a bloody nerve. Bitter ? I'm not bitter," Prabhu was very excited now, provoked to emotional excess, words pouring from his tremulous mouth. " I could smash you all to-day but I won't do it. I won't be provoked. I won't be got rid of. You'll live under me and in justice. I haven't come back here to fight people who believe in the things I believe in. I've waited for years to bring in reforms here in Jashimpur and I'll bring them in. If you want to help in this you can come in, but I won't put up with any hostility from people like you. There'll be a revolution but *I*'ll make it, legally and from the top. I've come down here to tell you that you've got to stop the disturbances in the town first of all. I'll have no violence. It's got to stop."

Hassan replied in Jashimpuri and Prabhu waved his hand irritably and said, " I don't understand that lingo so cut it right out." Then Hassan spoke in Urdu, and Prabhu, whose Urdu was deficient, said, " Speak in English."

In English Hassan said, " What language are you going to speak to the people in ? English ? That's no use. You've made yourself a foreigner here, not that any of your family are really Jashimpuri. You came here from the Punjab four generations ago and stole the country from us. I refuse to co-operate with you or any of your family."

" That's up to you," Prabhu said, cool again now. " Are you getting enough books to read ? Is there anything you want ? " He had come to the prison to free Hassan after having surprised him by revealing a Maharajah who was even more progressive than Hassan himself. But now he was angry and although he knew he was taking the first step in oppressive rule he decided to take it and to keep Hassan in prison.

" I want nothing, thank you," Hassan told him. The fellow was so smug, so very cool and sure of himself. Prabhu could not give up yet. He had another try.

" You said I was a socialist and that you were told from London about me. What does that mean ? Who told you from London ? "

" We have our contacts," said Hassan.

" Are you a communist ? "

Hassan laughed with genuine amusement. " Do you think we've struggled here in order to trap ourselves in an out-of-date ideology like communism ? " he said. " We don't need communism. If people get land and justice they don't want communism. Communism's finished."

Prabhu, who believed that communism was the power of the future, and wished he didn't, took off his dark glasses and let Hassan see his broody, staring eyes for the first time. He saw Hassan's sharp eyes examining his unmasked face and he hoped he could win Hassan over. He was a man whom he did not want to antagonise further. He respected him and was trying not to hate him for the cold contempt the prisoner had shown him. He was baffled by Hassan's unshakable air of freedom and self-confidence which made the small cell into something other than a prison ; it was as if Hassan was quite sure of running his revolution from here, cut off as he was from his people. He was ignoring his prison and was going to beg for nothing. It was as if he were unpunishable, unbuyable, beyond blandishment and compromise.

"You really believe communism's finished ? " Prabhu was laughing, thinking that perhaps Hassan was mad, an eccentric who had been too long in a cell. It was the coolness of Hassan which made him laugh.

"Have you ever been in America ? " Hassan asked him. Prabhu shook his head.

"No," he said. "Have you ? "

"Yes," said Hassan. "I worked in factories in America for a couple of years. Have you ever done any work yourself ? I mean *work*. Manual work."

Annoyed, Prabhu shook his head. "Why ? " he asked. "Does that cancel me out as a progressive ? Is manual labour the passport to righteousness ? What bloody nonsense."

"Now you're getting angry again," Hassan admonished him gently. "Since you came into this cell you've been making an exhibition of yourself and shouting in real Maharajah style. The reason I asked you if you've ever done any real work was to see how serious you are. You're one of these dabblers, a semi-intellectual progressive. We're going to have none of that here. Whoever heard of a socialist Maharajah ? You'll be despised by the people for it. Abdicate now and become an honest man. You'll be less ashamed of yourself then. If you want reforms then start with yourself. Abdicate."

Prabhu got to his feet and put on his dark glasses. He was choked with rage. He had always prided himself on being able to charm and win over other people, no matter how difficult. He regarded himself as a sincere, warm-hearted and reasonable man and he was frustrated by the solid arrogant calm of Hassan.

" I see we can meet nowhere," he said through his clenched teeth. " You're a fanatic. I came here to free you. Did you know that ? Well, I won't now. By God, I won't——"

" You're like a little child," said Hassan, smiling his friendly smile. " I don't want to be freed by you. I don't even want to be charged. I suppose you know I'm here without charge. That doesn't matter. The more tyranny just now the better. Send out the troops and shoot the people. Make more arrests. Follow tradition. It all helps. One thing we won't do is take anything from *you*. We don't want any presents from you in the way of reforms. You may be sincere but the best thing you can do is abdicate."

" That's enough," Prabhu said dramatically. " Shut up now. I've heard enough." He was so disappointed that he thought of making an appeal to Hassan, for he knew that without Hassan he might not be able to function in the way he had dreamed of, as the new kind of progressive, reforming Maharajah.

" I was going to explain to you why communism's finished," Hassan was saying, " but you keep getting angry and shouting. You're an autocrat. Now you're going to try and be a just autocrat and reform by force. We won't accept it. We'll accept nothing from you. The one thing we won't accept is one of your kind trying to ingratiate yourself because you know that the old days are finished——"

" That's not true," Prabhu cried heatedly. Because he was

sincere he must make his antagonist see that at least he, Prabhu, the Maharajah, was not a reformer out of craft or fear. " I intend giving up all my own family estates," he said. He tried not to sound ingratiating. " Land reforms will be complete——"

" With compensation to the landowners, of course," Hassan snapped ironically. " I'm not prepared to listen to any more of this nonsense."

" That's enough now," Prabhu shouted. He went to the door and opened it and the prison governor almost fell into the cell. Hassan sneered, laughing at the prison governor, who stood quietly and apologetically before Prabhu.

" You want me as an enemy," Prabhu said to Hassan. " Okay. I'll be your enemy," and on this dramatic note he left the cell.

" Tell them to send my food. I'm hungry," Hassan told the prison governor. " And I want no more visitors, thank you. Go and see to my food."

" It should be on the way now," the governor said fretfully. " I'm sorry it's late. Very sorry."

" Then clear off and leave me alone," Hassan said. " I want to think."

Chapter Seven

The twins sat, anxious and silent, while they waited to meet Miss Bullen. They had caught a glimpse of her in the corridor earlier on, and Roshan Lal, the elder by ten minutes, turned to his brother, Narendra Nath, and whispered, " She's even older than Mum said."

" If you call Mother Mum again," Narendra Nath said in a low, threatening voice, " I'm going to tell her. You know how she hates that word. It's low and horrible." He could not bear to think of his mother as Mum.

" It's going to be a living hell with this old woman," Roshan Lal whispered. " Wait and see. Why can't we go to a proper school like in London ? We'll be dominated. Wait and see. Mum "—he met his brother's hot eyes and added, " Mother —okay—Mother. Mother said we're not to sound too ignorant about religion if the old woman asks us. We're to say nothing. What I want to know is what's going on around here ? I mean between Mother and Prab. They've had another row. I can tell it was a bad one by the way Prab snaps at us. Why do these kind of people marry at all ? Why ? "

" Shut up," Narendra Nath said out of the side of his mouth. " And try and use some tact with Miss Bullen. Don't go shooting your mouth off about things." Roshan Lal talked about anything that came into his head, to anybody. He had no idea of the necessity for secrecy about some things, though he knew how to pretend about his sins and failings if caught.

" All right, oh, holy one," Roshan Lal said. " Don't worry. I'm not a complete fool." They could hear Miss

78

Bullen coming, the fruffing sound of her sari and the squeak of her sandals. " And why does she wear Indian dress. She's not Indian," Roshan Lal whispered.

" So *there* you are," Miss Bullen said. She smiled at them as they stood up. She shook hands with them. They were unidentical twins, completely different physically. She thought Lila could have come and handed over the children to her herself, but she was in her room with a bad headache. Still, it was a bit casual.

" How is your mother ? " she asked the two boys.

" A bad hangover," Roshan Lal replied. " Mother drinks."

Miss Bullen blushed and looked at the thirteen-year-old face with the big brown eyes looking keenly at her through horn-rimmed glasses. " You mustn't say such things about your mother," she said with gentle firmness.

" But it's true," the boy said, without impudence. " You're bound to find out sooner or later. Mum can't help drinking. We don't mind, do we, Nar ? " He looked at Narendra Nath, who was scowling at him and looking as if he were near tears.

" Don't speak about it," he said threateningly to Roshan Lal. To Miss Bullen he said, " Roshan Lal has no control over his tongue, Miss Bullen. He's always getting us into trouble because of it. He's a fool. He only thinks it's clever to sound grown up, that's all."

" Come along now. We'll go into the garden for a while," the old woman said to them. She must not start off by being severe, though as sure as God was her judge she could have given Roshan Lal a box on the ear right there and then. Perhaps the boy was backward, though, one of those innocents who spoke the truth always and caused such trouble in the world. She had never liked boys but she could start trying right now.

" A hangover ! " she kept saying to herself, shocked and amazed. She had come to know the word during the war when the whole world was full of soldiers looking for drink. Jashimpur had been popular as a leave centre then. They had even come into Kangla mission in their jeeps and had been kind to her but she never had much time for them. Men in the herd, without women, were too close to the animal. And here was a small boy saying that his mother, that beautiful and gentle girl, Lila, had a hangover. It was unpleasant to think about and she put it out of her mind and it came back at once.

" Did you like London ? " she asked the boys when they were sitting under a tall chenar tree.

" Like it ? *I*'ll say we did," Roshan Lal told her. " That was civilisation. I hate it here with all these phony old men who hate Prab's guts and pretend they don't. *I*'ll say we liked London, eh, Nar ? Then there's the language problem. Prab and Mum are fighting about that already. He says she should have brought us up to speak Urdu and she says he didn't want that, and he can't remember that. Anyway, we've got to learn it now. I'll never settle down here. I'm English in all but skin."

Miss Bullen smiled thinly while Narendra Nath told her that Prab was their father. He looked at Roshan Lal then and said, " Cut it out now, Roshe. It's not funny."

" I don't think you mean to be funny, do you ? " Miss Bullen asked Roshan Lal. He looked at her with a hint of gratitude in his eyes, but suspicious with it, and shook his head. " No," he said, " I'm not trying to be funny. Nar doesn't understand me. He never did. No one really understands me."

" That'll do now," Miss Bullen said, chilly with old-time distaste for self-pity, a curse she had had to fight in herself for so many years.

She was still happy from the warm and affectionate reception Lila had given her the night before. She had arrived late, tired and dusty from the long journey in the trade truck from Kangla. There was a party going on in the palace, and Lila, magnificent in a black and gold georgette sari, had invited her in to the party just as she was. When she had declined because of her dustiness and untidiness, Lila said, " As you wish, my dear. But don't stand on ceremony. You can't be expected to look like a picture after a long journey. I could do with an ally too. All the women in there are the usual subdued semi-purdah lot and it gets one down so much. Are you tired ? All right, I'll show you your room. Come on." In the room they had fallen into excited talk, forgetful of time until the Maharajah sent what must have been a stiff little note of reminder about the duties of a hostess, judging by the way Lila had pursed her full red mouth after reading it.

" Do you think there's going to be any fighting in the country, Miss Bullen ? " Narendra Nath asked her. " I mean real bloodshed ? " Eagerly Roshan Lal pestered her for information on this topic, adding, " We were right through the blitz in London, you know. War's nothing once you've tasted it. Do you think there's going to be a real revolution ? Prab's all for it——"

" You mustn't refer to your father in that way," she said. " It's most disrespectful. Do you understand ? "

" Okay," Roshan Lal said. " As you wish. But that's what he says. He's going to turn this country upside down. ' A stagnant heap of rubbish,' he called it the other night."

" Did he say that to you ? " she asked him lightly.

" Oh, no," Narendra Nath cut in. " He listens-in at key-holes. He's been punished for it by Father but he goes on doing it."

She smiled sweetly at them both. There was something wild about them, something uncared for in them. What kind of a life had they had in London ? " Tell me about school in London," she said. " What was it like ? Did you like school ? "

The two boys looked at each other, and then Roshan Lal looked away. " I liked it," Narendra Nath told her. " Roshe

F

didn't. He was going to be expelled if we hadn't come away when we did to India. He set fire to the headmaster's newspaper. The headmaster was reading it at the time. He's not allowed to have matches or play with fire at all now. Are you, Roshe?"

"No," said Roshan Lal sullenly, hopelessly.

Roshan Lal was taller than his brother and he was thin where Narendra Nath was stocky and well fleshed. He was nervous, chewing his lower lip, picking at his hair, twitching his nostrils, gnawing a thumb nail or sometimes shaking his right foot obsessionally. They both had thick shocks of glossy black hair. Narendra Nath was grave and handsome with a slight suggestion of fretful disapproval in his big black eyes whenever he looked at his brother. They had Lila's pale golden ivory skin.

"I'm being watched all the time," Roshan Lal complained to Miss Bullen. "It's bad for me. Only Mum understands me. But don't get the idea that I'm a problem child. I'm not. It's because I'm always expected to be like my brother that causes the trouble. Holy Joe here." He pointed to his brother. "Holy Joe's always sucking up to people and making out I'm a problem child. I never suck up. Grown-ups hate you for that, don't they?" When the old woman did not answer he said again, "Don't they?"

"Tell me about school in London," she said. She had seen already that these two looked on London as home, because their parents thought of it as home. Lila had often told her in letters that she would be happy nowhere else. She wondered if Lila still disliked India as much as in the past. Strange child. Fighting against her own people and full of undefined resentments. She remembered Lila's father, a small, intense, eccentric man obsessed by religion, by health and horoscopes and telepathy. He had gone a little mad in the end, it was said.

"Soon you were going to be expelled," she said to Roshan

Lal. "Do you like being naughty? Or do you hate it when you've been naughty?"

"Naughty?" Roshan Lal looked very put out as he said the word. "I'm fourteen next year," he reminded her. "I wouldn't call it *naughty*."

"Well, badly behaved then. Do you hate to be badly behaved?"

"Why?" he asked her. "Why do you want to know that?" He was puzzled and wary.

"You won't start setting fire to my newspaper, will you?" she asked him.

Roshan Lal looked hard at her thin, sunburnt face with its pink cheekbones and faint wrinkles at nose and mouth, and into her big clear grey eyes. He saw then that she was formidable, one who would dominate if she got her way. He could sense it, her will and her hardness beneath her smile. He felt hopeless then and said, "No. I wouldn't do anything to upset *you*. I hated our headmaster because he hated me. That's all. It's wrong for a grown-up to hate a boy. We need patience and understanding while we're growing up. Isn't that what Prab said last week after he'd given us all one of his shouting tellings-off, Nar?"

"Oh, shut up," Narendra Nath cried. "Miss Bullen doesn't want to hear all this." He was ashamed of his brother.

"Why did the headmaster hate you?" Miss Bullen asked Roshan Lal. "Surely you're mistaken. He probably quite liked you."

"He got hold of me one day after cricket," Roshan Lal said to her in an urgent, desperate way, "and he gripped my ear. He often did that to boys he hated. And he said, 'You'll finish up on the scaffold, sonny. And there'll be no appeal either.' That's the kind of headmaster he was. I was going to run away in the end. Nar liked it. Nar gets on with everybody. He has no complexes like I have. My troubles are mainly because I won't suck up to authority."

" I want to find a good school for them in India," Lila had told Miss Bullen the night before. " But I'd love it if meanwhile you can get to know them and keep an eye on them until we're settled down. They're feeling disturbed and upset. Roshan Lal worries me quite a lot. He's very nervous and terribly neurotic. You may find them a handful at first but I know they'll love you. I'm afraid I've neglected them a lot. I'm a bad mother."

Quite soon Miss Bullen had them talking about their ambitions and their plans. She began to like Narendra Nath and to cultivate patience with Roshan Lal's wild switches from subject to subject, and with his curious clinical self-pity and his precocious obsession about himself in relation to the world.

" Did you have any religion at school ? " she asked them when there was a lull. Narendra Nath gave his brother a significant look and then said, " Well, in a way, no."

" Tell the truth," Roshan Lal said wearily. " Father hates religion. We have no religion. There was a little religion at school but you could tell we were having it because it was an order. Father says religion has ruined India." He had stopped calling his father Prab, the old woman frowned so often at him when he had done so. She was foxy and he knew she was weighing him up and he could not help trying to make a good impression, though it went against his nature. The old woman had eyes like two electric drills and he knew she knew he had told a couple of lies about his doings at school. She had a way of nodding slowly and understandingly when he was lying which had made him feel very uncomfortable. As he thought about that he had a sudden impulse to run away and hide. But he sat quite still and answered all her questions.

" Are you a missionary ? " he asked her.

" I was," she said. " But not a very good one, I'm afraid. I didn't make any converts."

" Do you want us to go to church ? " Narendra Nath asked

her. " I'll go if you want me to. I'm not against church. Roshe is but he's against everything because it's smart. He doesn't really mean it. Don't be taken in by him. He's quite windy about everything underneath. So am I but I admit it. Does that sound as if I'm sucking up ? Roshe tells everybody I suck up. But I don't even if I sound like it."

" My God," Miss Bullen thought. " What *have* I done ? Why did I leave Kangla ? " " Shall we go for a walk ? " she asked the two boys. They agreed.

" There's a wizard temple at the end of the grounds," Roshan Lal said. " It's got a big mad-looking black woman in it with a knife. A god. Do you want to see it ? "

" A goddess," Narendra Nath corrected him. " Kali. It gives me the creeps. Shall we take you there ? "

In all her time in India she had never set foot in a temple or a mosque. She decided that now she would go with the boys. She feared Hinduism, connecting it with secret orgies and silent things and darkness. But she had always felt curiosity about it.

" Are we allowed to go in ? " she asked. She wanted to go into the temple now.

" It's ours," Narendra Nath told her. " Our grandfather used to use it, Father said. Father won't go near it. It's weird to think Grandfather used to go there and pray. Wait till you see Kali. It gives you the creeps."

" All right," she said. " I'll just have a peep with you."

She had studied Hinduism and had been impressed with many aspects of its philosophy, but she feared the strange bloody mess men had made out of it in the temples. These boys were Hindus and did not seem to know it. So easily did a generation of English ways disestablish the tradition of several thousand years. It was a shame that they knew no God, nothing. It was too bad of Lila, who had been brought up in a Christian home.

The temple was a building of massive red sandstone blocks.

They could see it through the trees after they had walked for a few minutes. Miss Bullen could hear music and she stopped. She could hear the low notes of a flute, the urgent yet un-hurried melancholy of the melody so moving that it caught at her heart.

" Do you know what that is ? " she asked the boys almost in a whisper. Impressed by the mysterious quality of the music, they shook their heads as they listened.

" That's *bhairavi*," she said. " *Raga bhairavi*, and it's being played at the wrong time of day too. But it doesn't matter. It's my favourite and I could listen to it at any hour." She had never heard the *raga* played with such feeling and skill, for this *raga* produced a sensation of unfathomable mystery, always giving her an impression of the load of eternity which man could never shift from himself, and at the same time it was full of a tenderness and sadness which stopped the tread of the mind. It was for the early morning, when man woke up out of his dreaming withdrawal from daytime, out of his sleep in which he had slipped the chain of his conscious living, and that was *bhairavi* time, dawn, sad but sweet, painful but glad, the re-entry into the world of struggle and appetite. It was a kind of sad gladness in the waking up for another day, instead of sleeping on, dead, gone. That was *raga bhairavi*, which she had remained attracted to since she had first heard it played by a Muslim *Ustad* in Delhi forty years ago.

The flute notes, liquid and dark, fluttered in the hot air and went echoing in the trees about them, the player shedding long cascades of his own design, and then building up slowly to the theme again, which was like a question, full of unanswer-able dolour, rueful and languorous. It was the music of estrangement and forsakenness made tender with hope and wonder. Its magic had never been so powerful for her as now while she stood in the midst of the flute notes so know-ingly woven, inducing a desire to shed tears, neither of sorrow nor pleasure, but for the feeling of mystery it always awoke, mystery and spiritual unrest. It was as though that cherished anguish which haunts the human being was given shape in sound, the ghost of time and living awakened in the body by the magic of these peculiar and special sounds which someone, centuries ago, had devised as the feeling of the tropical morning, those moments of languor between darkness and the first fire of the sun against the palm fronds.

They went quietly towards the sound of the flute and Narendra Nath said quietly, "It's Uncle Prem." She recognised Prem, whom she had met for five minutes the night before. He was sitting cross-legged, slightly hunched, with his black hair hanging down like the wings of a shot raven in the sunlight. He was playing a short bamboo flute and three of the temple priests were sitting opposite him, absolutely still, dressed in blood-red gowns of cotton, small turbans of the same violent colour on their heads. Two were grave and handsome, while the other one had an animal expression on his face, feral and aware and roused, his black eyes full of unguessable dreams, excited by the music. Prem swayed with the music, bending his head as if the better to coax out the marvellous weave of sound he had stored up in the flute. He finished with a long, low quivering note, holding it and then letting it slowly diminish in the hot silence.

"More," one of the priests said seriously, as if he had to hear more immediately.

"Yes, more," the other two said.

"You said it was the wrong time," Prem accused them, smiling.

"Even though it is the wrong time, more," one of them urged, smiling back at Prem. "You are a master."

"No more to-day," Prem said, and got up, brushing dust from his white cotton pyjamas. He turned and waved to Miss Bullen and the twins. "You can come now," he called, smiling at them. They were some way off and he went to meet them. Miss Bullen was confused, for she thought they had been unobserved and she felt like an eavesdropper.

" I hope we didn't interrupt," she said. " It was beautiful. The *raga* I like best too. We didn't want to disturb you."

" Really ? " Prem seemed delighted and surprised. " I heard you coming. I can hear a fly walking a mile away. So you like our twisty music, Miss Bullen ? Good. I had a friend in the bag with me in Malaya, an Englishman. He always called it twisty. He never really got to like it but he was always asking me to play it." He looked at the twins and said, " Having a good time ? You two little cockneys, we'll have to initiate you." He called to one of the priests and said, " Give the boys a piece of *gur* to eat."

The priest brought them two lumps of brown sticky *gur*, and when the boys had tried it they settled to eating it and forgot the grown-ups.

" What a magnificent door," Miss Bullen said. She pointed to the big silver door of the temple. It was glittering in the sunlight.

" Yes. It's rather splendid, isn't it ? I expect my brother will melt it down and build a crèche or a clinic with it. We live in stirring times. Would you like to see the temple ? " He eyed her for a moment. " You might find it a bit shaking. The idol, I mean." He smiled engagingly. " Are you an iconoclast, Miss Bullen ? " He had established a warm feeling between them already and she was able to laugh at his question, her head on one side, looking young for a second or two.

" I suppose I am," she said. " But I won't cast the idol down, I promise. Are you a devotee of Kali ? "

" Good God, no," Prem said. " At least I don't think so. I certainly bow to her. She reminds me of the underside of a few things I've seen, during the war. In fact she makes sense when you look at her. I often come down here and leave fruit or *gur* for her. Harmless stuff. She'd like a good pool of blood better, I'm sure. Come and have a look at her. You're nervous, Miss Bullen, aren't you ? " Their eyes met. His were warm and sympathetic. He looked thin and worn and gentle. " A nice person," she was thinking as his question struck her. He was reading her.

" Yes, I *am* a little nervous," she told him. " How do you know that ? " It was most strange, the ease she felt with him.

" Of the goddess ? " he asked. " Or of the whole Hindu religion ? I suppose we can call it a religion. Yes. I suppose it's all right to describe it as a religion. No, I thought that as a missionary you might disapprove. If you don't want to see her just say. It's perfectly okay with me. I've no feelings about it." Again he smiled at her. " I'm a Christian-Hindu-Muslim agnostic myself. So you can tell me if you're nervous."

" No," she protested. " I do want to see it. I'll admit I'm a little nervous. It's silly, I know, ignorance and prejudice." She had never spoken like that to anyone before.

" Come on," he said. He took her hand in his own in a way which had an innocent goodness of heart in it and which both moved her and embarrassed her, but his small cool hand reassured her and she went towards the door of the temple with him. " Kick your sandals off," he said. " No leather allowed in the temple." They kicked their footwear off and then Prem took off his wrist-watch with its leather strap and laid it inside one of his discarded shoes.

" Shan't be long, blokes," he called to the boys in an imitation of cockney.

" I think we're going to get on very well together, Miss Bullen," Prem said to her in a matter-of-fact way when they stood before the silver door of the temple. " Do you have that feeling too ? "

" Why, yes, I do," she told him. She wondered if she would blush but no blush came. He was holding her hand and smiling. His charm and his gentle way with her was uncomplicated and easy.

" That's good," he said. " You'd better call me Prem, Miss Bullen. I'd like it if you called me Prem. Eh? Now look at the door. Look at the designs on it. Someone must have spent years on that job. And all for nothing as far as I'm concerned. I mean I like how he did it, but not what he did. All that concern about slaughter and blood."

The artist's concern had been minute and detailed, the sliced-off heads, all etched in black on the flashing silver, and the gouts, torrents and spews of blood in scarlet, the colour as fresh as when laid on over a century before. There were men twisted in every sort of agony, tormented by every kind of mutilation available to the sword, even the severed heads picturing the extremities of pain the artist had guessed they had known, and worn on their faces after the destroyer's sword had finished with them.

" So much for our pathetic end to our golden age," Prem thought as he looked at the pictures on the door. He could wonder idly at the hundreds of hours, sped so long ago, which the artist had spent on these facets representing the cult of blood and death, which yet was not death but was the message of the violence in the universe, its tireless ungovernable power. He always thought of Kali-worship as the sun-broken peasant's surrender to the violent forces of the universe against which he had no weapons, and from which he could not hide. " Like us," Prem thought. " But he can't avoid it as we can. No electric fans, no fridges, no ice, no cushioned shade." But he *had* seen Kali's world, that dark murderous background of the real world from which the thin, cool mask of civil safety had been ripped. The world of defeat, which was Kali's world, the world in which violent death and suffering were in need of constant appeasement. Was that why he came here now so often to this temple, a man without religion but with an understanding of why others knelt down, and especially why they acknowledged this black demoniacal personality before which Miss Bullen was now standing in stunned and silent horror? Probably yes. He felt peaceful here in the big, cool, stone room, standing before the tall, savage, nubile, black goddess rearing above him, her long, wet, white teeth flashing and her curled, red tongue sticking out in that special and frightful exaltation of the death-image so beloved of the long-dead man who had fashioned her figure with devoted, religious care. She held aloft a huge burnished steel sword, its end curled into a terrible billhook, the beloved slayer of the world, the mother-destroyer who had a queer, mad love for her children whom she slew, the children of the world who were born to die of cholera and starvation and malaria. "But the hypodermic needle has bitched things for you, Mother," Prem smiled up at her, at her huge, staring eyeballs. "But never mind. You could have your old world of blood back to-morrow if things go wrong for us in Washington or Moscow." Yes. He had lived in her world, her special world of death and fear on the Thailand-Burma railway, built by the Japanese so that their troops could go and die in battle in Burma more quickly than by sea from Malaya. Yes.

The goddess was tall and naked and black, four-armed, garlanded with severed heads, skulls white and terrible at her waist, and her big pointed breasts seemed so full that milk might spring from them at any moment. The curved sword she held aloft in one of her hands had slain the headless man upon whom she was dancing. One of her long beautiful legs was raised in this dance, and her enormous eyes were full of a vision of madness and blood lust.

Miss Bullen stared up at her, terrified and sickened, but fascinated, and stunned into a dry-throated silence by the horror which loomed above her and which seemed as if it might descend and spread at any moment.

Prem went forward, knelt down, and then prostrated himself with his hands and arms stretched out before him and his forehead pressed to the ground. He stayed like that for some seconds and then got quickly to his feet again.

She had always been quick to take advantage of intimacy and friendship when she had known it, and she said without thinking, " Prem, how could you go down before this beastliness like that ? How could you ? You said you don't believe in her."

" For all the thousands of slaves who died on the railway from Thailand to Burma in 1943," he told her. " I always do it for them. D'you think that's silly ? " He was grave, his slender hand resting on her arm. He wanted her to understand, not to be too British and Christian about what had obviously upset her. But her eyes were fixed on the silent and raving goddess above them, as if she were defying Kali to meet her eyes. She believed in Kali, Prem thought ironically.

" You're impressed by her," he said. " She's a fact for you, isn't she ? You want to pull her down ? "

" She only represents the beastly little mind of the creature who carved her and put her up," she said. " Some tortured creature in need of true religion. That's all."

Prem sighed and scratched his head, a thin affectionate smile on his face while he watched her.

" She's a fact," he said. " She was very much with us on the Thailand-Burma railway. Whenever I think of what I saw there I think of her. She represents this world before we got control of it. Cholera and cruelty and filthy ways of dying. She makes sense."

" Yes. I suppose she does. I can't bear to look at her any more. Can we go ? "

" Yes. Come on. We'll sit down outside." He took her arm in his. She had turned quite pale and when she smiled there was a ghastly sort of tiredness in it, reminding him of how some men looked after being heavily shelled. He was very concerned. He regretted taking her into the temple.

She was old. She was of that generation which was so narrow and so worried about heathenism that . . . No. Not fair. But after all she was a missionary, and of a narrow generation. He kept forgetting that people of his generation had no fixed rule and no range-card and no compass bearing. His generation was on a long dawdling lost patrol, and was not worried about it either. Yes.

" I'm so sorry, Miss Bullen," he said when they got outside. " It's upset you, hasn't it ? "

" Of course it has," she replied, cross but friendly. " Seeing such a bestial sight doesn't happen every day. Like a walk through an abattoir with the devil. Ugh, what a vile thing to worship. And yet I can understand why it reminds you of horrible experiences in the war. Perhaps that's what the horrible thing was made for in the first place, to remind us of what brutes we can be. And yet, God knows, I can't see us as brutes."

" We're not brutes," Prem said softly. " At least not often." He tittered. He was dying for a drink. He had gone nearly two hours without one and it was no use. He had started to try and hold out for a whole afternoon without a drink, but already he was asking himself, " But why ? Why bother ? It's pointless. Either give it up altogether or drink whenever you want to." And as he was not going to give it up altogether, ever, he knew, he was annoyed with himself for bothering to try and hold out.

" Would you like some iced lime crush or something ? " he said. " Or something a little stronger ? We'll go back and sit on the veranda and talk. I'm very thirsty. Are you ? "

" I'd like something to refresh me," she told him.

She sat down on a bench of red sandstone by the wall while they put on their shoes. Prem began to talk about the Tamil labourers who had died in hordes while building the Japanese army railway from Thailand into Burma. He said they stayed in his mind as a symbol of a mystery. The Japanese had shattered the belief that the white men were unbeatable, but had also been given a chance to show that they were not better men than their defeated enemies. They had proved to be cruel and without mercy, and in their deep feelings of inferiority masked as perfection was the antithesis of that arrogance which had been the failing of their foe. That, said Prem, was the mystery. Was it the capacity for mercy and pity which, after all, made a people superior? He often wondered.

He asked her if she agreed with the departure of British power from India. Did she feel any different? Had she discovered anything since they had gone those few months ago?

" How do you mean, Prem? " she asked, knowing how he meant, but wanting time.

" I mean if you've been a member of an Imperial race and enjoyed it, and surely you all enjoyed it, do you feel strange to be in a country the size of India when your government runs it no longer? I hope this isn't a painful subject for you. Is it? " His voice was full of sudden sensitive concern and he looked at her with gentle and sorrowful eyes, making her laugh affectionately.

" Yes," she said. " I *have* thought about it." She wanted to tell him things she had never told an Indian, and which she had never wanted to tell an Indian. He saw her hesitation and he said, " Go on. Say it. It won't hurt me. You hate India being independent, even though you know she must have it and has a right to it, is that it? " His smile was winning, his eyes showing understanding. " Do you despise us very much? " he asked her. He heard her draw in her breath very sharply.

" Prem," she said with gentle severity. " What a thing to say. Do you believe I despise you? "

" What's the harm? " he asked her. " You can like a thing and despise it as well. Take Lila. She despises us all, and herself as well. She's a casualty."

" A casualty ? "

" Yes. A psychological casualty. People ruled by other people, conquerors, are all a bit twisted by it. None of us have ever told each the truth, have we ? I mean no Indian and no English person has ever spoken their hearts to each other, have they ? We talk among our own race and then switch to another usage for each other, you and me, I mean. Why don't you want to answer my question ? " He was looking into her eyes. She decided he was a truthful-looking and honest young man and she thought she could trust him. But she was cautious. What did she want to say ? That India was not ready for the freedom she had got ? What was " ready " ? India had been " free " for a long time before the British had ever built a ship or a cannon. What made her unfit to be free, and then when the foreign occupation was at an end, fit to be free ? But she did resent India no longer being ruled by the British. She admitted it, to herself.

" *Please* answer my question, Miss Bullen," Prem begged her, like a boy nagging for an answer. " I feel I can talk to you. Won't you talk to *me* ? "

" Of course," she said, puzzled and flustered.

" Well ? Are you glad we're free, or not ? "

" Are you ? " she asked. " Are you glad, Prem ? "

" Half of me," he said. " The atavistic half. The other half, the cricket-playing, Keats and Shakespeare-reading and whisky-drinking half, no. He's not glad, that half. But I accept it as inevitable. I know I'm a spineless sort of waster. I know I should be glad we're independent but I'm not. And yet I do understand how millions who are not varnished with British training are glad your government is finished. I've no beliefs, no religion, no background of my own which I cherish, no real patriotism. People like me are of no use now. We're traitors without wanting to be. We like to sit in the clubs and talk about Western things over a whisky, because that's our world. No, I'm sorry your government's gone, because it's the end for people like us. We've been on top until now, the satellites of the British order, and now the Gandhi-caps are on top. But the Japanese finished you in Asia, and I was glad and sorry for that."

" Glad ? "

" Well, only a little bit glad," he said. " The mean part of me. The easily insulted part. Have you noticed how touchy conquered races are underneath ? "

" I have," she said. " I'm touchy now too." She was smiling.

" Why ? "

" Because you've got rid of us," she said. " It's a curious feeling."

" So you feel it ? "

" Oh, yes. You do feel it. You do."

He took her hand and stroked it. " I know," he said con-solingly. " I do understand." He laughed, sympathetic and gentle. " It's queer, isn't it ? " he went on. " I mean how we feel these things which, really, are stupid, but important. Have you met my brother yet ? "

" Only for a moment."

" I don't understand *him*," he said. " Yet I know he's a better person than me. He does *care* about things. He told me he's giving all our estates away to the people. That may mean I'll have to go and work. What at ? God knows. Now why does my brother want to give all the land away ? Should I let him ? I mean, I have a say. I don't know what to do. I don't want to be poor or to go away from here. He said I can have five hundred acres. He's determined to make me agree that I should give up our estates. I know he's right. But why should I agree ? Why should I give up my rights and my income ? Now, you see, it's the same as the British rule in India. They felt the same. Why should they go ? I feel that, too, but I know our time's up here as the ruling family. And I hate that."

" I know," she said. " Why must your brother do it ? "

" You know why probably better than anybody in this State," he said. " You've lived among the people. It can't go on, can it, this medieval mess ? " He urged her, " Can it ? "

" No," she said quietly, " it can't."

He looked as if he had received a blow. " That's what I thought too," he said. " What a damned pity it all is. I wonder what's going to happen to us all. There's going to be trouble. The landowners are not going to agree with my brother. Why should they ? "

" What kind of trouble do you mean ? Fighting ? "

" I don't know," he said. " But they're very angry and frightened."

" Yes," she said, " the servants are all talking about it."

Prem smiled and was going to say something, hesitated, and changed his mind. Then he said, " Come and we'll have that cold drink." He was feeling weak and faint for a whisky.

Chapter Eight

The first long talk Prabhu had with his brother was at the Jashimpur Club, one of the hundreds of strongholds in which Englishmen had fought the long unrelenting rearguard action against the liberal teaching they could not afford to represent.

" I suppose you know Papa had the hell's own job to get into this club himself when they started it," Prem said, laughing, as they sat in the deserted club and drank gin and tonic. Jashimpur's fishing had attracted a few Englishmen and their mem-sahibs and some had settled in the State, getting permission to do so only on condition that the Maharajah and his friends be made members of the club. All the English were gone now, and already the club was looking grubby and depressed. Prabhu noticed it and he was wry about how right Englishmen had been and how wrong they were to be right. Everybody must make some concessions, surely to God. Prem agreed half-heartedly.

" They didn't mind Papa, really. It was his friends. The half-baked, half-tamed landowners he drank with. Curious the way Papa disliked cultured people. That dream he had about being a warrior and so on. Do you think the old man was mad, Prabhu ? "

" He was mad all right. We're all mad. I'm a little mad. And so are you. Look at you. You'd no need to let the Japs make such a mess of you. You could have strung along."

" I wanted to be a warrior too," Prem said. He looked

wistfully out at the deserted tennis court. Nobody had bothered to remove the net and it was fraying, falling apart. Nobody played tennis now.

" You've noticed, I suppose, that Lila's a soak like yourself, Prem. We're very tired of each other, Lila and I. You'll notice that too, Don't bother about it. I don't, much. I accept it. The war put the top hat on it, or was it the steel helmet? I'm not sure. Anyway, I was away over six years, and it was too long. We got over each other during those six years. Before the war, in London, when Papa wouldn't forgive me for marrying her, we were happy. We both had our jobs and a woman to look after the kids. We had such fun. But, you know, that life almost killed my mind for me. I didn't know it until I went into the British Army. It was heaven being a private soldier and sweating for a commission in the Indian Army. I grew up. I can't describe it properly, but my life with Lila had been too happy, too snug, too eventless. Can you believe that? I'd never have known that if I hadn't become a soldier. And the six years did the rest. I loved the war, and hated it too. I hate war and at the same time I look back to it with nostalgia. Lila's changed too. She became independent, truculent, full of this new woman stuff. You remember the outburst you had the pleasure of viewing? She works up to those after a few drinks. But that's the first one she's ever put on in full. That was for your benefit." He had taken off his dark glasses and he looked into his brother's eyes affectionately, adding, " She never wanted to come back to India. She hates being an Indian. And no one can help her about it. I've never been a passionate Indian, but Lila's a psychological case. And she thinks I'm one, about my ideas on politics and so on. India must be full of people like us, I mean people with money, of course, who got caught in the British culture-net. I liked it, and I still like it. But sometimes I wish I'd been a bloody peasant or an ordinary kind of Indian who knew where he was."

"I know what you mean," Prem said consolingly. "We're the lost generation. It's cock of course to talk about wishing you'd been born a peasant. You'd have cut your throat long ago. No guts. I'm the same. I can't go ten minutes without a drink. As for Lila, she's rather a dear. You don't have to prepare me for her fireworks and her moods. I'm okay. I don't give a damn if she sets fire to the palace. In about ten years I might care, but I'm so bloody contented not being a Japanese prisoner, and being alive, that just now I haven't a single moral lecture left in me for anyone. Tell me one thing, Prab. What's going to be the finish of all this reform you're full of? Are you really going to give the land back to the peasants? Why not just sell up and let's all clear off and let Hassan and company get on with it all? There's dynamite here, you know."

"I know about the dynamite. I'll take the fuse out of it that's all."

"You were always a bit gone about being free, weren't you? Just look out you don't get all our throats cut. This isn't Kashmir, you know. It's not important enough to send Indian troops into if you start trouble, Prab. I agree it's a mess and needs a wash, but I think you underestimate how much Hassan and company hate all our guts."

"You know why they hate our guts."

"Of course I do. But I don't want them to cut my throat. If they've had us here, then let's go. We could live in Madeira, or even go to America. I mean *I* could. Lila'll never stop sighing for London."

"Lila can take wherever my destiny leads us."

"Your *destiny*?" Prem was laughing as he poured out more gin. He looked into Prabhu's face. "Did you get hit on the head in Burma, Prab?"

They were too fond of each other to fall out, yet Prem saw how his laughing question had stung Prabhu.

"Yes, my destiny," Prabhu said curtly. "My destiny is to

clean this State up, and I'll do it, even if Hassan doesn't like it."

"Okay. Fine. Cheers." They drank. Prabhu looked at the long, deserted bar and wished it was full of red-faced Englishmen, and certain kinds of Indian. He missed the British Raj and was angry because he missed it, for he was a revolutionary. He thought of some of the things Hassan had said to him in the cell. Hassan was hardly ever out of his thoughts. Yes, he was the sort of socialist, as Hassan had hinted, who liked titles and decorations. He did not know what he was, only that he wanted to do something great in Jashimpur, and now, most of all, defeat Hassan. If he had been in any way half-hearted, he had become dedicated after leaving Hassan's cell.

"On the way back, Prem, I want to do something rather out of the ordinary."

"Oh ? For instance ? "

"I'm going to make a speech in the town to the people. I'm going to commit myself publicly, and set the landowners by the ears, and show the people that I mean business. Would you like to avoid seeing this exhibition of disloyalty to all that Papa held dear ? "

"Listen, Prab. Take my advice. I won't give any more, I promise. Get Hassan into your camp, on your side, or at least bribe him or buy him. The people adore him. I have my contacts in the town and I hear what goes on. They're watching you. You might even win them. But you've got to win Hassan if you're going to try and do what he's more entitled to do. I mean leading a revolution. *Must* you make speeches to the people before signing Hassan up as one of your boy scouts ? He'll be very annoyed."

"There's nothing I want more than to annoy Hassan. Hassan's got to come to me. I'm not going to Hassan. That's how simple it is. And if these landowners dig their toes in,

I want to be sure you'll stand by me, Prem." Prabhu was so earnest that Prem looked amazed.

"Stand by you? How do you mean? I'm not involved in this. Of course I'll stand by you, if you mean not interfering. Or fall down by you. I'm tight half an hour after breakfast."

"Breakfast?" Prabhu smiled. "I've never seen you eat at all. Watch yourself, Prem. Your liver. I like a drink, but you love it too much. You must try and eat." Seeing the concern for him in his brother's eyes, Prem shook his head and tittered.

"Breakfast for me is a cigarette and a vomit. Did the army coarsen you, too, Prab?"

"Yes, I suppose it did." It was Prem's acceptance of gradual alcoholic enslavement which made Prabhu go on to say, "Don't make Lila a boozing pal, will you, Prem? That's what she's always wanted. I mean—oh, hell, forget it. Come on."

They drove down to the town, Prem humming "Roll Me Over," and then he sang "Frigging in the Rigging."

"Ever sing that one in the mess, Prab? We used to make the palm trees shake with it. What good types one knew during the war, eh?"

"To hell with the war," Prabhu snapped. "I've had the war now."

"What you need is a few more drinks, Prab. You're moral-bound. You're too tense. You want to ease-springs, old chap."

Prabhu drove the car into Lord Stonehead Square, now called by Hassan's party, The Place of the Agreement. Lord Stonehead had helped Prabhu's grandfather to consolidate things after the great uprising of 1857 in India, and The Place of the Agreement was where Hassan and five companions had signed a covenant to revolt when all was ready.

"This is just the place," said Prabhu. "I'm going to make my first speech, and I hope to God my Urdu's up to it." He stopped the car. The square was swarming with people, laden donkeys, sacred bulls lying here and there among the traffic.

" Well, I only hope you're right, Prab." Prem shrank down in his seat as Prabhu stood up in the car and called to passers-by to come and listen to him.

" Get up on top of that hut, Prab," said Prem, so that he should not be stared at while Prabhu spoke. He was ashamed that his brother should do this strange public thing, and he wished he had not come. He was nervous lest the crowd do something impudent to Prabhu. Although he was half drunk, Prem never forgot that the people were " they " and that " they " were not a known quantity in a situation like this. He watched Prabhu climb up on to the roof of the vendor's hut. About twenty people gathered, and then more began to come as the word flew that the Maharajah was going out of his mind on top of a hut. Crowds began forming and became one. Prem took the wheel of the car and backed it away, signalling to Prabhu to show where he was.

" Brothers and sisters," Prabhu shouted. " My Urdu is even rustier than my Jashimpuri, but I have never forgotten our old Jashimpuri saying, ' The rusty sword can still cut a rope.' " There was laughter in the crowd. Prabhu took a deep breath and looked out across the square where the golden roof of the temple glittered in the evening sun. People were running to join the crowd. He had memorised three Jashimpuri sayings and he had used one of them. He would save the other two for the end. He spread his arms, swelled his chest, and shouted, " I, and Hassan's Party together, will cut the rope that binds you to poverty. That's why I came back from England. Not to spend you, but to free you, and to free you without the need for violence. I wanted to free Hassan from the prison where my father put him, but he won't come out." He let a silence hang for a moment and the crowd tensed, ready for the laugh when he added, " He doesn't like the prison, and he refuses to like me, because I

am the son of my father. That is my sin. I am my father's
son. So he won't let me free him."

All his being keyed up, sweat on his forehead, as the crowd
burst into a roar of laughter, Prabhu took a silk handkerchief
from his pocket and wiped his face. His nerves winced as the
thin silk caught and dragged on the fine needle stubble of
early evening. He waited, trembling slightly until the laughter
died down, and the crowd waited, ox-eyed again, but eager
for the next part of his speech.

"Hassan has struggled and suffered to free you," he cried.
"And I love him for that. There are some who thought I
came back to continue misrule. They were mistaken. They
hoped I would use repression and try and fight Hassan's
Party. But why should I fight what I have believed in for
years, justice and freedom. We will have land reforms, schools,
hospitals, and the poor man's son will have the chance to use
his talents as well as the rich man's son. The Party need not
hide any more. It can come out into the open. And I invite
the leader to meet me. When Hassan is ready to forgive me
for being the descendant of my ancestors we can work quickly
to change Jashimpur and make it worth living in for all.
Let the young men of the Party meet me so that we can
discuss these things and get on with the work of freedom."

He stopped and the emotional Jashimpuris, packed in the
square, uttered one fierce roar, like a beast, a roar of triumph
and agreement. They chanted, "Long Live the Maharajah
and the Party," after that, and Prabhu, spent and quivering,
looked down at Prem, who was standing in the car, laughing
with delight.

"Now let's see what Hassan makes of that," Prabhu
thought as he was helped down from the roof by hundreds
of hands. "I've arrived."

Chapter Nine

Miss Bullen had quarrelled with Lila. Lila had got her alone in a corner of the enormous veranda, drank half a bottle of whisky, and had unloosed a torrent of complaint about her unhappiness, about Prabhu's madness " which some people would call eccentricity," about the difficult conflicts going on inside herself about drinking, about religion and the many problems the lack of it had brought into her life, and about the general uselessness of being alive at all. Worse was having come back to India. She had been happy in London. But Prabhu had this dream of doing justice, and was becoming a laughing-stock to some and a menace to the landowners, who were showing their hostility.

In London they had had their different interests to absorb them, but here she and Prabhu were too much together, could not escape from each other, and every day Prabhu was showing signs of a growing fanaticism about becoming more Indian. He was going to wear Jashimpuri peasant dress. He had the tailors in now and was being measured for homespun baggy trousers and long ridiculous woollen shirts. His whole life was acting, acting.

" Where's it all going to end, for God's sake ? " Lila cried while she poured another whisky. " I have to talk to someone about it. That's why I sent for you. I need you. I must talk about these things. What am I going to do ? "

She described their runaway marriage in London, and how they had kept it secret from Prabhu's father until it had to come out when Prem came to London on holiday from Jashimpur.

"Prabhu was all right," she said, "until the war. The war ruined him. When he came back from the war he'd won the Military Cross. When I asked him how he'd got it he said, 'For bravery.' Just like that. 'For bravery.' No shyness, no modesty. 'For bravery?' I said to him. 'Prabhu, you can't go around talking like that.' I remember I laughed then, you know, trying to make it pleasant, but he was furious. 'I got it for bravery,' he said, terribly angry. 'And if anyone asks me why I got it that's the answer. You're too British for words, Lila.' Those were his very words. 'Too British for words.' My God, I was angry. I *am* British, but not too British for words. We had a terrific row. The first we'd ever had. You see, I'd grown up during that war, and Prabhu had grown down. Before the war he was the soul of gentleness and sweetness. He came back from the war a domineering, cantankerous, opinionated little captain who'd won the Military Cross for bravery, and on top of that he'd become a socialist. I suppose that's what one has to call it. Economics, man-hours, cement-production, justice, the man-in-the-street, the Atlantic Charter. From morning till night that's all he spoke about, and about how when the time came he was going to tear Jashimpur to pieces and give justice to the starving masses. The first time I ever cried myself to sleep was one night last year after seven or eight hours of a sermon about the colour bar and the way all war was fought for nothing but the problem of who was going to make shirts and underwear and who was going to wear them. That, it appeared, was all the war with the Japanese was about. Cotton-spinning and underwear. I was exhausted that night, and I fell asleep in the chair while he was preaching. He actually shook me awake, and shouted at me. 'We've got to live,' he said. 'We've got to help change the world. You, the converted Hindu-Christian's daughter, and me, the

Maharajah's son.' Then he told me what had decided him to begin thinking and to see where he stood in the mess of the world we were in. Apparently he'd lived in an officers' mess which was sixty per cent English and forty per cent Indian, and the Indians could never get any Indian food. They were outvoted every time. They got sick in the stomach and were always fighting and quarrelling with the British officers, who liked stew and bacon and eggs like sensible Englishmen. Do you know that Prabhu began to hate the British Empire for that? Isn't it incredible? And I had to lie awake listening to how the world had to be changed and justice brought to everyone. The Atlantic Charter! My God, that Charter. I can almost quote it word for word. And now we're here in Jashimpur to bring the light to the starving masses. Oh, how I wish I was like you, Miss Bullen, single, free, kind, not tortured like me in a marriage I'm sick of. And then the children. We fight over the children. Do you know, I think I'd like six months' holiday up at your mission with just the children and you, away from all this, and let Prabhu get on with this insanity. Thank God for Prem. At least he's here. He's like me, British though brown. I'm so split. So torn apart. Why, oh, why did you people ever let your government leave India? Life was so wonderful then."

Miss Bullen, simmering with rage and shock after hearing all this, had cut in to say, "Such nonsense, Lila, my dear. Such nonsense. Why, when our government was here you wouldn't live here. You hated India then as you claim to hate it now. You make me so angry, complaining like that, and saying these dreadful things to me about your husband, who's probably got so much responsibility to worry him. Have you no shame, no pride?" She had lost her temper for the first time in years, and she knew as she lost it that it was because Lila had nervously upset her with this assault on her quietness and peace which she had achieved during years of isolation. Also there was the matter of charity and loyalty and steadfastness, which Lila trampled across. Surely, she thought, a woman's first duty was the silence of loyalty. But no. As soon as she had shown her disgust and temper Lila started again.

"Where's your understanding, Miss Bullen?" she asked in a mournful, heartfelt way which angered the old woman even more. "Where's your Christianity? Do you think I speak like this to everyone? Can't you see what trust and love I have for you by the way I confide in you? Can't you remember how even in that short time together at Kangla years ago we liked each other? Is it my fault I'm embittered and unhappy? Would you like it if you had a husband who'd throw away Jashimpur because of a lot of stupid ideas he's got and doesn't understand? Am I to keep quiet and confide in nobody?"

"That's not what I meant at all, Lila. You know as well ——"

"Isn't it? Do you think I want a lecture about how I should be a good, meek, Indian wife and watch this kind of stupidity Prabhu's up to right now as we're talking? Do you know where he is? He's in the town preaching to the people. The Maharajah in the town preaching to the mob about justice! My God, don't you think I feel ashamed? You hate me, don't you, because I won't pretend it's wonderful? Is that friendship? Do you call that understanding Christianity? *I'm* more Christian than that. Oh, why can't you understand that I'm not criticising Prabhu, only what he's doing? Of course he's mad. But I have to bear it. Don't you understand? I'm beginning to hate him. Do you know what I want to do? I want to come and live in Kangla with the children and find my way back to God. Can you understand that?"

Well, that quietened and calmed Miss Bullen. She was immediately sorry for losing her temper. She took Lila's hand, and, hard though it was, said, "I understand, Lila. I'm sorry for saying what I said." (She was not sorry, she knew it.) " I only meant you shouldn't attack your husband in this way. It's wrong. I'll help you in any way I can. I'll help you find God if I can, if that's what you want. It's only when you're unhappy that you feel the real need of God. My poor Lila. Do you have to drink so much? "

" That's another thing," Lila cried. " My drinking. I'm drinking more and more because of Prabhu. He watches me. He searches my room and he searches all over the house to find if I've hidden whisky somewhere. But now he's begun to let me drink openly, though he's watching me just the same. He wants to see me crack up. He wants to see me a complete drink-victim, I suppose."

" Lila, do stop it," the old woman cried sharply. But Lila went on and the old woman thought, " I've got to get out of here. I'll go mad. I know it's selfish. Here's someone who needs me and I won't help. But I don't care. I just couldn't stand much more of this. She's drunk. Drunk. My God, this beautiful Christian girl, just a drunken woman, and those lovely children. And that handsome husband. Eccentric, yes, but worthy of loyalty. After all, he's the Maharajah. And she hates him. Her eyes when she speaks about him. She's full of some devil." Lila went on attacking Prabhu, saying that she was too far from him now in spirit for there ever to be any real reconciliation.

" And yet the flesh does bind us together," she said, vehemently, almost proudly. " There's always that. And that makes it worse, that awful bond, that slavery to each other."

Miss Bullen got to her feet. She could stand no more of this. Her face was hot as she spoke her anger to Lila.

" How can you *dare* speak of such a sacred thing to me, Lila? " she said excitedly. " How *can* you? Have you no shame at all? I want to go to bed. I can't stay and listen to this kind of thing. The most sacred things of marriage

treated like this. Oh, Lila! I'm so upset. I looked forward
so much to seeing you and being with you, and now to find
you like this. Pull yourself together. Do you ever pray?
Do you?"

"Oh, for God's sake!" Lila cried in a passion. "For God
Almighty's *sake*, don't let me down like this. Don't be a
missionary to *me*. It's friendship I want. Can't you even give
me a little of that? What about all those wonderful letters
we wrote to each other? Where's the friendship gone?
Can't you understand the misery I'm in? I need someone to
talk to, someone who'll listen to me. I'm dammed up. I'm
so unhappy." She wailed and poured another whisky.

"Perhaps she's mad," Miss Bullen thought suddenly,
afraid for her own lack of understanding and charity. "I
wonder if she's mad. Maybe the war, the bombing. Anyway,
there's something the matter with her. She's so changed.
She was so gentle. So kind and sweet. Now she's rather
horrible, poor darling, and so lovely to look at. I wonder if
her husband's done something dreadful to her? He wouldn't.
No. He wouldn't. He may be cold and distant to me but that's
no reason to think——" Prabhu's hostility towards her,
chilly and almost wordless, was another reason for not staying
here.

"I must go to bed, Lila," she said, making for the door.
Lila followed her, glass in hand, crying, "You can't. I've
waited so long to talk to you. Please don't. Sit down. You
must listen to me. There's something I must tell you. If I
can't talk to somebody about it I'll go mad." There was so
much urgency, so much hysteria in her voice, that Miss Bullen
paused. "What about me?" the old woman thought angrily.
"Haven't I got enough to worry me? Is there anyone to
listen to me talk about my useless life at Kangla? Can I find
someone to listen to me pour out *my* horrible petty little
miseries? No. My God, no." To Lila, she said, "Well, can
I lie down while you talk to me, dear? I feel if I don't lie

down I'll *fall* down." She went on towards her room, Lila following.

"You can do anything you like, Miss Bullen, if I can talk," Lila was saying. "Oh, if only you knew what it means to unburden myself after all I've gone through. If only you knew."

"Well, you mustn't talk to me about any secrets," Miss Bullen cried rather shrilly. "I won't listen to it. After all, there's a limit. Marriage is marriage after all."

"All *right*! All *right*!" Lila almost yelled the words in an exasperation which caused Miss Bullen to sniff and fume through her distended nostrils. She would simply have to put an end to this kind of shameful, drunken carrying on. The dignity of womanhood—God knows it was laughed at enough these days, but she was not going to put up with much more of this kind of thing. What made it worse was that a servant was sniggering at the end of the hall as they reached Miss Bullen's door. Miss Bullen glared at the youth and he shrank and sidled away.

"A servant *laughing* at you, Lila," she said in a voice steely with indignation. "Can't you see?"

"Oh, damn it all," Lila shouted, wrenching at the knob of Miss Bullen's door. "Don't worry so much. I wish you knew some of the things that have gone on in this palace in the past. I've had a couple of drinks. Is there any harm in that? Why must we pester each other all the time over these little things? Why?"

"Oh, all *right*. Very well, then," Miss Bullen said sharply as they entered the room. As she said it she knew she had struck up a peculiar kind of intimacy with Lila which was going to continue. She had failed to shame Lila. Lila was winning with her distressing and shameful coarseness and lack of restraint.

"All *right*, then," Lila mimicked her, shrieking with laughter. Miss Bullen lay down on the bed and looked at the ceiling, praying, " Oh, My God, give me strength to listen to this poor creature and not to start loathing her. Help me to be kind and patient. And, oh, I forgot, understanding. Help me to be that. Help me to help her. Help her to pray, and to know you." But she was in too much of a rage to go on in this way, adding to herself, " As if God's going to listen to me while I'm in this state of nerves." Lila was singing in quite an attractive voice, " When the Saints Go Marching in," which Miss Bullen had never heard before.

Lila finished the song and turned to the old woman who was sighing on the bed.

" I'm in love with a man called Clegg-Bray," she said. " That's what the matter is with Lila to-night. A few drinks and my heart opens again and I want to die. Do you understand ? Die. That's what it's like. Wanting to die. He's a man you'd love. Tall, fine, rich, kind, not one of these excitable madmen like Prabhu. But the man I was born for. Have you any idea what it's like to meet the man you were born for when someone else has got hold of you ? Someone like Prabhu. Bags of cement per hour, man-hours, calories, justice. That's what is the matter. Now you know. Now I've said it. Now I've told you. Hate me. You can hate me if you like. Despise me. It won't alter anything. I love this man. He's in London eating his heart out waiting for a letter from me. Shall I write it ? Shall I ? After a few whiskies I'm ready to write it but don't write it." She sat down and burst into tears. Miss Bullen lay on her back and said, " Oh, my God. What a world. What a world." She took a packet of cigarettes from her handbag and lit one.

" Go on, my dear," she said. " Have a good cry and tell me more if you want to. Does this man love you too ? I mean——"

Lila sobbed for a while and then dried her eyes. She drained her glass and said, " It's been going on since the flying bombs started in London. We met in the doorway of Harrod's when one of the bombs was coming down. The engine had cut off and I was shivering there, ready to screech. I'm a coward, you know. I gibbered all the way through the blitz. Well, here was this fine-looking man in uniform saying into my ear, in Urdu, ' It won't hurt us. Be calm.' Then it exploded a couple of streets away. He went on speaking in Urdu, *pukka* Urdu, and I felt so ashamed, not being the kind of Indian he thought me, that I said, ' I never speak that language. English, please.' We started to meet after that." The old woman sat up on her elbow and looked into Lila's eyes. Lila eyed her back with a hostile expression on her sullen face and said, " Well, you're wrong, see ? Nothing of the kind took place. The whole affair has been strictly honourable, save that I've said nothing about the man to Prabhu. He'd strangle me. He's so jealous that he hated the milkman in London because I used to pass the time of day with him. Our men are nearly all infantile, Indian men I mean. Do you know that ? It's the system. It's the fault of the whole mess we live in here."

" Oh, do stop attacking India, Lila, please," Miss Bullen said sharply. " It's so tiresome of you. Well, what about this man ? You must drop him. You can't——"

" I'm damned if I'll drop him," Lila shouted. " I love him, and he loved me. You can't just *drop* things. Don't you know *anything* at all about people and life? I love him. What am I going to do ? "

" You've got to give him up." The old woman was pale. She was horrified and was showing it.

" That's what I'm talking about," Lila said. " You've got to help me. But narrowness and intolerance won't help me. There's got to be broadmindedness and understanding. I suppose you despise me now as an adulteress or something, but let me tell you again there's been nothing of that kind between us. He's an honourable person and knows about our ways in India, I mean he thinks Indian women are all, you

H

know, pure and everything." She uttered a shriek of laughter. "I mean he respects me and only wants to marry me. And I'll say this for him, he's the only Englishman I've ever met who's absolutely without *any* colour prejudice. He said my skin reminds him of honey and gold. That's a change from cement and calories, isn't it? I'd like to give him up, but why should I? I wish I could be a good Christian again. Then I'd want nobody. I'd give marriage up and all the men too. I hate most men. But Derek's wonderful. I've got a couple of weeks left before I give my reply to him. He's waiting in London for me to make up my mind."

She told the old woman that she had promised Clegg-Bray that she would make up her mind within a certain time and then write her decision to him. After Miss Bullen had hinted and nagged for a time Lila admitted that Clegg-Bray was already married, " Unhappily, of course. He's had a life of hell. Rather like I've had from Prabhu. I tell you, we're made for each other. My God, it hurts so much."

"What you need," Miss Bullen said, with an intensity that struck like a whip. " What you need is a good beating. You want bringing to your senses, Lila. It's just disgusting—mean and disgusting. You're surprised, are you? You should be ashamed to look me in the eye." Then she lay down again on her back and Lila wailed into maudlin tears again. The old woman let her cry for over a quarter of an hour until they heard voices. They could hear Prem shouting and laughing. Lila dried her eyes and said, " They're back. Prem's drunk. Oh, why does he drink so much? He's hardly ever sober." She went to the door and shouted, " Prem. Bring the whisky. Is Prabhu there? I'm in Miss Bullen's room. Come on."

Prem came first, the bottle of whisky in his hand, glasses in the pockets of his white dinner jacket, and a siphon of soda-water in his left hand. His tie was undone and his thick black hair was hanging over his eyes.

"Prabhu's bringing some ice," he said. As usual, though drunk, he appeared to be sober, only a wildness in his black eyes telling of much liquor within. "He made a speech to the people to-night that makes it certain I've lost my income for the future. Drink-money is all I want. Lila, will you talk to Prabhu for me and make sure I have enough drink-money in the bank for the next fifteen or twenty years. I won't live longer. Will you? I mean, I don't care what the hell he does with all the estates and the rest of it, but I've got to have booze-money. Say you'll talk to him for me."

"All right," Lila said quietly. "Sit down and pour me a drink."

"Sorry, *Mataji*, for kicking up such a racket," Prem said to Miss Bullen. "Loaded again, you know. My God, even though he was signing my death warrant—unless Lila fixes me up about drink-money—even though he was signing my death warrant, I must say Prabhu can hand it out. He can hand the bull out without pausing for breath. The people were cheering. After all, it's not every day the Maharajah comes down to the town and stands on a building and tells how he's going to make himself a beggar by giving all his lands and money away. You can imagine the interest they showed."

"You see?" Lila said to Miss Bullen. "You see?"

"See what?" Prabhu asked. He was standing in the doorway.

"Ah, you're wearing your rubber shoes to-night, darling," Lila said, laughing with false gaiety at her husband. "I thought you only wore those when you were searching for my drink ration among the bookcases and under the beds."

"See what?" Prabhu asked again, coldly. He turned his black glasses on Miss Bullen and said, "My wife is drunk, Miss Bullen. I'm sorry if you've been annoyed."

"Quite the contrary, Maharaj Sahib," Miss Bullen replied,

unperturbed. She had decided to stand up to Prabhu in future. Otherwise he would walk over her.

" I'm very glad to hear it," Prabhu said as he came into the room. He looked into Lila's face and then leaned forward and kissed her. It was one of his gestures, meant to bewilder and surprise. " My little drunken Maharani," he said. " Pour me a drink, please." He sighed as he threw himself into an arm-chair. Prem watched everybody and tittered, and then sat down.

" We're getting out of this barracks of a palace by the end of the month," Prabhu announced. " We'll live in the house at Mangra. I want this place to become a school. I'm giving it to the people."

" Oh, give me a whisky, Prem, will you ? " Lila cried with angry friendliness, looking into Prem's mocking eyes. He laughed with her.

" What's funny ? " Prabhu asked.

" Nothing," said Lila, taking the whisky from Prem.

" I was thinking about the joint family to-night," Prabhu went on. " It was after I'd finished speaking to the crowds. I was thinking how right India was to hang on to the joint family for so long, the country's insurance system against disaster and poverty. And the *panchayat*, the village council. How right that was too. We must keep it. We must preserve all that for the future."

" You're not planning a joint-family system for us, I mean you and me ? " Lila said acidly. " I hope not."

" That would be rather difficult, Lila," Prabhu told her coolly, " with your hysterical temperament. I wouldn't think of it. Did you pour me that whisky, my darling ? " He stroked the last two words with his softened voice. She poured him a whisky and gave it to him.

" How do you find the twins, Miss Bullen ? Difficult ? " Prabhu raised his glass to Miss Bullen.

" They're wonderful children," she said. " Wonderful."

"How nice," he said, playful, yet not absolutely so. "How fine to know that. Lila and I thought they were just two little toughs. By the way, you can teach them about religion as long as Christ is made just a man, none of this Son of God business. And Islam, Hinduism, Buddhism, the lot. I want no bigotry. Will you do that?"

Miss Bullen sat up. She was feeling at home with them all. She did not feel it incongruous to be sitting on her bed while Prem and Prabhu watched her. If there was one thing she felt at this moment it was that she would master Prabhu, if she stayed.

"I should tell you, Maharaj Sahib," she said with gentleness and firmness, "that I'll do no such thing. I'm narrow-minded and intolerant about such matters. I believe Christianity to be the only truth. I'll teach that, if you wish, but no other religion. I respect firm Muslims and Hindus. I don't like Muslims to teach Christianity and a little Hinduism, and so on. I'm sorry."

Prabhu clapped his hands together and said, "Splendid. A fanatic. Miss Bullen, I like you for that. You'll teach no religion at all to my children, please. Forget the matter."

"I shall be returning to Kangla at the end of this month, Maharaj Sahib. I want to discuss the matter with the Maharani." Lila's lips parted and she looked at Miss Bullen in a hopeless sort of way and began to cry again.

"Crying drunk," Prabhu said affectionately. "Don't let's discuss these matters to-night, Miss Bullen. My wife is upset. I can always tell. Her lips swell when she's upset." He went to Lila and stroked her hair. "Poor darling," he said. Miss Bullen turned pink at this unIndian exhibition by a husband to his wife in front of others.

"Take me to bed," Lila said, sobbing. "Miss Bullen, I mean. Take me to bed, Miss Bullen. You can't go. Don't go. Please."

"Stinko!" Prabhu said to Prem, quietly. "She must have

drunk a bottle of Scotch. Where's it all going to end ? That's Lila's favourite expression. It's a good one too." He watched Miss Bullen with her arm round Lila's shoulder, leading her from the room.

" Now, you were saying about this Hassan, Prem," Prabhu began when they were alone. " Tell me all you know."

Chapter Ten

It was at breakfast the next morning that Miss Bullen and Prabhu began to understand and respect each other. The twins were sent off to go on with their unpacking as soon as they had eaten their breakfast.

"Forget them for a while," Prabhu said impatiently when Miss Bullen rose to follow them after a few minutes. "Have some more coffee." He snapped his fingers to the servant standing near the door.

"My wife's got a bad hangover," Prabhu said silkily. "Now don't go and think, 'Poor man, having a drunken wife,' will you? Don't think that. Lila's just a little mad, you know. No harm. She began to drink in London during the war, while I was away. Unbreakable habit now, I think. As you're one of the family now, so to speak, you'd better know these things. They can't do any harm. I hate any form of hypocrisy, don't you? Now I do hope you're not serious about giving us all up as a set of drunkards and degenerates and socialists and so on, and won't go back to your wilderness at Kangla." He smiled. His dark glasses were beside his plate. His solemn eyes were attractive. She had to stop herself from staring into them. He used them so well, so compellingly. Only with Lila did he wear the dark glasses, she thought. Why?

"You'll change your mind, then?" he said. "Go on. Say you've changed your mind." There was an annoyingly boyish charm in the way he pressed her to agree with him. She agreed and he smiled.

" Good. You mean a lot to my wife, to us all. I think you're charming; the way you put up with us all last night in your room was sweet. I mean it. You know, Prem was telling me you knew this Hassan man quite well some years ago. He said that he was at your mission at Kangla, and that Kangla was his village. Is that correct ? "

" Yes," she said, " I'm afraid so, Maharaj Sahib. I'd no idea he was going to turn out as he did. Is he going to be kept in gaol much longer ? " She could not understand it when Prabhu said, his eyes staring out of the window, " I wouldn't mind having been born Hassan. How marvellous to rise up out of the mud and have someone like me puzzled. I can't make him out. He refuses to leave the gaol. I want you to go and talk to him for me, Miss Bullen." He smiled as he met her stare. " Yes, seriously," he said. " I want you to go and get him out of that gaol. Was he ever interested in becoming a Christian ? "

She shook her head. " Never," she said. " But I always knew he had something powerful in him. I haven't heard much of him for years, except that he was in gaol. Somebody told me he'd actually gone to America to study." She put down her coffee cup and said, " Maharaj Sahib, you've been very kind to me. May I ask you a question ? "

" Fire away," he said. " Cigarette ? " For the first time she accepted a cigarette from a man and let him light it for her. "I'm done for," she thought. "What next, I wonder. Whisky?"

" Is it true, Maharaj Sahib ? " she said, " that you want to give all the land back to the people ? Isn't that what Hassan wants to do, and the other young men like him ? "

" Yes," he said. " But I want to do it first, and with their help, if they'll join me. But Hassan hates Maharajahs, on principle, even when they're mad, like me. I'd give anything if Hassan would work with me. All I want is to form a modern government of the best brains in the country and start giving the people a decent life for a change. Do you think that's insane, Miss Bullen ? " He was laughing, but not at her. He was getting quite fond of the old thing.

" If there's anything I can do," she said, " I'll do it."

" Please answer me," he insisted. " Do you think it's insane for a Maharajah to want to better his people ? Do you think it's mad to give the people their lands back ? "

But he could not draw her. She said, " It's not for me to pass opinions on such things, Maharaj Sahib."

" You don't approve, I know," he said. " You're used to my father's ways. But I'll show you. Talk to Hassan for me. Tell him he's free to come out of gaol. Do you know why I'm asking you to do that ? " She shook her head and said she did not know.

" Because I found out that he regards you as the first useful influence in his life. He told the gaol superintendent that, who passed it on. Now, that makes you practically a revolutionary, Miss Bullen. You see the dangers of this Christianity when men take its message seriously ? " They laughed, each for a different reason. She agreed to see Hassan, and was rather stirred at the thought of meeting him again under such circumstances.

Prabhu talked to her for a long time, about his sudden understanding of the poverty of Asia, and its spineless acceptance of the white men who took Asia and looted it. " You can't blame the white men for that," he said. " Only for preaching Christianity while they looted and consolidated. It was the famine in Bengal in 1943 that finished me off as a starry-eyed member of the brown-British. That, and two English friends in my regiment, non-regular soldiers, of course, who told me about the value of socialism as a hammer for smashing up out-of-date things. I can see no other value in socialism."

He managed to draw her out and she began to admit that she, too, realised that things could not have gone on as they were, but she would not admit that the people had had enough of Maharajahs.

"Maharaj Sahib," she said, "you don't know how much the people like to have a king, even a bad one they can hate. It's the landlords they want to see changed, not you."

"You think so?"

"I assure you," she said.

"You must have seen a great deal in your time among the people," he said, looking at her closely, into her eyes. "Do you think the people will ever get up out of the muck, if they get the chance? Or do you think they like it as it is?"

She was about to speak her mind on sick religions, on the need for spiritual regeneration among the people, about the cynical *Mullahs* and the devious pandits, and of how Christ's message held the key, but she felt suddenly weary of the whole business. Centuries of misery and dirt and fanaticism weighed her heart down as she considered the history she lived in.

"I think they'll get up out of the muck, as you put it, Maharaj Sahib," she said.

"What *were* you going to say, Miss Bullen?" he asked her, catching her eye.

"You'd call it religious fanaticism," she said, hoping he would press her to speak, but he looked irritated and said, "Don't let's be serious about religion, if you don't mind. It means just nothing to me, though I know it's everything to you. What time would you like to see Hassan?"

"I'm not sure he'd like to see me at all," she said. He had noticed the way she had hesitated, the blush in her cheeks, and he fastened on to it and began to question her.

"Why?" he asked. "Why shouldn't he want to see you?" But she evaded the question, and said she would be ready to see him in the evening after taking the children for a walk.

"About six, then," Prabhu said. "I'll warn the superintendent of the prison. By the way, you needn't do any propaganda for me, if you don't want to. Just see Hassan for old time's sake." He tried once more to sound her. " Why shouldn't Hassan want to see you ? " he said. " Was there something he did in the past, perhaps ? "

She got up from the table, cooler now. " No," she said. "Nothing like that." And she knew he knew she was not telling the truth. His sensitivity was quite worrying. No wonder Lila fought against him. But she liked him. She had a feeling she could have considerable power here in this palace, if she wanted it. She felt thrilled when she thought of how she had begun to enjoy life. If only Lila did not drink and become such a nuisance in the evening.

She was driving into town with the children in half an hour. She was taking them to the great market where the races of India and Central Asia met to haggle over the price of tea and chillies and wool. She had decided to speak to them in Urdu from that morning on, half an hour every morning. It was a disgrace that they spoke no Urdu. It was interesting for her to notice that such a thought would never have occurred to her in British times, a year ago. Already, old defences and prejudices, no longer useful, were decaying. It was very strange. Would she end up a fanatical Indian nationalist ? She felt as if she had come out of a prison, but she missed that prison, the mission, and her heart seemed confident that it would return there eventually.

She spent the day in the market with the twins, and Roshan Lal's precocious comments on this and that finally forced her to reprimand him. He went to pieces at once and was so miserable that she told him she was not nearly as angry as he thought. She had never been able to put up with old-headed children. They brought a devil up out of her, a malicious and vindictive devil.

As she fought for control over Roshan Lal, and influenced Narendra Nath, she decided that she must be herself, and if it did not work out, then it was a pity. So she showed no mercy when she told Roshan Lal off for sneering at some of

the beggars, and making what he thought were clever comments on harmless people about them.

"You'll grow up into a nasty brute," she said, "if you
don't learn to control your tongue. It's quite sickening to
listen to some of the things you say about people. Now just
stop it at once or I'll tell your father. I won't have cruelty,
especially clever cruelty. It's just revolting. Now, remember
what I said, Roshan Lal." This so demoralised him that she
understood him at last. He was a softy in a state of terror, a
neurotic in training. From then on she was kind to him but
he punished her by refusing to give an opinion on anything
to her. When she asked him what he thought of an exhibition
of jade carvings at the stall of a Tibetan trader, Roshan Lal
looked at her with resentful eyes and said in a crushed sort
of way, "I'd rather not say, if you don't mind."

"You little beast," she thought, her eyes on him while
he read her thoughts. After a day of this she was tired and
was not in the best of moods when it was time to meet Hassan
in prison. She made up a bundle of magazines and newspapers
and took them with her to the gaol in the superintendent's
car. He was one of those soft-spoken, insinuating and frightening people who cannot help giving the impression that they
have read a secret file on their companion. Miss Bullen quietly
resented the way the man hinted that it was well known she
had had a great deal to do with the making of the revolutionary,
Hassan. She could not decide if the superintendent was not
a secret revolutionary himself, but she never forgot the many
lessons in intrigue she had learned in her long life in Jashimpur,
and was silent as the man talked. "They're all beasts, these
officials," she thought. "I hope the Maharajah sacks the lot
of them. The whole lot need sacking. There's not one of
them who's not corrupt."

"You see, Miss Sahib," the superintendent said in his soft,
rich, dripping voice, "we know all about you. We know
you've always favoured change and progress, but not the

kind Hassan wants, of course. But he claims you taught him to think. Perhaps he'll be a great man one day. Look at Pandit Nehru. A few years ago he was a villain to the British, and now they love him. Do you think Hassan will rise to power one day?"

"I never think about these things," she said. "Never." He was silent after that. "Tap the old woman," someone in the secret police must have said. "Try and find what she thinks about this and that. You never know, you know."

The stale smell of imprisoned men seemed to cling to the superintendent as they walked through the prison yard. Hassan was sitting in a small whitewashed room near the main offices and he rose when she approached. She watched a pink flush spread into his face as he looked at her and smiled. He greeted her in the increasingly popular way, Muslim though he was, with his hands pressed together in *pranam*. She knew it was British prejudice in her bones which did not like to see the Muslim using this ancient Hindu greeting. "My God," she thought, "I'm becoming quite a neurotic myself." It was curious how the departure of the British Raj had opened up so many closed areas of her mind. India was getting in deeper than ever before, trying to flood her, and yet she was relieved these days to know that the stuffy mem-sahibs had gone, although she had liked them. All this she thought of while Hassan was saying, still blushing, "So you remembered the stubborn peasant, Hassan, Miss Sahib?"

"I remember everything, Hassan," she said dryly, taking his hand and shaking it. "You've become a big man. Did you ever get a message I sent to you down in India telling you not to preach hatred of the British?"

"I did," he said. "I'm afraid it made no difference. I was too far gone in perdition by then. And now the British have gone, and we're all delighted, and a little lost, and feel very fond of them, the nice ones among them, that is. Like yourself, Miss Sahib."

" You've become very smooth in the tongue, haven't you ? "
she said. " And that touch of American accent. Did you like
America, the great world power of to-day ? They think they
own the whole world now."

He laughed at her, affection in his eyes. " How you suffer,
you old-time British," he said. " You had such a good time,
and you don't like anyone else to be the boss. Yes, I loved
America, except for the dishonesty about the colour bar. At
least Russia is going to force them to alter that. One thing
I'll say for the Americans, Miss Sahib. They do *want* to
practise what they preach, which is more than we could say
for the old British diehard." She knew he was trying to annoy
her, as he had done in the past when they had talked as he
worked in the compound of the mission. But she would not
be annoyed.

They sat down in the cane-chairs and talked about Hassan's
life while they both thought about that time when she had
saved Hassan from disgrace and had then helped him to get
away to India.

Yes, she thought, she had had a lot to do with the making
of him.

After he had described his two years of hard work in a
factory in America, a short silence fell between them, and the
load of the past pressed down again and waited for discussion.

" Miss Sahib," he said suddenly, his eyes on the floor,
" did anybody ever find out about my part in that—" he
paused, sought a word, and used it—" that contemptible
business I was involved in ? I mean my part in it ? " " Look
up at me," she tried to will him, but he kept his eyes on the
floor.

" No, Hassan," she said. " Nobody found out your part
in it. But the woman was finished, of course. Her husband
threw her over. The child is still with her. A big strong girl
now. Do you want to talk about it ? "

" No," he said miserably, shaking his head. He sighed,

drummed his fingers on the table beside him and then looked up at her with sad, doggy eyes. " No. I don't want to talk about it. But it was not all my fault, Miss Sahib. The woman pursued me. She was in love with me."

" I know," Miss Bullen said bitterly. " All the same, you broke that marriage and ruined the woman."

" You're being hard on me," he said. He looked as if he might get up and go away. " Do you know I might have become a Christian if that hadn't happened? You had a great influence over me then. I was thinking about Christianity so much in those days. How long ago it seems now. How good you were to me. Did you ever expect to see me in gaol, Miss Sahib, for trying to free my country from this pack of parasites we've had over us all these years ? We're going to win. And when we've won I shall come to you with an offer, an offer after your own heart. Don't ask me what it is. But I've always admired you. Yes, don't say anything hard to me. I mean that. Don't you believe me ? " She stared into his eyes and said, " Yes, I do believe you. Have you never married ? "

" No. I'm one of those men who need only one lesson. I had that lesson, I shall never marry. But I'll free this country. Will you tell me something, Miss Sahib ? "

" If I can."

" It's this. What do you make of this Maharajah ? Now you must see a lot of him. They think he's mad. Do you think he's sincere ? Do you think there's any sense in a Maharajah who wants to destroy his own throne, and go on being the big man ? What do you make of him ? " He was watching her eyes as she listened to him. The short, pointed beard suited him. He had always been good-looking, but now he wore that kind of vanity which dissolves the farm boy's innocent humility, and which went well with the will and the ardour she remembered. He would never be ruthless but he would want to be. He would never be subtle but he would have cunning. She could recall his hatred of the land-lords and how he had said it was his wish to see them all hanged, one in every miserable village. Was that longing still alive in him, or had reading and thinking and the steady grind and polish of experience killed it?

"He has a great admiration for you, Hassan," she said, studying him, watching the light come into his eyes, and then how he laughed, and she knew he did not care if the Maharajah admired him or not.

"And I hate him," he said. "Isn't that strange? I hate him for coming from the people he comes from, and I hate him for not being what he is, the Maharajah, the chief land-lord. I despise him for his lack of shame. I'd sooner see him trying to tyrannise over us, like his ancestors, than trying to be loved by us as a revolutionary Maharajah. And you can tell him that, Miss Sahib, if you want to."

"I'll do nothing of the sort," she said firmly.

"Did he ask you to try and sound me out?"

"Now you're being impudent, Hassan," she said. "Is there any need to be like that with me? Is there?"

"No. I'm sorry. One thinks too much in a gaol."

"Then why don't you leave it?"

"I'm not sure," he said, smiling at her. "The last thing I want is an act of clemency from a Maharajah. It's very awkward, you know."

They laughed. A peon brought them two cups of tea and a plate of sweet biscuits.

"Why don't you work with the Maharajah, Hassan?" she said. "He means well. I know he does. He's sincere. Why can't you stop hating him because he's a Maharajah's son? Can't you be reasonable?"

"No. They were never reasonable with us. We want him to get out of this State, voluntarily too. We want him to abdicate, and we'll see that he does it too. A people like ours is entitled to a certain amount of reveneg. We're not

Englishmen. Did you know I drew the dole for two months in London, by the way? Very interesting. No, we're Jashimpuris, and we've been trampled on too hard, for too long. And we want to see an end to all Maharajahs in this State. And do you know, Miss Sahib, I think you know enough about us to understand why we want that?" He offered her the plate of biscuits and she took one and nibbled it. "You know," he went on, "why we would like to put an end to that family here." He looked out of the door into the glaring courtyard where some crows were bouncing and clowning. "If India will allow it, that is," he finished. "India might suddenly feel tender for the Maharajahs, the long noble line of rulers, et cetera. I wonder."

For half an hour she tried to soften his hatred for the ruling house, but he clung to his spar of revenge in the sea of reason. No, the Maharajah would have to go, and he, Hassan, would be rescued by the people from this prison, or at least in some way the people would show their will, once they found the courage.

"You know my views about our cowardice," he said, flashing his angry eyes at her. "I said enough about that while I was building that wall for you at the mission." He brightened up into that happy sadness of memory, of good times enjoyed long ago. "Do you remember how we used to drink tea at a quarter to five? I was very happy then. Why is it that that kind of happiness isn't enough for a man?"

She gave him the magazines and newspapers and said, "There's something I'd like to ask you, Hassan. You haven't given up your religion, I hope, and become one of these empty people who think all man needs is another suit of clothes and an extra ration of sugar. You're still a Muslim, a proper one?"

"A better one than ever," he said. "And you, Miss Sahib. Did they break your heart at Kangla? Did you have to leave it?"

"I think they cracked it, at least," she said, giving him a thin bleak smile. "I tried and failed."

"No. You didn't fail. Goodness always lives on. They'll be talking about you in a hundred years from now, Miss Sahib. I'm not being soft soapy. They will."

"I'll come and see you again," she said. "And listen. Pray. Ask God if He wants you to hate the Maharajah. Yes, ask Him. Say to God, 'God, am I hating the Maharajah enough because of his ancestors? Are You pleased with me, God? Am I hating enough?' Ask God that, Hassan, and let me know what He says." She held out her hand. Hassan looked uncomfortably into her eyes and smiled in shame.

"You always knew how to hurt, Miss Sahib," he said. "Please come again and talk to me. One day I'll offer you something you want. Won't you ask me what that is?"

"No," she said, going to the door.

"What an iron will you have. Good-bye, Miss Sahib."

"Good-bye, Hassan."

Chapter Eleven

The road into Jashimpur town ran along the edge of the river for a while, straggling, and then suddenly came to a stop and piled up into a packed mass of buildings which ranged from seventeenth-century sandstone to modern lath and crumbling plaster. This was the old town, burned and sacked and rebuilt again and again, and the city wall, almost intact, was broken down in one place to allow the thin stream of bungalows to creep out along the river. On hot days a heavy stench arose from the centre of the city. The river was inches deep in a scum of old filth. Into it fresh vegetable matter was thrown daily from the thousands of small windows below which the river slowly moved. Here lived the tailors, the makers of shawls, copper, bronze, enamel, and iron-workers, in hovels running up to three and four rickety stories. From dawn onwards the centre of the town was deafened by the sound of thousands of small hammers across which the heavy strokes of the iron-workers clanged at intervals, and thousands of voices were raised all day in advice, surprise, denial, instruction, and always there was laughter. Donkeys laden with charcoal for the forges passed in streams to and from the city, and the narrow streets seethed with people in their white and yellow cotton clothes. Tibetans holding trays piled high with blocks of tea passed along in search of those who would barter spices in exchange, their packs of scrawny dogs yelping on their heels.

The main Jashimpuri pastime, conversation, was a low and

continuous roar in these streets, steady and never quite drowned by the hammers, the creak and squeal of wooden ox-cart wheels, or the shouting and yelling of wandering traders. It was an exciting place to live and once you had lived there, it was said, you were lonely anywhere else. For there was always one or a dozen anxious to talk with another and exchange gossip, stories, advice, scandals old or new.

" If you have not heard it in Jashimpur town then it is not worth hearing," traders would say. And, " This can't be true, I heard it in Jashimpur," was always the introduction to a ridiculous fantasy based on a forgotten fact. After all it was in this town that Christ had lived while studying Yoga and where He became a Master Yogi, Master enough to die and then live again after the soldiers had killed Him in some distant country. Places were pointed out to the stranger. He had lived there, spoken here, lectured over there. Then one day He went back home to confuse the world with His death. And to-day one had these palefaces still claiming Christ as a stranger here, as one of theirs. Men shook their heads and said, " Aye, these Europeans have a terrible impudence. They think they invented the world."

Buddha was here, too, for a while, under his real name, Sakya Muni, and he had learned much of the evil of the world, " for even in those days," it was explained by the story-tellers, " your companion was selling your clothes piece by piece as he spoke to you. Even then it was a wicked town."

Fa-Hsien, when he made his great journey from China through India over a thousand years ago, had stopped here for a drink of tea and had gone on, refreshed by conversation and wit, and minus his shoes and staff. " The place where they were stolen from him is just over there," a story-teller would say, pointing, " Just where that confectioner is over-charging that man for that adulterated candyfloss. Everything is like yesterday, and to-morrow will be like to-day, full of the adventure of loss for one and gain for another. So it goes."

A claim had been made that Marco Polo had lost a cloak and some money here but a learned historian had denounced this story as historically impossible, Marco Polo never having come this far south, but the story was still told.

The enamel-workers, among the finest in the world, lived from day to day in the hope of being given a large order from abroad which would make their fortunes, but in dread of it too, knowing that they could never raise the capital and pay the assistants to fulfil such an order. For all were in poverty and made barely enough to subsist. Their name was famed for the beauty and quality of their art, and cursed for dishonesty. It was safe for the stranger to buy one piece of enamel work, the one which he held in his hand and admired, but he should never order a dozen, for the other eleven would be pieces of trash hammered out by underpaid starving apprentices and then despatched in excellent packing. It was the same with fruit, cotton goods, embroidery, sandals. The sample was splendid, and when the case was opened the top layer was good. Beneath lay the trash. In the battle to live it was said in Jashimpur, "True charity is to forgive the unfortunate thief. He reminds the good man of his splendid virtues."

Over their forges while they squatted and rolled the sticks of coloured wax into glowing blues and scarlets, the craftsmen argued about the way the world was looking with the agitators on one side promising heaven, and now, spit on a devil's grave, the new Maharajah promising even more. Tramp on a sleeping tax-collector, but what was a man to believe?

The day after the Maharajah's speech to the crowd hardly any work was done in the city. Men sat all day and discussed this shattering and unbelievable happening. What were the young book-reading ones going to say about that? Here was a young Maharajah who had spoken in the town and promised a new life, and more, he was going to give his land away. He had been hit on the head in the war and was not himself. He had been drunk. He was smoked up with *bhang*! He was in some way trying to blind the people to some new plan for taxes. No, he was simply mad. It was generally agreed by midday that the Maharajah was mad.

"Yes, mad!" Hassan's lieutenant, Nabha, yelled to the crowd who listened to him that evening in the warehouse at the old Serai of the Tibetan caravans. "The Maharajah must be pitied because he is mad, and suspected too. Let us examine the actual situation." He had the crowd laughing after a while as he described how the Maharajah had decided to give back each blade of grass, one by one, to each Jashimpuri, and then each tree in the forest, and then the stones and rocks and mountains, under the impression that he owned it all. "He might then give you back your wives, and then your children, one by one, for he owns all those too," Nabha said. "He is a man of great power, this Maharajah. We will send him and his family off into exile where they can drink together. Be charitable to this harmless madman. We have now formed our own government and we are ready to rule. It is merely a matter of time before we rule this country. But first we have to make our move of courage. We must rescue Hassan from the prison. The people must act, and make a sign of courage and unity."

While he spoke to them, seemingly confident and happy, convincingly lighthearted and amusing, Nabha was very troubled, for more than anything he wanted his leader, Hassan, to remain in gaol. Since Hassan had gone to gaol he, Nabha, and his friends in the Party had been able to get things done. Hassan was so meticulous, so painfully honest and narrow because of it, so scrupulous and careful and rigid. Nevertheless, in the meeting of the Party committee he had just come from, Nabha had been defeated (though he had never once said that Hassan should stay in gaol).

It had been a difficult and painful meeting. Hassan, though not present, was very much there while the members of the committee spoke their pieces if not their minds. Hassan seemed to know that a battle would be fought over him, over his release from gaol. He had sent out a message from the gaol which had been read out at the meeting. It was a simple message, but loaded and powerful.

" I know," his message said, " that there is nothing easier than to forget me and behave as though I am dead. I know, as you all know, that the one thing you wish to do is avoid taking direct action of any kind, such as storming the gaol and rescuing me. Well, I am sitting here and waiting to see you rescue me. And when you have done that I will lead you, for you will have shown yourselves worthy of leadership. Are you worth leading to freedom ? Show me. Show Jashim-pur. Show India. You will be tempted to do nothing, especially since the young Maharajah's speech to the crowd in the city yesterday. That is our national, and long-ingrained, cowardice working in us. Ask Nabha why he is not leading you to rescue me from the prison. You will blame each other, of course, and the rich, led by the new Maharajah, are watching you. I, too, am watching you. We have very little time left in which to seize Jashimpur, our country. The Maharajah came to me in my cell and offered me liberty. I refused. Why ? Because I insist that you, my Party, take action and liberate me. This is your country and my country, and I am your leader who has spent his life in your service, in the plan to free us all and give us a happy life. What are you going to do about it ? "

They all knew that nobody wanted to do anything about it if they could avoid it. Even so, Nabha could not say so, for he feared Hassan, and more than that he feared actually challenging Hassan's authority and taking over the leadership of the Party, for only Hassan dead would not be known as leader. All wanted him free but none wanted to do what Hassan goaded them into doing, to free him themselves by storming the gaol.

So Nabha was very disturbed while he spoke to the craftsmen in the Tibetan caravanserai, while laughing with them and watching their faces below him as he manipulated them. He was a small, thin, good-looking man of about thirty-five, and there was that sullen, proud look in his face which is often to be seen in the face of an ex-slave when his character is carrying him up out of the mud where he was too unhappy to stay. He had something in him of the clown, his ruthlessness hidden by a ready laugh and a face which mirrored perfectly emotions he did not feel, and just as readily those which he chose to show. His ambition had been eating at him since boyhood. His target was to be Prime Minister, to have a Chevrolet, and to make money, plenty of money, while seeing to it that the poor got a little more than they were getting. He knew this was wrong, that he was too ambitious and that he was not truly idealistic at heart, but he could not help it. It was regrettable but not to be conquered. Hassan was a real idealist and that was what was wrong. Look at this business of forcing the people to rescue him from the prison. Sheer vanity. It was known everywhere now that the Maharajah had visited him in his cell and offered to free him. But no, said Hassan. He was in no hurry to go. No. The people must rescue him, showing that they had enough courage to care and to act. Never mind. The Party was on a journey just now, a journey to power in this little miserable State, and when that journey was over there would begin the sorting out of who was who. Idealism would be no use then, though it was vital now. When the Party began to govern it would be time for the realists, like Nabha.

" So there it is," he shouted. " We have to rescue Hassan from the prison. And we will do it to-morrow before midday. The craftsmen's guild will supply a hundred men for the task." He almost laughed aloud when he saw the swift shiftiness move into the dark faces below him, that curious rolling back of all the eyes as they glanced at each other and then stared back at Nabha.

"We cannot have freedom without risk and effort," he warned them. He almost said, "Terrifying though it is for you all," but he had to control the laughter which was bubbling up in him. There were about three hundred men listening to him, and when he announced that he wanted a hundred men to step forward now as volunteers there was a deep silence and a solid, glum, ox-like expression settled on every face. Nobody moved. Only the hundreds of eyes moved, looking everywhere but at Nabha.

"Why don't you push each other forward?" he snarled at them, for he had suddenly recalled that he hated the famed cowardice of his race, and that he had campaigned against it, and that it was not as amusing as the people liked to make out. As now, for instance, when a howl of laughter went up from the crowd of ragged men and they began to struggle with each other, trying to force each other forward as volunteers. For none of them wanted to rescue Hassan. They loved Hassan. They wanted Hassan rescued. But they did not want to get into any trouble for him. So they clowned and laughed in the warehouse below Nabha while Nabha watched them with bitter, smiling eyes, feeling that perhaps they were never going to be free, were unready, undeserving, unworthy. He watched them playing and acting for a couple of minutes, while they shrieked and laughed, shouting to each other, "No. You go. Not me. I'm only a coward. I'm not worth such honour. You go," and "I'm willing to give my place up if you insist. But I want payment. After all, I've waited for years to do something brave," and everybody screamed laughing.

"Very well," he cried in his special voice for the crowd when it was time for pressure, "I'll count out a hundred of you." He called to one of his assistants and told him to pick out the first hundred that came handy. After some nervous shuffling the crowd became still, resigned, and those of the chosen hundred who could would shift for themselves when the time for action came, shouting defiantly and hanging back. Never mind, it would have to do.

Later in the evening Nabha moved through the town, addressing crowds, arranging for the mob who would storm the gaol in the morning. Nabha had always looked up to Hassan but since Hassan had been in gaol he had tasted the pleasure of leadership and he liked it. He had discovered that he was not only as good as Hassan as a leader, but was more intelligent, more subtle and he was not as severe and as stern as Hassan. It was only when he had the chance to use his authority in full that Nabha saw that Hassan had been a fanatic. He was too narrow, too suspicious, too uncompromising. For his own part, Nabha was even willing to follow the lead of the new young Maharajah, as long as he was made Prime Minister under the Maharajah. The Maharajah was not mad. He was only ambitious, and determined to stay Maharajah, even a landless one, as long as he could be loved. As Hassan had written in a letter sent out of the prison, " He is very vain, this Maharajah, and a tyrant in reverse. I would say there's nothing he wouldn't do in order to be loved. He is a boy, but a dangerous one."

At eleven that night Nabha arrived at the house belonging to the only rich man who saw that change was inevitable, Doctor Kholi, where the other members of the provisional government were waiting for him.

As usual, Doctor Kholi was in an excited state, lecturing, expounding, flinging about the crazy ideas which poured in a ready stream from his small, brown, bald skull. But mad though he was, Doctor Kholi was genuine, courageous and sincere. Nabha had come to love Doctor Kholi.

" The Maharajah is a typical case of early deprivation," Doctor Kholi was explaining to the intellectual group in the provisional government. "A classic case of the non-breast fed. I've gone into the matter and it's a fact that he never had the breast. There is no menace in the world, gentlemen, like the man of intelligence and personality who cannot forgive the world for not having had the breast, and who does not realise what is the matter. You smile, Hari Lal? Let me assure you that the records are full of proofs of my statement. Hitler was almost certainly a bottle-fed child. Possibly Jenghis Khan too. The whole aural-fantasy is distorted and the pattern is broken. Part of the modern Western obsession with the female breast is rooted in this early deprivation. Cigarette smoking is only an extension of the yearning for the breast. Don't hate the young Maharajah. Pity him. He means well." When the lean, spry doctor saw all the dark eyes flicker at him he raised a little dry brown hand and said, "Don't start imagining that secretly I'm a lover of the *gaddi*, or a monarchist or a believer in autocracy. I'm telling you not to worry too much about these fantasies of the young Maharajah, speaking to crowds, striving to dominate and so on. Pity him. The big, warm, brown breast of the mother which is denied haunts the soul of the deprived ever after. There can't be too much pity in this world, gentlemen."

"May someone else speak for a moment or two now, Doctor Sahib?" Hari Lal asked acidly. "Not about the breast this time, but about something more important."

"There is nothing more important than the breast," the doctor murmured. "Nothing. As they will find out in the rotting West before long. See how sensibly narrow and old-fashioned the Russians are becoming? Remember how they started off? Free abortions, free divorce in the post office, clinics, machine civilisation. And look at them now, splendid specimens. They've gone back to narrowness and good sense, that's why. Everyone breast fed. Everyone. And no shame about pulling a breast out in a railway carriage. Nothing like that. Did you think Bernard Shaw was joking when he said that the starving Russians during the famine of 1932 should keep their children on the breast until the age of twenty-one? Not a bit of it. Shaw must be read. Beneath each jest is a sharp arrow of good sense." He went on murmuring while Nabha opened the meeting.

Kholi sat down and watched the young men while they discussed the rescue of Hassan. He was sorry for them, knowing that their adventure must soon go stale for them once they got power, and then the jealousies which were alive among them now, but held down and hidden by their common idealism would burst into flame and their struggle with each other would begin. He warned them often of this and they laughed and slapped him on the back and said, " Never fear, Doctorji, we are above that kind of petty behaviour. We will give you a Jashimpur worth living in."

Some had come up from the poor and were shrill or vengeful or erratic, and four from the very rich, who had to spend most of their time proving that they had been thinking about revolution since childhood. Others were from the middle-class who had had two meals a day instead of one, or none. They were about equal in the agony which had India by the throat just now, about sixty per cent Muslim and the rest Hindu. Only seldom did their religious differences get in their way, and then Hassan would crush it with brutal sarcasm. Nabha was not so good at this as Hassan, not so swift in scenting childish irritations before they became storms of quarrel. Nabha tried, but he could not manage as well as Hassan.

When the matter of rescuing Hassan had been decided in detail, discussion began on the proposals for elections throughout the State, the first elections ever to be held in the territory's history.

It was Hari Lal who stunned his companions by saying that he proposed the Maharajah should be offered membership of the Party, and later should be allowed to become Prime

Minister. Hari Lal had always been a free-thinker, conscience-ridden, and coolly determined when he believed in an idea. When Nabha spat with rage after Hari Lal had spoken, and after the enormous silence, Hari Lal smiled and said, " Now, Nabha, remember you're a man of authority, not a member of a mob. I want my proposal considered not spat at."

" Never. Never in a thousand years," Nabha cried. " You traitor. You toady. Have you lost your senses?"

" The Maharajah has authority," Hari Lal said, calm and unshaken by Nabha's outburst. " I'm thinking of India and the Indian Government. They're not prepared to see us blacken a Maharajah's face too much. Don't forget we have to reckon with India in the end. And the Maharajah's sincere. I'm certain of it. I've never condemned a man because his father was this or was that. To have the Maharajah in our Party would be a triumph. The Party would be unable to go wrong in the State. Don't forget he's in a difficult position. The landowners are frightened of him and hate him already. In our Party, the landowners couldn't do much against him. You must consider my proposal. It's sensible."

" That's your Brahmin blood speaking, Hari Lal," Nabha sneered at him. " Craft and cunning trying to cover up the real issue. Sectarianism and the traditional love of the *gaddi*, the worship of the king. Conservative to the soul. Yes, your Brahmin blood. Our blood betrays us at times, doesn't it?"

" You can be a silly little man at times, Nabha," Hari Lal said. " But I forgive you. Let someone else speak for a while."

A serious quarrel began after that, and Nabha was hurt to see how much support Hari Lal's proposal was getting. It was finally agreed that the matter should be shelved until Hassan was free to preside over the meeting. Only then could there be a full discussion of this outrageous idea, Nabha said as he closed the meeting. Doctor Kholi was convulsed

with almost silent laughter on the couch and when Nabha
saw this his face darkened.

"It's not funny, Doctorji," he said. "How can you laugh
about such a thing?" He raved a little then, waving his
clenched fists before his face. "I always knew we'd have
trouble with this slavish streak in us. Now, because that
family of plunderers produces a cunning member who wants
to cash in on the new ideas, everyone wants to crawl along
the ground and worship him. And you laugh. It's nothing
to laugh about."

"Oh, but it is. It is," Kholi said, bouncing up and down
on the settee. He called to the young men who were filing
out, still arguing, "Don't go yet. Tea is coming. Sit down
all of you." But they knew he wanted an audience. The doctor
could talk all day and night and never exhaust himself. They
thanked him and said they must get some sleep, and then went
on their way, leaving Doctor Kholi a little disconsolate, while
Nabha went on cursing the slavish nature of the Jashimpuri
soul. His mood of pessimism increased as he attacked the
Brahmin soul of Hari Lal, and he told Doctor Kholi that he
thought everything would come to failure in the end, that the
people of Jashimpur would never be free because they were
slaves and feared freedom more than their slavery. Kholi
listened to every word, and as always when he listened to an
aggrieved person, heard what was not said, heard the fear in
Nabha himself, for Nabha was often appalled by his own
participation in the freedom movement. He was a third
generation Muslim, his grandfather, a Hindu of the lowest
caste, having embraced Islam rather than go on any longer as a
piece of ordure disguised as a man. Sometimes Nabha's
ancestral rage with the chaos of Hinduism overcame him and
he had to struggle against a desire to see Hinduism swept
away. His own faith in God was secure and he tried hard to
live up to the tenets of Islam. He could not understand
Kholi's cool tolerance, his dry amusement with the world of

men. All the young men looked to him as to a father, understanding about his streams of fantasy and his curious opinions.
He listened to Nabha's doubts now and seemed to agree with
them all.

"Yes," he said. "It's possible that all this may come to
nothing after all. It's all very delicate, like an elephant tip-
toeing across a sheet of glass. You're all so liable to turn
round and feather your own nests when the time comes.
You'll be tempted. As to the slavish soul of the Jashimpuri,
I have it too. And you have it too, Nabha. Are you willing
to die for freedom? You're not, are you? I know you're
not and you know you're not. Don't get angry with me now.
It's not easy to shake off centuries of slavery. You're all
talking to yourselves when you curse the people's cowardice.
But would you die to-morrow outside the gaol, to free
Hassan? Would you?" Kholi's merry brown eyes centred
on Nabha's face. He laughed at Nabha's anger. "Would
you?" he asked again.

"I'd die to-night for freedom," Nabha's voice echoed in
the room after his shout of defiance. The doctor collapsed in
laughter on the couch as the servant came in with a tray of
tea. Nabha was scowling, his face a dark bronze-red.

"It's true," he cried when the servant had gone. "I'd
die to-night for freedom. It's insulting to laugh like that,
Doctorji."

"Oh, you liar," Kholi shouted through laughter. "You're
such a liar. You know very well you wouldn't die for anything. You've got all your plans worked out for your future,
haven't you? Hassan would die. But not you, Nabha. Now
look at me and swear you'd die for freedom." They stared at
each other, into each other's eyes for some time, the doctor's
thin shoulders shaking as he tried to stop laughing. The
doctor imitated a hero defying the police and tore open his
shirt, snarling contemptuously, "Shoot me, then. Go on.
I defy you. Shoot me. But not too hard, please. I've a wife

and three children to support," and Nabha burst out laughing with him, at first ashamedly, but he began to play the part of a police officer, and standing against the wall he shouted, "I refuse to shoot anyone unless my wages are raised. I'm a Jashimpuri with a wife and family. I refuse to shoot you. Ask the inspector. He's better paid than I am."

"Go ahead and shoot me," Kholi called in defiance. "What's money compared with justice? Shoot me. Help us. Spill my blood and help the revolution. Please shoot me. Be a man. Don't be a Jashimpuri coward. Shoot me." They both bent down laughing again, but Nabha became remorseful and said, wringing his hands, "We shouldn't *do* this kind of thing." He was quite grieved with himself now. "It's contemptible. We shouldn't do it. Oh, God, we're hopeless. We're a rotten people at heart. Rotten."

"Vile," the doctor said, laughing. "Not merely rotten, but vile."

"We never seem to grow up," Nabha complained. "None of us. I happen to know for a fact that my own father laughs at me and does imitations of my speeches, while it was he who taught me as a boy to look forward to freedom, to want a better life. How can we be such a contemptible people? What's the matter with us all?"

Never stuck for an answer, in fact unable to leave a question of any kind unanswered, Doctor Kholi said, "Vanity. Pure vanity. The whole race from the richest to the poorest is vain. They laugh at themselves so as to spoil anyone else's laugh at themselves. And this vanity is due to a deep feeling of inferiority, because essentially we're quite pointless and utterly hopeless. Any starving Indian's a better man than a Jashimpuri because he's not vain, not so destructive with his laugh. We're all frightened of each other here, frightened of laughter, the other fellow's laughter. The only one of us who's not frightened is Hassan."

"Hassan! Hassan! It's always Hassan! You're always

praising Hassan to me, Doctorji. I know he's a fine man. I know he's clever. I respect him. But why are you always praising him to me?" Nabha regretted his outburst as soon as he had finished speaking.

"You hate Hassan, I think," the doctor said. He began to pour the tea. "Do you know why? Because he's going to make you do what you only think you want to do. Free Jashimpur. And he's willing to see you all die, and himself, in doing it. Because he's serious. You hate him because you don't really want to be free. That's a fact, isn't it? It was fine fun when it began, but now it's getting serious, possibly dangerous. That's what's the matter. You must steel yourself, Nabha. Your testing time is coming. Hari Lal may have more courage and leadership than you have. How do we know?"

"That's a lie," Nabha shouted, knowing the doctor had diagnosed well. "That's a mean thing to say to me."

"You may get killed in the morning, leading the people. Are you ready, Nabha? Do you want to free Hassan? You want to be a hero but you fear the dangers involved. So you've got to fight against cowardice. To-morrow morning you must go to that gaol full of determination. To-morrow will decide many things. That's why Hassan insists on you rescuing him from the gaol. He knows you're mostly cowards but only need to perform one act of bravery to become as vain and ready as tigers." Nabha shivered and sipped his glass of lemon-scented tea. He nibbled one of the cardamom seeds floating on the top of the glass.

"You're a good man, Doctorji," he said, looking into the brown, smiling face of the sprightly, emaciated doctor. "You've been so good to us. I wish you liked me more. Do you despise me?"

"Ask me to-morrow night," Kholi began to laugh.

Nabha looked hopelessly at the wall. He suddenly saw then why some men devoted their lives to making money,

K

caring nothing for other's opinions, for rights or wrongs. Making money was simple, direct, and money could be trusted. He had cared in the beginning, had truly believed in freeing Jashimpur but lately he had lost some faith, gained ambition, and it seemed sensible. And to-morrow someone might hurt or shoot him while he was engaged in freeing Hassan, whom he wanted to see kept in gaol. Let come what was to come then. Having retired into the Jashimpuri cloud of waiting in which most things could be borne, he asked the doctor to prepare a *hukkah*, and when it was ready they smoked it together, handing the mouthpiece back and forth and talking about everything save to-morrow.

Chapter Twelve

In the gaol hourly reports were delivered to Hassan from breakfast time onwards. The superintendent of the gaol, now fully converted to belief in Hassan's programme, was in such a state of morbid anxiety that Hassan had to console him and assure him that he would look after him in future.

"You must remember that my family have served the State for four generations," he had pleaded with Hassan. "That's a long time. It's hard to break with tradition, even though I now see that your cause is right." And he had even begged Hassan to work with the new Maharajah. "What could have been more reasonable than his attitude when he visited you here?" he had asked. "Why must you consider such a man your enemy merely because he is his father's son?"

"For that very reason," Hassan had replied. "Because he is his father's son. Go off and see what is happening at the gates. People must be gathering by now."

"But they were not. Not even by ten o'clock was there any sign of a crowd. Hassan walked up and down his cell, fretting, and the prison governor tried to comfort him.

"They'll come," he said. "They're bound to come. Sit down and drink your tea. You'll be rescued, I know you will. Everything is ready. The guards are all prepared. Every rifle is unloaded and all the ammunition is in the armoury. There's no danger. They've all had their instructions. The rest depends on the people." It had taken many hours of argument for him to convince Hassan that it was better to withdraw ammunition from the guards and issue them with blank rounds. He was terrified of spilling blood, whereas Hassan wanted some spilled, just a little would do, a blood sacrifice. The cause needed a few martyrs. He knew he should have been firm and insisted on the guards firing into the crowd and killing a couple of people, but he was shaken to find that he had not the will. Was he then, after all, just another timid Jashimpuri? He was afraid so, and the discovery had done him no good.

He had insisted, though, that the guards, after firing blank ammunition, should use their rifle butts on the crowds. There must be people left lying about on the ground, preferably in some pain. There must be shown to have been resistance, struggle, sacrifice. But after discussing the matter with the guards, the prison governor had to give Hassan the news that they had refused. They were not willing to hit anybody now as it looked fairly certain that the People's Progressive Party was going to rule the State and they wanted no trouble. They had their futures as guards to consider.

" I'm sorry, Hassan Sahib," the prison governor said. " I've done my best but it's no good. The guards won't use violence. They say they'll put up a convincing defence and then retreat into the courtyard if the people will advance after the firing of the blank ammunition. But never mind. The main thing is that the people will show the will to rescue you. That's what you want, isn't it ? "

" The whole business is just disgusting," Hassan said sombrely. " I've a good mind to call the whole thing off. The whole thing makes me feel ashamed. It's revolting." He looked into the clear, innocent, official eyes of the prison governor. " I shouldn't have let you have your way in this," Hassan went on. " It's a miserable business, sickening, and so very like Jashimpur. You're afraid, aren't you ? "

" I haven't slept all night with the worry," the officer admitted; no shame, no pride, no manliness, just a Jashimpuri at heart. Hassan could have slapped him across the face for his frank timidity, though he himself was glad and relieved there was going to be no violence, as glad as the prison governor. So in a way he was a failure, a Jashimpuri. He thought he might weep with despair and he turned away from the official.

By eleven o'clock about thirty people had assembled near the gaol in charge of one of the Party organisers, Dokra Singh, a young man devoted to Hassan and very proud of his martial Rajput ancestry. He had had to drag the thirty protesting men out of their houses and had all but beaten them along the narrow lanes leading to the gaol. Dokra Singh raised his fists high at eleven prompt and yelled, " Free Hassan ! Tyrants, we have come for Hassan."

" Shout, you frightened dogs," he growled at the gloomy men behind him. Low croakings and small yells so comic rose from the men that some of them began to laugh, and the others joined in.

" That's no use, is it, Dokra Singh ? " one of them shouted. " But the fact is this could lead to trouble. It's all right for you, you're educated and can use the gab if you get caught. It's not the same if you're just a poor, frightened, illiterate like me. There's nothing the police like more than beating up an illiterate. I've got to go home. My child's sick."

" What about me ? " another one complained. " I've been dragged out of a sick bed. Look at me." He grinned when they all looked at him standing there as healthy as an ox.

" The next man who complains I'll hit him," Dokra Singh warned them. " Now, remember, I'll put up with no more nonsense. I'm going to count three and then you'll shout, ' Free Hassan.' Is that understood ? "

" Answer me this first," one of the older men said. " Did the Maharajah or didn't he offer to let Hassan go free ? Now, the Maharajah said that to us when he spoke to the crowd in the square. Now, what about that ? Why then, must we risk our precious blood, family men, mind you, to free Hassan ? Now why ? "

" The Maharajah was lying," Dokra Singh said without hesitating, and with firmness. " There was no such offer made to Hassan." He began to count.

" *Ekh !* "

" I do not believe the Maharajah has lied to us ! " someone shouted.

" *Do !* "

Others began to shout. They said they believed the Maharajah. " Even if he lied I'm determined to believe he told the truth, because I'm not going to attack that gaol," another voice cried. There was a burst of laughter.

" *Teen !* " On reaching the word " three," Dokra Singh threw his fine head back, his black hair shining in the sun, and screamed, " Free Hassan ! " Not a single voice was raised to join him.

" You see, we're not sheep, Dokra Singh," one of the men called out. " Why must we rescue Hassan ? Why ? "

The sentry on the gaol gate about twenty yards away had been standing at ease with his rifle, solemn and official, but now he burst into the sniggering, Jashimpuri laugh of the initiated. The group of men behind Dokra Singh laughed back until he turned on them, cursing. He decided to wait until the others began to turn up. He needed support. But the men would not be silent and continued to ask why they must rescue Hassan when he had refused to be freed by the Maharajah.

" Take us to the Palace and let the Maharajah tell us himself," they said. " Someone is lying."

By one o'clock the Party organisers had managed to get over a hundred men collected near the gaol. Scouts were appointed from Party members and posted in the rear to prevent men sneaking away after several had vanished into the alleys. Large numbers of women and children and old men gathered nearby to watch.

" What do you think you're doing in there ? " one woman screamed at her husband. " Why aren't you at work for your children ? Come out of it and get off to your work." She tried to get through the cordon and seize her husband but the scouts prevented her. Her husband shouted that it was all a mistake, his being there. He had been forced to come. " You fool," his wife called back. " You were never any use. You'll finish in the gaol."

Nabha arrived in a trade truck with Hari Lal. They had a conference with some of the Party members, and Nabha listened patiently while Dokra Singh said that the men forming the crowd were clinging firmly to the idea that there was no reason to rescue Hassan and that they were convinced the Maharajah had told the truth about wanting to free Hassan.

Nabha lifted his shrewd eyes and looked at Dokra Singh. " Could it be that you agree with these men ? " he asked accusingly. " That you would like to avoid storming the gaol ? "

" You dare to say that to me ? " Dokra Singh kept his voice low but his eyes were glittering with fury. " You, a base-born sweeper's descendant accuse me, a Rajput, of being afraid ? "

" That kind of talk's not going to help anybody, you know," Nabha said, shaken by the Rajput's anger. " If you're very anxious to give your Rajput blood a chance, then storm the gaol on your own. Lead the people. The sweeper's descendant will watch with interest."

" They will not go," Dokra Singh said. " I can assure you of that. They're in a state of terror at the idea."

A dozen policemen with rifles had lined up outside the wall of the gaol. It was a long, massive eighteenth-century building with a high wooden door. The policemen were standing about twenty feet from each other and were looking ready and determined. An officer smoking a cigarette lounged nearby. He showed no sign of agitation, knowing his part as he did.

Nabha turned to the crowd and spoke to them. " We will be ruling here quite soon," he said. " So step forward any man who thinks Hassan is not worth rescuing."

Nobody moved. " So you are all ready ? " Nabha went on. Sweat had broken out all over his body. He had decided to lead the crowd against the gaol, to show what a base-born sweeper's descendant could do.

When he turned and was about to raise the Party yell, *Jashimpur for the People*, he saw the police raise their rifles and he paused, his throat drying. " Why am I doing this when I don't want Hassan free ? " he was thinking. " Why ? Is that a manly thing to do ? Isn't it cowardly of me to be doing what I don't want to do ? Then why am I doing it ? "

" So you feel pretty certain that the crowd believe what the Maharajah said ? " he said as casually as possible to Dokra Singh.

" Absolutely certain," said Dokra Singh. " I'll lead them right now if you order me to. But there'll be bloodshed. If you want that, say so. I'm ready. But why not find out about this mysterious offer of the Maharajah's ? Why not telephone him and ask ? "

" *Please* don't walk up and down this cell any more," the prison governor said hysterically, for each time Hassan passed him where he sat in the narrow cell he had to lean to one side to avoid the bed and knocked against the tense official.

" It's *my* cell," Hassan cried. " I'll do what I like in it."

" Very well," the official said apologetically, but in an exasperated whisper, wringing his hands, running them through his oiled hair, staring at the ceiling. " I'm sorry. If only you'd relax, just for a while. It'll be all right. They *will* rescue you. Why can't you sit down and wait? You're so worked up. It won't help."

" *I'm* worked up?" Hassan said contemptuously. "Me? What about you? You've been shivering since you arrived this morning. And what have you done for the Party? I'll tell you what you've done. You've made a disgrace of me. No one was ever able to do that before to me. No one. But I trusted you. I had to. I'm your prisoner, after all. You know very well that the people should be left to attack the prison and face the firearms. Otherwise it's all a lie, a dirty Jashimpuri trick. Why didn't you consult me first? We can't hide a thing like this. It'll be known all over Jashimpur that the guards were disarmed so that I could be rescued. You fool. Why didn't you discuss this with me before you did it?"

" They're not disarmed. They've got their rifles," the governor protested. "No one will know. You know no one in Jashimpur believes *anything* they hear. Please don't worry, Hassan Sahib. And don't be angry. You've been angry all morning."

" I know that this morning has finished me," Hassan said, looking at the whitewashed wall with brooding eyes. " I've made a mistake. For the first time I've made a mistake."

He had always been careful, and had never trusted his affairs in hands not thoroughly known to him, until now, and this frightened maniac had done for him, disgraced him.

" Call it off," he cried. " Go out and call the whole thing off. At once." He grabbed hold of the sweat-wet collar of the man's khaki silk shirt and pulled at it, but the man held on doggedly to the chair on which he was sitting. After all, he was an officer and not used to this kind of treatment. He bent his little head as Hassan wrenched at the shirt-collar. It finally came away in Hassan's hand with a thin, ripping sound. Hassan held it in his hand and looked at it, made a curious kind of sobbing sound, short and disgusted, and then flung the collar to the floor. It was too much. He went and sat down on his bed, and looked at the wall, quite desperate, dangerously silent.

"Is that your gratitude to me?" the governor asked coldly. "After all I've done for you? What have I done to have my collar torn from my shirt? Give me my collar." He held out his hand in such a cold and commanding way that Hassan half rose on his way to retrieving the collar, but he remembered who he was and sat down again. He looked so dejected and hopeless that the Prison Governor forgave him and began to apologise for losing his temper. He saw that a collar was nothing, a collar ripped off by a great man like Hassan should not be allowed to become a barrier.

"I must go and see what's happening, Hassan Sahib," he said. He wrung his hands together and asked to be forgiven.

"Go away," Hassan said sombrely, absently. He waved his hand. "A race of slaves," he murmured. "A race of slaves." He was thinking about his long journey which had brought him to this place, to this sensation of disgust and despair. He was not big enough to win. He had not even the resolve to see a few slaves killed so that hosts of other slaves would feel pride, and courage, and belief. He had let himself be made a Jashimpuri coward by another coward, one of the little, terrified men who wanted freedom but dreaded the getting of it. "And how well he knew me," Hassan thought bitterly. "One Jashimpuri knows another one. He knew I feared violence. I wonder do we all smell of that fear, of that craven love of peace and of being liked and thought well of? How well he knew me. I'd like to punish him for that, for knowing me that well, and for acting without discussing it with me. It could only be here in Jashimpur that such a miserable and spiritless thing could be arranged." But he was glad. That was what hurt, being glad.

When the official had gone Hassan sat on, withdrawn and

detached from his surroundings, resigned to admittance that there was no Jashimpuri spirit of courage or defiance. Such a people were not worth struggling for. He knew that had he been a communist he would have had the necessary courage to have struck down the Prison Governor for making such craven arrangements with his guards, and would have gone himself and countermanded them. Had he been a communist he would have had sufficient contempt for the people to make them suffer, and learn to hate from it, but he had shuddered to think of the bullets piercing the flesh of the poor, and yet he had steeled himself to it, but the Prison Governor had read him and arranged the farce, and they both knew that Hassan was glad.

"One day you'll thank me," the Prison Governor had protested after Hassan had spent a certain amount of rage on him.

After a time he heard running feet in the corridor. Excitement began in him again and he ran to the door, ready to believe that the mob had stormed the gaol for him. It was the Prison Governor who met him at the door.

"They've gone," he said, his eyes pleading and sorrowful. "They've all gone. There's not a soul left outside the prison."

"That English colonel was right," Hassan said dully, his hopeless eyes not looking at anything in particular. "We're a useless, spineless, lying race. I always knew it, but I always denied it, because I'm one of them, and I'm like them."

"We're just cattle," the Prison Governor said, relieved now. "Cattle. Nothing but cattle."

The crowds began to shout slogans, cheerfully, as they moved off towards the palace on the hill. Nabha and his friends were in front arguing bitterly in undertones, Nabha saying whenever he got a chance, "We're splitting. Even now we've learned nothing, you see. We're splitting, because the great Maharajah has spoken. And now because we lead a gutless people we have to go to the Palace to satisfy the crowd, so that we shall know what the Maharajah really meant."

"Then why come, Nabha?" Hari Lal hissed at him impatiently. "Why come if you feel like that? Why don't you admit that you're glad we're not storming the gaol? I'm glad. I admit it. I want to live. That's why."

"You've no shame, have you?"

"I'm what I am," Hari Lal said proudly. "We have to do with what we've got, what we are. Why pretend that we're a violent, fighting people? Why bother. We want reforms. I'm convinced the Maharajah is ready to bring them in."

Others of the young men agreed with him. They were all glad to be able to speak their minds without Hassan's presence. They loved and admired him, but they wanted him to stay in gaol for a little longer.

The sun glared down on them in its midday fire and the sky was cloudless, a thin, dry, powdery blue aching with summer heat.

"It's beautiful to be alive to-day," Hari Lal said, unashamed of his relief to have left the area of the prison and the rifles.

"There'll be trouble about this," Nabha warned his friends. "We have to face Hassan one day. We've left him in the gaol. We've done nothing. And now we're going to speak to our enemy, the Maharajah. Well, it's not my idea. I want everyone to know that I disagree with this. Everyone."

"It's the will of the people," Hari Lal replied in his quiet, ironic way. "Let the people have their way. They've never been allowed to have their way." He had impressed himself and he dropped the irony. "They'll always be grateful to you for giving them their way over this. After all, it's democracy we want to bring in here."

Grudgingly pleased, Nabha said, "You mustn't do anything about this suggestion of inviting the Maharajah to join

the Party without consulting Hassan. Hassan can be frightening when he's properly angry."

"Frightening for you," Hari Lal laughed as he looked
down into Nabha's small clever face. "Not for me, Nabha."
Hari Lal's father had money. They were so confident, so
free. Money was wonderful.

"Still, you must consult Hassan first," Nabha said.

"But you like the idea yourself, don't you?" Hari Lal
knew how to goad Nabha while informing him. "The idea
will grow on you. Wait and see. Perhaps Hassan's job is
over. The rest is up to us."

"Well, here we are," said Nabha. He was not going to be
drawn. He stopped and the chattering crowd of men drew
up behind the leaders. "Here's the palace." He knew what
they were doing was not in the revolutionary tradition, was
opposed to all Hassan's teachings and to his own sentiments
which he had put on like a jacket when he joined the Party.

Through the massive wrought-iron gates they saw a jeep
coming at speed down the drive. The Maharajah was driving,
cigarette-holder in the corner of his mouth. Behind him were
two servants holding a ladder. The jeep drew up with a
squeal of rubber and metal, and Prabhu jumped out. The
crowd heard him tell the servants to put the ladder against
the wall. All disappeared for a few moments and then Prabhu
appeared on top of the wall.

"I'm delighted to see you all," he said, smiling down at
them. There was no mistaking the real pleasure he was feeling
and the crowd began to shout greetings and good wishes to
him. He so obviously enjoyed the crowd that they warmed
to him at once and some called out, "Long Live the
Maharajah!"

"I couldn't agree with you more," the young Party men
could hear him murmur from where they stood below him.
He was so sure of himself, so at ease, so completely happy.

"I heard you," he called down to them. "So I thought

I'd come down and listen to you. Now, what's it all about? Anything I can do? "

He had just swallowed a couple of gins and he felt fine. He had had a cold, refreshing shower, changed into thin silk underwear, sensuous with their chill on his skin, and then put on a pair of thin brown linen trousers and a green tee shirt.

" So it's Hassan? " he said, laughing, when Hari Lal had finished speaking. There was a little fellow standing next to Hari Lal. He had his hands on his hips and was glowering up, defiant and angry-looking. Annoyed, Prabhu pointed down at Nabha and said, " What's upset *you*? And what's your name? You look very cross about something."

Men began to laugh and shout. " Speak up, Nabha. Why are you angry? Tell the Maharajah why you are angry."

" Tell the Maharajah you're angry with us because we wanted to hear him speak."

" Yes, he is angry because we wouldn't die at the gaol for Hassan."

" Why should we die, Maharajah Sahib, if it's true you'll let Hassan out? "

" You can have Hassan out any time you want him," Prabhu then described his meeting in the gaol with Hassan. He found it hard to keep contempt out of his voice. He had grown to like being Maharajah, and the more he considered Hassan's cold and hostile attitude to him the more it hurt. The best thing would be to break Hassan. There was nothing he could do with a type like Hassan.

" Even though he's right," that other voice said within. " Even though you agree with him, and even though you know why he hates Maharajahs."

" I admire Hassan," he told the crowd who were listening in silent absorption, their eyes fixed on him like one, still, patient and watchful eye. " He's had the courage to struggle for justice, and I have the ability to grant justice. Why don't we all get round a table, the leaders of the Party and the ruler, and discuss these problems? There's no conspiracy. There's no need for mystery now. We need to talk facts. Now, what do you want me to do?"

The crowd were yelling that they wanted Hassan freed without violence. They did not want to break the law or annoy the government in any way.

"Hassan prefers it that we shed our blood," one voice was complaining. "He is free to go, yet we must risk our lives to free him."

"He means well," Prabhu shouted above the noise. "He only wants you to act, to show courage. But why should you when you have no need? I'm ready to start reforms to-morrow. We'll have a conference. I shall free Hassan to-day if you agree." They agreed with cries of relief, some shouting for Hassan's blood, hoping to please the Maharajah, but he turned on these and said, "Hassan is one of your leaders. I have a use for him. We will go and get him out of the gaol. Then you must carry him on your shoulders into the town. That will make Hassan very happy."

They were eating right out of his hand. They were all his, set upon following him. As far as he could see he could not go wrong. "Lead us," they were demanding. They had walked all the way to the palace to check on his word, to see if they had heard aright about his statement on Hassan. Real love for them welled into his heart, so he made another promise.

"I have a plan for our only real export industry," he announced. "For the enamel-workers. Every enamel artist will have work and income. With our artists we'll put Jashimpur on the map of the world again. Now, to the gaol. We'll free Hassan. I'll give you Hassan." He lit another cigarette with shaky hands while they cheered. He was so short of breath he could not inhale the cigarette smoke. Life had never been so good, so rewarding, and so full of proof of the underlying splendour of the human spirit. The wonderful way people seemed to know a good man when they saw and heard one. And he was the man. This time they had come to him, not he to them. He knew he was their man. They were acclaiming him as such. " Long Live our Maharajah," they were intoning as he drove the jeep out of the gates and headed for the gaol. The crowd poured down the hot road after him in a hurrying stream of rags and waving arms.

Chapter Thirteen

Hari Lal was about the best educated of the young men. He knew how dangerous it was to think emotionally, and he thought emotionally ; and he knew, too, that Hassan would never lose his hatred for those who had battened on the peasants for so long, and would always see Jashimpur emotionally. He knew that this hatred was Hassan's real driving force, and Hari Lal was conservative enough to know that his own turn would come, for Hari Lal came of a rich Brahmin family. He wanted his own father to make a sacrifice, for God and Jashimpur. By that sacrifice many things could be achieved, and he thought the old man was about ready. What Hassan would not believe was that you could not make a revolution with cowed and broken peasants. And there was no need for it. Change would be enough. A beginning was needed, a sacrifice.

Hari Lal knew as well as Hassan that many of the land-owners, moneylenders and merchants, including his own father, deserved hanging, but he was determined to see that there would be no hanging even if peasants could be found to do it, which was unlikely. " Moderation in all things, except pleasure," the peasants said, and he did not quarrel with that. Hassan, though, despised such cynicism. Hassan was narrow, Hari Lal thought, and he knew that a time would come when he would voice some of these thoughts to Hassan.

To some of his friends, Hari Lal would say, " After all,

what's Jashimpur? A few hundred square miles of India. What Hassan can't see is that we're about to become a part of India, a part of a new country called Independent India. That's all. Nothing more. But he thinks of us as a pilot scheme, as a daring example to India, and says we should put through by revolution now everything that conservatism will try and prevent in India. For after all, he's right about that. The Indian Congress Party isn't revolutionary about social problems, only about British rule. But that doesn't mean we've got to have bloodshed here to please Hassan. We must vote on this matter. We must have the courage to oppose Hassan. He can't see past the callouses on his hands."

Hari Lal's opinions made the others uncomfortable, for they knew that if they once began to compromise with the rich they would lose. They knew Hassan was right when he said, " The task of the rich is to melt us down, buy us, or shoot us. It is we who must give in to them, they maintain. Whereas, I want *them* to give in. But the people must act."

The talk stage was passing now and the people would not act. For a week the Party had been waiting to hear of risings among the peasants in the countryside, but there was silence. Orators had gone out to put a little fire into the people. Hari Lal laughed whenever he spoke of " the revolution." He had an inborn contempt for the beaten and oppressed. He had once said to Doctor Kholi during a discussion on psychology, " The reason why so many people have inferiority complexes, Doctor, is because they are inferior. Why make a fuss about it ? " He distrusted all the new jargon, the pigeon-holing of people and types, the phoney philosophy and the bent psychology.

He found it hard to assess the new Maharajah. He envied him his casual ways, his air of experience, his long cigarette-holder and his good looks. How sincere was this curious man who went to the trouble to show how much he disbelieved in who and what he was? What was a man to make of such a Maharajah? And more important, what was a peasant to make of him? Hari Lal did not approve of the Maharajah's doings, for deep in him was a veneration for position and responsibility. There was something clownish in the Maharajah's doings, something brutally hurtful to the peasants' feelings about the past. They were not laughing at the Maharajah yet, but that would come. That cruel Jashimpuri laughter would come when it was ready. Only a few more public antics from the Maharajah and it would come.

It had been interesting working beside the self-made, like Nabha and Hassan, who still smelled of soil and were liable to eat their food with their mouths wide open—for Hari Lal almost as disgusting as the thought of another person's spittle. He knew his early conditioning in Hindu disgusts and disapprovals would never honestly die, would only pretend to. He admired Hassan for his courage, for going abroad as a common seaman, becoming a coolie in fact, and for working in America as a labourer. His experience of life showed itself in surprising manifestations of charity, yet the hatred for all those " on top " never diminished. He extolled America as the only truly genuine experiment in human freedom ever tried. He despised the French and Russian revolutions, but could grow wistful about the way those revolutions had done away with those " on top." And he could be timid when attacked unexpectedly. Hari Lal had discovered that the way to tackle Hassan was by brutal verbal assault, for under all his calmness and certainty Hassan was tender and liked to love and be loved. His emotional attitude to revolution was at its most ludicrous in the way he insisted on being rescued from the gaol, " making the people act." " A blood sacrifice," and so on. But need the Maharajah have dealt with the business so cruelly, so heartlessly, playing to the crowd as he did?

Now Hari Lal watched the Maharajah address the enormous gathering opposite the gaol. He stood on his jeep and told the people that he was going to give them Hassan. He had been approached by a deputation and he was responding. He would bring Hassan from the gaol and deliver him to them.

" After all, he's your leader. He worked for you and strove to better your lives. Now that I'm here in Jashimpur to do just that, Hassan should be among you to co-operate with me. I know he wanted you to go and rescue him, but you wouldn't go. He was perhaps asking too much." He paused to let them laugh and they laughed. Here was a leader who was not going to be for ever lecturing them about courage and bravery, nagging about how it was necessary to despise danger. They laughed again when Prabhu went on to say, " You have all been wise this morning, as wise as these men who didn't lead you against the gaol," and he pointed to Nabha, Hari Lal, Dokra Singh and the other members of the Party. Dokra Singh was trembling, his fists clenched, and he looked as if he might take off like a rocket at any moment.

" An insult," he yelled. " An insult and you laugh."

Angry cries answered him and fists were shaken.

" Quiet while the Maharajah speaks."

" Have you no manners ? "

" Long Live the Maharajah."

Prabhu let the crowd have its say for a little longer until Dokra Singh turned away. When it was quiet again and the crowd had turned its vacant mass-face to him for more leadership, Prabhu said that he would now release Hassan.

" But if he won't come out then what are we to do ? " he asked them, spreading his hands. He smoked while they exploded into replies.

" We will make him come out."

" Yes, we'll bring him out."

" Very well," Prabhu said. He got down from the jeep and told Nabha and Hari Lal to come into the gaol with him.

He had the main gates opened wide and told the sentries to stand well back and to allow the prisoner, Hassan, to walk straight out. Nabha, looking hunted and unwell, said he would wait outside with the crowd. He wanted to put off his meeting with Hassan for a little longer. He looked as if he might run away.

" Not at all," Prabhu said brusquely. " You'll come in and report to Hassan and tell him what's happened. Come on." Through his dark glasses he could see Hari Lal's intent eyes studying his face. " You must come for a drink at the palace later," Prabhu said to him. " And Hassan. We must have a discussion."

" Hassan won't come, Maharaj Sahib," Hari Lal replied instantly. " Do you mean Hassan to come as well ? "

" Of course."

" He won't come."

" Then come without him."

Nabha and Hari Lal looked at each other. Hari Lal smiled and said, " Hassan will be very angry with me, Maharaj Sahib."

" But you'll come, I hope," Prabhu liked the look and sound of Hari Lal, his respectful manner and his air of maturity, so different from Nabha's furtive, worried ways.

" Gladly, Maharaj Sahib. I always do as I wish."

" And you, Nabha ? " Prabhu gripped Nabha's arm, sending his will down into it, almost shaking the little man in impatience.

" I'd like to, but——"

" Look on it as a command," Prabhu said coldly.

" But——"

" Eight o'clock at the Palace." He would sever Nabha from Hassan, break up the Party, lead it. He caught a glimpse of a look in Hari Lal's eyes that was like a gloating. Here was an ambitious fellow with no love for taking orders from upstarts like Nabha, and he warmed to Hari Lal. Friends everywhere, only waiting to be discovered.

The Prison Governor, pale and red-eyed, came out into the glare of the courtyard, saluting, straightening his tunic, his eyes shifting from Nabha to Hari Lal, and then fixing on the Maharajah. He looked all in, eyes like a *bhang* smoker, nervous hands, dry lips.

" Hallo," Prabhu said. " I want to get Hassan out of here. Where is he ? In his cell ? Go and get him. Tell him the people are waiting to welcome him."

" He's in his cell, Maharaj Sahib."

The crowd had advanced right up to the gates and had begun to shout, " Long live Hassan. Where is our Hassan ? Bring us Hassan."

" Bring him," Prabhu told the Prison Governor.

Hesitating, the officer stood before Prabhu and began to twist his hands. " Maharaj Sahib," he said, " Hassan wants force to be used. Could we not have a little force used ? It means so much to him. He's a good man, Maharaj Sahib. Couldn't some of the people be allowed down to his cell to rescue him ? There'd be no trouble. He was expecting to be rescued. He's very depressed. He won't come voluntarily. He's been a model prisoner." The man was almost in tears.

" They all love him," Prabhu thought bitterly. " Go and get him," he said in an iron voice. " Tell him the gates are open and all he has to do is walk out. The people are waiting for him. Now, hurry up, please. Go and bring him. I've had enough of this nonsense."

" Bring Hassan," the crowd began to chant.

Just then two Europeans or Americans appeared in the courtyard and began to set up a ciné-camera on a tripod. One of them took out a light-meter and started measuring the

light. They worked with that peculiar steadiness and de-
liberating coolness which, Prabhu felt, they would use whether
photographing a murder, a bloody riot, or a miracle.

" Okay ? " the cameraman shouted to his assistant. The
noise of the crowd was increasing.

" Just about right, I'd say, Jack," the assistant replied.

Muttering annoyance, Prabhu walked up to the cameramen,
and Hari Lal, all his inherited instincts awake, followed him,
knowing that his advice was going to be needed.

" What's the meaning of this ? Who are you ? " Prabhu
looked into the blue eyes of the two men. They were wearing
the new white man's tropical dress, brightly coloured, loose
Hawaiian shirts, thin linen trousers and sandals, Parker Fifty-
Ones in their breast pockets.

" We're going to shoot the rescue," the cameraman said.
" We're covering Jashimpur for *Global News*. Okay ? "

" You can get to hell out of here," Prabhu said angrily.
" The bloody nerve. Go on, get out of it, and sharp."

" Wait, Maharaj Sahib." Hari Lal touched his arm lightly
and lowering his voice, said, " May I speak to you a moment
over there, quietly ? " He was urgent, and Prabhu went aside
with him, head bent, listening. " What is it ? " he asked.
" Do you know these bloody people ? "

" Maharaj Sahib, there are several pressmen in the town
now. If you get angry with them you'll appear in the Press,
and on the films, as an autocrat and a reactionary. Let them
take their pictures. Pictures of Hassan being brought out of
the gaol by the Maharajah would be a tremendous blow against
your enemies. The progressive Maharajah of Jashimpur.
Give a party for the pressmen. They love drink and being
treated as important. It costs little and will do a great deal
for you."

" I think from now on, Hari Lal, you can handle all Public
Relations. Thank you. That's good advice." He was very
impressed with this advice, for of course the Press could finish

him in a few articles, or help to show him for the progressive leader he was fast becoming. " Trust a Brahmin to give the right advice at the right time," he thought as he nodded to Hari Lal, whose eyes were bright already with the pleasures of intrigue and planning. " No wonder they ran every kingdom of India. They never get excited, never get cross, always see the opportunity as it opens. Marvellous."

The cameramen were delighted and surprised by Prabhu's friendliness as he offered them cigarettes. They could not see his suspicion through his dark glasses, suspicion which was a kind of fear, for he knew how easily he could be made a fool of by a fellow at a typewriter. They loved writing about Maharajahs and their strange ways, their cruelties and manias. This Hari Lal was certainly able. Listen to him with the two Englishmen.

" Have you been accredited ? " he was asking the older of the two Englishmen.

" In India, yes. At Delhi," the cameraman replied with that expert curtness of the British with all possible wog-types, but Hari Lal's fine English and his careful friendliness put them at their ease. Here was no Babu, and he was not aggressive with inferiority feelings. He was pleasant and reassuring, almost like an Englishman.

" Well, you'll need to be accredited here in Jashimpur too," Hari Lal said, his white smile splitting his dark, smooth, lean face. " Can't have you wandering around photographing slums and your other favourite Indian subjects, can we ? No, we'll accredit you and the Maharajah will be giving a press conference this week."

" Thank you," the Englishmen said. " And can we shoot this Hassan character coming out of prison ? "

" Certainly," Prabhu said. " I didn't realise who you were. I thought you were a couple of Americans at first. They know nothing about India. I didn't realise you were British. Will you excuse me now ? In future, if you want anything just get in touch with Mr. Hari Lal here, at my office in the Palace." He had learned one thing in the post-war world. If you have a brown skin, then ride the British when you were with the Americans, and ride the Americans when with the British. They loved it. Then laugh it over later.

" Thanks, Your Highness," the cameramen said affably. " We'll do that. By the way, would you pose with the prisoner as he walks down the courtyard ? Just stroll along beside him straight on to the camera, talking and so on ? "

" Certainly," Prabhu said. He was delighted with the way things were going. He could see the film shots on the screen already, the Maharajah giving freedom to politics at last in Jashimpur, big enough to free a man who was trying to be his enemy.

" Excellent. Excellent," he kept saying as he walked with Hari Lal to join Nabha. " I'm most grateful for the way you handled that, Hari Lal. You must open a Public Relations office right away. I liked the dig about the slums and so on. They appreciated that."

" One great British secret, Maharaj Sahib, is to publicise the dirt and backwardness of their dependent peoples and show it as the kind of thing Britain is in the world to remove. Not mentioning, of course, that their own misrule has helped to create it. One can't but admire such propaganda. It'll be years before we learn to handle things like that. But the secret is a sense of humour. We're not very good at that yet."

" Yes," said Prabhu, " they are a brilliant race, no doubt about it. The finest propagandists in the world. I wonder if we've learned from them."

" There is one important matter I wanted to ask you about, Maharaj Sahib. If you will agree it could change everything for the good."

" Oh ? And what's that ? "

Hari Lal halted so that they were still some distance from Nabha. " It's this, Maharaj Sahib. My advice to you is to join the People's Progressive Party right away and take over the leadership. Nothing could be simpler. If you do that, Hassan comes under some kind of control. Plenty of us in the Party will give you the warmest support. If it could be announced to the crowd when Hassan comes out of the prison it would have an enormous effect. I do advise you to do it, Maharaj Sahib. I've wanted to approach you for a long time about it. The people trust you. They want to trust their Maharajah. And I don't need to tell you that once at the head of the Party *all* your enemies would be disarmed. I include, of course, the landowners." He smiled as Prabhu turned his dark glasses at him.

" Are you so sure that the landowners are my enemies ? " he asked Hari Lal sharply.

" My father is a landowner, Maharaj Sahib," Hari Lal replied.

" I see. I see. Yes. No doubt about it. Yes. In the Party I could do a lot. Why not ? Yes. Come back to the Palace with me when this little mess is over. You think I should announce it to the crowd, do you ? But *do* I become head of the Party ? Will there be a vote ? I can't risk being defeated, you know. It's got to be a certainty."

" You tell the crowd, Maharaj Sahib, and I and my friends can assure you of the Party leadership."

" All right," Prabhu said. " I'll do it."

" Here they are, Maharaj Sahib." Hassan had appeared at the end of the courtyard. He was trying to free himself from three policemen who were dragging him.

" Clear the courtyard," Hari Lal shouted in a voice of command which made Prabhu start. Hari Lal began giving orders to Nabha to get people out of the way so that the cameras could shoot the scene. He wanted that scene on film of Hassan trying to get back into gaol.

" What a bastard," Prabhu thought admiringly as he watched Hari Lal pushing people out of the way. " He thinks of everything." He had never shaken off a respect for the Brahmin abilities which had kept them in the lead even when slowly growing literacy among non-Brahmins should have lessened their command. They had survived every upheaval through centuries. They survived everything. They adapted, accommodated, watched, and then took the lead again in every generation of change. They had many virtues, one of which was their vice as well, a consuming ambition to be respected and listened to. And why not when they produced Hari Lals who knew exactly when to compromise, and he was compromising madly right now, helping to destroy his leader, Hassan, whose task was done and who must be pushed aside. He would be doing it in the name of the welfare of society, not in its right name, the ambition of Hari Lal. The test would be about his father's lands when it was time for them to go into the kitty of the land reforms. It would be interesting then to see how Hari Lal would behave. When that time came there must be no favouritism, no playing about, no fiddling. No, only fair shares for all.

The roar of the crowd when it saw Hassan was deafening for a time.

And then Nabha did the strangest thing. He burst into tears as he ran up to Hassan and knelt on one knee. He got hold of Hassan's right hand and placed it against his own forehead, repeating a phrase over and over again in Jashimpuri.

" What's he saying ? " Prabhu was tense and nervous as he plucked at Hari Lal's sleeve.

" Forgive us, Hassan. Forgive us. We are all cowards," Hari Lal translated for Prabhu.

Hassan flung Nabha away from him and straightened up. He surveyed the whole courtyard until his big eyes rested on Prabhu. On his face was a tragic but dignified expression.

His grey prison dress made no difference to his dignity. He was one of those men who were seen before their clothes, one of those who could look well in anything. "If only the bastard would stop hating me and judge me as a person instead of as a Maharajah," Prabhu thought regretfully.

"Aren't you going to make a speech?" Hassan asked him in a loud voice which rang from the white walls of the sunny courtyard. A close-lipped sardonic smile was on his red mouth.

"I can wait," Prabhu said, cigarette-holder in mouth. "It's your turn; you make one. There's the crowd." He pointed to the chanting mob. Within him joy in Hassan's defeat was clashing hard with sorrow for having caused it.

Hassan looked calmly out at the crowd. He swallowed hard.

Hari Lal spoke next. "Address the people, Hassan," he said. "Then we'll all go off to Doctor Kholi's house. There's a lot to discuss. But you must address the people first. They've waited a long time. They're shouting for you."

"Yes. They've gone through a lot for me, haven't they?" Hassan said. "Waiting out there all the time. And you and Nabha and the rest of you rescuing me like this. Yes, I must address them after all they've gone through."

Hari Lal gave a sigh of exasperation and then calmly wiped his perspiring face with a handkerchief.

Hassan watched him for a while. In the silence the camera was whirring, and Hassan looked at Prabhu and said, "You've thought of everything, haven't you?"

"Don't argue with him in public, Maharaj Sahib," Hari Lal whispered without moving his head. "Say nothing." So Prabhu smoked and was silent, an enigma in dark glasses. The tenseness of the atmosphere in the courtyard mounted rapidly. Even the camera was silent. Action was wanted. Everyone was waiting on Hassan. When the stillness had become unbearable, for even the crowd's shouts had died down to a low murmuring, Hassan walked across the court-yard towards the gates, the squeak and scuff of his sandals the only sound now to be heard. He climbed up the iron gates with the speed and agility of a monkey. When he was standing on the wall over the wide arch he spoke to the crowd slowly in Urdu, so that Prabhu could under-stand.

"I haven't much to say to you," he said in solemn tones. "Perhaps I gambled and lost. I have only ever struggled for your welfare, yours and mine, for *we* are the people. You must make up your mind whom you want to lead you. I don't want power for power's sake. I want the best for the poor. No more than that. You must say whom you want. Me or the Maharajah. Say now whom you want. I am willing to withdraw if you don't want me. So speak."

Prabhu felt the sweat come out on his body and the hairs on the back of his neck tingling. Beside him Hari Lal was chewing his lower lip, his black eyes without expression, under tight control, detached. The crowd was quite silent. Not a voice was raised. The cameramen panned across the crowd, then moved the panning handle until they had focused on Hassan.

"Top shot now," the cameraman said. The two English-men climbed up the gate slowly and deliberately and set up their camera on the wall. Soon they were shooting pictures of the hundreds of upturned faces.

"Well?" Hassan cried. "Who do you want?" But they would not reply.

"I wish to Christ I knew what was going on around here, Jack," the assistant cameraman said. "What did this type say? Why's everybody silent?"

"We'll get the dope later for the shot lists," the cameraman answered him. "Just more mysterious India. God, I'm dry."

Hassan got down from the gate. He looked forlorn, puzzled, and Prabhu was sorry for him. He went up to where Hassan stood and said, " We're going to have to get round a table sooner or later. Why not sooner ? We want the same things."

" Why not ? " Hassan shrugged his shoulders.

" Get the jeep," Hari Lal told Nabha, already a little imperious with success.

" You get it," Nabha said. " Who are you talking to ? "

" Get the bloody jeep ! " Prabhu shouted at Nabha, and Nabha rushed off to obey. Hassan smiled as he watched this scene and then looked at Prabhu with ironical eyes.

" Well, I must say you've learned a lot since you got back here. You'll have to learn not to despise too quickly. Your father made that mistake. It's easy to despise cowards. They're just a bunch of poor jerks who've never had enough food to have guts."

Prabhu laughed hard. " Jerks," he said. " Yes. You were in America, of course. I read *Time* regularly and I know the language, you know."

" Yes," said Hassan. " Sometimes I wish I was back there. But don't worry, I'm not going. I'm staying here. I'm staying and I'm going to see that the wolves don't get away with it once more. Oh, I know what's going on. But we'll *have* the land reforms, *without* compensation to the wolves ; schools; an end to the bloodsucking moneylenders, and a system of elections. And we'll have them no matter what tricks are tried." He fixed his sardonic eyes on Hari Lal and said, " Even your father's lands will be reformed, Hari Lal. I know you're working hard to save them, but let me assure you you're wasting your time. The people are cowardly but they know I know what they want. Don't forget that, will you ? "

Hari Lal's thin face turned a reddish bronze but he said nothing. Hassan watched him blush and laughed at him.

" *I*'ll compromise," he told Hari Lal. " But I'll see you don't." He looked at Prabhu then and said, " All right. We'll have to talk." There was no sign of hatred in his eyes, though Prabhu searched hard to find it.

" I'm joining the Party, Hassan," he said. " I'm going to tell the people that. You could fight me on that if you liked. But if it's the good of the country you want, you won't try and oppose me. You're going to have to believe me in the end. I *do* want progress here. Now I'm willing to shake hands with you here, in front of the crowd, and work with you from now on."

" Accept it, Hassan," Hari Lal urged. His eagerness was obvious only in his eyes. " It's for the country. If you refuse we'll all know what it is you care about. Yourself. But I don't believe that."

" Don't you ? " Hassan said ironically. He smiled knowingly at Hari Lal. " Beware the Brahmin who speaks humbly," he quoted the Jashimpuri saying with relish. " For he may be about to sell your trousers. We'll put it to the vote. I know you mean well, for yourself, Hari Lal. But we'll discuss it later."

" Then I'll tell the crowd," Prabhu said. He could hardly hold himself back. He had his speech ready on the end of his tongue. He was winning all along the line.

" Tell them," Hassan said wearily. " But be quick. I'm hungry. Where are we going now ? "

" To Doctor Kholi's," Hari Lal told him. " He'll be expecting you." Only in repose as he turned away could Hari Lal see the dejection in Hassan's face. He wanted to go to him and offer some words of comfort but his training held him back. He knew that Hassan would reject his comfort as embarrassing, and as a Brahmin subtlety of triumph, for Hassan could not root out of his heart a suspicion that all Brahmins were the friends of the rich, of the established order, and of ever-waiting Hinduism which must digest all down into a common soup of Hindu ways and customs.

They waited for Prabhu while he told the crowd that he was becoming a member of the People's Progressive Party. "If Hassan will have me," he said, clowning. The crowd laughed and cheered. Hassan stood with Hari Lal, looking strained and worried.

Chapter Fourteen

A few hours before the press conferences to be given by Hassan at Party headquarters, and by Prabhu at the palace, Hari Lal dressed himself carefully before the big mirror in his father's town house. He had a good soft, honeyed voice, and liked it best when he was singing one of K. L. Saigal's Urdu film songs. He was one of the million worshippers of Saigal's voice and method, and he ravished himself at times with the melancholy he could achieve in his imitation of Saigal's sadder mood.

He looked at his dark, handsome, smooth face in the mirror, his mouth opened, not too wide, to let out the last poignant notes of the song. Then he examined his even, white teeth, smoothed his eyebrows, gave a swift curling to his thick, lustrous black eyelashes, patted his well-brushed pad of gleaming black hair, and said aloud in English, "I agree with you. I quite agree. Property is property. But some change is inevitable. Nothing can stop it, not even bullets. If you'll only let me carry out my ideas you'll at least finish up with *half* your property. If you don't, you'll lose the lot. I have influence with the Maharajah. And Hassan respects me, and fears me a little too. Be calm and let me cut right through between Hassan and the Maharajah. Remember the old saying, ' If you cannot eat the whole cake then pick out the raisins.' " But his father was his real target.

He began to sing in the style of Bade Ghulamali Khan, closing his eyes to get the right mood. The mood soothed him, brought happiness quickly, and he finished the song in confidence. He buttoned the tight collar of the black *atchkan* and bent to adjust his sandals, humming and whistling.

He was twenty-seven, lean and fit, well educated enough to save himself a lot of trouble in his reading and in his pleasures. He had tried communism during the war, when he had been often tearfully proud of the heroic struggle of the Russians to defend their country, but he had gone back to Byron and Shelley, and Ghalib and Firdousi. Extremely emotional, he had learned to ride instead of being ridden but he dreamed still of a world in which all men would love each other and share their produce. He knew it was never to be, that it would only partly be, and he thought he would work for that much. He had struggled patiently with his father against several proposed marriages. There was a girl in Lucknow. He had met her at college in India. They wrote to each other twice a week. Neither his parents, nor hers, knew of this relationship. She was a Muslim, and he was a Hindu, and a Brahmin, and they feared the doing of what they wanted to do. They wrote scores of pages to each other weekly about this problem of a marriage between Muslim and Hindu, and he knew that this was the relationship they enjoyed most, and that they would never marry, and would not regret it much. God for him was an animistic spirit, and the laws of Manu belonged with Sanskrit, a rich forest where scholars could picnic in happiness all their lives. He did not believe in caste and yet smells, spittle, dirt, acrid sweat, made him shudder in the groves of his atavistic body-image ; he was the scrupulous Brahmin who could take a thought and shave a thousand variations from it, and who could grade the million forms of dirt and describe each pollution. He laughed whenever he thought of his precious blood, his trained ancient seed, his immense heritage of knowingness and of hidden maniacal sensitivities. He was glad he was a Brahmin, even though it would take fifty years of ceremonies to cleanse him back into the pure vessel shining on the apex of the pyramid of castes and groups. His father liked a plate of roast beef, too, but now, ageing, beat his fat breast and tried to bend his Western-varnished mind back into what had refused to die, the longing for sanctity and innocence.

" Poor old chap," Hari Lal thought as he pinned a small rose on to the breast of his *atchkan*. He did this because he was an admirer of Panditji Nehru, who had shown how to span the gulf between Shelley and the quivering sound of the sung *Bhajan*, between engines of steel and the cracked brass temple bell. " Poor old chap," he thought again, remembering his father's bewilderment during a recitation of the young Maharajah's speech to the crowd in the town. The speech had been taken down and printed by the thousand for distribution. He was certain his father was ready.

" We can obviously have the Maharajah certified for this," Gudha Singh, one of the most powerful landlords, had told Hari Lal's father after hearing Prabhu's speech read to him.

Again Hari Lal rehearsed his speech to the landowners, stepping back from the looking-glass to gesticulate. " Poor creatures, how terrified and desperate they are. They'd like to kill everyone in Jashimpur who doesn't own land, just to solve it," he thought. Even his father said Prabhu might be mad. Anyway, they had all taken a dislike to him, and to his wife, at that chaotic dinner at the palace just after the Maharajah's arrival. And the Maharani had made no secret of her dislike for what she called " crushed women." She had been drunk, it was said by those with a keen nose for whisky, but she carried it like the Maharajah's brother, masterfully. She had outraged all the landowners' wives, masterfully.

" No, mistressfully," Hari Lal thought, laughing.

When he had reported his success with Prabhu, his new job as Press Relations officer, his father had sniffed and said, " I see great trouble ahead. Violence and rebellion. It'll finish with rifles. Where is God in this awful century ? "

Hari Lal had never been able to explain his love for Hassan, even though he knew that the deep hatred underlying Hassan's generosity and kindness demanded some form of revenge. He was confident that he could master Hassan's crippled heart in the end, and put reins on the Maharajah too. He had seen quickly that Prabhu was sincere, neurotic, and yearning for friendship.

On the telephone that morning after hearing Hari Lal's proposition, Prabhu had sounded worried and cantankerous.

" It sounds very risky to me, Hari Lal," he had said. " You must promise nothing to them. Mix a lot of words together and promise nothing. Whose idea is this ? "

" Mine, Maharaj Sahib. If you will allow me, I can confuse matters so completely between Hassan and the landowners that it will give you time. The reason ? They're planning to send a delegation to Delhi. It's the land reforms. You've terrified them. Hassan's one thing. The Maharajah's another. But I may bring off a great surprise."

" Why didn't you tell me about this ? " Prabhu had become neurotic at the end of the telephone, his voice full of self-pity. Interesting, that vanity of his.

" You must trust me, Maharaj Sahib."

" Oh, must I ? "

" I have a lot to do. Your membership in the Party. That's the hardest." Prabhu had agreed, grudgingly, murmuring something about " Brahmin intrigue."

" Without Brahmin intrigue there'd be nothing," Hari Lal thought as he left his father's house for the meeting. " There'd be just a pack of howling savages eating raw human flesh from Calcutta to Bombay, and all the warriors looking for a Brahmin to end it for them. Patience, that's the thing. Patience, and what looks like compromise."

The meeting was held in the annexe to the Pandit Beni Prasad Reformed Hindu Hall. Beni Prasad was one of Jashimpur's most unusual sons. He had worked for the French in India, gone over to the British, and had become one of their greatest spies. He had helped establish British rule in the Punjab, made a fortune in speculation, kissed Queen Victoria's hand, eaten beef in London, danced in Paris, and had then come back to be cleansed in Jashimpur, where he died, very old, penitent, and left his fortune to further a form of religion he had devised for himself. The hall was now used for meetings, travelling theatres, and by groups of Buddhist monks who met there every ten years.

The landowners looked glum and grim as they sat with folded arms below the small stage from which Hari Lal addressed them. He had enough contempt for them, and enough pity, not to lash them at first. Instead he told the people of the rich miser who had starved himself to death rather than waste good food, and who, when he was dying, asked for medicine, and the physicians had said, "It would only be wasting it." After that he told them the story of the French revolution, and of every other Revolution he could think of.

"There is not much time left," he said sadly. "Between the People's Progressive Party and the Maharajah in this changing world you can only offer up some of the loot. Yes, loot, and I include my own father's loot. It's no use appealing to India. She has to defend the revolution of the people in Kashmir against the tribal invaders. It's up to us, not India. You can all hang by the neck or live with less than you have now."

There was uproar in the hall as twenty or so landowners got to their feet and began to shout their protests and their indignation.

He let them shout for a while and then held up his hands and pulled out the safest card in India, and his trump for his father. He talked about Gandhiji, whom many of them detested, but who dare not say so. It had been agreed long ago that Gandhiji was a saint, and Hari Lal used him now, reminding the fat men below him that Gandhiji possessed only a five-shilling watch, a pair of sandals and a staff and *dhoti*. No one had the blasphemy to get up and say that that was Gandhiji's business. They were silent, many looking pious and shaking their heads, and wondering what was coming next from this supple and infuriating young man dressed to kill on the stage.

"You can imagine the contempt Gandhiji has for people like you," Hari Lal called out to them, and meaning it. "You can imagine how he will hear of your doings up here in the most famous poverty-stricken state in the sub-continent. Your greed, your hypocrisy, your lack of religious principles and your ill-gotten gains which the people may use violence to take from you. Yes, violence, the thing Gandhiji hates above all other things. Well, you will bring on that violence, and I want you all to think about it for a moment." He was silent and everybody in the hall was silent with him.

"I've done what I can to tone down the feelings of the People's Progressive Party," Hari Lal continued. "That's why I'm in the Party, not just for my beliefs in freedom and justice, but because I loathe violence. But if one landowner, one rich man made one great warm and religious sacrifice, people like Hassan would be moved, and so would Gandhiji, and so would God." He was speaking to his father now, who sat in the corner of the room, well back, almost hidden by a red curtain.

"As for myself," Hari Lal went on, "I give up my rights in my father's estates." Pandemonium began as the land-owners got to their feet. Hari Lal shouted them down. "I give them up," he said, and looked at his father. Had the old man been able to screw up his courage, or had he funked it? No. The fat old man with his white hair lifting in the breeze from the opened window rose to his feet and said, "I agree. I offer my lands to the Maharajah. We got them from his ancestors, and I hand them back." Then he fell down into his chair and stared gloomily before him as his companions turned on him to threaten, cajole, plead. But he had

gone through too much, from his son, and from a longing
for God.

"Do you deny Gandhiji's teachings, then?" Hari Lal
yelled at the top of his voice. "Do you mean you forbid my
father to follow Gandhiji? Shall I telegraph and ask Gandhiji
if my father is right?" There was a dead silence after these
yelled words. Everybody stood where he was, stunned,
fretting, harassed, and most of all, looking pious.

"I've done it. I've begun it," Hari Lal exulted silently as
he stared into all the faces looking up at him.

"I shall telegraph Gandhiji anyway," Hari Lal said. "And
tell him of this great moment. The meeting is closed. Thank
you all."

It had taken him four years to manœuvre his father to this
moment, and his hopes had grown as the old man's journey
back to religion had increased. Now he was satisfied. He
would call the pool of land he planned to accumulate *The
Atonement Land Fund*. He left his father to work out his future
with the gabbling landowners and took a tonga to the press
conference at Party headquarters. All the way he sang Saigal's
songs, the *tonga wallah* clicking his tongue in admiration,
a Saigal fan himself.

Chapter Fifteen

Prabhu had spent hours in his study poring over police records, Public Works department files, secret reports from agents all over the State. It was a study of corruption never checked, never frightened. He pieced together the dynasty of the contractors and the landowners, the men who had control of the rice crop, the orchards, the public works, the potato crop; of transport and irrigation canals, animals, rivers, fish, birds, men and women.

Everything that went on in the State was known, reported, filed. His father and his grandfather had never interfered with it and now he knew why. Everything would fall apart if the big men were brought to book. They would have to be dissolved slowly, by lawyers and patient administrators, these men who owned Jashimpur. To nationalise the land would break the dynasty, but not the point of view about the righteousness of monopoly over people, over contracts for cement and the farming of taxes and labour. It would be a hundred years before a rich or a poor man in Jashimpur could refuse a bribe, and refuse it angrily. " But first," thought Prabhu, " I could take the land off all of us, the big boys, and give it to the people, and I must do it before Hassan's crowd do it."

This man Kholi. He appeared in some of the police reports as a dangerous man, rich and cultured, who was behind the People's Progressive Party. There was a form attached to one report, a harmless-looking census form of three years back, which Kholi had dutifully filled up. At the bottom of the form a police inspector had noted, " This is typical of the insulting behaviour of Doctor Kholi in all matters pertaining to government." Prabhu read the doctor's replies to the questions set out on the form.

" Name : Gopi Nath Kholi. Caste Name : Mere Once-Born. Place of Birth : Bed. Age : Fifty-one. Profession : Doctor of Medicine, and Student of Police Methods. Married or Single : Ask the Maharajah. Name of Wife : Ask the Maharajah. Children : Ask the Maharajah. Reasons for residing in State : Ask the police. Income : Private."

The Chief of Police, Nasrullah Beg, a little, grey, tired man in neat khaki uniform, smiled thinly and bleakly when Prabhu showed him the census form and asked him what " Ask the Maharajah " meant. He had worked all his life to see that the various dams and sluices in Jashimpuri society functioned safely and well. His job had been to ensure that the rich lived happily and the poor patiently and dutifully, and he had done it well. He had not had much excitement in his life. He had broken up a bandit gang which had flourished for ten years in the wild mountains to the west and his jaw had been broken by a bullet. He had killed the leader of the bandits with a knife. He had the policeman's devoted and narrow fanaticism about human wickedness and could not have gone on living in a world of goodness and peace. He understood criminals and rebels better than ordinary people. Ordinary people had no interest for him. They were dull and worthless, spunkless and tiresome people. He said so to Prabhu over a cup of tea while guiding him through the fantastic maze of the police web revealed in the reports from village and town.

" There's nothing like police work, Maharaj Sahib," he said. " It gets a grip on you. When times are dull I actually find myself praying for a band of criminals to turn up. I've come to despise the ordinary plodding fellow who never does wrong. There's no challenge in them ; nothing. Crime's not nearly as interesting here in this State as in parts of India. Now take gold smuggling. That's the great thing in India just now. We miss all that here. The better your police work the duller your life. We've ruined crime here in the State. You can laugh, Maharaj Sahib, but your own father said that. He liked a bit of good crime. He read all these reports and used to hope we'd come on something really big, like a mass murderer or something like that. It's politics now, nothing but politics."

He twice avoided answering Prabhu's questions about Kholi's census form, until Prabhu took off his dark glasses and gave him a cold and imperious look across the table.

" Come to the point, please." Prabhu saw some relief in the policeman's nervous eyes. He wanted to be ordered to speak and now he spoke.

"' Ask the Maharajah ' means that when Doctor Kholi was about twenty-eight or so your father forced a certain landowner to hand over his daughter to him. She was to have married Kholi. She sells sweets now somewhere in India, I'm told. A hag, they say. It worked on the doctor's mind. He's one of these men who've never found out that one woman is like another after a time. Never gave himself a chance. He's a virgin to-day as he was then. He took a vow of *Brahmacharya*, complete abstinence. That warps the mind, you know, Maharaj Sahib. Delusions, outbursts. I've tried three times to get him out of this State but your father would never allow it. And yet this man is known to have sworn to finish your family as rulers in this State. That's the meaning of this People's Progressive Party. All because of not having some woman or other. He's a clever one, this Kholi. I hope you'll watch him, Maharaj Sahib, if you'll pardon my suggesting it. He took this clodhopper, Hassan, and financed his Party. Are you thinking of making mass arrests, Maharaj Sahib? You've only to say the word. Everything's ready." The man was tense as he asked this question, like one ready to leap out of the room and ring the bell for the machine to go into action.

There was one sealed secret file on Doctor Kholi, personal property of Prabhu's father, which had made Prabhu laugh with a kind of pity for the doctor. He said nothing of it to the Chief of Police. He would save it for another occasion.

As he looked at this faithful and devoted servant of his ancestral régime Prabhu thought what a pity it was that he had come back here to wreck all this perfection, this ordered little segment of decaying society which asked only the peace in which to enjoy the poor. The policeman's honest and willing loyalty was a marvellous thing, sworn to protect the sacredness of property, the rights of the poor to their poverty, and living in boyish hope of one more great crime to give interest to the dullness which his ability had achieved.

" No," said Prabhu. " No mass arrests, thank you all the same. It's very kind of you to have everything so ready. A credit. No. I have other plans." The policeman saluted smartly, proudly, his eyes not revealing any of the sultry and disturbed thoughts which some of Prabhu's actions had evoked during the past couple of weeks. It was being said among officers of the small State forces and the police that Prabhu had been educated in Moscow and had been a spy of the Comintern in London and other places. The Chief of Police did not believe that. He believed Prabhu to be some kind of British agent whose mysterious task was as yet beyond understanding. Like all British plans, it appeared to be doing what it was not actually doing. The shape would emerge only when the British secret service was ready to act. He said nothing of this to the other officers. He was a man who could wait, but would obey orders right to the end. Duty was duty, and it was not for him to go beyond his dreams and hopes. He had never taken a bribe but he allowed his officers to take them, and kept a record of them in a safe in his home. His power was complete.

Hassan's file made Prabhu jealous. He could not help it. He would have given much to have been born Hassan and earned these long screeds of rage and hate and fear. There was even a report from America written by a Jashimpuri business man to the old Maharajah, giving a detailed account of Hassan's daily life for close on a year. A harmless enough daily life, yet dangerous because of his interest in trade unions and radical societies. The dossier was enormous and it took Prabhu many hours to read it. One report from Kangla said that Miss Bullen was teaching revolt to the peasants but that constant hostility by the elders of the villages would wear her down in the end. There had been some intrigue or trouble in which Hassan had been involved and Miss Bullen had got him out of it and had given him the money to get to India. Something to do with a woman. No one in the villages would speak of it, not even under pressure. Loyalty to Hassan was one hundred per cent, and was silent and stubborn. The agent promised to root out the meaning of the hidden intrigue and report. But he had obviously failed.

" I wonder what that was ? " Prabhu murmured, his human instinct for scandal and intrigue stirred. He closed Hassan's file and picked up the latest reports from all over Jashimpur, beginning with the weekly report on the city.

It angered him to find no mention anywhere of his passionate speech in the city's main square. It was the most tremendous thing that had ever happened in Jashimpur, and it was not even hinted at. He knew the whole town was talking about it, that the landowners were gibbering with fury over it, and that the police were almost out of their minds because of it. But not one single word was written about it in the reports. It was too much to put up with. He got the C.I.D. on the telephone and asked for the superintendent. The man's steady evasion, his denials, his surprise, so angered Prabhu that he began to shout into the mouthpiece, accusing the superintendent of a most unseemly and misplaced cowardice.

The man promised to find out all he could about the effect of Prabhu's speech and apologised so much that Prabhu flung the telephone across the table and got up to walk to the window. Lila was standing in the doorway of the study, smiling at him.

"My, but we *are* worked up to-day, Prabhu, darling," she said. "Anyone would take you for a Maharajah, flinging your telephone about like that. What's the matter? Won't the people approve of your public speeches?"

Prabhu put on his dark glasses and laughed, taking her arm, his hands quivering with the spending force of his rage.

He was just about finished with Lila. He knew it. She knew it. Soon it would be time to have a big explosion, either in bed or in a shouting match over a bottle of whisky. The bed business only delayed things. The drift and the erosion was too great and too swift now to ignore much longer. But he kept his temper and stroked her smooth arm and thought, "My God, what happens to us? Men and women? I mean, what goes wrong, and when, and why? If two human beings can't get on with each other after years, after ten thousand years of practice, then what's the use of trying to get to the bloody moon or Mars? This is the real mystery, right here, in here, in this flesh, hers and mine, only it's not in the flesh. It's in the jungle up here in the mind. If I had time, and if I really cared, I'd have a go at solving it. But why bother? Unhappiness is the great fuel of doing and being. Happiness almost killed us until I went off to the war. Yes. There's no killer of men and women like happiness."

Chapter Sixteen

Shaken by the silence of that crowd outside the gaol and smarting from the hurt Prabhu had done him in the manner of his release from gaol, Hassan could hardly think about these things because of his contempt for himself, his cowardice, his Jashimpuri failure over the failure to spill blood.

He was not a violent man, nor had he ever been known to engage in a brawl or to strike anybody. He had merely wanted what the times needed, a little blood, peasant blood spilled against tyranny. He knew Prabhu had given orders to the police and to the troops that in no situation should they use force without his personal order. He knew the people believed in the Party, were loyal to Prabhu, but looked to Hassan for action. They would take no action themselves. They waited, as they had waited for centuries. They had obeyed his order to refuse payment to the moneylenders, but they would not attack the police posts. Not even the Militia, waiting in hiding in the hills, would come out. Doctor Kholi, with whom Hassan had had five minutes' talk before going to the press conference, had smiled and said, " Patience. Everything's on our side. I have one or two little things up my sleeve. Patience."

The press conference was held in the hall of the Party headquarters. Before the reporters came in Hassan quarrelled with Hari Lal and threatened to have him thrown out of the Party.

" Try it," Hari Lal said calmly. " If you manage to throw me out, then I'll start a party of my own. Remember you were the one who taught us to stay together, one Party.

Until you lose this stupid hatred for the Maharajah we can get nowhere. He's popular and you can't do anything about it. Neither can I."

"Neither can you? That's strange, isn't it? Neither can you. You'd lick his boots if he ordered it." All the young men watched this exciting exchange of words. Hari Lal said nothing about his father's surrender of his lands. That bomb-shell could wait for the meeting when they discussed the Maharajah's application for membership of the Party.

"You won't keep the Maharajah out of the Party, Hassan," said Hari Lal. "You can't. I happen to know that most of the committee feel as I do. They say let him in."

"Do they? We'll see."

"The Press," somebody called.

There were three Indian reporters, an American and an Englishman. All of them had come here for a rest after the rigours of covering the fighting in Kashmir. This story would be light and crisp, just a small part of the enormous Indian revolution taking place in the princely States. Hassan began by insulting them all, losing his head as he talked. This was his first press conference, and, Hari Lal thought, possibly his last. Usually urbane and pleasant, the happenings of the day had knocked Hassan's controls to pieces. It was despair and humiliation which lay behind his sarcastic address to the pressmen.

"So here are the vultures," he said with mock welcome, sweeping his right hand as if to offer them the hall. "What shall we have first? My sex-life? Or what I eat for break-fast? Or would you like some tales of child murder, rape, *sutti*, or about caste? What about caste? Now you, sir, from the British Press, you can't go away without some examples of our backwardness in matters of caste and sexual orgies. And, from America, you'll want to find some communism, some red spies, or maybe reports on the desire for American washing machines and lipstick among our women. As for the gentlemen from India, there's the young Maharajah, very progressive, not quite a follower of Gandhiji, I'm afraid, but mad about progress and the peasants and all that kind of thing, especially since he came back and discovered the People's Progressive Party in the saddle. Now, are there any questions ? I'm in a hurry, gentlemen."

The reporters were unmoved. They had been watching Hassan, and making notes. One took a few photographs.

The American said, " Well, that's very kind of you, sir. I notice you have a slight American accent. Did you go to school in America ? "

" Yale and Harvard," Hassan said sombrely.

" The land reforms, sir," the Englishman said, his voice loaded down with patient understanding. " What about the land reforms ? "

" What about them ? " Hassan replied truculently.

" I mean, are you going to have land reforms here ? Would you like to make a statement about that ? "

" No. I didn't ask you here. You asked to come. You're here. I'm waiting for you to go now."

" I see. You don't feel the need at all for any reporting of your views in the Press ? "

" None at all."

" You don't feel you need any ? " one of the Indians asked him.

" I've never had any up to now. Why should I want it to-day ? "

" You spoke a lot about rape and sex and so on," the American said, dead pan, sincere. " Are you particularly interested in those subjects ? " One of the Indians laughed and then covered his mouth. Hassan was unmoved.

" I read your papers," Hassan said.

" I see."

" You wish to make no statement of any kind, sir ? " another Indian reporter asked him, notebook ready.

" Yes, I'd like to make a statement," Hassan told him.
" A short one. It's as follows, and I mean it for all of you.
Get some worth-while and honest work. Follow your real
convictions instead of the salary. Get off the corpse and give
the jackals a chance. If you all did that then we'd have a lot
less trouble in the world. That's all."

" That's most interesting," the Englishman said, nodding
thoughtfully, as if impressed.   " You'll ban the Press in
Jashimpur then ? "

" We only have two small newspapers," said Hassan. " One
Urdu and one Hindi. They belong to your friends, the rich
men. They're quite harmless. A little poetry, one or two
reports on what happened here two or three thousand years
ago. Occasionally one of the writers will go into a restaurant
and threaten the manager with a satire in the newspaper unless
he's fed. That's about all. No, I won't ban them. People
here are interested in old history. We don't go in for news,
or who killed or raped who. We're very dull here. Well, I
think that's all. Good-bye."

And that was the end of the press conference. Everyone
stood quite still and quiet while the reporters went out
laughing.

" They'll say you're mad, Hassan," said Hari Lal, shocked
by what had gone on. He had a reverence for the Press and
for information of all kinds. He wondered if Hassan was
fighting against some hysteria following the prison scene.

" They'll say that anyway," Hassan told them all.   He
laughed, throwing his head back, laughed for a long time.
They waited for him. When he had stopped laughing Nabha,
grave and impressed, said that he thought Hassan had made
a mistake.

" No, no," Hassan said contemptuously to Nabha, whom
he suspected as the real coward in the morning's doings.
" The reporters are only here for a bit of comedy. Jashimpur's
nothing to them. They'll do some fishing, visit the brothels,

N

drink some whisky at the Jashimpur Club and then go away and get on with their work where it matters. Now that's enough about that. I want to say a few words about this other comedy. The one about the Maharajah joining the Party. The meeting will be at seven o'clock sharp, at Doctor Kholi's house. And I'll take no excuse for lateness. None. That's all." He left them and went into his office, where Doctor Kholi was waiting for him.

Hari Lal left for the palace.

Chapter Seventeen

As soon as he got inside the office, Hassan locked the door, put his face in his hands and broke down, weeping, but with hardly any sound. His big frame was shaking hard and Doctor Kholi, sitting at one of the two desks near the open window playing patience, sat back and watched him with an expressionless face. He waited until Hassan's storm was over and then said, " Depressed ? "

Hassan nodded, wiping his eyes with strokes of his long, hard, brown hands. He sucked in his breath and smiled at the doctor. He sat down at his desk and lit a cigarette. The doctor waited, throwing a couple of cards down one after the other. He kept a record in his diary of all his games of patience. This was game number seven thousand five hundred and forty-one, which added up to eight, which was useless, and it would not come out. Eight was never any good for the doctor.

" This race should be taken and put into chains and sent somewhere where it can work under masters for the rest of its life," Hassan said in a hard, bitter voice. " And I should be sent with them."

" And what about me ? " The doctor threw another card on the game.

" You're all right, Doctor. You don't give a damn as long as you can sit back and watch the fun, and see the Maharajah's family finished. Yes, it's true. This race is no good. It's spineless, utterly spineless. I saw that at the gaol during the great moments of liberation. And I see it in myself. My mistake has been caring, really caring. You don't care. The Maharajah doesn't care. But you have your plans and can take it quietly. All I wanted was to see the people *act*, for once. But they haven't the guts for anything."

The doctor was wearing a spotless white *kurta*, so fine that the shape of his vest showed through it, and the darkness of his brown shoulders and arms. It was buttoned with three small jewelled studs which glittered and glowed redly in the sunlight pouring into the room. His small, brown, polished, bald head was shining with health and well-being. He looked at Hassan with tender eyes and laughed softly.

" I heard you with the Press," he said. " Excellent. I wished I'd said it myself. It was a mistake, though. They'll say some nasty things about you."

" You liked it, but you didn't like it. Is that what you mean ? "

They had known each other well for many years. The doctor had been like a father to Hassan. Sometimes Hassan hated him, in gusts, for his unfathomable sense of fun disguised as seriousness, and for eccentric seriousness which was dressed up to sound like fun. He had never solved the problem of whether the doctor believed in " the people " or not. One of the doctor's favourite sayings was, " The trouble with the people is that they're making new people while we're talking. And there's no such thing as the people, therefore. They're like time."

" Yes. I liked it and disapproved of it," Kholi said, throwing more cards on the game. " Is the Maharajah getting on your nerves very badly ? "

" Yes."

" Don't forget you're getting on his."

" No, I won't. So you've accepted his invitation at last. What are you going to say to him ? "

The doctor was going to the palace for drinks. Kholi threw the rest of the cards down and then swept them all up into his hands and began to shuffle them.

" I have one or two surprises arranged here and there," he said. " I won't talk about them yet. I'll chat with the Maharajah about anything he likes. His subject will be joining the Party, I imagine. Seven o'clock to-night, isn't it, the meeting ? You won't let him join ? "

" No."

" What about the others ? They're wavering, you know. How are you going to deal with that ? And Hari Lal's smooth. It's quite interesting, isn't it, watching you all change as the big moments come ? " He laughed, shaking with it, and began to deal the cards again.

" He won't get into the Party. I'll see to that."

" Good. By the way, I've bought Brigadier Kapra Singh, genealogy and all. The price was high, but I bought him. So the army's practically yours. No rush, though."

The doctor looked at Hassan with twinkling eyes, smiling with his small red compressed lips, and quite unmoved by the flush of anger which crept over Hassan's face. After all, this was the great and seldom discussed difference between them : Hassan's boyish hopes of a militant Jashimpuri people and the doctor's honest, cynical, and charitable knowledge that the only hope was in buying the army. Before Hassan could give voice to the anger in his face Kholi began to make serious fun of Hassan's old dream.

" You think I haven't tried to support you in all this crusade of yours ? You can't say that." He began to shuffle the pack of cards again. " I've helped right the way through. I've always told you, though, that you're unfair in trying to make revolutionary fighters out of swindled beggars and slaves. I've always been touched by your belief in them. But I warned you. When you were sitting in the gaol and we wrote to each other about this mania of yours, the mob smashing the gaol down to rescue you, I didn't laugh. You've got to admit it. I didn't. I went along with you. I knew last night what would happen this morning. You're tyrannising over your people. You know it. You love them, and you hate them because they won't be what they can't be, what you want them to be, what you can't be yourself. Their grandsons will have more courage. It takes time, diet, freedom, confidence. Can't you see that? So I bought Brigadier Kapra Singh for you. The people love you. Why can't you let them love you and leave them alone and forget this blood business of yours? When they hear we've bought that noble personage, with his moustache and his long genealogy of murderers and warrior princes, the people will cheer. Admit it, Hassan."

" You'd no right to do it," Hassan shouted at him, rising from his chair, his fists clenched. " No right. And you know you had no right. I'm the Party. I'm the Jashimpuri people. I'm the clod with ten generations of sweat and misery behind me, and I'm the people because of it. I'll make them come out and fight. Unless they do that they'll remain what they are, trampled, humble, timid mud. You can unbuy the noble brigadier. D'you hear? "

" Things can't go on like this, Hassan. Everyone worked up. The Party ready. People waiting, but unwilling to come out and fight, and the Maharajah's two battalions in the city, and the two battalions up-country waiting to open fire. You'll lose if we don't act at once. We've got to see the Maharajah off in his car with his family on a tour of abdication. And we can only do it with the army. And, damn you, son, do you realise all the trouble I've gone to to buy this idiot and his troops? Do you? "

" You know very well the Maharajah's forbidden the troops to fight. He actually wants the Party to come out into the open everywhere, and he wants to join it, and then lead it. He's winning. I want the people to show their will, just once."

His voice broke with the boiling emotions risen in him.
" You'd no right to do it. None."

" So what next? Are you going to lead an attack in person
on the barracks? Blood on the ground and so on. Your
blood? "

" You think I wouldn't do it? " Hassan advanced towards
the doctor's desk, his nostrils quivering and his fists held
before his chest. " You think I'm afraid to do it? "

The doctor sprayed cards on to the table from his small,
quick, brown hands, intensely, as if everything depended on
it, and Hassan knew he was in a temper and was holding it
for a moment. They had never agreed on this matter about
the blood, about the heroes being shot down, the people
dipping their clothes in the blood and running screaming to
the city shouting, " Martyrs. Martyrs." The doctor laughed
at it and refused to admit that this blood mystery was what
had smashed kingdoms and tyrannies again and again.

" You know what the trouble is, Hassan," the doctor said
in a tight, cold voice, going on with the almost obsessive
dealing of cards in neat rows. " You know well. The
Maharajah won't tyrannise. He won't play the old game. He
won't shoot anybody. He's making a fool of you. He's
offering everything you've preached for years. And because
he won't be a tyrant and has made himself popular, you're
desperate." He hurled the rest of the cards on to the desk
and sprang to his feet, showing Hassan his small, blazing
eyes. " I want the end of this pack of princes here, more
than you do. Yes, more. You want it too, but most of all
you want to get into some little history book in the future.
Hassan surrounded by the pictures of the martyrs who died
for freedom. And you know damn' well you're not going to
get any martyrs. The Maharajah's cut off the supply, and the
people are delighted."

" Take that back about me and the martyrs," Hassan was
wounded to his tender heart. They had never brought their

differences to this kind of ravine across which Hassan felt he would soon reach and seize the doctor by the throat, his friend, his surrogate father.

" I take nothing back. We all have our fantasies. I have mine too. Mine's Kholi, the vengeful virgin who lost a woman to a Maharajah who could buy them by the dozen. I've nourished it, lived on it, while working, delivering babies by the thousand, in hovels and palaces. And it's ridiculous, and I know it, because I got over the woman three years after I made my vow." He laughed sorrowfully as he spoke, trying to put his hand on Hassan's shoulder, but Hassan moved away, keeping his hard eyes on the little man who poured out more laughing, cynical truths.

" Stop it," Hassan cried. " Stop it."

" Well, I have my little fantasy, like you. It's useless. It's pointless, but it's been my hobby for years now, and I'm seeing it through to the finish. I'll wreck the Maharajah here, even though the whole cursed thing means very little to me any longer." He could not go on. He threw himself down on to his chair and bent double, screaming with laughter, a laughter so infectious that Hassan nearly laughed with him, hysterically, for he felt delirious with conflict. He felt he might suddenly explode, or run about crying. He sat down and put his head on his arms while the doctor howled laughing.

When the doctor picked up his cards again and began dealing, laughing softly as the fit died in him, Hassan looked over at him and thought, " We've come to some kind of stop and I don't know where to go. I know I'm right about the blood, but what can I do when this little man expresses my own doubts ? I can't laugh about it like that. I'm not that Jashimpuri. What'll I do ? What next ? "

" I've got to go now," Kholi said. " Will you meet Brigadier Kapra Singh after the Party meeting to-night ? "

" Do you still stick to your old opinion, that you don't want any part in the government when I form it ? " Hassan said. He was chilly now, trying to remove himself to a distance, but the doctor was not going to put up with that.

"You're going to try and break with me? Is that it?" He had always been swift, following in a rush behind his intuitions.

"Yes. I think we ought to break now. I'll finish the revolution, without Kapra Singh. You've gone too far, Doctorji."

"And without me?" Kholi was smiling warmly at him, dealing those cards tirelessly so that Hassan wanted to take them from him and fling them out of the window. "You'll finish the revolution without me?"

"You're dishonest. Did you mean what you said? That you're only against the Maharajah as a sort of game? That all this vow you made never meant anything to you after all? Don't you believe in *anything*?"

"I'm in the grip of my unconscious, Hassan. Like you. You've never had any time for that kind of thing, have you? The unconscious and the grooves of habit we make in our minds? I want to win now. It's become like cards. Here we are right on the edge of winning. The winning hand is Kapra Singh, and I've bought him. All we have to do next is take over. Think of it. Banners, bands, troops with your Party armbands on parading the streets, so much bought revolutionary material, but it works. The people will come out in the streets cheering you. That's all it is, one more move. I've got to go now, Hassan. Will you think about it for a couple of hours while I'm meeting my ruler for the first time? Give me your decision when I get back before the meeting."

"I haven't waited all these years to use a bought military idiot to free Jashimpur."

The doctor was at the door now. He turned and lifted one eyebrow, as he looked at Hassan.

"You'll never rule, Hassan. You'll take command for a

while, but you'll never rule. You're too cruel. There's no one so cruel as the good man who won't let people be themselves. You'll torture them. If you give up smoking tomorrow you'll run about the streets snatching cigarettes out of people's mouths. If you cease believing in God to-morrow you'll forbid religion. And people won't stand for it. I'll see you when I get back."

Chapter Eighteen

Since Lila's drunken outburst to Miss Bullen about her unhappiness with Prabhu, and the shadowy English lover called Clegg-Bray, there had been a coolness between the two women. It was not friction, or that strained unspoken hostility between two women which can fill the atmosphere for those about them with electric, brooding tension. It was in fact a tender, puzzled, nervous stumbling in words, in the middle of statements, the old woman wondering if Lila knew how much she had spoken in drink, and Lila withdrawn, somehow humble and pathetic, but at times sullen and tearful. It was a kind of atmosphere which the two boys watched and discussed while they were playing with their electric trains in the room Miss Bullen had arranged as a playroom.

"Miss Bullen's rumbled Mother," Narendra Nath said to his brother as they rearranged the railway lines across the room. "Poor Mother. She just can't get on with anyone, can she? D'you think it's the boozing? D'you think Miss Bullen's given one of those lectures about sin? Do you think Mother'd let her give her a lecture?"

Roshan Lal took off his glasses and wiped off some thin smears of jam, with spit on his handkerchief. He was sitting by the main tunnel on the railway line. Lately he had become very friendly with the old woman, but he watched himself all the time in case Narendra Nath would accuse him of sucking up. The old woman had revealed many mysteries about himself to himself, and had even told him that the mysteries continued in manhood. All grown-ups, too, were suffering and in trouble, but they had got ready for it and had learned how to try and be good and happy. While there was a certain sloppiness and a frightening little woolly lamb feeling about some of the old woman's sayings, she could be as hard as nails too. He defended her now.

" She's right if she's lectured Mother," he told his brother. " Prab could do with a lecture too. And yet the old woman said once to me that every grown-up knows damn' well when they're being bloody-minded and stupid, like Mother and Prab. I think they must have had a fight about something, probably about the boozing. Did you look at the letters on the table this morning ? Mother comes down very early and searches through the letters every morning. But I'm there first. This morning there was a letter from guess who addressed to Mother ? Guess who ? "

" The galloping colonel." As he said it Narendra Nath was gazing at his brother, watching his eyes. They looked into each other's eyes, understanding each other, as Roshan Lal nodded and said, " Right first time, cock. And he's in India. In Delhi. It was post-marked Delhi."

" Stone the crows." Narendra Nath looked at the wall and swallowed. They had used to lay bets of a penny in London that one day Prab was going to catch on. The colonel used to come frequently to the flat right up to the time Prab came back from the war. After that Mother began going out a lot. They followed her once and saw her meet the colonel in the park. She had got into his car and they drove off.

" I thought that business was finished, didn't you ? " Roshan Lal put on his glasses and folded his arms. The two boys were silent for a time. From the front of the palace they could hear jazz. Their father and mother and the old woman would be with the guests now, drinking and talking. Newspapermen hearing all about Father's plans for Jashimpur, for the bloodless revolution, Miss Bullen had called it.

" You think Mother'll leave Prab ? It looked like it long ago, didn't it ? He wasn't a bad bloke, was he ? "

" You mean slipping us half-crowns and books and toys ? " Roshan Lal, who had been the first of the two of them to make friends with Colonel Clegg-Bray, wanted to forget. And Narendra Nath let him.

" Okay. Have it your way."

" What d'you think's going to happen ? I mean after we've been packed off to this school in India? You think Mother'll give Prab the good-bye and leave him ? "

" And marry the galloping colonel ? "

" Yes."

" I don't know. Let's stop talking about it. I don't want to hear any more about it. That's what you get for snooping. We wouldn't have known this if you didn't snoop."

" I wasn't snooping. I just looked at the letters."

" Yes. Every morning."

" You've got to face things. Miss Bullen says if you don't face things and be honest you become a pest to other people."

" Ah, shut up."

" And you shut up too." They were silent again.

Lila had read the letter so many times, her heart pounding and her throat dry and tight, that she knew every word of it. Whole sentences of it stood up suddenly and marched across her mind. She was trying to concentrate on what the American reporter was saying to Prabhu about the present world situation and the atom bomb. Miss Bullen was teaching the English reporter how to say, " I refuse to pay more than one rupee " in Urdu. The Englishman had involved himself in a quarrel with the *tonga wallahs* in the town and, while sure that he had paid what was just, had come to the palace sweating and raging about the East in general. Later he said he was being unfair, but even so it was another example of how the barrier of language caused trouble and war.

The press conference was over. Hari Lal, with whom Miss

Bullen and Lila were charmed, was giving a final touch to
his briefing of the reporters about Prabhu's plans.   There
would be a handout ready to-morrow.   They were being
printed in town now.   From now on there would be hand-
outs.   The reporters nodded sulkily, sorry that the curse of
the handout had come in here in crackpot little Jashimpur.
They were all of them, the American and the Englishman as
well, sympathetic to Prabhu's plans for Jashimpur, which he
had described feverishly and with his usual relentless mass of
detail.   Hari Lal had taken the rough jewel and polished it to
great brightness, underlining the bigger problems with
inherited subtlety, chopping down the reporters' unspoken
doubts before they could be expressed.   Prabhu had admired
one thing in particular which Hari Lal had said to the reporters.

" You could all write a terribly funny story about us here
in Jashimpur, behaving as if we matter.   But somehow I
think you won't do that."   He had smiled that dazzling
friendly smile of his and added, " We laugh about ourselves
here quite a lot, you know.   Perhaps you could make us
sound serious in your papers."   And he was good with gin
and whisky, gliding about seeing to glasses.   He had sent the
servants away beforehand, telling Prabhu to remember the
old Jashimpuri saying, " Deafness in the good servant.
Dumbness in the beloved woman."

" I think I'll show it to Bella," Lila fretted.   The letter was
rolled up into a thin tube and was resting, warm and fragrant,
between her breasts, where it did not belong, but was safe.
Or did it belong there ?   " Oh, my God," she thought.   " I'll
ask Bella about it."   She called Miss Bullen Bella now and
had begun to do so in the hope of warming their dampened
friendship, for Lila had never been able to apologise to anybody about anything.   She was struck dumb when it was time
to apologise and knew it for one of her incurable curses.

Hari Lal looked at his watch and glanced at Prabhu.   The
party was over and Doctor Kholi was due.   Hari Lal had

given Prabhu a briefing on Kholi, but Prabhu had read every police report on Kholi for the last ten years and knew more than Hari Lal, but said nothing about it.

Prabhu stood up. The reporters stood up. Hari Lal, as he had promised Prabhu, now pulled his final bird out of the bag and let it flutter up into the warm atmosphere created by good talk and good drink.

"You may be interested in meeting one of the biggest landowners here," he said. "My father. A devotee of Gandhiji. To-day he handed all his estates to the Maharajah as the first part of *The Atonement Land Fund*. Congress never did very well here but Gandhiji has great influence. It's the beginning of something wonderful. Land reform by spiritual means."

The reporters seized the bird and examined it, asking many questions. They were enthusiastic and took the address of Hari Lal's father.

"He'll see you any time," Hari Lal said as they all walked out to the veranda. "It was a terrific decision for him, but it proves that the landowners know the Maharajah is right. If you wrote a good story about my father's decision it could do wonders here, and maybe in India."

When the reporters had gone Prabhu took Hari Lal's hand and said, "You could charm a cobra with that tongue and manner of yours." He had tried hard to get Hari Lal to have a drink, whisky or gin or beer, but he refused. He drank tomato juice or fresh lime, saying that his wits needed no oil.

They all had another drink, chatting about the world situation and the reporters' opinions of it. They talked for a long time about Kashmir and the war there.

"Dear old Kashmir," Prabhu said. "I had good times there on leave during the war."

"*Very* good times?" Lila asked lightly, her black eyebrows raised. She knew she had fascinated Hari Lal and she acted small parts for him now and then. He watched her like a *saddhu* staring at the central point of nothingness.

" Not *that* good," Prabhu replied, smiling at her. He had his dark glasses on and was safe.

Miss Bullen was feeling about as usual under their dialogue and thinking, " My God, the way people waste each other. The way they stick knives into each other. I suppose Lila's right. I missed nothing by not marrying." But sometimes she regretted not marrying and having children, luxuriating in the regret, for nothing could be done about it now, thank God. They heard Kholi's car on the drive.

" Now for it," Prabhu was thinking. " The master mind has arrived."

Lila had watched Prabhu all evening, thinking about him and about the essential difference between a man's unfaithfulness and a woman's unfaithfulness, and knew the difference, and struggled with it to change it. She knew that men were immature about this matter, were maniacally unchangeable about it, even when they preached free this and free that, even when they were most progressive. A woman could give them a wound which a lifetime of nursing could never cure, wounding herself only if she admitted it. Men were not like that. They all had delusions of grandeur, of one and onlyness, of the goddess who must worship and never stray. It was really too infuriating for words, even thought-words.

Did she love Clegg-Bray ? What was love ? Fifty per cent Don't Know. Thirty per cent Not Sure. Twenty per cent What the Hell ? She missed Clegg-Bray, though. His warm voice, his ready and never failing kindness, his patience, his waiting, and his grant of freedom to her to be completely herself. And she hated that self, and yet when she was that real self she was happy. With Clegg-Bray she could swear, drink as much as she liked, give any opinion, behave idiotically, and never get squashed, never feel crushed and ashamed. And Clegg-Bray loved her no matter what she did or said.

Surely that was the real and genuine love. Be yourself, he said. I don't give a damn. I adore you. I adore everything in you. He had stood ready since 1945, when he had made his mind up to smash up his miserable home and finish with his chilly, mad wife. He had never talked much about his wife, but when he had his voice had changed to a kind of cold, steely weapon, as if he were talking to her. And now this fearful and shattering letter rolled up between her breasts, lines of words on a piece of paper, but a bomb hidden in her bosom. She had the impression she often had in times of crisis or danger, that time had stopped. The threat had been given, she absorbed it, and then thought, " It's all away out there, not happening yet. Only *I* know about it. It's not happening yet ! " But all the pieces were flying silently together, every minute, growing into the quiet thing that would be the situation, the fearful situation in which the characters, this time Clegg-Bray, she and Prabhu, would face this thing and begin to talk and do and destroy. " My God," she thought. " What'll I do ? Shall I talk to Prem ? He loves me. I know he does. He can't keep his hands off me some- times when he's had too much, and yet they're nice hands, not those kind of hands which make one feel sick and ready to smash the owner. No. Prem's lovely, a lovely person. A wreck, but a lovely wreck. Shall I talk to him ? Or to Miss Bullen, Bella ? Yes, Bella. Which one shall I go to ? I must talk about it or I'll go mad. Mad."

Doctor Kholi was coming into the room with Prabhu. She got up quickly and went forward to go through the formal motions which led up to the hallos, sitting down, drinks, chatter. She loathed so much being hostess, mama, Maharani. She was so homesick for London that she sometimes said to the twins that one day they would all be back there. With the twins she always called London " Home," and they understood. Doctor Kholi was standing before her.

" My God, he looks like a little brown demon out of a

pantomime," she thought as she shook hands with Kholi. No nonsense about palms being pressed together with this little gnome, none of that simpering over the pressed palms. No, a tight, dry, and somehow meaningful handshake. The doctor was looking into her eyes with a sort of wicked smile in them. She almost retreated from him. Prabhu had said that this character was a virgin who had " never known the empty mystery of the full bed." What a beast Prabhu could be sometimes. Jashimpuri to the last snigger, and she knew he knew it.

Chapter Nineteen

Prabhu's plan had been to let everyone have about half an hour's conversation with Doctor Kholi over drinks, and then Miss Bullen would float away to the twins, Lila would entertain Hari Lal and Prem, who was due back from the club any time now, and then Prabhu would take Kholi to his study. In the study he would take Kholi to pieces and find out what was what. But there was no need for anyone to go away, or for Prabhu to take Kholi to the study, for the doctor opened the conversation by looking at Prabhu intensely and asking him how long he thought he had left in Jashimpur.

"Would you say about a month, Maharaj Sahib?" He was elegant and at ease in the arm-chair, not lying too far back, or leaning too far forward, but relaxedly right, his glittering gin in his little, perfect brown hand with its flashing gold ring. His polished bad manners, perfected over the years by practice of this technique of the direct attack, were impeccable as he nodded slowly and gravely to Prabhu's angry, "You're not bringing the tumbrels out *to-night*, I hope, Doctor."

Everyone except Kholi had sat up as if they had heard a shot fired in the grounds.

"I mean no offence, Maharaj Sahib," Kholi said gently, eyeing everyone quickly to include them. "It's being said here and there that you may abdicate." He wanted to get the feel of the young man who was running everywhere making speeches and performing in public. He admired him, but what was he made of? Was he just Prem's brother, but who did not drink so much? Need Hassan worry so much?

"Are you a member of the People's Progressive Party?" Prabhu asked him. The softer tone of his voice, under control now, let everyone relax back into their chairs. Miss Bullen was fanning herself with a booklet called *The Way of the Seer* which the World Mission of the New Yoga had sent her. She fanned herself as if demented, her mouth prim as she stared at the little doctor. Lila caught her eye and winked at her. Miss Bullen showed Lila her feeling of outrage with the doctor by glaring at him and then back at Lila. "You're delicious, Bella," Lila thought, sighing for yesterday's innocence, before the mail delivery.

Kholi smiled slowly, letting the smile slowly split his small, intense, brown face, his eyes shifting over them all until they rested on Hari Lal. He nodded to Hari Lal and then looked at Prabhu.

"There's the man," he said. "Hari Lal. He's the only member present, and likely to remain the only member."

"You mean I won't be elected?" Prabhu smiled and proferred the silver box of cigarettes. Hari Lal took the box over and began to glide about, pleasing people without their knowing it, lighting cigarettes until all were happy, and then glided back into his chair.

"You won't be elected, Maharaj Sahib. Hassan will see to that. He dominates everybody, except your new Press Officer here."

"You haven't heard the news, about Hari Lal's father, Doctor Kholi?" said Prabhu, hoping not. The doctor raised his eyebrows and waited to be told. When Prabhu told him that Hari Lal's father had given up all his lands he took it well, though Hari Lal knew the news had struck him right in the centre of his hatred for Gandhiji. The doctor hated Gandhiji so much that he could not laugh about him, which meant a lot.

"Really?" he said.

" Yes, really, Doctorji." Hari Lal watched him take it down into his mind for digestion.

" The Mahatma will need a very big handkerchief when he hears that piece of news," Kholi said, dry of voice but dead pan. Only his eyes showed how hard the news had hit him. They had clouded and the slightest of frowns had come over his face, like a shadow which would seep up through the skin if he allowed it. He brightened then and sneered at Hari Lal, saying, " I could cry myself, right here, over that piece of news. Is your father going into a *dhoti* as well, with spinning wheel or are we to be spared that ? "

" You must ask him, Doctorji."

" You don't believe in Gandhiji, Doctor ? " Prabhu asked.

" No more than you do, Maharaj Sahib." He waited until Prabhu had taken the full force of his quiet delivery of this insulting truth, and went on, " I had no time for British rule at all, but I got rather fond of it after watching the Mahatma. If a man has a fixation about lavatories and sweepers there's no harm in that, but one must draw the line when it becomes national policy."

" How dare you ? " Miss Bullen's voice, hardened by the mention of lavatories, and by the grudging admiration grown in her over the years for Gandhi, struck the air like a wet whip. Prabhu put his handkerchief to his mouth and forced his laughter into a cough. Lila looked proud and glad for Miss Bullen, and Hari Lal was impassive. The doctor looked at Miss Bullen and smiled.

" He put you all across his bony knee and smashed you, Miss Bullen," he said casually. " And then he sang his favourite hymn, ' Lead Kindly Light.' How dare I ? I never joined the conspiracy of worship that's grown up all over India. I like drink, boxing, wrestling, machines, clocks, science, factories, and I'm honest about caste. I won't sit down to dinner with sweepers, not even if they bring all Gandhiji's books to the table with them. The man's a confounded nuisance. I refuse to worship, that's all."

"I see," said Miss Bullen. She had taken a violent dislike
to the little man, and she had a lot to say, but what she thought
of as "manners" forbade her to reply. The subject dissolved
in a small silence while the doctor took a sip from his glass
of gin.

He had alienated himself from all of them, except Lila, for
even Prabhu admired Gandhi. Lila had always been ashamed
of Gandhi and wished he would wear trousers and a shirt.
A man who hated Gandhi had something wrong with him,
Prabhu decided. He began to hate the doctor, especially for
his unshakable attitude of contented relaxation. To the point,
then. About what? He realised that the doctor was domi-
nating him without much effort. There were a hundred things
he wanted to say but they had all flown. Lila came to the
rescue, but with a piece of the stupidity which on another
occasion would have made him clench his teeth.

"Do you think *Brahmacharya's* a good thing, Doctor?"
she said. "I heard you'd taken a vow of it. Is that right?"
This unsettled the doctor. He sat up in his chair and looked
at Lila in what was almost surprise. Miss Bullen had put her
hand over her eyes and looked pink.

"It can't be described," Kholi said. "You must try it for
yourself. May I ask you a question, a personal question?
Were you a breast-fed baby?"

Lila and Prabhu exchanged glances. Lila had a half smile
on her red mouth. She was embarrassed for a moment.

"Yes, I was, Doctor. Is that a help in any way?"

"You were *not* breast fed," Kholi told her with a brutal
hardness. "Inquire again and you'll find you were *not* breast
fed. If you had been you would be a very different person.
The only two people in this room, beside myself, who were
breast fed, are Miss Bullen and Hari Lal. And I'll wager a
hundred rupees on it."

"Mad," Prabhu thought. "Mad. But entertaining. You

wouldn't think the little bastard was so dangerous, scheming and running things against me."

Miss Bullen was looking at Lila as if to say, " Just say the word and we'll leave. It's manners alone that keep me quiet." Lila was laughing, honestly amused. She preferred it when there was a bit of shock in the conversation, a touch of the bizarre. The long diet of cement and factories and man-hours had almost destroyed her palate for useless happy talk. " Prabhu's killed me," she thought. " Actually killed me. I almost like this horrible little gnome."

" Can I count on your support, Doctor, in my plans for reforms here ? I imagine you have no fixation about me because I'm a Maharajah." Prabhu had got it out at last. Now for the reply.

" My whole life, Maharaj Sahib," the doctor told him gravely, " has been devoted to ending your rule here. You must know that from all the police reports you've read. My own file is that thick, isn't it ? I have a copy of it at home. Friends, you know. In the file you'll have read that while my interests appear to be the same as those of Hassan and the Progressive Party, they're not in fact. I want to see a republic here in the State. You couldn't count on me, Maharaj Sahib. Without me things couldn't have gone nearly as far as they have. I forecast your abdication here and now. It's inevitable. And being the realist you are I know you won't take it personally. It's merely that I have always hated your family. Petty, you might say. Even vindictive. But there it is."

" That doesn't sound very breast-fed, Doctor," Prabhu said. He could have got up and punched the little man in the middle of his calm and attractive brown face. The doctor threw himself back in his chair and let out a scream of laughter. Prabhu jerked his head at Lila, Miss Bullen and Hari Lal, and his mouth was so tight that Lila got up. She and Miss Bullen left first, Hari Lal pointing at his watch and holding it for Prabhu to see. Prabhu nodded and Hari Lal left.

Chapter Twenty

When they were alone Kholi and Prabhu looked at each other and Prabhu smiled. Kholi smiled in reply. Prabhu took off his dark glasses and put them on the bookshelf beside him.

"You must find things rather different, Doctor Kholi, since my father's death. He was the last of the muddled Victorian minor-Maharajahs. Holy men nagging him, pilgrimages, dozens of concubines, and the hard work of having a good time. That's all gone now. How would you like it if I offered you the post of Minister for Land Reform?"

"I wouldn't like it at all," said Kholi. "Is that why you wanted to see me?"

"No. But my hope was to win you over to my side, Doctor." Prabhu handed him another glass of gin and tonic. Kholi took it and waited for Prabhu to pour his own drink. Kholi lifted his glass and said, "To your future, Maharaj Sahib, wherever it may take you."

"Thank you," said Prabhu. They sipped their drinks. "As I was saying," Prabhu went on, "I hoped I could get you on my side. You seem to me to be a reasonable man."

"Thank you, Maharaj Sahib," Kholi said with gentle sarcasm.

"Quite all right, Doctor. Do you mean to tell me that all this fable about your hating my family over some girl or other thirty years ago is true?" Prabhu flashed his eyes and his voice rose. "Am I expected to believe this idiotic story as if I'm some local peasant interested in folklore ? And all these lies about being sworn to celibacy ? Am I expected to take this pack of nonsense seriously, and sit back and let you go on playing politics as if my stupid father were still alive? What do you take me for ? You have your women when you want them. I'll show you the reports. Not police reports. Much more private than that."

While Prabhu had been speaking Kholi's face had tightened as he clenched his teeth. When Prabhu had finished Kholi's face was dark red with anger. He looked as if he would throw his glass at Prabhu. When he spoke his voice was husky and rasping. He was choking with temper.

" Lies," he said. " There are no such reports. Dirty contemptible lies." He was quivering now as his voice gathered power. " Are you accusing me of keeping women ? Are you trying to say that I'm a hypocrite ? "

" I don't give a damn," Prabhu said. " You can do what you like. I only object to this nonsense because it's supposed to be a noble task you've taken on. To get rid of me here. You want me to bring proof of what I've said ? Oh, you've been careful, I know. But how would you like to know that your old and faithful servants were on my father's pay-roll, and that a complete dossier of the occasions you've broken your bloody phoney *Brahmacharya* is in my office ? "

Kholi sat down. He looked crushed. He opened and shut his mouth, but no sound came. But he managed to whisper, " It's impossible. My servants."

" *I* didn't do it," Prabhu said. " I detest this kind of business. But the files are there. The well-known ascetic, Doctor Kholi, who swore to renounce women as a public accusation against my father, has one brought in twice weekly by his old and trusted servant. You have a damn' nerve, Doctor."

" It's impossible." Kholi looked as if he had just been sentenced to death, and Prabhu was touched. He knew what meticulous care Kholi had always taken. The girl came hidden in the boot of his car just after midnight, on Tuesdays and Saturdays, the same girl for the past six years.

" What does it matter ? " Prabhu said, and it may have been the way he said it, but Kholi began to laugh, bending over as if to hide his face. He laughed hysterically while Prabhu watched him, half smiling, thinking, " I like this little head-case. What next, I wonder ? "

" You want to see the reports ? " he asked when Kholi was making less noise with his laughter.

" No, but thank you. Thank you, Maharaj Sahib." He had to laugh himself out, ending with gasping and shortness of breath.

" It's a serious matter," Prabhu said.

" I know, Maharaj Sahib. That's why I'm laughing." He wiped his eyes with a big handkerchief and then, picking up his gin, looked at it with hard, solemn eyes.

" A vile world," he said. " Vile."

" You think so ? " said Prabhu. " Because you can't keep secrets in it ? "

" I suppose that's it. I'll tell you, Maharaj Sahib, you've given me some bad news. You've surprised me. Is that why you sent for me ? " He had put his head in his hands and was making a strange whimpering sound.

" Partly," said Prabhu. " I'm getting tired of the situation here."

" Are you trying to blackmail me, Maharaj Sahib ? "

" Yes. I want an end to this nonsense of yours. I want to get on with my work in the State, and I want you to help me. That's all."

" By blackmail ? "

" You have no secrets from me, Doctor. You can't fool me. Your private life's your own, as long as you don't cash in any more on your phoney legend. That's the curse of this country. Legends made out of lies."

" Yes." Kholi's shoulders began to shake as he laughed.

" Yes. Legends made out of lies. Yes." He lay back to laugh in comfort.

" You think it's funny ? "

" Well, it's not tragic, is it ? " Kholi could hardly speak for laughter. His eyes, though, were broken, tragic. " The little bastard's taken a wallop," thought Prabhu.

" I'm not in the mood for fun, Doctor," Prabhu shouted in a sudden temper.

" Oh, aren't you, Maharaj Sahib ? " The doctor stood up, a little figure of menace with his tragic eyes turned to hardness. " Aren't you ? May I know why you've invited me here ? "

" I'll expose you if you work against me any more," Prabhu said. " That's why you're here. To hear that."

" I see. And you have no fears that I can hurt you too ? "

" None."

The doctor began to peal with laughter again, bending double, with his little right hand pressed against his mouth. Prabhu drank two quick gins while Kholi got through his new attack of laughter. The doctor blew his nose, gasping again, drank some of his gin and then began to speak in a quiet, persuasive tone, but Prabhu could see that he was trying to hide great agitation. He was pressing his little finely-sandalled right foot into the carpet, twisting it about and sometimes shaking it.

" I admit it, Maharaj Sahib," he said, his fine eyes unblinking as they met Prabhu's. " But I'm no hypocrite. For over twenty years I *was* a celibate. Eight years ago I broke my vow. It was one night during the *Holi* festival. Do you want to hear about it ? " An expression of misery had come over his face.

Prabhu looked at his watch. " Yes. Go on."

" Twenty years feels like a long time the night you make it all pointless. The night, that is, when you fall. Can you imagine what that's like, Maharaj Sahib ? Making twenty years of effort and training useless and wasted ? Those twenty

years were all right until that night. They were valuable ;
they were mine, and I was going to make them twenty-five,
and then thirty. Do you know that even *saddhus* and *fakirs*
used to come to me for advice, for help in conquering the
flesh ? Do you think it was a pleasure for me to fall ? *Do*
you ? " He had almost shouted the last two words. Prabhu
was staring at him, fascinated by the shifting glints of madness in Kholi's eyes. " I say ' *Do* you,' Maharaj Sahib ? "
Kholi demanded heatedly.

Prabhu began to laugh now, helplessly, and as if in rage
Kholi turned his back. Having offended him, Prabhu controlled himself and apologised.

" I'm sorry, Doctor. I wasn't laughing at you, but at something you reminded me of in my own life. Please go on. I'm
terribly interested." Kholi turned round. There were unshed
tears filming his eyes, making them lustrous and glowing.

" You can laugh," he said. " But you don't know what
it's like to fall after twenty years of struggle. It's not easy,
you know, celibacy. But I'd won, I thought. But you've
never quite won. There's no end to the battle. No end."
At that moment he looked desolated and utterly alone.

" You were telling me about the *Holi* festival eight years
ago, Doctor. What happened ? "

Kholi showed the fixed, obsessive trap that fall had made
for him. He showed it in the way he seemed to be suddenly
alone, talking excitedly to himself, his eyes glittering while
they stared into nothing before him.

" I'd got my diet right," he said, the words falling against
each other as he rushed them from his tongue, " the food not
too spiced, not too rich, not too much. All sensory reflexes
under control. The mind clear and calm. I was happy.
Twenty years of routine. I had my temptations to remember.
If only I could have believed in some God or other. Yet I'd
done so well. My work. My habits. My hopes. Yes, I was
happy. But I was too confident." He looked sadly into

Prabhu's eyes, back with him again. " It was *Holi* time. I was in Delhi at a conference discussing *ayurvedic* methods of medicine. We were to report fully on all aspects of indigenous methods, quackery and all. Everything. Day after day listening to idiots from the villages describing how they could cure everything from cancer to heart disease with a few herbs and a recitation in Sanskrit. The mind feels as if it's been trampled upon after a few days of listening to these ignorant sorcerers, and it's their terrible pride which hurts most. I used to spend the days in such a rage that I felt I was going to go on fire. I've always had a very short temper and controlling it has made me tired. Self-control is a never-ending struggle. That's what's wrong with the whole of Asia, the massive repression, the jigsaw of taboos and prison rules. . . ."

" Yes, yes," said Prabhu impatiently. " And then ? *Holi* time in Delhi. What happened ? "

" Yes, I was saying. I was saying. What was I saying ? *Holi*. Eight years ago. Yes. *Holi*. Yes. That day—that day. It was hot. I began early in the morning. I was very hot." He wiped his hand across his forehead. " I must sit down, Maharaj Sahib," he said weakly.

" He's in the throes," Prabhu thought. " Do," he said. " Do sit down, Doctor." " Yes. Poor little fellow. He's like all of us. Bent."

They sat down. The doctor flung the rest of his gin down his throat, hardly knowing Prabhu was taking his glass and filling it again.

" It was very hot," Prabhu said, one eye on his hands pouring gin, the other watching Kholi. " Delhi. Eight years ago."

" It was so hot that I felt ill. You know, living in these cool mountains softens us. Delhi feels like an oven to us. And I had a horrible day before me. This *ayurvedic* medicine ! My God ! It's so like everything that chains us down to what you called the legend made out of a lie. History. What's history ? How one god strangled another in the name of some king who couldn't afford an army to kill his rival. It's worse in Europe, of course. They have professorships in it there. Professorships of falsehood, a chair of lying, dons of deceit. What about here in India . . . ? "

" Will you for God's sake tell me about how you broke your vow ? " Prabhu pleaded angrily.

" I'm coming to it." Kholi flushed into anger. " Can't you understand how painful it is for me ? Can't you understand I have to make myself face it ? Do you think it's easy to talk about it ? Do you ? "

" No."

" Then let me find my own way to it. I've never spoken of it before. But your filthy policemen have written my life down, and my servant has sold me. Do you think it's nothing ? Do you think it's just words ? "

" No."

" No ? "

" No."

" I'm so glad. Where was I ? Can I have another drink, please ? "

" Certainly. You were at the *ayurvedic* conference. It was *Holi*. It was hot. You were unhappy."

Kholi's attitude had changed so much that he was pitiful. Prabhu handed him the glass of gin and tonic.

" Thank you, Maharaj Sahib," he said. " Where was I ? "

" Delhi. Eight years ago. *Holi*. *Ayurvedic* conference. You felt trampled upon." " He doesn't want to talk about it, and he wants so much to talk about it," Prabhu thought.

" Yes," Kholi said, animated, awakened again from his doleful quiet. " Yes. That's it. That day. What a day. You know I used to drink when I was training in Dublin as a young man. I gave it up for a while. But never completely. I always had a whisky if I felt like having one. And in Delhi we had a very difficult time. We had to go out to a Maharajah's palace, the one he used in Delhi. I think he was from one of the more backward of the States in the Deccan, rather like Jashimpur. Anyway, he'd collected a whole lot of witch-doctors for us to interview. One of the group with us was an American woman. One of the Besant-cum-Blavatsky devotees. You know the type, but sex-mad disguised as a seeker after uplift." He began to peal with laughter again, looking mad, with his eyes staring back to that hot day in Delhi. His laughter was genuine amusement but there was a pity and self-hatred in it which made Prabhu feel sorry for him, and yet he could not help laughing himself. He felt that Kholi was like himself, a lover of humanity who feared he was about to lose his faith at any moment, and seeing life as a joke veiled in heartrending sorrows. He had not found any-one who could make him laugh like this, merely by laughing at what was sad, comically sad. It disturbed and frightened him.

" She was writing a book about Indian magic and medicine," Kholi said. " She was brainless, and beautiful. Almost as beautiful as your wife, Maharaj Sahib, but white and blonde, and made to break people like me. As soon as we sat beside each other in the hotel where we were all having cold beer, or tomato juice for the Gandhi-fanatics, we began to tremble. We had not been introduced but we sat there in silence and trembled. I felt as if an iron band had been screwed round my heart. Sweat broke out all over me. I was in such a state of nerves that I didn't dare lift my glass of beer from the table. I had to wait for a while before I could lift it. I could feel the woman beside me radiating electrical forces between us that set us shivering. I thought I was going to faint. I caught her eye and we were *there*. Do you know what I mean by *there* ? I mean we knew we had been travelling to that spot together for ten million years. You laugh ? But it was so. She put her hand on mine and pressed it. It was like an electric current in me. I could hear her saying to me in a low voice, ' Yes, I know. I know, I feel it too,' and while she was saying it to me she was pretending to listen to a professor who was describing rituals used after snake bite in certain communities. You know there are certain genes which scream out to other genes, and you can hear their screams through any amount of flesh. Nature gets feverish and disturbed when these pairs meet, and from then on there is no rest. There was only one thing to do. Go away. Leave the conference. But how was I to know I was up against a magician?

"I got up, left my glass of beer, and excused myself to the professor, saying I was unwell. I rushed to my room, packed my suitcase, got a taxi and told the driver to take me to Maidens Hotel in Old Delhi. It was miles away and I felt I must be alone. I was so upset that I could hardly speak. I was actually in love with the woman. Can you imagine it? A brainless woman whose talk bored me. All I had been able to do while she talked to me was say to myself, 'No! No! Stop it!' And I knew that I couldn't be tempted so long as I went away.

"At Maidens I met two British army doctors and they were interesting and I drank more than I should have done. I drank like you smoke, Maharaj Sahib, compulsively, and it quietened me in a way. They made me have lunch with them. It was a hot mutton-curry, something I usually avoided, but I ate it and asked for more. I felt better, sleepy, and even safe. When I went to my room to lie down the woman was there, typing."

"Typing? You mean the American woman? Typing?" Prabhu looked at his watch. He still had a little time before the meeting of the Party about his candidature.

"Yes, typing. She nodded and smiled. She said, 'I've borrowed your typewriter for a minute or two, Doctor. My room is across the way. I won't be a minute.' And she went on typing. She was dressed in a grey-blue silk dress. I wanted to tear everything off her, knowing she would smile and help me. I stood there almost fainting. She lived there, at Maidens, and to get away from her I had come to her. Where should I go next? She finished typing, pulled the sheet out of the machine and gave it to me. Then she said, ' Don't forget we're all due at the Maharajah's palace for a meeting to-morrow morning at eleven. I have a car. I'll be waiting for you at the main entrance.' She got hold of my hands and kissed them, saying, ' Master! Master! Let me be your *chela*.' And then she went. I was feeling very faint, ill. I had to sit down and rest before I could read what she had typed.

" It was a letter to me. A heartbreaking letter of appeal, saying she would commit suicide if I tried to ignore her again. She could not live away from me. I was her spiritual master. She was my slave, my servant, my *chela*, my pupil, and my lover. Her adopted Indian name was ' Pryamvidda.' "

" Tell me the rest in the car, Doctor. It's time to go," Prabhu interrupted him.

" If I don't tell it all now I shall never speak of it again," Kholi cried piteously. " You *must* listen to me. I've got to tell you about it."

" Why? "

" Because you've found me out. And now you must listen to me." He was begging to be heard.

" Oh! All right." " He's mine," thought Prabhu. " Mine. He's handing himself over. He's mad. We're all mad here, I think. All except Miss Bullen. She's watching us all. We're all mad." " Go on," he told Kholi.

" I couldn't sleep that night. I went out and walked in the moonlight for miles. I went to the Chandni Chowk, and I wandered through all the streets until it was dawn. Then I went to a Sindhi restaurant and got some breakfast. I knew that if I didn't leave Delhi I was finished. And I didn't want to leave Delhi. I wanted this woman. I wonder if you know what it's like for an ascetic to find himself thinking his life a waste, and knowing it's the flesh talking, and yet listening

P

gladly to the flesh talking ? I found I had a hundred reasons ready for having this woman. It was that night that I knew I loved your father for what he had done, for taking the girl I was to marry. I'd never have been happy as a married man. That night I knew that the fame I had in Jashimpur as the doctor sworn to celibacy and revenge was only my hobby, the pastime of my juvenile self. And each of us retains a juvenile self until we die. Are you surprised, Maharaj Sahib ? "

" So you don't hate me as Maharajah ? Then what is it ? Why do you work against me ? " Prabhu seized Kholi's slender wrist and shook his arm.

" No, I don't hate you. I like you, Maharaj Sahib. I give in. But how am I to do it, Maharaj Sahib ? I have some pride, after all."

" You had breakfast at the Sindhi restaurant eight years ago. And then ? "

" You can't wait to hear of my humiliating fall, can you, Maharaj Sahib ? " Kholi cried bitterly, his face racked with self-pity and the inner pain of incurable wounds. When Prabhu burst into wild laughter Kholi joined him. They laughed until Prabhu said, " That's enough. Hurry up and tell me. One last gin for the road. We've got to go. Come on, hurry up with the story." He gave Kholi another glass of gin and tonic.

" That day was *Holi* festival. The usual gangs were swarming through the streets with handfuls of *Kumkum* powder and dye, splashing the red stuff on everyone's head, and cheering. I had on my best suit. I'd forgotten it was *Holi*. If I'd remembered I'd have put on some old *pajamas* and *kurta*, but there I was, in the streets with the gangs running about marking everybody with bright colours for *Holi* and happiness. Have you ever been caught in Delhi, Maharaj Sahib, even prepared in old clothes for *Holi* ? You know how one has to pretend to be enjoying the accursed business and how one's heart is full of murder when you are face to face with the gang ? Well, that *Holi* they were doing something I'd never seen before. The gangs had big buckets of mixed dyes, green and blue and red, and bicycle pumps to squirt it with. I was running like a fox through the lanes, stopping to listen to the cheers of the gangs.

" As I ran across the main road I saw a business man in tears. He was screeching for the police. He was dyed from head to foot, even his beautiful yellow brief-case was spattered with purple and green. The gangs were cheering all round him. I had not far to go to the hotel. They saw me and began to run after me. There were about twenty of them, several had buckets of dye and nearly all of them had bicycle pumps. They were laughing and cheering as I ran like a fox ahead of them up the road. It was not funny. I had on not only my best suit, but the only suit I had brought to Delhi for the conference. And it was about nine o'clock and I was to leave for the day's work at the palace in Delhi at eleven. So I ran like a madman along the road with the gang after me.

" ' Come back,' they were yelling at me. ' Come back and celebrate.' I'd made up my mind that I wouldn't let them put even one drop of their dyes on me. And I would have been all right if another gang hadn't appeared at the end of the road. They had bicycle pumps and buckets ready for me. I was trapped."

" But what's this got to do with the fall in the garden of Maidens ? " Prabhu asked. " We've got to hurry. What's it got to do with the fall ? "

" Everything," said Kholi curtly. " Everything. Great sins always have humble and even stupid beginnings."

" Doctor Kholi," Prabhu said, looking crafty and suspicious, " you're not trying to keep me from going to the meeting, are you ? "

" Why should I, Maharaj Sahib ? You won't be elected. Don't you want to hear my story ? You started it. Now you must hear me out. It's very important. Am I boring you ? "

"No, Doctor. But I'm feeling very jumpy. I can't relax. But go on. Tell me what happened." The Party members would be meeting now in Kholi's house. He was too nervous to consider what he would do if they rejected him as a candidate. But they would not dare to reject him. He was still the Maharajah, and they were still Jashimpuris. Hassan, he did not doubt, would vote against him. But the rest were not so certain, not so spitefully determined to humiliate him. "Go on, Doctor," he said.

"I was surrounded," said Kholi. "They took a special revenge on me because I'd nearly escaped them, and because I fought. I lost my temper. I lost it completely when the first bicycle pump full of dye was squirted straight into my face. The others were squirting me all over, back and front. I was crying with anger and despair. I was sodden through and through with red and purple and green dyes. They followed me up the road, cheering and squirting me. One was shouting in English, 'Happy time for gentlemans sahib.' I knew my suit was ruined for ever. Do you know I was composing a letter to the Press while I ran up that road sobbing with rage? It was a wonderful letter, full of biting sarcasm about our ancient spiritual culture, especially during *Holi*, the festival of friendship, love and joy.

"In my room Pryamvidda was waiting for me. She led me to a chair, and was so tender to me that I began to cry. I asked her to get a bearer to bring me some whisky and soda. She served me like a slave. I knew I loved her then, but I had to fight it. When the whisky came she locked the door and then, I shall never forget it, flung the key out of the window. The trembling began in me again.

"'Now we are alone, Master,' she said. She knelt at my feet and took off my shoes and socks. She kissed my right big toe several times, whispering, 'My lord and master. Command me.' Then she got up and helped me off with my sodden coat. And then came the affair of the trousers. I hung on as long as I could, begging her, imploring. But she was very strong, and determined. She dragged them off me, upending me in the chair and more or less emptying me out of them. I shall never forget the silent way she went about it, not grim or passionate, but quiet and determined, and the most tender expression in her big blue eyes. It was to that tenderness in her that I appealed and begged. But it was no use. I managed to get out of the arm-chair but she threw herself on me and seized me, and dragged me to the bed. She lifted me up. I could feel the swell of her breasts against me, and the perfume she used was everywhere. I got hold of the end of the bed and hung on. I think I was shouting implorations. I can't remember. I can remember getting a grip on the end of the bed and saying to myself, ' Hold on. Hold on or you're finished. Twenty years of achievement will be finished.' She held me with one hand and picked up an ash-tray with the other and hammered my fingers with it until I let go. She flung me on the bed and threw herself on top of me. She was reciting a Tantric *mantra* over and over again. I knew I was finished when she kissed me on the mouth and then said, ' Master, your wife is with you now and for ever.'

" I had one last try to escape. I tried to get out of the bed but she pinned me down by the wrists. I said, ' Can't you have pity ? I've struggled for twenty years against this. Please let me go.'

" ' We're in the grip of the forces, Master,' she said. ' Forces that have waited too long. Why should we tremble beside each other when I am to be your wife ? ' We began. I was in tears, of joy and bitter sorrow."

Prabhu fell on the couch howling with laughter. Kholi, who had been giggling sadly, began to laugh too, but he was sobbing, tears flowing down his face, while he laughed. He was shuddering and gasping, his eyes demented. He was having a nervous breakdown at last.

Seeing him from where he was laughing on the couch, Prabhu got up and ran to him, putting an arm about his slender shoulders.

"Get her," Kholi was sobbing. "Get her. Get my wife. I give in. Get her. Bring her. Send for her."

"Wife? Your wife?" Prabhu exclaimed. "Where?"

"Pryamvidda. She's in Calcutta. Send for her. I give in." He began to collapse. Prabhu lifted him and put him on the couch. He rushed to the wall and rang for a servant. "Bring the Miss Sahib," he said. "And hurry. Bring Miss Bullen. Quickly."

Chapter Twenty-One

Miss Bullen had prayed for Lila every night, every night since what she thought of as the night of " Revelations," when Lila had revealed all the stains of the world she carried inside her.

Her prayers to the God who had withdrawn Himself during the last few years were the prayers of a woman who had never quite forgiven God for arranging the propagation of the human race through such sinisterly tempting and degrading forms of behaviour. She had never understood why it had to be like *that*. And human beings rushed, tumbling over each other, to indulge in this depressing behaviour, even people like Lila, whose beauty and gentleness should inspire to purity and to goodness. She felt revulsion and compassion about it. Despite all the painful and ugly things life up in the mountains of Kangla had revealed to her, Miss Bullen still believed that only the poor and degraded had an excuse for this kind of extra-sin, not people of sensibility and education. For Lila to involve herself with another man, to drink too much, to be loose-tongued about secret things, was more sinful than the grubby, miserable sins committed by some puzzled peasant. She prayed hard that Lila would feel a proper shame for her condition and renounce the evil which was trying to strangle her soul.

Prayer was not easy, and it had to be worked up to over a few days until the heart was aching to voice it. Then it was delivered to God for consideration and judgment. On occasion she prayed angrily, in a cold rage with some of the things God allowed to go on down here, for she was by no means convinced that God kept proper accounts. She believed that prayer sent up powerfully could give God a jolt, and she had had proof of it once or twice, even though that tireless devil of chill scepticism would whisper, " Pure coincidence, and you know it." Her prayers for Lila, though, were working. Lila was trying to change, was realising that she must come to account and draw a line under the old, bitter, useless life she had fallen into.

" Oh, I know I'm a bitch," she would say mournfully to Miss Bullen. " I know. I can see by your eyes when you look at me. I know I'm a bitch. I've become hard. It's only when one is close to a person like yourself that one realises how bitchlike one has become, how one takes it for granted that everyone in the world's hard and callous."

Never had Miss Bullen contradicted Lila, never had she put out her hand and said, " You're not, Lila. I can't bear to hear you say that of yourself." Never. For Lila *was* a bitch, that horrible word which Lila used so frequently, and which was used nowadays on every page of a novel, and in every radio drama. Even Prem used it, actually used it to Lila, as when he had said, " Lila, what a bitchy way you have of putting things sometimes." That was the world of to-day, the world which had lost its way and was screaming with despair. Women had made this world, by lowering themselves and by allowing the brute, which was ready in every man, to walk about openly and without shame. She had told Lila and Lila had looked thoughtful and said, " There's nothing more brutal than a politically-minded husband, Bella. I blame the suffragettes for that, but secretly. That's what incites a woman like me to murder, a boring, political husband. That's a bigger sin than some others." Lila trying to be clever, trying to dodge the issue.

Within the last couple of days, though, Lila had been

looking very down and depressed, and had actually said,
" Bella, I need prayer or something terribly badly. Pray
for me. Pray that I make a right decision about you-know-
what."

Imagine it ! Pray for a right decision about you-know-
what ! But she had prayed about it, prayed about praying
about it.

Now, nervously strained after helping Doctor Das to give
a sedative and calm Doctor Kholi, who had broken down into
a quiet little good-natured wreck, Miss Bullen wanted to be
alone. Lila, who had been forbidden by Prabhu to see Doctor
Kholi, had said, " Of course he's had a breakdown. Why
shouldn't he when Prabhu got at him ? He probably
dominated him so much with some figures about Jashimpuri
statistics that the little creature has folded up. Poor little
man. A charmer, though a bit of a beast, I'd say, on the
quiet. Is he sleeping now ? Like a little doll on the settee.
You look tired, Bella. Oh, Bella, I must talk to you." Her
whole manner had changed then, her black eyes clouding
and her red mouth trembling. Miss Bullen had looked into
her eyes and said, " In ten minutes, my dear. I *must* lie down
for just ten minutes. I'm not a young thing, you know." In
this madhouse she never felt relaxed.

" But I must talk to you. I *must*. Oh, I must. You've got
to help me. All right. Ten minutes. I'll bring you a cup of
tea myself, in ten minutes." There was something torturing
Lila, and about time too, poor child.

Miss Bullen wanted ten minutes in which to come to a
quiet decision, to be alone in her room for a last revision of
her plan to change Lila. She was greatly tempted to leave
Lila to go her own way, and to give up her job here in this
place and go back to Kangla. Each time, though, she was
ready to make up her mind the bitterness of her fruitless years
at Kangla brought on her old anger with God again. She
fought the temptation to return to Kangla, fought it daily.

Seeing Prabhu smiling beside the prostrate Doctor Kholi and saying, "He's all right, Miss Bullen. A self-administered psycho-analysis and a collapse afterwards, pure relief, in fact. Get Doctor Das," had made her want Kangla again. Kangla where there was at least some spiritual peace.

Kholi had looked up at Miss Bullen and murmured, "Not psycho-analysis, Miss Sahib; purely nervous exhaustion. I've merely given in."

"What have you given in about, Doctor Kholi?" she had asked him. Then he had started that fantastic laughter of his again, and Prabhu had said, "He's too tired to talk about it, Miss Bullen. Phone Doctor Das and ask him to come up here with a set of opium pipes or a bottle of ether or something. Doctor Kholi needs a long, peaceful sleep. He's exhausted."

She had had about enough of this palace and these people. The peasants at Kangla had assumed proportion in her mind again. They were good and useful hardworking people when compared with this collection here in the palace. Except for Prem. She loved Prem, weak though he was. And Lila. She loved Lila, and must not give up her soul. And the Maharajah, a worried, lonely, unstable person, in need of loving. Damn them all. No. Yes, *damn* them all. "My God, I *am* selfish," she thought angrily.

Lila let her go to her room. She lay down on her wide bed and closed her eyes and whispered, "Alone, thank God. Alone. Now, God, help me to think and decide."

Now what would happen to the Maharajah at this meeting which Lila had called, "the thing that's going to knock him rigid. He knows they're going to turn him down, but he goes on and on. Wait till you see, Bella. What a damned *fool* the man is." The Maharajah had been pale when he went to the car with that nice, well-behaved young man, Hari Lal. "Come on, Hari Lal," he had said. "Let's find out the worst." It seemed very important to him.

Lila actually *wanted* her husband to be hurt, wanted him to "be brought down to earth," as she put it.

"Oh, thank you, God," Miss Bullen murmured, "for allowing me to stay single. I know I'd have been no good at it. I'd have been far worse than Lila. If I despised a man I was married to I'm sure I'd do something frightful, kill him or something. I'm so impatient. And I feel so old these days, especially since coming here and watching all this terrible business going on. They're all well behaved, except for Lila, but they're all like volcanoes, no peace or restfulness in any of them. You're punishing them, I suppose. You know how to punish all right, I can vouch for that. You punished me enough. And did I ever do anything against you? Did I? Did I ever weaken or commit any awful sins? Never. But you punished me. You wasted my life. Yes, you did. You did."

She was nearly crying but she choked it down again into her thin throat, swallowing painfully in the soft light of the bedside lamp.

"I shouldn't have said that to you. I know I shouldn't. But what do you expect in my state of nerves, after a wasted lifetime? I suppose I envy Lila, being beautiful and everything, poor Lila, the fool. She has everything and wastes it. But she's young. Not like me. A damned wasted life. Yes, *damned* wasted. You punished me, and I'm damned if I know why."

Sorry for this, and ready to pray now, her heart surging with it, she got off the bed and knelt down, folded her thin hands, closed her eyes, and got in touch. The prayer came straight up out of her, passing up through her closed eyes into the darkness above where mystery swayed stars and unknown deserts of night she thought of as eternity.

"Dear Lord and Master," her spirit breathed, "You know how I have doubted you and suffered because of it, and you know my rebellious heart forgets itself, and you know how

I have been pulled this way and that by the torments of the petty little reasoning you have given me, and with which I fight you daily. What shall I do with the pledge? Shall I make Lila sign it? Has she the moral courage to stand by it if she signs it? I'll make her sign it all right, don't worry about that. But what about afterwards? Is she strong enough to win the battle? What do you want? Do you want to break her yourself, or do you want me to do what I feel you're goading me to do—set my will to change her and bring her back to the fold, a whole woman again? Give me a sign. As to myself, I admit to you that sometimes I hate you, God forgive me, yes, hate you, and I know it's wrong. But what do you want me to do? Go on with the battle for souls? But could I have done more than I did for forty years at Kangla in your service? Could I? Admit it, I couldn't. Admit it, Lord. Forty years of failure. Those years are gone for ever, and I'm not going to get them back, and it's no use me pretending I'm pleased about it. Do you blame me for being bitter? Doesn't it show you how much I cared that I feel so bitter? Forgive your wayward servant who cannot forgive you the waste of her life, a life, let me repeat, in which I have not one single sign of your approval. Nothing! And yet I have to go on praying and believing. It's no good, I can't get rid of you, I can't send you out of my heart, and you know how often I wish I could.

"Well, what about the woman, Lila, taken in spiritual adultery? Am I to fail there too? Am I to leave her? Am I to go back to the grind at Kangla and die there in some little unknown grave, buried by the same pack I came among forty years ago, a pack of lost, miserable creatures with not enough to eat and with no courage to fight for their freedom? What am I supposed to do? I can save Lila. If I once decide to take a grip on her I'll change her, but is that what you want? This is the first time I've spoken directly to you for some time, I mean spoken quite freely and honestly about some of the things which trouble me, and not only me, but many more like me.

"For instance, what are you doing with this world these days? Are you handing it all over to the communists and the papists? What's going on? You sent people of my race all over the world to bring your message and to build and do and give law and order and justice, and we laboured in the fiercest heat and bitterest cold. And yet what do we see to-day? After all our great work in India, Africa, Burma, everywhere we've toiled, you let us be driven out, and to-day heretics of all kinds flourish, not to mention the brazenness of the papists, who work tirelessly for our downfall. What's the meaning of it all? The Pope is spoken of on the radio and in the press to-day in headlines, and the communists are entertained to dinner by men who should know better. You know who I mean. Are we to stand by and see the world handed over to Rome and Moscow? Do you blame me for being angry?

"To-night I feel tired and desolate, Lord. I know it. But I mean everything I've said. I'm bitter, yes. I simply cannot accept that I'm to write off my forty years at Kangla, and the disappointment I've had there, and pretend nothing's happened. I want some explanation. And I suppose, as usual, that I'll get none. But I can bear it. I've borne worse things, as you know. I'm not complaining. Simply stating facts.

"Well, what am I to do about Lila? I'd better say right here that if I go after that wonderful soul I'll pursue it to the end. Is that your will? Do I start with the pledge?

"Oh, Lord and Master, here she is. She's at the door, her hand's on the door-knob. She's crying. I hear her crying. I accept, Lord. I accept the sign, the sign of tears. I shall pursue this soul for you and bring it back to the fold."

She got up hurriedly from her knees and sat down on the

bed. She could hear Lila sobbing, calling her name, " Bella. Oh, Bella, let me in."

" Come in," Miss Bullen called, somewhat coldly, for she had come to a decision.

Lila came into the room looking distraught, saying, " Oh, Bella, help me. I haven't had a drink of whisky for four hours. Only those two small gins and tonic. I'm desperate for a drink but I can't. I've got to think. I can't stand it. What am I going to do ? Read this." She took a letter out of her black and red Sindi bodice which glistened and flashed with a thousand tiny pieces of smoked glass sewn into its superb embroidery. " Read it, Bella. Please read it and tell me what I'm to do."

" It's about this man, isn't it ? "

" Of course it is. It's dreadful. Oh, Bella, don't look at me like that. I can't stand it. Be kind to me."

" Before I read anything, Lila dear, I want you to read something." The old woman got up and went to her chest of drawers. She returned and stood before Lila with a hand-written sheet of paper.

" Read it, dear," she said, " and then sign it. And when you've signed it I'll fight beside you to the end until you have control of your own life again, until you're happy and at peace again."

" What is it ? " Lila was tragic-eyed, holding Clegg-Bray's letter against her breasts, reaching out for the paper in Miss Bullen's hand. " I couldn't stand any more bad news, Bella. What is it ? I don't want any more blows. I'm going out of my mind as it is. Oh, my God, where's it all going to end ? What's this paper ? "

" Read it," Miss Bullen said firmly. " It's your first step on the road to strength again."

Lila read it slowly, the old-fashioned copper-plate hand-writing running without faltering to the last words, and then looked up at Miss Bullen in astonishment, and fear.

" But I can't, Bella," she cried pathetically. " I can't. Why should I ? I'm not a wreck or something."

" Sign that pledge, Lila my dear, and begin your battle. You can't put it off any longer. Sign it and I'll turn this world upside down if necessary to help you. But you've got to help yourself too. Read it aloud to me and then sign it."

Lila appealed to her dumbly with her beautiful eyes, looking like someone who has received some fearful blow and cannot recover.

" Go on, Lila. Read it. I've prayed about this matter for days. There's no way out. Read it aloud, and then sign it."

They fought a silent battle with their eyes, one pair of eyes black and melting with pain, and the other pair grey, cool, determined, lit up with the soft glow of spiritual certainty. In a husky, sullen voice Lila read the pledge, astonished unbelief coming into her voice as she understood it all.

I renounce all alcoholic drink from this day forward. With God's will I shall succeed in breaking the slavery of alcohol, and become a credit again to my religion, my husband, and my children, and to the noble womanhood to which I belong by right, and from which I have so nearly fallen. I solemnly swear that from this day I shall never partake of alcohol again.

Signed. . . . .

" You wouldn't make me sign this, Bella ! " Lila almost whispered the words. She knew she was going to sign it if the old woman was determined enough, and she knew she wanted to sign it, but hoped that somehow she would not have to.

" My dear," said Miss Bullen, her eyes tender with love for Lila. " I wouldn't *make* you do anything. How could I do that ? But I know what you want to do, and I want to help you to do it. Do you want to sign it ? "

What was Lila to say ? Did she want to sign it, this terrible Victorian sort of document ? She had begun to feel burdened with vices. She had an idea she had read of this kind of thing in books about the stuffy world in which Miss Bullen must have spent her childhood and youth, a cruel, lying, two-faced world of terrible and malevolent goodness, yet far more sure of itself than this one.

" Well, Lila dear, do you *want* to sign it ? " Miss Bullen took her hand and stroked it. Lila looked into her eyes and trembled. She knew she was going to have to fight but wanted to evade it. She loved the old woman and knew that in the frail, handsome old body in its grey-blue sari, behind those sensitive, cool, grey eyes, was a will of unbreakable steel, and she feared to challenge it and bring it out in all its terrific strength.

" I wouldn't mind if it were true," said Lila weakly, yet feeling she was on the right track, that she was finding a way to escape the trap. She was longing for some whisky. She had denied herself whisky all afternoon and evening so as to be able to think and plan about this letter from Clegg-Bray, and now she was almost whimpering for a drink, and must fight her friend, her steel-willed friend from quite another generation, from another world altogether.

" If what were true, Lila ? " Miss Bullen stroked Lila's golden arm and enjoyed with forgotten, buried appetite the feel of the warm, tender flesh, loving its owner whole-heartedly.

Lila lifted the pledge and said, " If it were true what this paper says about me. None of it is true. None of it. Why should I sign it ? I mean what's the point of it ? This is the kind of thing an alcoholic signs, not me. I'm not an alcoholic. I like a drink, yes. In fact I drink quite a lot. But I'm not an alcoholic. It's different for an alcoholic. It'd be dishonest for me to sign this paper. Surely you know that, Bella ? "

Miss Bullen smiled, still stroking Lila's arm, her smile affectionate, motherly.

" The next thing you'll be saying, Lila, is that you can give up alcohol any time you like. That you drink it for pleasure only, and that you have no craving for it. Is that all you meant when you said the paper's untrue ? "

" No. I mean all of it, Bella. These words, *the slavery of alcohol* : I'm not a slave to it. *A credit to my religion* : I've no religion. You know that, so how can I become a credit to it ? *A credit to my husband* : I *am* a credit to him." She was escaping from the feeling of crushed shame, from the readiness to give in. Her voice was changing, her eyes lighting up. " I was never anything but a credit to him. Look at me. I'm a beautiful woman. I'm satisfying. I know it and he knows it. He doesn't have to go to another woman. I've got it all here, all of it, and he knows it and I know it. As far as sex is concerned, I fear nothing and nobody. Oh, don't look shocked, Bella. It's very important. You're shocked because I'm saying it, not because it's untrue. In your world a thing may be true but it mustn't be said, if it's about the *secret* things. That's what I mean about being a credit to him. Look at me. If I were a man I'd follow me across the world, because I'm beautiful, and I know it. Follow me across the world—— Oh, Bella, Bella ! " She was crushed again, her eyes pitiful.

" What is it, Lila ? "

" I came to beg you to help me and you stick this horrible paper in front of me and bully me into signing it. I want help. I'm in terrible trouble, Bella. Please burn the paper. Don't make me sign it."

" You've got to sign it, dear, and you know it. You've got to make a start against the drink. Be strong and sign it. I'll help you every moment afterwards."

Lila worked herself up again, looking at the paper in her hand. She remembered what she had said about being a

Q

credit to Prabhu, and now she turned to the matter of the children. "*A credit to my children*," she said in a low, vibrant voice. "I *am* a credit to them. Look at them. Look at how wonderful looking they are, their brains and their understanding. That's all me. They were torn out of my body in pain and suffering. You've never known that. You've never known what it is to go and have a look in the glass and see yourself loaded with two children inside your body. And you see yourself looking like an ox, all smashed looking, for a man, not that you're not proud and glad of it. No. But you feel it, you know. You feel it standing there seeing yourself with that special look of an ox, patient and *got down*. That's what you feel, *got down*. He's all right, Prabhu, or the man. He's getting on with his weekly *Time* magazine and his statistics about the sheep in Peru or something. Credit to the children ? My God, I don't have to sign a thing like that. I've suffered for my children. I lay for hours like a beast on a bed with an idiot of a nurse saying, ' It won't be long now, ducky, just bear down. Keep bearing down.' You don't know anything about that, Bella. That's *living*. And look at this, *credit to the noble womanhood to which I belong by right*. That's shocking to write that and expect me, your friend, to sign that. You know it's shocking. Noble womanhood. How can you, Bella ? *And from which I have so nearly fallen* : that's the mean part. You're trying to get at me again about what I told you about Derek Clegg-Bray. You're trying to insinuate that I've been unfaithful to Prabhu. I haven't. There's been a little bit of nonsense now and again, that's all. There's nothing *like* that in it. And there couldn't be. That's the mean part. Trying to make out I'm just a *thing*. Is that fair ? Is it ? " She held out Clegg-Bray's letter and said, " Oh, Bella, read it. It's horrible. He's here. He's here."

Although she was shaken by those last words, Miss Bullen would not be drawn away from the pledge.

" Sign it, darling," she said with great tenderness. " Go on. Just sign it and start the new life."

" Change it, Bella," Lila pleaded. " Change it just a little. Make it six whiskies a day. I'll sign it if you'll let me have six whiskies a day. That's not much Three after lunch, say. And three in the evening. Be fair, Bella. Don't be cruel about it."

" My dear Lila, I'm not trying to stop you drinking," Miss Bullen said, moved by Lila's pleading. " You know you want to sign it. You know you want to start afresh. If you sign it I'll listen to everything you want to tell me, and I'll help you. But you're going to pieces and you haven't much time left."

" Haven't much time left ? " Lila breathed the words and peered into the old woman's eyes. " What do you mean, Bella ? "

" You'll go mad if you go on drinking, Lila. Mad. You're not a real alcoholic yet, but you've not long to go."

Lila, worn down by worry since the letter from Clegg-Bray had arrived, and all her nerves baying for a drink, sat down heavily on a chair at the foot of Miss Bullen's bed and looked at her with beseeching eyes.

" I'll go mad *without* it, Bella. I don't mean I can't do without it. I can. But I mean I'll go mad without it because I love it. I just love it. That's all. There's no harm in that. I don't fall about or vomit or throw things or do anything disgusting like that, do I ? Now do I ? " Miss Bullen would not reply. They held each other's eyes for a long time, until Lila said almost inaudibly, " Very well. I'll sign it. I'll sign that cursed thing." She got up in a temper. " I'll sign it for you and then you'll be happy. You'll have won. You'll have got your way and then I'll suffer and you'll pray for me. It's wicked, that's what it is. Wicked. I don't know how you can do it. I don't know how you can be so pitiless to me, who loves you and only wanted your help. That's all. Your help. I wouldn't go to anyone else. There isn't anyone else I'd go to. And then you show me this horrible piece of paper and say, ' Sign it or I'm finished with you.' " She was winning. Miss Bullen had sat down now, perplexed, doubtful, and sorry for what she had done, knowing she had been narrow and cruel and Victorian. And yet if ever she had had a sign it was at that moment of prayer when she heard Lila sobbing at the door. She looked so tragic and sorrowful that Lila, after looking hard at her, said, " I didn't mean any of that. Oh, Bella. Please read this letter. It's so urgent. Don't make me sign that paper first. I mean I've got to go through so much yet. I'll need some whisky, I mean—you know, Bella, the strain and everything. Won't you read it ? "

But Miss Bullen had rallied, had remembered that Lila not only had a powerful will about pleasure and enjoyment, she had immense patience as well, but would give in when faced with unbending determination.

" I'll get you my fountain pen, Lila," she said, getting up. " And when you've signed it we'll go into this other ghastly thing about this man. But we've got to put some moral force into you first. You've got to make this act of will and deny yourself."

She handed Lila the pen. Lila took it and looked at the pledge in a stupefied sort of way, blinked over a threat of tears, and then signed. She flung the paper and the pen to the floor and sat there like a child, with half-closed eyes, her mouth quivering.

" That's not very nice, Lila, is it ? " Miss Bullen said gently, " You'd think I was your enemy or something. Tear up the pledge. Go on. Tear it up. I don't care. If you want to tear it up then do so. Go on." She picked up the pledge and handed it to Lila. Lila took it, stared down at it, and then looked up into Miss Bullen's eyes with a look of the most fierce hatred.

" You bloody old bitch," she said, her face quivering with

the clench of her teeth. " You merciless old bitch," and then
bent her head down until it rested on her knees. She stayed
like that while Miss Bullen burst into tears.

They could hear a car coming up the drive. They both
began to get ready to face other people. Lila looked at Miss
Bullen and began to tremble as if she had a fever, all the
immense struggle and worry having drained her.

" You know I don't mean it," she said. " You know that.
I'm the bloody bitch, not you. I wish somebody would kill
me. I do. I do."

Miss Bullen, white and stiff-faced, her eyes big and cold
with this curious experience she had evoked, said, " I'll make
you a woman again if it's the last thing I do. . . . Now go and
see who's coming. And remember this pledge. I have it here,
and I know you'll stick to it. I'm leaving it without witnesses.
But if you go back on this pledge we'll have it witnessed, by
the children."

" By the children ? " Lila clutched her smooth, dark, golden
throat and thought about it, inwardly, her eyes on the old
woman yet not seeing her, struck with this sudden realisation
of the two boys who watched everything, said little, and
played with their trains.

" Some kind of shame is what has always kept us human
beings on the straight and narrow, Lila. Nothing else. You
have to commit yourself in such a way that to fall will utterly
shame you. Unless you prefer to show what you can do on
your own." Miss Bullen, still frozen by that flash of repellent,
childish hatred revealed by Lila, softened her voice as she
nagged at Lila's ready but resisting wish to live the good life.

" Bella, sit down. I'm going to read you this letter, and
then you'll be sorry for me. You'll see how cruel you've been
to me with this awful piece of paper." She waved the pledge
at the old woman. Miss Bullen sat down on her bed.

" All right, dear," she said. " You've signed that pledge,
don't forget. Now read the letter. But if it's horrible and

secret I shall leave the room. I feel quite ill already at the way you've spoken of your marriage. I beg you to spare me any of the secrets."

"Don't worry," Lila said, her voice husky again. "Don't worry. It's nothing like that. It's just terrifying. Listen to this."

She began to read the letter in a low, desperate voice, her ineradicable innocence, her wonder at the vengefulness of the world, all trembling in her hurrying voice. As she listened Miss Bullen pressed her hand to her mouth and exclaimed, "My God! Oh, my *God*!" And "Oh! Oh, God! How dreadful. How dreadful." Although she had no Irish blood her unsuspecting settler-mettle had absorbed in childhood that ancient and mindless feeling for the drama in words, the intoxication of emotion which banished dull reasoning, and which could make a bicycle ride to a village into a journey deathwards of the unsuspecting soul. It expressed itself in these heartfelt cries, the heart fearful but the mind excited and wild with the romance of terror underlying ordinary living. She knew she had this curse which would have been a great possession in an isolated community on the edge of the Western world, or in the nursery of some emigrant slum, but while she cried out and went through early environmental attitudes her cooler Protestant mind was sieving the material coming from Lila's nervous mouth.

Here was wounded human love again, but garbed in the grey rags of hatred, showing itself through the convulsed and timid words of the shaken lover, this mysterious Derek who was at last making himself fact for Miss Bullen with his pitiable letter. This was the kind of thing that frightened Miss Bullen most, this wrecking and tearing people committed in order to give and have what was not really theirs, their dangerous, untamed selves.

This, for instance: "I've been in Delhi for twenty-four hours and I'm coming to Jashimpur. I'll stay at a hotel called The Moghul, which I believe is fairly bearable. How am I going to tell you what's happened? It's so horrifying I can hardly think about it. Brenda's found out, not only found out but has had us watched since just after the end of the war. Not a word all this time, over two years. Think of it. I told you she was cold and frightful. She sprang this on me last week after breakfast. We'd had some words about the salt or the way the eggs were fried or some stupid thing, and I said, 'You're becoming rather a nag, you know.' I was so tired of everything. And then she looked very peculiar, almost cross-eyed, at me, and dropped it. I can tell you I froze sitting there. She said, 'For three years you've been hinting at a separation. And now I'm going to play ball. And I'm going to drag you backwards through the newspapers, with your Indian tart, photographs as well, the lot. I've had enough.' She walked straight out of the flat. I sat there feeling dead. You can imagine. The phone rang about ten minutes later and it was Brenda. You never heard anything like it. Quite insane, and horrible. She knows everything, every time we met, where and when, everything. I told her it was quite innocent, that I was genuinely in love with you and so on. It didn't matter. She laughed at me. 'When I'm finished with you,' she said, 'you'll know how to value a devoted wife.' Yes, a devoted wife. She even has a photograph of us taken that time we were in the boat near Maidenhead. Do you remember? My God, Lila, I'm so terribly sorry about it all, for your sake. Yet it's forced things, hasn't it? I kept my part of our bargain and didn't pester you, but now we've no alternative. If only it weren't for the frightful mess it's going to make in the papers. Me the war hero and Brenda who she is, and as she put it herself on the phone, 'I wouldn't have minded so much if it had been a white woman, but I object to being thrown aside for a wog.' Mad with jealousy. She *is* mad, you know. So I chucked everything up and took a plane to Delhi. Deal with your end of things as quickly as you can. We can fly to America as soon as possible. I ought to have known she was up to something by certain hints she dropped now and again, but one always thinks the best of people, I'm afraid. Things like, 'Do you ever eat curry these days, dear? Do you still like it really *hot*?' That was six months ago. On another occasion she said, 'You look quite Asiatic when you get cross, dear.' I never dreamed of all this happening. Lila, my dearest, I'm so terribly sorry. But we'll weather it out together. I'll buy a hotel or something. I don't care what we do as long as we can get to hell out of her way. I actually thought of murdering her, which shows how shaky one can get. 'Don't worry about your money, Derek,' she said at the end of this phone misery. 'I won't touch your money. I just want to hurt you so much that you'll learn what a dead love can do when it's dead. The rest is with the lawyers.' Then she rang off. I've no room left on this air-mail sheet. I'll be at The Moghul by midday the day after to-morrow."

Lila was in tears now, tears falling with a grey, wet sound on to the letter. Miss Bullen, paralysed with the menace of the world, sat quite still, staring at the wall, murmuring, "My *God*! The disgrace of it. My *God*! The poor Maharajah. The poor Maharajah."

"What about *me*?" Lila sobbed bitterly. "What about *me*? I'm the one that's going to suffer. I'm the cause of it. Well, half the cause of it. There was no harm in it. Just a romance, just a deep friendship, someone who understood me and never lectured me and crushed me with those awful looks Prabhu gives me. That's all. A romance, a harmless romance. And now look what happens. This fiendish bitch. That's all she is, fiendish. What'll I do, Bella? What'll I do?" She came and sat down beside Miss Bullen and held her hands. "What'll I do?"

"A war hero," Miss Bullen said absently. "A war hero. It's too terrible. It seems impossible."

"What's impossible? Because he was a war hero? They're the worst of the lot, the war heroes. Oh, I'm not saying anything against him. But they think everything belongs to them, these war heroes. Prabhu's the same. He says he got his Military Cross 'for bravery.' For bravery. No shame! Vanity. In his way, Derek's the same. He tells you about the war in that flat, sideways kind of way some men have, making out it was nothing, and then at the end you find he'd killed a hundred Germans. And he *was* brave. Oh, Bella, don't make me say rotten things about him. Tell me what to do. He's arrived in Jashimpur to-day. He's at The Moghul Hotel now. I'm so afraid he'll ring me up or do something violent. What shall I do?" Now it was all voiced she looked like a woman who had been rescued from drowning, her face all wet, her eyes staring and her hair wild and rumpled. Miss Bullen embraced her and rocked her, in a kind of delirious maternal tenderness, saying, "I'll have to think, dear. I'll have to think. But no more drinking from now on. That's final. If there's been no harm in this thing, couldn't you confess it to your husband? He's such an understanding person. He'd forgive you, surely. Would he forgive you?"

"He'd kill me. He's insane with jealousy. You wouldn't know it, but he is. Infantile. I read a psychology book about people like Prabhu. They're not integrated. They're infantile. He'd kill me." She began to declaim and to shout. "All this is the fault of my upbringing. Christianity. It's not suited to Indians like me. It destroyed me. It's mixed me up. I don't know what I am or what I'm doing. No wonder Prabhu hates me and despises me. What am I anyway but a mess? A twisted mess. That's all Christianity did. Guilt and needing a hundred years to grow up after it, after all the narrowness and horrible suspicion about sin and everything you do and think——"

"That'll do," Miss Bullen said frigidly. "That'll do for now, Lila dear. We must think, not talk nonsense."

Lila did not argue. She put her face in her hands and said thickly that she wished she were dead, had never been born, and had never even heard the word " men." Men were the curse of this world, even the nice ones.

" A man is what a woman lets him be, and wants him to be, Lila," Miss Bullen said. " That's what's the matter with this world to-day. The women are treated like dirt and it's their own fault. Men are just brutes, poor creatures, if they're not kept in their place. And it's the women who must do it. You mustn't see this man. Or even write or telephone to him. You must have nothing to do with him."

" He's such a dear person," Lila said pitifully. " And anyway that's not the point. The point is that his wife's going to disgrace us both. I'll kill myself. I'll kill myself."

Miss Bullen took her arm and shook it angrily. " Stop talking nonsense," she snapped at her. " You really must control yourself, Lila. You've got to get out of this, that's all."

They could hear a car on the drive. It stopped. They heard Prabhu's voice, loud and uninhibited, shouting that he was finished with placating now, finished with all that idiotic pandering to Hassan. From now on there would be a change. They could hear Hari Lal and Prem trying to console him.

" They've smashed him," Lila said, staring through her wet eyes at the letter. She folded it up and put it back in her bodice. " They've voted against him. I know by his voice. That's his *thwarted* voice. And I'm sorry for him. I *am* sorry for him. Isn't it strange ? I wanted him to get a good taking down and now he's got it I feel I could cry. That shows you the state I'm in. Where's it all going to end ? "

" Go and do yourself up quickly. I'll go out and keep things going until you appear."

Impulsively, with a little cry forced from her by the violence with which she seized Miss Bullen, Lila embraced the old woman, saying, " You're so lucky being you. Free. Free. How I wish I could be you. You darling."

" That'll do, Lila. Hurry off and get ready. Don't show you've been crying. I'll try and think of something to do about this business. Give me your pledge now. From now on you've got to fight the drink." Miss Bullen's eyes had brightened with hope for Lila.

" Oh, Bella," Lila moaned. " Bella. Let me tear it up. I'll cut down my drinking. I promise. But don't make me stick to this pledge. I can't. I'm too weak. I'm too hopeless."

" You've signed it, dear. Now give it to me. And from now on no more drinking. You've pledged yourself."

Dejectedly Lila handed the pledge to Miss Bullen. Seemingly without pity for her Miss Bullen took it and folded it up.

" Oh, Bella, how hard you can be." Lila looked as if she wanted to die.

" If you knew some of the battles I've had to fight, Lila," the old woman said, eyeing her with a suddenly mocking expression, " you wouldn't say that. You know there's only one way, total abstinence. Now I'm going out to hold the fort for you. Do yourself up and then come and console the Maharajah. He sounds very upset."

" You think he's wonderful. Why is it that everyone thinks a woman's husband is wonderful except the wife ? Everyone thinks Prabhu's marvellous. And all he is is pitiful. Pitiful."

It was true and Miss Bullen stared at Lila as she realised it was true. There *was* something pitiful about the Maharajah, though perhaps tragi-comical was a better description.

" All right, Lila," she said. " Shall I order some tea for them ? "

" Tea ? " said Lila sardonically. " They won't want tea to-night." She shook suddenly like a malaria patient, crying, " Oh, Bella, I want a whisky."

Miss Bullen took a couple of steps forward and put her arms round Lila and kissed her warm, tender cheek.

" You think I'm hard, don't you, Lila," she said, knowing she was hard, knowing how much harder she could be.

" I think you're as hard as steel, Bella. Hard as steel." It was not funny but they laughed, Lila pathetically, with pleading eyes. " Why am I letting her dominate me ? " she was whimpering to herself. " Why ? "

Chapter Twenty-Two

Prabhu seemed finished. He looked haunted, completely dispirited. He was sitting hunched up in an arm-chair looking cold and ill when Miss Bullen went brightly into the big living-room with a false little welcoming smile on her prim mouth. Hari Lal was pouring drinks and Prem was putting twelve records on the pick-up, Prabhu almost snarling at him, saying not to forget that he wanted to hear no corny New Orleans stuff. It would be the last straw.

"Hallo, Miss Bullen," he said. He got up and smiled wearily at her. "Where's Lila? Drunk again on one of the verandas?" He swung his dark glasses in his hand. His eyes were without light.

"No, Maharaj Sahib," she said coolly. "She's coming now."

"You know that protégé of yours, Miss Bullen," he said. "You know what he did to-night in the way of democracy? He threatened to cut his throat if the other members voted for me. He saw they were going to vote for me and he said he'd kill himself. Do you call that a Christian, democratic act?" He had been drinking. He had lost his confident and nervously happy manner, that manner which had always seemed set on the next move, the next moment.

"Hassan?" she said, aghast. "Said he'd cut his throat?"

"Yes. Hassan." He slumped down in his chair again and lost all further interest in her. The jazz suddenly blasted against the walls from the pick-up. Prem clicked his fingers, swayed his head, and then came to Miss Bullen.

"Yes," he said. "It was a ghastly business." He began to describe to her what had happened two hours before in Doctor Kholi's house, where the meeting had been held.

Trying to hear what Prem was telling her against the noise of the jazz filling the room, Miss Bullen clutched his arm and he began to stroke her hand.

"*Mataji*," he said softly, "three of your converts have arrived in the town from Kangla. They're on their way to ask you to go back to your mission. The people want you back."

"Three converts?" she exclaimed. "From Kangla? But what's that got to do with Hassan and the Maharajah?"

"Nothing," he said. "I just thought you'd like to know. I have my own spy organisation in the town. I was told to-night that these three chaps from Kangla arrived at about six. They're staying out near The Poet's Bridge. Aren't you happy? Three converts." His delight for her in this news touched her. He was drunk.

"How extraordinary," she said. "They want me to go back to Kangla. Are you sure?"

"It's pukka gen," he said. "I have a chap with his ear down to the ground there. Have to, you know. The moment the balloon goes up and Prabhu sees the light, I have it all arranged to change every cent he possesses into precious stones and gold. I've read every book ever written about refugeeing. And to-night's little *tamasha* is the red light as far as I can see. Look at Prabhu sitting over there. It's really knocked him for six. You can see it, can't you? Did you know that Hassan was such a maniac?"

"What actually happened? Did the Maharajah quarrel with Hassan?"

Hari Lal brought her a tomato juice and handed a large whisky to Prem. He stayed with them and they told her what had happened at the meeting in Kholi's house. Hari Lal's eyes were hurt and bewildered as he described the meeting.

Hassan had opened the meeting with a lecture about the past, and about the history of the Party, and about how he had led them, not forgetting to mention the invaluable backing of Doctor Kholi. The Party had come through thick and thin, and now was more or less in control of the State. The Maharajah, anxious to cling to power, now imagined he was going to join the Party with the help of turncoats like Hari Lal " and some others." That would be easily settled by a crushing and overall vote against the whole nonsensical behaviour of the Maharajah. Hari Lal then spoke and stirred up feeling for the Maharajah's case, and others spoke their minds after him, pressing Hassan to be reasonable and allow the Maharajah to become a member. He was one of themselves, a progressive, anxious only for the welfare of the people under new and reformed conditions. The people were for the Maharajah and were impressed by his sincerity and his genuine feeling for their future. Even Nabha had spoken up and said it was best not to split the country at a time like this. The people did not want the Maharajah to abdicate. Therefore the Party should work with him for one united Jashimpur. After that Hassan had worked himself up into a cold and sardonic rage. He told them that they would vote against the Maharajah. They *must* vote against him. He then threatened to cut his throat within the hour if they voted for the Maharajah's acceptance as a member of the Party. Before that fantastic threat most of the members had yielded to Hassan. Well over half of the Party's officials present at the meeting had been willing to accept the Maharajah's membership, and some had even attacked Hassan's sentiments. They had looked to Hari Lal and he had fought well for Prabhu.

" I'll kill myself within an hour if the Maharajah is allowed to enter the Party," Hassan told them in a quiet, matter-of-fact way when the atmosphere had been talked into strain and hostility. He had stood up and made himself clear. " For me life would not be worth living if I were to lose in this matter," he told them all as they sat round the long table in the living-room of Doctor Kholi's house. " I cannot afford such humiliation, or to lead a Party which wants to hand itself over to the enemy. Yes, the enemy." He had talked for a long time about " the enemy." The enemy never showed himself with his teeth bared or with his knife in his hand. No, the enemy had a smile and a way of aping what he was not, pretending to be a friend of the people. " I'll kill myself within the hour unless you vote him down."

In the next room Prabhu had sat smoking with Prem, Hari Lal taking his part in the heated meeting in the living-room. Prabhu could hear the voices through the closed door, the voices sometimes raised in question, in disbelief, in anger, and he could hear Hassan's voice raised above the others. He knew they were fighting over him and he knew when he heard Hassan ranting that he would lose. But he was staggered to find he had lost by a suicide threat from Hassan.

Hari Lal had come into the room, looking drunk, or drugged, his eyes staring, murmuring, " It's incredible. It's frightful. What are we to do with such a man ? And he *meant* it." He had looked at Prabhu, his eyes glazed with a sort of exhaustion of his belief, his trust in Hassan's good sense. " Yes, Maharaj Sahib," he said in a low voice, " he threatened to cut his throat. And the others collapsed and voted you down."

Prabhu had turned pale and his face thinned before Hari Lal's eyes. He appeared to lose weight, to become ravaged. Like many healthy introverted-extroverts his spirit all but strangled his body in a time of nervous crisis.

" Cut his throat ? " he whispered. " You mean he hates me that much ? Is he mad ? " Then he shouted, " Is he mad ? "

" No. Not mad," Hassan had shouted back from the doorway of the living-room where he had just appeared. Prabhu looked at him. There was a cloud of drifting cigarette smoke behind Hassan, and Prabhu could see the other members standing furtively, in shame, behind Hassan, not wanting to come out into Prabhu's presence.

Prem spoke then. "I always suspected you were mad," he said to Hassan. "I believe you *would* cut your throat over a thing like this. I believe it." Prem was appalled, contemptuous. Hassan was leaning against the door frame, at ease and relaxed in his triumph. He was wearing a grey, double-breasted flannel suit with a snowy white shirt and blue tie. His short, black beard was neatly trimmed. He looked like some intelligent and handsome lawyer or businessman to be met in Cairo or Teheran or Delhi.

"I'm glad you believe that," Hassan said. "I could have got on with *you* as Maharajah, but not with this one here. You'd have abdicated reasonably and got on with your drinking. But this one has no shame. Your brother is the new kind of old rich, willing to be trampled on as long as he's still saluted." He looked at Prabhu. "Well, what'll you do now, Maharaj Sahib? It's the end of the road, as they say."

Out of control, Prabhu had begun to shout his contempt, his disgust, his amazement that such cowardice and hatred could live in one man. "You narrow peasant," he cried. "From now on there'll be a change. I've had enough. As for the rest of them, they're tired of you too, but they hadn't the guts to take you up on your threat. Just as you haven't the guts to cut your throat." Hassan smoked a cigarette and leaned against the doorpost while Prabhu made an exhibition of himself. Hassan watched him, unmoved.

Hari Lal had let Prem do most of the talking to Miss Bullen, but now, when it came to the part where Hassan had actually taken a razor out of his pocket and showed it to Prabhu, he had to interrupt. The shock of that scene affected him visibly all over again. As Miss Bullen looked into his grieving eyes she understood how affected he was by Hassan's

R

strangely cool attitude to violence. Hari Lal looked as if he were staring at that razor now as he described the scene.

"He took this old-fashioned razor so casually out of his inside pocket and held it up for Prabhu to see," he said. "Then he flicked it open. We were all standing there dumb. I thought he was going to kill himself in front of us. He said, 'There you are, Maharaj Sahib, there's the razor. You see the width of the blade. It's nothing much, not even an inch, yet that's all that stands between you and becoming the boss; that's all that separates you from membership and from eventual leadership, and from the popularity you love so much. Because the people like you. They'd sooner have you than progress. That's a fact. You have glamour, and you're a change from your father and your ancestors. I can't deny it. So there's the razor. I can assure you I'd cut my throat with it to-night rather than see this pack of spineless jerks lying down for you to walk over to the top. I'm the top, not because I like it but because this time we're going to have a revolution, a real one, peaceful and absolute. Now what do you think about that?'"

"My God," said Miss Bullen. "He must be mad. He must be."

"He's not," said Hari Lal. "He's far from it. It's had a terrible effect on the Maharajah. We went to the club to try and cheer him up. It's hopeless. He's in a terrible state."

The jazz beat up against the walls. It was blues now, slow, licking, cold flames of it among the double bass and the trombones, a sick trumpet squealing through a mute, and a drugged, ecstatic negro gabbling hoarsely about how he had to get right out of town. The deadly artificial splendour of its sorrow comforted Prabhu hunched up in his chair. He had drunk two thick whiskies since he had sat down and was settling into his pain, that pain of defeat. All he had to do was start arresting everybody, Hassan, all the Party chiefs, and have done with the game. But he was not going to do it, and he was not sure why. He felt a nausea, a sickness of the world, but most of all he felt astonishment at Hassan, knowing that Hassan would kill himself for his idea if necessary. There was nothing Prabhu would kill himself for, as he had told Prem and Hari Lal angrily, drunkenly at the club an hour ago—nothing.

"And when you find that out from someone like Hassan you've got to think again," he had told them both.

"Think again about what?" Prem had asked, interested.

"How the hell do I know?" Prabhu had shouted in a rage. "It just matters, that's all. Being able to stand there with a razor and mean a thing like that. I've had it. I'm finished. I don't know what to do."

"Arrest Hassan," Prem said.

"Don't be stupid." And they let Prabhu say what he liked after that. He had talked himself out and now he was empty in the chair, waiting for nothing to turn up.

Miss Bullen and the two men watched him covertly as they talked. He was oblivious to them. The almost boyish despair he wore, not quite sullen, far from fierce, was all the more poignant for Miss Bullen, for she saw more clearly now how pointless and luxurious had been his dream of being the impossible thing, a revolutionary Maharajah. There was no need for a revolutionary Maharajah, only for a revolution.

And at about midnight, while the jazz pounded on, and while Lila was arguing quietly and hysterically with Miss Bullen about the need for just one small whisky, the revolution broke out.

Chapter Twenty-Three

Miss Bullen's three false converts whom she had christened Mishak, Shadrach and Abednego, arrived at The Bridge of the Whipped Poet just as it was growing dark. The bridge spanned the wide river and across it nearly a hundred years ago a famous satirical poet had been whipped by the Maharajah's soldiers. He had written a poem of thanks to the ruler for all the benefits and comforts he had bestowed on the people during his reign, praising the Maharajah for every virtue which he did not possess. In the shabby restaurant near the bridge story-tellers would still recite the poem for coffee and tobacco.

Mishak, Shadrach and Abednego got off the trade truck with their bundles and went into the restaurant. It was crowded with ragged men who were all arguing as usual, but very heatedly to-night, for none could agree who had the finer brain, the Maharajah or Hassan. Because there was shame over the failure to rescue Hassan from the gaol he was being attacked and the Maharajah was being praised.

The three men from Kangla sat quietly in a corner and asked for a *hukkah* and a samovar of the cheapest tea. Mishak, the leader of the three, and the one whose counsel the others had followed in coming to Jashimpur City, was a nervous, furtive young man, the son of a scavenger reputed for his dirt and sloth. Mishak was clean and as neurotic as an orthodox Brahmin about dirt and smells, and Miss Bullen had left her mark on him for ever. Lost without her after her departure from Kangla, the three had agreed to come to her and declare they were true Christians. They were willing to bear the terrible stigma of shame which this could bring upon them publicly, but they had agreed that they would bear witness openly. In fact Mishak was willing to die as a martyr. Living with the old woman had infected them with her stern virtue and her tender emanation of Christ's gentleness. Loneliness without her had been too much, and it was Mishak who had had the courage to give the other two courage in speaking out what was in their minds ; that they were truly Christians. The shame brought upon them by the declaration of the elders to Miss Bullen, when they had explained the role of the three false Christians, had made Mishak ill, Shadrach tearful, and Abednego sleepless. Finally all three had gone to the elders with Mishak as their spokesman. They confessed that they had been false in pretending to be false Christians.

It had been a very solemn and painful meeting, the old men listening with stern faces and exchanging secret looks with one another. They too longed to have the old woman back. She was theirs and they wanted to have her last years and then bury her at Kangla and possess her for ever. That she had gone from them was spoken of now as a thing so shameful that everyone's face was blackened, and those with beards said they had been made beardless by it and disgraced.

"Very well," the elders had said when they had weighed the grave announcement of the three Christians. "We will agree on one condition. You will go and bring her back to us here. And if you fail then never return to us. We cannot have you here as Christians unless the old woman is with us too." All knew that it was impossible to speak out and declare what all knew, that there were one or two more who would have declared for Christianity, but they lacked the courage and therefore, God be praised, society was not going to be upset. It was agreed, silently, among the elders, that Mishak, Shadrach and Abednego should continue to be regarded as false Christians, even should they announce their new faith from the tops of the mountains, for face must be saved. The people's love for the old woman, though, was genuine, and Mishak promised that they would bring her back with them.

The mission buildings and the gardens had been swept and tended daily as though Miss Bullen had never departed. The three Christians promised to give the old woman a full report of the villagers' stewardship and of the welcome awaiting her on her return.

" Tell her that we know we are vile and weak," the eldest elder said. "But we will try and improve if she returns to us. And tell her we are sick and need her help. Break her heart. Make her weep. Make her ashamed of betraying her trust to us, and of denying the mission to us which her Christ put upon her. Leave no word unspoken which will distress her. You can even tell her that we are spoken of sneeringly now as the people who drove our benefactor away."

" No," another elder said. " Don't tell her that. She will think it is only shame which makes us send for her, whereas it is friendship and affection." Agreement on all points was reached and the three departed.

While they were waiting for the *hukkah* and the samovar in the restaurant by The Bridge of the Whipped Poet, Mishak's face had assumed the worried, apprehensive look that always came when he was disturbed. The other two were watching him and waiting for him to say what he would say when he was ready. Mishak was a genuine mystic and suffered for it. He had seen a giant figure in the sky one day near the mission and had fainted. On another occasion he had told people where to go and find an old man who had died in the snow of exhaustion up in the mountains. These things caused him anxiety and he often wondered if God had some frightening plan for him. Obviously yes, for here he was with two companions, far from home, and following his nerves which were tied painfully to Miss Bullen and her friend, God, whom she had so often said was a poor man called Jesus. That He should be Issa (the false prophet !), the Jesus of minor achievement as the *Mullahs* agreed, had never been shocking to Mishak, and he had worried at first because it was not shocking to him. Now, though, there could be no doubt that Jesus had something frightening in store for him, and he did not know what it was. He was feeling it while his two companions watched his face in tense silence.

" What is it, Mishak ? " Abednego asked, always the most impatient one of the three. He felt he had waited long enough. Mishak was worried and it was time to know about what.

" We were watched getting off the trade truck," Mishak said in a low voice. " And we were watched coming in here. I feel something is going to happen here. I can't decide if we should get up and run away from here, or wait and see what's going to happen. My throat is drying up and I feel afraid." The drying throat was always a sign.

" Who watched us ? What do you mean ? " Shadrach asked. Shadrach was a big, heavy, simple man who was always unhappy if someone was not ordering him about and giving him tasks. Abednego was thin and tall and had a short, black beard. He was addicted to quarrelling and lying and gambling and he was fond of being lectured about these failings by Mishak.

" A soldier came out of the shadow of a building and watched us when we got off the truck," Mishak said. " It may not be anything, and yet it must be. My throat is drying up and I feel afraid." And as he spoke three soldiers with rifles came into the restaurant and stood looking about them. Silence came down on the noise of the excited talk at the long tables and the eyes all turned to look at the soldiers with the still, dark, ox-like look authority always received.

Long after that night the incident at the restaurant by The Bridge of the Whipped Poet became known as another case of *Shaitan ki ungli*, of how small things make noises like thunder, of how the Devil uses his finger.

The classic case in which the Devil had used his finger was on an occasion three centuries before. One day the Devil was strolling with a friend in the town and they were discussing cause and effect. The Devil had been very patient in trying to explain the machinery of the business to his friend, but the friend was dull and the Devil sighed and said he would give an example.

They happened to be walking along through the crowded bazaar of the big, prosperous town, and when the Devil decided to show the working of cause and effect they were beside the stalls of a *halwai* whose cauldrons of simmering toffee, and tables laden with sweets for sale, attracted many customers. A few soldiers of the Emperor were standing nearby and one of them had a fine dog on a leash. The Devil dipped his finger into one of the cauldrons of toffee and drew a sticky line with it along the dog's back. Thousands of flies swarmed down on to the dog.

" And now let us stand back and watch the fun," the Devil said.

The dog went mad with the flies and broke off his leash and charged into the *halwai's* stall, upsetting trays of sweets and scattering people right and left. People fell against tables and knocked them over. Cauldrons were upset. The *halwai* screamed and a turmoil began. The *halwai*, incensed by the damage which was increasing in the pandemonium, picked up an iron bar and killed the dog with it. The soldiers drew their swords and killed the *halwai*. The people attacked the soldiers. More soldiers came. They fought with the growing crowds. The stoves were knocked over and the bazaar went afire. The whole city was soon engulfed in the flames. When the place was a heap of smoking ruins the Devil turned to his friend and said, " You see what I mean ? "

That was " The Devil's Finger."

While Shadrach, Mishak and Abednego were drinking their tea and passing the *hukkah* from hand to hand, a tall, thin mountaineer in rough homespun came in, his yellow turban glowing in the lamplight. He had a face like one of the wild mountain tribesmen, haggardly handsome, and he walked with long strides up to the counter and asked for a bundle of *biris*. When they were given to him he took one from the bundle, lit it, inhaled deeply and then blew the smoke straight up into the air. He smiled with his big, white teeth on the watching company, for mountain men were always watched (one never knew what they might do next). He had been without a smoke all day and now he relaxed as he puffed at the green, crackling *biri*, chewing it in his teeth like a cigar.

He threw a silver rupee on to the counter and said, " Now that that man's writ no longer runs whose head shall we see on coins in future ? A moneylender ? Or a landlord ? Or our own Maharajah ? Or this upstart called Hassan that we hear about ? Whose head shall it be on the coins ? "

" Which man's writ no longer runs ? " the hotel owner asked testily. He disliked mountain people. They sat on the floor when there were chairs, licked their plates, scowled about the bread, and were liable to draw their long knives if upset.

" This king fellow on the coin, man," the mountain man said. " His writ's finished here in India. Now who next ? What's this about this Maharajah speaking in public ? Is he trying to get on to the coins ? "

Mishak stood up and began to declaim, holding out his hand and making it quiver as he gave out the message about that which was due to Cæsar and that which was due to God. Then he told of the money-changers and how Christ whipped them out of the temple. These were his two favourite visions of Christ, who would have cleansed Jashimpur in one day with his blazing person.

" Do you understand ? " Mishak cried to the staring crowd.
" Do you understand ? "

People began to shout angrily that no, they didn't understand, and who was this villager, this stranger who got up
and preached without being asked, and about a false prophet
into the bargain ? Some of the men were angry and had
taken steps forward. Others had clenched their fists. The
mountain man went over to Mishak, gripped him with his
hands and then shook him so hard that Mishak's teeth knocked
together several times.

" You devil," the mountain man shouted into his face,
amazed by Mishak's brief and puzzling performance. " You
devil. What's that got to do with the coin ? And what right
have you, you mongrel, to teach foreign religions here when
a man comes in to smoke a *biri* and drink some tea ? What
right have you ? "

Just then a patrol of soldiers under a lieutenant came into
the room. One of the soldiers pointed to the three converts and
said, " Those are the men, sir. They jumped off the truck
before it got to the check-point. They're spies."

The crowd quarrelling round the mountain man and the
three strangers were too excited to notice the soldiers. They
were trying to drag the mountain man off Mishak. Mishak
had gripped the big man's lean throat and was trying to push
him away. Shadrach and Abednego appealed for fair play,
begged everyone to understand that they were good men
who had just arrived from Kangla, and not to hurt their
friend. Mishak was calling the mountain man a savage brute
born of unknown parents and then his adversary drew a
knife and raised it while about ten men piled on to him and
tried to drag him down. The more they pulled on him the
more he tried to stab Mishak. One of the soldiers, after calling
for peace several times, let off his rifle and shot down one of
the ragged men. The noise of the shot in the room was
deafening. The officer screamed for order and sought to

push aside the frightened soldier who had shot the innocent man. Perhaps it was the sight of blood, and the pathetic picture of the pallid face contorting as the man tried to die, but all the dark eyes turned on to the soldiers. The mountain man cried, " Enough of this now," and sprang at the soldiers with his knife. Like a wave, the roaring, tramping crowd followed him and fell upon the nearest soldiers. They took their rifles and clubbed three of the soldiers down. The other three soldiers, under the orders of the white-faced young officer, opened fire wildly and the room turned into a shambles of struggling bodies. The junior officer withdrew but the crowd followed him, three of them with rifles, and several fell as the frightened soldiers fired and ran, across the dark bridge and along the road into the town. The mob grew. It seized one of the soldiers who had emptied his rifle and hanged him up on a tree by the road, and while this was done the hundreds of people were baying and screaming. Some men carried the bodies of those shot down by the soldiers and they half ran into the town, sobbing, some shouting, " Witness this. Witness this tyranny of the soldiers. Vengeance. Vengeance." In a few minutes buildings were set alight near the barracks and like a dark rumbling wave the mob poured into the gateway and swept over a line of sleepy soldiers with unloaded rifles. The word had got around now that a prophet in the city had announced that the money-changers were all to be killed before morning because they were getting what rightfully belonged to the king, the Maharajah.

" What's that again ? " some would cry impatiently when this news was gabbled at them. " The moneylenders ? "

" I've told you, you fool," others would yell. " The thing now is to finish with everything, for ever. That's the order now. An end to everything. You see our dead ? An end to everything, for ever."

Other men gave it out that a Christian fanatic from up-country had arrived and said that Christ was come back into Jashimpur. Where? What did it matter now? Look at these dead.

Others told others that the moneylenders were to be put into the Hindu temple and tried publicly and then whipped out of it. Look at these dead.

The barracks was set on fire and the armoury looted. Soldiers upstairs opened fire on the mob, which was a mistake, for it simply flooded up the stairs and killed everybody it could find in uniform and then threw the bodies down into the courtyard. " An end to everything," they screamed. " An end to all uniforms. Now to the tax office. Burn it to the ground."

Inspired by this call, a call to the wrung blood and the never-ending sense of hopeless struggle and ruin, the mob went out of its mind and surged down into the *maidan* where the government buildings stood. The police took one look and disappeared as the yelling wave reached the buildings.

People arrived with a battering-ram, a whole stripped tree taken from the log-jam in the river by the timber-yards. Others came with axes, hammers, clubs. One man had a saw and began to saw some wooden railings down without any particular reason, but shouting again and again, " What about my pension as a second grade *chaprassi* for fifteen years? What about it, eh? " His teeth were bared. His friends were tramping their feet beside him in rhythm to his chanted words about his pension.

The noise of the battering-ram was drowned by the crash of the enormous doors. In a few minutes it was snowing documents from the upper windows. Whole filing systems came falling through the air and burst on the ground. Hills of paper mounted as the laughing and screaming mob dodged about in the rain of files. They set fire to the papers and soon the *maidan* was covered with blazing fires, the people dancing round them and announcing an end to everything at last. No leader arose. None was needed. The damped-down rage of generations, smouldering in controlled sullenness during work and dreaming sleep, had exploded.

Brigadier Kapra Singh arrived during the burning of the files. He was in a jeep, driving himself, dressed like Field Marshal Montgomery: a black beret with two badges, a long khaki pullover and yellow corduroy trousers. The bright blue, silk scarf round his neck was his own idea, and it was specked with small designs of his personal coat-of-arms—two curved swords surmounted by a rearing black horse, with the motto, in Persian, *Strike for Justice*. For years he had smarted because of a whispered version of the motto put about by Doctor Kholi, *Strike for Justice and Higher Wages*, for it was well known that the brigadier could not live on his pay and his family had lost their lands with a pack of cards two generations ago in the good old days. The brigadier had sixteen children, and another one on the way. He had sent the family to Delhi as soon as the Maharajah's fantasy about Hassan revealed itself in the former's visit to Hassan in gaol.

Behind the brigadier's jeep came three truckloads of his best troops. Of all nights he had had to pick this one to practise night manœuvres, and on receipt of the news about the riot had driven non-stop for twenty miles from the manœuvre area. He was soaked to his scalp in military history and military traditions but, owing to the determined opposition of Prabhu's father, had never seen action. He had applied continually during the war to be allowed to serve with a regiment in the Indian Army, but the old Maharajah had liked him too much to allow it. The grief of this lack of the soldier's absolute necessity, experience in seeing large numbers of trained people massed and killed, had told on his character. Sometimes a bitter note came into his talk about war and generals. One of his favourite anecdotes for telling to friends nowadays was, " First I put in my vocal application. Then I threw in my three requests. I followed up with a dozen more applications, thrown piecemeal into the show. Then I struck with my threat of resignation. I followed this with a pincer movement by getting my friends to recommend me from headquarters, Indian Army, in Delhi. But the enemy broke off the action and left me in possession of the field, and with no medals." It was not funny at all, and none of his friends laughed. They knew he was courageous and, more important, had striven hard to keep his loyalty to the old Maharajah despite everything. Of late, though, he had been heard to voice quiet criticism of the whole business of princes and tradition. The atom-age had put an end to all that stuff. It was only a question of time before world government was evolved and he was thinking of applying for a job with the United Nations. He was an expert, self-trained, in the pedigrees and inter-marriages of all the defunct royal houses throughout the world. At present he was working on a history of the Indian embassies to ancient Rome, a subject about which little had been written.

He was a spare, querulous, vital, swift-moving little man with a toothbrush moustache, an unearned-income-group British accent, and a driving personality which had never quite spent itself in the pursuit of military knowledge.

Beside him in the jeep was Colonel Arif, a tall, silent man with mocking eyes. He had become silent because he had fought in Italy and Burma with an Indian regiment and could never discuss it with his jealous chief. He had sympathy with the brigadier's position and genuinely liked him. It was hard to like him but Arif was a patient and good man. His row of medal ribbons made him ashamed whenever the brigadier's eyes sulkily settled on them. He hid them with his arm whenever the brigadier was discussing military history with him over a drink in the officers' mess or the Jashimpur Club. Arif took one look at the mob cavorting around the mounds of burning documents and said, " Well, sir, do you want to try the tear gas or go straight in with the troops? They've killed, according to reports, fifteen soldiers."

" Tear gas," the brigadier said as the jeep came to a stop about fifty yards from the scenes in the *maidan*. " I've never seen the stuff used. But then, of course, I've seen nothing at all, have I? Just training and so on. Go on then, get stuck in with the tear gas. Arrest any smart-aleck-looking characters as well. Very clever of Hassan's Suicide Commandos to keep out of things, I must say." The brigadier and his officers always referred to Hassan's Party as " Hassan's Suicide Commandos."

Arif, whose father had been born a slave-peasant, knew how much the brigadier hated the idea of democracy, or as he called it, that pooling of humanity's superstitions about money.

The tear gas was no good. The grenades would not go off. They lay among the crowds and sputtered and fizzed themselves into silence. But the mob grew quiet and gathered in a large, menacing half-circle about the jeep and trucks, standing about fifty yards from them. The troops had deployed under their junior officers and were waiting at the kneeling-load position. Good-humouredly, the crowd cheered the last grenade which fizzed out about twenty feet away from them. What was chilling for Brigadier Kapra Singh about that cheering and the laughter which followed it was the lack of fear and respect it showed. There was a humorous and waggish calling of names and suggestions going on, some of of the people calling out, " What about you, Brigadier Sahib? Are you in the hands of the moneylenders yourself yet? We're trying to help you." But immediately after these sallies men carrying dead people came out of the ranks and placed the bodies on the ground. While they did this the silence was eerie. They then withdrew again, sinking into the huge quiet animal of the crowd. There were ten bodies lying there, some old men, others young, nearly all poor and ragged-looking.

"Now shoot the lot of us," somebody screeched in the crowd. "Go on. Shoot the lot of us." Somebody wailed. The wail was taken up. It became terrible, like bitter grief done to the rhythm of the handclapping which began, slow, steady beating together of hard hands. The chanting grew louder as the whole mob began to lament for the dead, and sometimes one hysterical voice would cry, "Life is four annas to the rupee." It was well known that life had once been fourteen annas to the rupee, but that was generations ago, out of human memory. And even so, life had never been sixteen annas to the rupee, the full total, the complete rupee. That would be in heaven. Yet four annas to the rupee was too low, and was not to be borne any longer. The front rank of men picked up their dead and then the wall of people slowly moved forward, chanting. The brigadier, fascinated into fear and respect, backed his jeep, calling to Colonel Arif to climb aboard. The troops withdrew before the crowd. They withdrew as far as the river bank and stood there in silence while the thousands of people filed past and beat their breasts and cried to God to have a look at this down here and to remember that it was time for a change of government.

"Well, that's that," Arif said in a low voice. "No use shooting, sir."

"No," Kapra Singh said tensely, his eyes watching the disappearing mob. "But you should have arrested some of them. You know that, don't you?"

"Do you want me to go and arrest some now, sir?" Arif pretended to be about to spring out of the jeep and start off with the soldiers. He knew his man, and his people. He knew as well as the brigadier that the mob had silently agreed with them both that the riot was over.

"No. No," the brigadier said harshly. "It's too late now. If we arrested anybody now they'd burn the city. No, they've had enough. And so have I. We'll put patrols all over the town. If anything starts again then shoot to kill." But he could not feel his old self again. That macabre scene with the dead bodies had banished his ardour for the scene he had planned—a line of troops advancing with fixed bayonets, he at their head, and driving the mob like frightened cattle before him. He knew that he should have done that, and he knew, too, that he could not have done it. Pity and fury were fighting desperately for his heart. He settled instead for sullen determination and he began to give his orders to Arif and told him he would be at the palace if needed. When he had finished his orders he drove at full speed for the palace. It was nearly two o'clock in the morning, and he was on his way to report, and to hand in his resignation.

It took Colonel Arif only half an hour to discover that Hassan's militia had occupied the town, and that all telephone communication to and from the palace was cut, and that Hassan and the Party had complete control of the situation. He put up his hands in bored, cold resignation when nervous militia pointed dangerously trembling rifles at him and demanded his surrender. He was taken to have tea with Hassan on the top floor of Doctor Kholi's house.

The troops laid down their arms and listened in a calm and soldierly manner while Nabha, dressed up as a colonel, told them from the top of a commandeered bus that as from to-morrow their pay was going up ten rupees a month and that rations were to be improved.

Chapter Twenty-Four

While Prabhu sat there in the big comfortable arm-chair, hunched up in his stillness, that grey, misty stillness which acceptance of defeat can bring so mysteriously, he let anything that appeared out of the unfillable file of memory have its performance before his inner eyes. He did not move while the jazz shook and throbbed all about the small, frail, beleaguered castle of his skull. He let everything appear in front of his inner eyes and watched it dispassionately until it was done, seeing it for what it might be as well as for what it was, or what he had thought it to be, or what it might only appear to be.

" *Am* I right in thinking that all this matters, this operetta in Jashimpur with myself as the factotum in a ruler's mask ? Why am I here in Jashimpur ? Did I truly want to come ? Is it my blood ? My little meal of political stew still undigested in my brain's belly ? My need to *get outside* of Lila and *do* something ? Who's the maddest one ? Me or Lila ? Or Hassan ? "

He thought he understood now that the trouble between Lila and himself was that he would not accept ordinariness, because he was not ordinary. Eight till twelve in the office or factory, then a break for lunch, and then on till six o'clock —that was the life for those who had yearned for that life since the Stone Age. They loved the terrible feel of the steady and comfortable march of doom in their safety. But for people like himself who ran along the precipices of the unsafe and the adventurous there was the thrill of being the self, of not being chained and of not bowing to that powerful clock of comfort in accepted order. Lila had made him unhappy. She had never understood that he was not to be understood. What was left to you once you were understood? Yourself without your fantasy.

He shivered when he saw the scenes again in which he and Lila had participated in one of those painful rows about things that were agreed to matter, things which did not matter and were all used outside the desert as distraction, as facts to be solved. "Oh, the mind, the bloody mind," he thought desperately. "This mind business, and then this set of acts we go through in obedience to this mind, and generally to no purpose."

He stared in surprise when Lila knelt down at his knee and looked into him with those enormous stricken eyes and said, "There's something I must say to you, Prabhuji, darling." She was trembling for a drink, but he had no pity for her.

"Prabhuji, darling!" That sounded like a long time ago.

"What do you want to say?" he said gloomily, almost bitterly.

"That I love you, and that I'm sorry for you, and that I wish everything had happened the way you wanted it to happen."

"Are you slipping?" he asked her. "Are you going out of your mind? Do you mean that?" Seeing a wound appear in her gaze he was sorry and he patted her hand and said, "Darling, you can be terribly surprising sometimes, can't you? I mean can't you?"

He had never been able to cherish a bitterness, or nourish a coolness, and now she saw that look in his face, that look of thin, sharp urgency as he said, "I suppose we'd better get off to bed. Eh?" That was not the cure to-night for her, she knew, and had never been the cure for him. She had resolved at last to open the safe and show him the small, fear-dried bones of her affair with Clegg-Bray, who, with that controlled self-possession she had begun to hate to-night, had not even telephoned the palace or hinted in any way that he was in the town. He was taking his time. She was relieved to the point of exhaustion that he had not telephoned, and was hurt and angry because he had not, and she knew it was stupid but there it was. And it had to be faced, this thing had to be discussed with Prabhu and then put behind for ever, and from then on she would be his slave. It was sickening but that was what she was going to do, be his slave, for that was what he wanted. And it was what she wanted now too. Impulsively she began to tell him about Clegg-Bray, qualifying every few words, and seeing him get angry, his eyes chilling as she made a mess of it, so that she was not sure if it was the news or her way of delivering it that was making him stare at her with stony, angry eyes.

"I know all about it," he hissed at her. "You bloody fool. I know all about that character. Is that what you've been mooning about the place for, that bloody, brainless guardee with the half-crowns for the kids? For God's sake, pull yourself together, Lila. You mean he's actually in this town now, to-night? Here in the town?" But she had fainted away, slipping with a comical but pitiful sigh to the floor. Everybody came rushing while the jazz went on flooding to the ceiling in bursts of drumfire and the massed braying of saxophones trying to kill the insistent needles of the trumpets.

While they were laying Lila down on the settee, with Miss Bullen in cool command, a sleepy servant staggered in to say that Brigadier Kapra Singh had arrived and needed to see the Maharajah on urgent business.

Lila half opened her unfocused eyes and whispered to Miss Bullen, " *Now* can I have a whisky?"

"No, dear," the old woman said, compassionate but firm and loving. "We're taking you to bed and you can have a nice cup of tea." And Lila broke down into resentful and relieved sobbing.

Chapter Twenty-Five

It was during the strange scene with Brigadier Kapra Singh and Doctor Kholi that Prabhu saw where he stood, once again, and this time maybe for good. He stood in a slightly different place from all the others he had occupied from time to time, but in the new position he at last knew that he was only an amateur in the human pastime of complicating the otherwise simple life. He knew at last that he was a fool. He thought of old Tolstoy, the genius who discovered the simple, complicated life in the end and died in a railway station waiting-room because of his Lila, his wife, who had known him better. He had wanted to capture the peasant simplicity and tie it to intellectualised spirituality, and there was a long, slow explosion because of this impossibility. No woman, and no genius, could stand it. There was no having the simple life when you were not simple.

Take this character, Brigadier Kapra Singh, dressed up for a role in *Desert Victory*, explaining the revolution at two o'clock in the morning in Jashimpur. Revolution! For the first time Prabhu wanted to laugh about it all, but he was depressed by the thought of the dead. Hassan's unordered martyrs.

There was only one modern man who had managed the simple life while being as complicated as two Swiss watches, each keeping different time, and that was Gandhiji. While he let Tolstoy and Gandhiji pass through his mind Prabhu listened to Kapra Singh and knew that he had had enough of Jashimpur history, and of Jashimpur as well.

But the man went on, lecturing, reminding Prabhu of himself occasionally, though he had never made things as dull as this little chap, knowledgeable though he was. Theories rolled out of the little man's mouth. He talked harshly, as if lecturing young military students in some impossible military college where the curriculum was Jashimpur in all its historical aspects.

"I realise as well as you, Mahraraj Sahib, that the driving force behind Jashimpuri inertia is lack of martial tradition, a tradition which they once possessed but which was destroyed by long neglect——"

"Driving force behind their inertia?" Prabhu said, laughing insultingly. "Surely you mean the inertia behind their driving force." But the little man took it straight and shook his head patiently.

"Don't misunderstand me, Maharaj Sahib," he said respectfully and yet with reproof in his eyes. "I mean an inertia with a driving force, a driving force which goes downwards deliberately as a revenge on itself. Remember the Jashimpuri saying, 'I am strong when I am weak. I am a hero who runs away.' There's nothing more dangerous than that kind of force when it finds its feet. And they've found their feet here in Jashimpur to-night——"

"And so you're going. You're resigning."

"Only because I've failed, Maharaj Sahib. No other reason. I failed to-night. I know I did. I should have hit them for six when I had the chance. But I didn't. I suppose it was the way they messed about with the bodies and the rest of it. One couldn't shoot. It was a pretty frightful show all round. In military terms one might call it an unexploitable situation, a calculated risk which couldn't be taken. Had I opened fire on them during the body business they would really have gone amok. My fear was that they would have attacked the palace, Maharaj Sahib. No. I think, in military terms as I said, one could call it an unexploitable situation——"

" Why not call it what it was ? A complete bollix-up. That's what we used to call it during the war when we lost." He knew he was being unfair to the little brigadier, but he meant to be. He disliked him because the little man reminded him in so many ways of himself, but without the sense of humour, without the touch of true Jashimpuri ridicule.

" I beg your pardon, Maharaj Sahib," Kapra Singh said with considerable dignity. He was white with anger as Prabhu waved his hand and told him to be quiet.

" We've all been found out here, that's all it is, my dear brigadier," said Prabhu. " You dressed up like Montgomery and with your mania about having no medals—who *cares*, damn it, about your medals—and me here with my little drama about uplift and changing the life of the people and going down in history for it—which I accused Hassan of, by the way. Yes. All of us. Messing about here while the people are so bloody tired of us that they'd cut our throats to-night if they could manage it. And as for your military forces, all I can say is that the sooner you take up gardening or knitting the better, for all concerned——"

" Maharaj Sahib, pardon me, but we're not living in feudal times now. I'm not obliged to stand here and be insulted in this way——"

" You're damn' right we're not living in feudal times, my dear brigadier. If we were you'd be hanging up by the feet right now over a slow fire. And I'd have ordered it. And I'd be leading my idiots in a massacre of the people so as to be sure of my rents in the future. But it's not like that to-night. It's all changed. Would you like a drop of whisky ? There's no need to stand there trying to look like a turkey cock. I'm not impressed. I've got enough on my mind without listening to a lot of balls about unexploitable situations. Hassan's got the town, I expect, and the least we can do is have a whisky and wait and see what happens. You might have at least seen to it that my bloody telephone line wasn't cut. That was a situation you might have kept unexploitable. Well, whisky or gin ? " Even though he had worked himself into an artificial rage, Prabhu was still cold and dead inside, except when he thought about Lila, when he wanted to laugh with pity and love. He was sorry for the little brigadier who was standing there in his dashing, casual Montgomery outfit, a man who had never faced a single crisis but was chockful of the history of such crises, and who, when faced with some tatty excited peasants burning some old paper, had come to resign. He could not even explode one tear gas bomb. It was the tear gas part of the mess which had made Prabhu contemptuous.

" Gin, please, Maharaj Sahib," the brigadier said despondently.

" Okay. Pour out two." While the brigadier obeyed, Prabhu attacked everything he could think of, soldiers, politicians, landowners, genealogy, Sandhurst and West Point and the Frunze Academy, and then remembered St. Cyr and sneered at that as well, and when he had finished with the soldiers and politicians he cursed all forms of hereditary rule and title. The brigadier, who had met Prabhu only twice, and briefly, stood sipping his gin and saying occasionally, " Yes. Too true. Bad show. Bad show. Yes. Rotten to the core, all politics are rotten to the core. I agree."

They heard the door at the end of the long room open, and when they looked round they saw Doctor Kholi in a dressing-gown. The doctor pointed straight at Kapra Singh and said, with his flashing eyes on Prabhu, " That man is due a cheque from me. Miss Bullen has told me about the riots. This man could have stopped all of it if he'd stood by his word. I bought him a couple of days ago." He lifted his chin and stared at Kapra Singh. " Why didn't you collect your cheque ? " he asked.

Then began a bitter wrangle between the two men about

who had done what. Prabhu sat down and watched. What the doctor was most bitter about was the way in which Kapra Singh, after long prevarication, had finally agreed to take his troops over to Hassan's side and capture Jashimpur for the Party, and had sneaked out of it ; and now, when still representing the Maharajah, had made a mess of that too. This was too much for Prabhu, who leaped out of his chair and rushed at the doctor. He stood before him and said, " You've a damned piece of cheek, Doctor Kholi. Accusing the brigadier. What about yourself ? Didn't you rat on Hassan and then snug yourself away out of sight here in the palace. I sent the cable, by the way. Your wife's coming to Jashimpur. Soon you can end your *Brahmacharya* respectably, openly. What a nerve. The whole damned lot of you need shooting. There's no need to look sheepish about it. You sneaked out on Hassan. So shut up on that subject and go back to bed."

Kholi, still fuddled with drugs, had actually forgotten that he had deserted Hassan. His mind, so long tortured by his false position and by his longing for the woman he loved and feared more than anybody on earth, was unable to function properly any more. It stirred feebly in a smoke of sedatives. He kept clutching his forehead while Prabhu's hard words cracked about his ears, murmuring, " I can't just sit down and listen to this kind of thing. I can't do it."

He sniffled and then some tears appeared in his eyes. Prabhu rushed to the door and shouted for Miss Bullen.

" Take this lunatic away to bed, for God's sake, before I throw something."

However, Doctor Kholi went sadly away on his own to the bedroom, still muttering, still unable to comprehend what had happened. The brigadier was saying, " Bad show, the whole thing. Bad show."

" So you sold me," said Prabhu when they were alone again. " You were bought. You see why these peasants have got tired of people like us ? How much did you agree to take ? "

" Half a *lakh*, actually," Kapra Singh replied, not meeting Prabhu's eyes. He was not ashamed, for he had not actually taken the fifty thousand rupees. He was, instead, proud that he was still incorruptible. He stood up to Prabhu's icy smile and justified not only the taking of bribes in certain circumstances, but the refusal of them in others. Perhaps the long military studies had helped in this objectiveness, the seeing of the enemy's forces and then of your own—Enemy—Own troops—seeing the other chap's position before assessing your own. Whatever the reason, he convinced Prabhu that there was no real badness in the world, just as there was no real goodness. It was merely a matter of how you put the stuff together, the clues and evidence and so on, and what you wanted to make of it all.

In his own case there was the education of his children to consider, a growing drain on his meagre finances, and even now, when only seven of the children were at school he, a brigadier commanding the State forces, was smoking the cheapest cigarettes. He had even sold his car last year. The children were going to cost more and more money. He had been tempted, he admitted it.

He challenged Prabhu with his actor's eyes and said, " I'm not one of these birth control fiends, Maharaj Sahib. There's no need for delicacy about such things between us. I've a full quiver, one might say. I think we're the same kind of people, though I have sixteen children and you only have two. We're going down in the world and steadily, our class of people, and yet we still want the best private schools for our children. It's the same in England, my friends there write to me. Mass-man in the saddle. What's the difference between robbing a bank and stealing a country and sharing it out with a lot of landowners ? What's robbery ? What's bribery for that matter ? Do you think a man in my position would stoop to such arguments as these a generation or so ago when there was the money and the future to look forward to ? What do I do ? I've accepted the kind of life my father taught me to like. The Western way, and I've got no money to follow it up. That's why I nearly took the money."

"All I want now is a confession from Miss Bullen that she's an ex-night-club queen and the thing's done," Prabhu said wildly. "One more confession from somebody and I'll resign. Why the hell do I have to listen to these things ? "

"You have that nature, Maharaj Sahib," Kapra Singh said, meaning it. "That's the true aristocrat. I'm the same. It's the curse of people like us, magnanimity, charity, under-standing. Look at my own life. I let your father bully me and I stayed here and haven't a medal to wear in front of my officers, half of whom are plastered from head to foot with campaign ribbons. I can't show myself in public sometimes, I feel it so much. I was a bloody fool. I apologise, Maharaj Sahib, for being tempted about that bribe. I apologise for everything. As for tonight nothing I could have done would have made any difference. This country's shown its teeth and Hassan has won. I knew it the day I heard of your going to see him in gaol. We all knew it. Well, there it is."

"Well, you've offered me your resignation. The thing is am I the person to take it, or is Hassan ? And does it matter whether you resign or not ? I mean does Hassan care ? Per-haps you ought to take it to the United Nations. What are you going to do ? Hand me your sword or your beret ? What shall I hand Hassan when I resign ? My sun-glasses ? But seriously, Brigadier, I've had the lot of you. Don't take it hard. But I have. I've had the bloody lot of you. And I've had politics as well. What are you going to do ? To-night was the great situation of your life. Remember that. And all you're doing is prattling away to me here in the palace about schools for your children and so on. That's what I get from my military commander. A chat about the problems of educating his children. Doesn't it strike you as just a little off-beat ? A little lacking in the martial tradition ? "

" You accept my resignation, Maharaj Sahib ? " Kapra Singh had had quite enough of Prabhu now. They had shown each other without meaning to that in themselves they represented something no one could afford any more, unless made to, and in their different ways this vision had depressed them.

" I accept it. Perhaps it might be as well to make sure and go down and offer it to Hassan as well. He'd love to have it. Unless Colonel Arif has shown he deserves to be brigadier. But I doubt it. My bet is that Hassan has the town."

" You could do something if you drove into the town, Maharaj Sahib. The people will listen to you. Shall I drive you in ? "

" To do what ? Make another speech ? A juggling act, or the rope trick might have an effect. But I doubt it. No, thanks all the same. I suggest you make a pincer movement towards your pillow and await events." And on that they parted. Prabhu listened to the roar of the tired jeep engine as it went down the drive.

" The thing now," said Prabhu to his gin as he swirled it in the glass, " is, do I scram with the State funds like some South American general ? Or do I just go to bed and drag poor Lila through this comedy about her demon guardee lover ? I never would have thought that clot would come running out here after her from London. Poor bastard. I'll look him up to-morrow and shake the guts out of him with a few ill-chosen words. A little bad form would be the thing to shake him. Poor bastard. He must be in love with her." He began to laugh and the laughter took him so sharply that he spilled his drink all over the floor. It was strange, but now that he had made up his mind that the operetta here was finished he felt almost happy. And he was very tired, which was another reason for going to bed.

He picked up the volume of Tolstoy's writings on the simple life which was trying to obsess him. He wanted to read more of it so as to be stirred by indignation again, but he put it down. He knew he was going to have a convulsion with Lila, one physical, one mental, both inseparable despite his efforts. Tolstoy could wait for another day. However, he knew he would have to read something when Lila had gone to sleep. He chose *Time*. He had noticed a particularly well-written-up air-crash in it, and a promising article about the new war to come which had been promised via Moscow and Fulton a little over a year ago. The armaments industry had to go on. Thinking about war he went to join Lila.

Chapter Twenty-Six

" You could have come home in nineteen forty-five, but you stayed on in India instead until nineteen forty-six." Lila said. " That showed me what you thought of me." She was about to stop but remembered the children, and added, " And the children." She had meant to be soft and yielding, behave as contritely as she felt, but God, it was hard.

All had been going well, gently, almost tenderly, and Prabhu had been reaching a mellowed mood. He had come into the bedroom holding *Time* open, planning to read to her later the fine bit about the American version of what was going on in the Punjab smoke and flame. She had welcomed him softly, asking after his head. He had said earlier that he had a bad headache. He had asked how she was feeling, was she going to stick it out in this—he had been about to say ridiculous, but forbore—thing about giving up drinking? She looked pinched and as if about to start shivering, her eyes lustrous with varied sufferings and thought-over wrongs. She was sitting cross-legged, her black silk dressing-gown wrapped about her, and as he looked at her he had a momentary vision of their very separateness, everybody's separateness, and of all the splendid, frightful troubles caused by the effort to abolish this separateness. That was all it was, an impossible effort, performed willingly, desperately, necessarily. She looked so very far away from him in person and in spirit, sitting there on the bed with her black eyes watching him as if from afar. Their mysteries were awake, feeling for each other, come stealthily out of the accretions of habit, and of time, and of pretence, tangling with each other across the room. As soon as he felt the unfleshly touch of those occult longings they had always cherished for each other, most powerful now between the stare of their eyes, he knew that one more great effort was being made to meet, to understand, and to accept. Pity for both of them filled him, tinged with hate and contempt for their unfailing selfishness, for their iron platforms on which each waited for the other's surrender of personality, thinking it right and just and deserved. He scattered several questions around her, about Clegg-Bray, lowering his voice gradually, remembering that anger was no good. And she had been ready for this, and was cool while earnest, making what was ridiculous for him seem of great value for her, while diminishing for him now all of the value she had once thought it to possess for her. She was finished with the Clegg-Bray nonsense. She began to tell him about her relationship with Clegg-Bray. He sat down on a couch and smoked while she talked. As he listened to the tale of nonsensical goings on, part of which he knew from his own covert observations in London, he marvelled once more at the way Lila had always hidden her real self from him, a chaotic, childish, harmless self which had trembled always before his harsh laughter. Clegg-Bray took her seriously, cherished her nonsense, he could see that now while he listened.

She threw in the piece about how he, Prabhu, had stayed on in India after the Burma campaign and had not returned to England until nineteen forty-six—during that period she had fallen in love with Clegg-Bray, in anger. The way she threw it in, and threw it in again and again, gradually sharpening its edge, annoyed even while he silently admitted its truth. He could have come back to her in nineteen forty-five but he had not wanted to—he had got over her, got over missing her some time in nineteen forty-three. The war had been too long, too long for everybody in the world. He could have come back to her, rushing back to her, after all those letters, but he had grown up, away from her, and when they did meet in nineteen forty-six they were not the same people at all. He thought of that while she answered questions asked by the other side of his mind.

He knew nothing like *that* had happened between Clegg-Bray and herself. The way she called it *that* made him smile sadly. He agreed he knew that nothing like *that* had happened. It was not *that* which upset him about this Clegg-Bray character—no—it was the stupidity and the nonsense of it, that was all, and now the trouble it was causing. This idiot had flown out here from London because the game was up with his own wife. Did she see the nonsense of it all now? Yes. She did, but she was defiant, flaring up into accusation again.

" He gave me tenderness, whatever you say about nonsense," she cried. " That's what he gave me. He respected me and treated me with understanding. You never did that. When a man treats a woman with respect and tenderness, a woman like me, she responds to it. You don't need a woman. You need a woman with a man's mind and personality. What do I care about vitamins and rebellions in South America and factory hours? I want to find myself. I want to know what's the matter with me. I want to be understood. You sneered when I told you why I went into churches in London with him and sat there for hours. How could anyone like you understand why I did that? " She slowly wrung her hands and won a struggle with shame while she suffered through that sneer of his about the churches.

Clegg-Bray used to take her into churches in various parts of London, churches of all denominations, and talk to her by the hour about his soul and her soul, and about things she had understood absolutely while he had talked but had forgotten soon afterwards.

" What things? " Prabhu shouted. " What things? "

She could not tell him. Deep things, things about life and about sorrow and everything. Prabhu was tensed up with rage and she could see it. He said what she expected him to say.

" That's what kills me," he cried. " That pretence about understanding everything. You understand nothing. *Nothing.* What's wrong with understanding nothing as long as you are a beautiful woman worth loving ? That's all I want. That."

Now she cried and said, " I know that. I only wish I were clever and could understand you and all your business about things that don't matter to me. I never had to feel small and horrible when I was with *him.* I did think I loved him. I don't. I love you. You won't let me. You hate me. You despise me. You treat me like dirt. I hate everybody in the world." She threw herself face down on the pillow.

" A Scotch, darling ? " he said. " I'll bring you one."

She shook her head, thin sobbing losing itself in the pillow.

" What I can't understand," he shouted, his fists clenched on his chest, " is what this is all about. I mean, why you and me have to fight all the time. It's got to stop. You want me to pack this character off, send him back to London ? " He lowered his voice, coaxingly. " Is that what you want ? You want an end to this nonsense now ? " Yes. She was nodding, piteously into the pillow.

What was the use of her explaining to Prabhu that her loneliness had begun with her marriage to him ? Before that marriage she had had herself for company and had loved it. Marriage to him had split her into two pieces of nothing. There was nothing so lonely as being married to a man who did not need you, but who swore over and over again that he needed you, swore it in tempers after long periods of tension between them. A man who despised you for what you were, an idiot with a beautiful body and a heap of scattered errors for a brain. She could remember the day he had used that expression. It was on a day six months after his return to grey, war-sodden, spam-gagged Britain when she had been trying to make an omelette out of a packet of chemicals called *Eggo*. Prabhu had wanted to lecture her in the kitchen about nationalisation and the proper use of controlled manpower, and she had wanted to make an omelette which could not be made, with *Eggo*, the product of the world Prabhu looked forward to—a world of masculine planning in which house-wives were expected to produce splendid meals with *Eggo*.

He made her get up out of the pillow and talk to him about " this church business with Clegg-Bray." Was she looking for a religion ? What was the game ? The game ? Yes, the game. There was and is no game. Well, this church business. What was it all about ?

" The only place left in this world where you can be alone now," she said to him, " is in a church. That's all ' the game ' is, as you sneeringly call it." He said he was not sneering.

" If I get rid of Padre Clegg-Bray," he said, " do we have another go ? Do we start all over again, as they say ? " He wanted to start all over again. He was always willing to start all over again. There was never going to be happiness with her. There would be marriage instead, that process of forestry which ever looked forward to the settled clearing with the snug homestead set up in it, all storm winds blown out on a greyish but comforting plain of mutual forgiveness called affection. The forest, though, was primeval, and all clearings were temporary. In a way there was a masochistic excitement for both of them in their desired and unendable union, their pains and wounds their very own, not even Clegg-Bray sharing one of them. So they embraced each other, still full of unbroken silences, worlds of misunderstanding unspoken of, deserts of small jealousies, hatreds, envies, resentments, all covered again in red clouds of mist as the death-force took one more fall in the bout which would never end.

Chapter Twenty-Seven

" Of all of us, of all these various excited and heated planners, I'm the only one who knows that life consists of a series of compromises, and that history is a stairway made of them. Only I know that there can never be black, and never white, in things which are to be pawed about and twisted and finally lived with by people. We have to have a grey, a compromise, and what better than the oldest one of all, the one that's hardest, and the one that will never be completely denied, even by the iconoclasts who roam about with a hammer in each hand looking for gods to smash." Hari Lal's head sang with such thoughts as he made the rounds of the holy men in their shrines by the river, up in the hills piled in blue masses beside the town, in the *ashrams* where old men were preparing for the fearful wintry ascent into the Himalayas on their yearly pilgrimage. Yes, they said, they would support a religious and non-denominational movement for reforms, a hateless and non-violent crusade in which Hari Lal's father had already made his astounding first move. One of the *fakirs* was an old, frail, handsome Muslim who was said to have done something dreadful in his youth. When he agreed to come out in his trembling age for the procession planned by Hari Lal the news travelled fast, for he was very holy.

Hari Lal's father, after a good many tears, tears of remorse and happiness for the new life, as well as tears for the searing pain of the wrenching away of himself from his property, now wore a new look of hope, a wan sort of happiness. Even Hari Lal himself was so affected by this change in his father

that he found himself reading the Gita again, trying to con-
nect, to see it as the source of ignored wisdoms, of unlearned
lessons. His father had begun to assume true humility. Had
he nagged his father for five years about the need to surrender
his riches in order to be struck down by religion himself, in
order to become a person even smaller than he knew himself
to be? The thought was not frightening. He knew that
when he had had his fill of the world's adventures he would
leave it for silence somewhere—but that was a long way
away. It was unlikely he would ever marry. Already he was
involved up to the throat of his ambition's appetite in the
arranging and ordering of men's lives. He did not feel that
urge to live with a wife. He would need no son to light his
funeral pyre. None of that custom and tradition meant very
much to him. It was terrible but true.

He knew that the Maharajah was sagging, that his thrusting
excitements which had been flinging themselves into patches
of nowhere, were mortally wounded by Hassan's bizarre
success with the suicide threat.

Organising the procession became for Hari Lal a consuming obsession as soon as he heard that there was to be a clod
and straw-rope demonstration by what might be the last
slave crowd to assemble in Jashimpur to show their ironic
self-contempt. These customs would vanish in the many
new uncensored winds blowing into the continent of India
now that the British walls were levelled. Castes would
crumble faster as men learned to lie brutally about who they
were not. Women would become worth quarrelling with in
marriage, companions instead of being meek listeners. He
thought of the Maharani, her suppressed angers. Age would
have to explain itself, youth be able to prove itself. The complicated prison of folk-custom built round the two real powers
of religion, charity and humility, would collapse and leave
men to themselves instead of to public village opinion—a
terrible revolution. Men would become hopeful Indians

instead of mystified caste-members, all the millions who had smashed themselves generation after generation on the hard, sun-beaten earth for the tax men and the middlemen who operated between God and their own treadmill of almost hopeless struggle. Whatever the king, he had held out his hand and had it filled, whatever the monsoon did, whatever the agonies of the far villages. The many ancient communities which had made their noble struggle to live together, and to eat, and to thank the gods for that right, since misty Ayran times, would have a chance to show bloody-handed but still inspiring Europe some new way to refuse battle and catastrophe, some way of facing the juvenile, masculine fear of being thought lacking in guts about murdering people for honour and power. Hari Lal would bend his head and whisper shame when he thought of the killings going on between Muslim and Hindu in the Punjab. How the world which had been forced to admire Gandhiji, how it must laugh now. No matter. India would rise again as she had risen before, in response to the cold thought pulled from her hot heart. She was the mightiest of mothers.

His British varnish thinner than Prabhu's, Hari Lal knew he had less to forget, less to regret, less to lose than Prabhu, who had been flung back on himself, the imperial umbrella which had sheltered him from the patient, waiting tumult of India, vanished in the terrific wind made by the passing of the viceroys and their hunting packs of lawyers and, more important, by the departure of their peerless administrators. They had administered their own invention called British India and had administered it well, and now India was coming back to sift the ruins of the past and inspect the frame of the shaking present.

Of all that had gone, of all that had been bent down into new shapes and plastered with stucco newness, religious fervour remained, with its hollow eyes still fixed on the darknesses beyond the ache of the burning sky. He had read many books in which a certain form of British insolence explained year after imperial year, the miserable, hypocritical superstitions of their conquered races, for the trained palates of the elementary schoolboys who had done the fighting far from their slum bases to support their insolence. All that was finished now. The roar of its crumbling filled the world. He had regret for it, and gladness too. Sometimes, newspaper in hand, his spirit wandering in a mushroom-shaped cloud, he prayed that there would be no more conquerors, even benign ones who could not resist tinkering with, and smashing, what was not theirs, from language to custom to religion. They had left religion here, their stoutest ally, afraid of losing the valuable inertia of its superstitions, writing little insolent books about it instead. See how Harry Wugg, though, had climbed on to Hassan's back and rode him still, Hassan's thin Jashimpuri skin taking the Colonel's whiplashes for all, made an acrobat for his people by this underlining in print of his patriotic shame. Hari Lal stopped in the road to laugh.

Yes, religion. When the superstitions which protected it were there, that was shiftlessness according to the insolent ones. When the superstitions were gone, that was godlessness, a most dangerous situation for the unrestrained mobmind. India was now free to make her own mess, her very own, and he, Hari Lal, was doing his rounds in order to build a little wall round Jashimpur's mess, a little religious wall behind which men could find time to chill their passions down to reasoning level. Everyone had had quite enough of the Hassan-Maharajah morality play about vanity, well meant, constructive vanity.

He arranged his religious procession to clash with the clod and straw-rope performance. His glee was too great to hold. He simply must tell it all to the Maharajah, who was so depressed and listless, make him laugh again, and take an interest in the coming tangle he was preparing for Hassan.

Chapter Twenty-Eight

It was thought by some that that swift, wild night of protest against the soldiers, the burning of the documented sweat of centuries, and the ending of soldier-police rule would become known as the strangest day of the century. But the next day was even stranger, and when it had ended some thought it was a punishment from God while others said it was his approval, his signature of agreement to the end of an era. But the general opinion was that He was displeased.

First there was The March of Repentance. This began as a procession to the Party headquarters to salute Hassan, to shame him for his treatment of the Maharajah, for the word had gone round about his gesture with the razor. This story was not believed when it first made the rounds, no one believing that Hassan would cut his throat, or even threaten it. But there were men who described the razor. It was black with a red blade and carried the words " Made in Germany." Hassan had bought it seven years ago for four rupees eight annas, second-hand from an American professor who measured the skulls of living men. His servant remembered it well. It was with this razor that he had threatened to cut the Maharajah's throat if he was let into the Party. That was more like it. It was well known how much he hated all kings, and particularly their own young, mad one. That was his one failing, that hatred of a perfectly good young Maharajah whose only fault was his insanity about his own property. And this insanity was catching. Now one of the richest men in the country, admittedly known to be turning back to God, had surrendered his land. This piece of news was so extraordinary that crowds had squatted down outside Hari Lal's house to get a *darshan*, a sort of touch of the garment, of this man. Holy men hearing of this said it was wrong to use the word *darshan* already of this man who was not yet holy enough for such a word. Let them look at him, yes, for he had made the first great step, but let there be no hysteria. Undoubtedly the poor man was as insane as the Maharajah, but their insanity was of the kind favoured by God.

The March of Repentance was done in a style not seen in Jashimpur since the very old men were young. No one ever was able to find out just how it began. The request went out for short pieces of old straw rope. By ten o'clock in the morning the whole town seemed to be on the move with pieces of straw rope in their hands. Thousands of people, young and old, men and women, assembled by the river and put on " The Yoke of Penitence," " The Clod of Humility," the thing had many names all signifying the same thing, a lowly badge of lowliness. It could be used for satire, for mockery, for true and false sorrow, and for accusation. A man could go before a tyrant moneylender wearing the lump of mud hanging from his neck on a straw rope halter and hand over the grudged money in silence, and with half-closed eyes and hanging head. It took a brazen creature to stand that treatment twice. The custom was seldom abused by either side.

When the clod on the straw rope was carried round the neck in procession, silent, shambling, mournful-looking procession, it was intended as a show of penitence and of disapproval. The penitence was for the killing of the soldiers, which, happy occasion though it was, splendid though it might be as a warning for a century to come to all soldiers everywhere, was to be regretted for the bloody business it was. The disapproval was for Hassan, who had threatened to cut his Maharajah's throat so as to shut him off from the new kind of power which had now fallen into the gutter for all to have a kick at.

"Long live Hassan, yes," a solemn wag said, "but a bearded man needs no razor." Hassan's perfect, small, neat beard was much admired.

The procession started at half past ten. The thousands in their drab, grey wool and faded brown cotton made up what looked like the greatest collection of mourners in the world, as if all the beggars on earth were out to follow their beggar king to the burning *ghat* or the burial-ground. The pace was slow, the only sound the slow dragging scuff of thousands of sandals. In its uneven surge and fall it was like the noise of the sea caught in its own echo, and there was a drab and mystifying grandeur in the sight of this seemingly endless train of silent people. Around every neck hung a big brown clod of mud or clay, the yellow or reddish coloured straw of the rope catching the sun like shreds of tarnished gold.

Everyone seemed to be there in that slow trudge of genuine but superbly acted sorrow, from Mohamed Lefthand, very aged now, the famous man who had sold his brother to a friend for six months in return for eight pounds of Rampur tobacco, and bought him back for two rupees, to a ten-year-old boy who had rescued an English tourist from drowning a year ago and had refused all reward (either to finish as a saint or a lunatic, none could say).

As the procession passed the battered barracks there was some whispering. "The uniforms won't forget that place in a hurry." "By God, no. The uniforms will be polite for some years to come." "I agree it was terrible, but birth is terrible, so is death. So is living. What is not terrible?"

"Yesterday we were dirty and ragged. To-day, though, we smell of blood as well. That will have to be paid for." After that whisper had been whispered around everyone was silent so as to think about it. They thought with bowed heads as they tramped through the city, crowds watching them from each side.

" They are going to punish Hassan," people called to each other. " It was he who sent those three Christian turncoats to kill the soldiers. They were disguised as British officers."

" No. That's wrong. You should have a stopper put in your mouth."

" Oh ? Then, what's right ? "

" It is not known. The city is driven mad with lies to-day. But Hassan needs punishing. He was too proud to the Maharajah with his sword."

" His razor, you dolt."

" All right. Razor, then. Razor ! Razor ! Razor ! Are you satisfied now ? "

The militia were on the streets, whole and confident with their slung rifles and their coloured armbands. Their pride was great and they exchanged warm, friendly looks with some of the marchers who stole glances at them, brotherly mockery, too, in many of their eyes. Friendly cynicism was in the air. Is there anyone more conquering than the second-line troops who have come up to occupy the already captured territory ? The youthful delight in being armed and in command was sweet to the militia, and understood by the marchers, who glanced up at them without lifting their mourning heads.

The foreign correspondents, and Clegg-Bray, and some Indian business men defiantly reprimanding their own capitalism in their Gandhi homespun, leaned on the second-floor veranda of The Moghul Hotel and watched the long procession going by.

Clegg-Bray who had soldiered in India for some years and was feeling a detached and restful interest in a people he had loved but had never been able to meet on equal terms, until now. It did not matter any more if there was a riot below. He did not worry about it, or go down and mess it up further, or solve it. He did not have to bother officially any more about what was good form or what was good for the natives. The Indian business men, impressed by Clegg-Bray's polished Urdu, such a change from the usual barrack Hindustani, conversed with him about such things as proportional representation, revolutionary aftermaths, Krishna, the battle of Kurukshetra, the love of Rama and Sita, and he batted the ball back expertly. Although he knew far more about India as a whole than they did, he never made the mistake of implying that he knew what it was to be an Indian. His civilised care with their sentiments and their prejudices was far removed from diplomatic subtlety. It was brotherly, so brotherly that they invited him to take tea with them again. He was a tall, lanky, bald man of about forty-five, thick, loose, yellow hair bunched above his ears and separated by the pink ball of his time-polished skull. His unworldly, blue eyes were large and sad. He was scrupulously shaven except for a faint, thin line of greying moustache. His mouth was always clenched, not in temper or unthinking bitterness or regret, but as a result of intense thinking, a sort of clenched, desperate thinking. His khaki shorts and the khaki drill jacket were vintage, holes in the shoulder-straps revealing a defunct rank. He was easygoing despite that grim-looking mouth. He looked the kind of man, especially with those eyes, who might explain that he was off to climb Everest. He had the far-seeing, slightly disembodied look of the fanatical mountaineer, the man who thinks he climbs the mountain because it is there.

The procession trudged on until it reached the Party headquarters, a three-story building of blinding white stucco, which was rented from one of the bitterest enemies of the Party.

It was a humiliating experience for Hassan to have to come out on the veranda and look down on the silent masses of people who did not lift their heads to look at him. He had walked up and down his cluttered office, into which he had just moved, debating whether he should not have the demonstration broken up by the militia. His coolness, though, a coolness permanent and secure below his many angers, assured him that he would manage this business all right if he could find the right words. The temptation to rush and hurl down a barrage of accusations about slavishness and degrading customs was very strong. More than anything, those lumps of clay hanging on the straw ropes incensed him. Colonel Wugg had written a whole chapter about those, and had even become mystical about them, claiming that they represented the origin of such expressions as "common clay," "humble clods," and had then blasted it all by calling the custom "the very epitome of snivelling serfdom." It was hard to forget those whiplashes of the demented colonel. In his heart Hassan knew that this colonel had destroyed part of him while appearing to raise it from the dead, from the cemetery of degradation. His obsession with the colonel's ravings had caused him to love what he hated and hate what he loved. This conflict of pity for his people, and hate for their patient defeatism had exploded in him in flames when he had peered out carefully from behind a curtain at the appearance of the thousands of clod carriers below. His love and his hope for them was pitiless for some moments when it considered the sly, masked wit hiding behind that massed penitence of the bowed heads. "The March of Repentance," he thought, sarcasm pulling at his set mouth. "They should be celebrating their moment of fury last night, not pretending to be sorry for killing a few uniformed ration-eaters who were there to shoot them." But when Dokra Singh appeared with a hand-written reproof for him, in fine Jashimpuri (at least it was *that* nationalistic) accusing him of offending the Maharajah, as gravely as they, the people, had offended God by killing the night before, he bowed his head and cursed for some time in whispered Urdu.

"Their leaders handed it to me," Dokra Singh said. "If I may say so it is disgusting and slavish."

" It's about the razor incident," Hassan said quietly. His face was set in an expression of exasperated perplexity. " I can guess the distorted stories that are going about."

" There are plenty of stories," Dokra Singh replied. " But the real one is enough. Threatening to cut your own throat to defeat the Maharajah took things a bit far."

" Oh ? " Hassan met his eyes with a forbidding stare, a look of one who has received impudence. " Oh ? You don't approve ? You think I was too brutal ? "

" It was a mistake, Hassan. Now you are the chief. I just want you to know that I for one, now you are the chief, reserve my right to my opinions. I'll serve you loyally, as always, but will remind you from time to time that being chief does not make you a god. You made a mistake and you ought to do something about it. You've won. Now invite the Maharajah into the Party."

" That's Hari Lal talking. That's pure Hari Lalism."

" And it's Dokra Singh, too, and all the people waiting downstairs as well. It's you, too, but you won't admit it."

" Well, thank you, Dokra Singh. Thank you." Hassan dismissed him and brooded about Prabhu while the crowds still poured into their places below. As usual, coolness came to him again, a speech came ready, and he went straight out on to the veranda to deliver it, inspired, and taller than usual with certainty.

" Brothers," he cried. " Brothers in victory as in the struggle, I thank you for your message, and I greet you fraternally in your penitence about the blood that was shed. But we must remember that two bloods were mingled last night on the soil of Jashimpur, the blood of the bought hire-lings of the dead régime and, sacred to us, the blood of the innocent poor, shot down by the soldiers. That is the blood to remember when you have mourned for your small sin. We shall not pretend. We shall be honest and admit that this demonstration is merely an old custom in which you make token penitence. For we know that your killing of the soldiers was only your reply to the killing of innocent men just as much as it was the prelude to your destruction of the tax records. All the exploited generations who have gone salute you for that action last night. Away with sham and fraud from this day." He began to listen to his blood now. He began to thrill to rage for he had remembered the most insulting and puerile portion of that address they had sent up. He read it out in wild ringing tones, sarcasm edging the words as they fell on the warm air. " Our loyalty to you, Hassan, is as strong as ever, as strong as our affection and loyalty to the Maharajah who has done us no wrong. Though he is not in your Party he is in our hearts. Though he is threatened he has not imprisoned you. Rather he liberated you, we being too cowardly to shed the blood you claimed in rescuing you. We bow our heads in shame for all these things." When he had finished reading these words Hassan's voice was breaking with the force of his contempt and despair. " This kind of sickening thing must stop," he cried. " You must stand up like men and face your vices and your false and degrading pretences of the past. Humility is one thing. But wallowing in hypocritical shame is another. From to-day this clay hanging from the neck is at an end and must go into the dirt where it belongs with your chains. To-morrow I set up the commission on the land reforms. Next week the courts for the moneylenders will commence. In those courts they shall tell to the world who owes them what and for how long, and how much interest they have sweated from ancient unpayable debts. These are the things from now, not this play-acting with pieces of clay." He had been speaking into the sky, not a movement or a sound from below to disturb the rapid flow of his words. Not a head had lifted.

His love for them killed the voice in him. He had to contend with his pity and love which was aroused by the sight of their drab and shabby clothing, their close-shaven skulls, the handsome, worn faces which he could not see but knew so well ; manly, rugged faces masking generous, timid hearts which he despised and feared. They looked like a swarm of helots come to listen to their lord, and it was because he knew so well the almost hopeless, deadly poetry of their cynical dreams, their hidden, rancorous romanticism, their love of children and their distrust of men, that he could forgive them their two-faced love for him. They had come to reprimand him, and more, to show him that they were sorry for the deaths of the men they had so exultantly killed, that they denied their right to take the lives of those tyrant-symbols, the poor venal soldiers who had worked for rations.

It was Abdulla Hussein who lifted his head and spoke for the crowd. He was a tall, handsome man, his fine features melting at last in this generation into weakness and shiftiness. He wore a torn, grey, woollen shirt and white, cotton *pajamas* so frayed that they looked like fine muslin from a distance. He was one of a family of copper-workers which had survived on the edge of the town since they were driven off the land in the year " They " had taken to bird-shooting and needed more space. He had the look of a condemned man as he began to speak, hopeless yet defiant, vain, but unafraid of the militiaman who strolled ostentatiously close as if to menace him.

" You up there, Hassan," the pale-faced man said in a dry, chesty voice. " You despise us, and you love us. We all know that. And we love you and don't trust you. Why should we trust you, a man like us full of hatred and bitter memories, when we forgot ourselves yesterday and slew the brainless soldiers ? Yes, brainless, like these new men here with the rifles waiting for you to tell them to arrest us. While you and the Maharajah have been hurting each other for our sakes, the State Council of four men has run this country quietly. They are the men in the secretariat who run this country, and they are waiting for orders, fresh orders. It will be the Maharajah who will give those orders, Party or no Party. We would sooner see a good Maharajah undoing the work of his ancestors than kill all his ancestors' tyrants. That is because we are cowards——" The crowd laughed downwards at the ground, not a head lifted. It was like a deep, baying sound, fading away into chuckles at this lying truth, this painless, sardonic contempt they felt for themselves.

" But," Abdulla went on, " we have produced you, Hassan, a man who is not a coward, and yet you held up a razor in front of a good young man, whom we approve of, and told him you would cut your throat if he was allowed to join the Party. You did that for us, you will say. But I tell you you did it for yourself, just as much as the cruel landlord does a similar act against us—for himself, but in the name of this, that or the other good of the country. It was agreed in the early hours of this morning by the guilds we still have left to us, that compensation shall be paid to the families of the army ration-eaters who were killed by our passion last night. That is the will of the guilds. We are not pleased with you either. We agree with your wish to better our lives. But we will not stand by and see you begin to fight with your friends, and with your ruler, the Maharajah. Already there are some men who are saying that only Muslims must have the country because the Maharajah is a Hindu, and only Hindus must have the country because they were here before the Muslims. Well, we will not have any of that here. If we shall compensate the families of the dead soldiers, then you must apologise to the Maharajah and from this day work with him——"

Hari Lal could not have chosen a more perfect moment to appear with his own procession. He had tried vainly for two hours to take Prabhu out of his bitter mood and make him join the procession, but had been refused. It was his father, though, the rich landowner who had given up all for God, who was the star-turn of the small procession which now appeared from a lane up the wide street and walked slowly towards the crowd. It halted in a trickling, uneven sprawl of ranks, about two hundred men, and met the eyes of the tattered hundreds who lifted their heads at last from their performance of repentance. Hari Lal was holding a banner, an enormous white sheet of cloth stretched across a bamboo frame. Black lettering announced in Urdu, Jashimpuri and English that this was the " Voluntary Land Pool of Jashimpur," and that only by " Spiritual Methods not Hate " could men do good. Everyone was staring at Hari Lal's father, who was wearing only a loincloth and a loose, ochre-coloured shawl. He had a rosary of big *rudhra* berries wound round his right wrist and there was a look of peaceful resignation in his eyes. The breeze blew softly through his thick, white hair. He was on his way to the mountains, in complete retirement from the world at last, as Hari Lal began to explain in fine but simple oratory to the people.

" And all his acres now belong to the people," he told them. " My father has renounced his ancestral lands, and has renounced the world of gain and toil. Many years he has taken to reach this great decision—for who likes to leave his family, even for God ? And he reached this decision because of the sincerity of the young Maharajah who wants nothing of gain or riches, and who has told you so himself. The violence of political hatreds are no use to us. We are an ancient people in this State, brothers in a common history. You see in this procession Hindu *Mahants* from the temples, priests who welcome my father's renunciation of the world, and you see Muslim *fakirs* who have not left their retreats for many years. They have come to approve. This is the way to change Jashimpur, in the ancient way we have ignored and forgotten, not by the way of hatred and bitter speeches. We are on our way to the river where I shall describe the aims of the new way of softening the landlords' hearts, loosening the moneylenders' clutch, and giving honour to the religions we have all but forgotten——"

Up above, grim and unmoving, Hassan watched it all, knowing that this was his real enemy, the right way which would never work, the just solution which rich men would laugh at until the end of time; the religious dream which could never admit that the rich relied on it, and used it, as their eventual protector in all crises when " law and order " were threatened by the lower classes. The rich would listen to the religious men who preached justice and soft hearts, and then would nod and drive away in their Cadillacs. It was always the strike by workers, though, which finally forced the higher wages out of the rich men, for the rich men were not here to practise religion and the sharing out of their loot. Hassan marvelled at the sincerity of Hari Lal's delivery, and why not, for he was moved himself by what Hari Lal was saying, even though he knew it was all useless. He was too cold inside and too sickened to protest, and he had only to look at the suddenly innocent eyes of the hundreds below as they listened to Hari Lal to know that he had lost them. There were several things he could do, break up the crowd, follow the old Jashimpuri official tradition; but he was too disgusted, and too touched in his deeply religious core to be able to act. Despair made him want to laugh. Had he been a Marxist he would have laughed so loud that Hari Lal would have been silenced. Once again he envied the communists, just as his opponent, the Maharajah, had said he envied them, for their narrow, shut certainties which watched coldly while the West kicked its own moral order into the dustbin, where the East had had theirs kicked centuries ago. The communists had only to wait until the rich in all lands had finally used religion to death and had filled their banks too full, for there was nothing the Communists liked more than to see rich men working for them everywhere with unswerving, unchanging greed. Even here in this little State full of used-up, ragged people that system worked, and he listened to Hari Lal with understanding and pity, pity for all of them, particularly for himself who liked much of communism but could not swallow it all, and could not, therefore, truly deny its force. He had too much respect for religion to break up Hari Lal's spell-binding, ancient call to man's longing for the truly impossible. Most mysterious of all for him was that he felt love for them for this tragic, ignorant innocence which began to turn them as one man to follow Hari Lal and the others to the river. Soon the street was quite empty except for the militiamen after the last scuffling sounds of the crowd's sandals had drifted away. Hassan had not moved. Dokra Singh was standing behind him in tears, tears of anger, and of genuine religious excitement, and he was unable to speak.

Chapter Twenty-Nine

Prabhu's meeting with Clegg-Bray was so curious an experience that he regarded it afterwards as a mysterious turning-point, something he could never describe to anybody even had he been able to discuss it.

In an ironic mood he set off to "have things out" with Clegg-Bray at The Moghul Hotel. It was late afternoon and he was still wearing his peasant garb of loose, light-grey woollen shirt reaching to his knees, and he was feeling strange in the baggy white *salwar* which ended at his shins, the trousers of poverty. His feet were happy in the light sandals, free of socks but threatening to blister during the long walk from the palace. He was finished with motor cars from now on, unless he made long journeys up-country for the new crusade of voluntary surrender of lands. From here on it was going to be the simple life. None of that Tolstoy stuff, the smart-aleck simple life with the unravelable tangle of literary explanations of what Christ had never said. How would Tolstoy have liked it if Christ had turned up at Yasnaya Polyana one day for tea, and was found to be a short, heavy-shouldered, dark-skinned, sweaty Jew who was proud of being a carpenter and who wiped his mouth with the back of his hand after a glass of tea? And then shattered everything with a miracle, out-talking Tolstoy. Why stick at Tolstoy in this matter? How would Miss Bullen like to meet that Christ? There must be quite a lot of Christians who would refuse that Christ entrance into their clubs. They would have

sent that Christ to the Jewish Working Men's Institute, or
to the gas-oven. What was it Hari Lal had said about Gandhiji
this morning? Yes. "Gandhiji's heart is broken with the
Muslim-Hindu killings in the Punjab. And yet killing is as
important as sex to men. Is that why Christ let them crucify
Him? So that He should be the symbol of all regiments and
all armies in the future, the target for all time? Like man?
What *was* the meaning of the crucifixion?"

"You must ask Miss Bullen that," he had told Hari Lal.
For his own part he did not want to know the reason. More
than anything he feared religion and the load of guilt it put
on that mysterious substance Miss Bullen often mentioned:
the soul. But he knew it was going to come to him one day,
and through Lila. Lila did not know how religious she was,
but *he* did, and he did not look forward to the day when
she would let it work in her without opposition.

Something happened during his walk from the palace to
the town. He knew it was very Tolstoyan of him to walk
about in peasant dress so as to be seen by the people, who
were to marvel, and who marvelled, those who recognised
him. They were genuine about their marvelling, and he was
not genuine about his simplicity, but he forgave himself.
Very soon he would accept himself in peasant dress just as
he would accept the new simplicity he had launched himself
into, and then all would be well with him. One needed time
to get well into a part.

Half-way to the town the thing happened, his discovery of
how difficult was the simple life for those who had to live it
whether they liked it or not. Half-way to the town he saw a
ragged, aged man with a sick, scabby child whining in his
thin arms. The old man was rocking it slowly and singing
to it in a quavering voice. There was a little boy nearby,
almost as ragged as the old man, with a begging-bowl in his
hand. Prabhu tried to avoid them so that he should not
embarrass them by being embarrassed by them, but the boy

pursued him and pushed his begging-bowl up almost to Prabhu's face.

"Give now, *huzoor*, while there is still time," the boy told him. Brought up in beggary he showed no shame. His honest eyes looked up into Prabhu's, who was frowning down at him. At that moment Prabhu remembered that he had left his dark glasses in the bathroom and had not thought of them since. He had forgotten them. He stood quite still, the boy forgotten, while he tried to interpret the meaning of the thing. Spattered with vague superstitions misinterpreted from odd readings of digested writings on psychology, he tried to find the symbol of the probable symbolical meaning. Was it a symbol of rebirth, the unconscious flinging aside of the eye-masks so that in his peasant dress he need not hide any more? Had he been hiding? Was it Lila's laughable unburdening about Clegg-Bray, the bald demon-lover, which had pressed some waiting trigger in him? Only habit in him fretted for those dark glasses as he stood before the forgotten begging boy. He did not miss them. There must be some meaning in the thing. He had never forgotten them before. More likely it was because he had defeated Hassan, and yet the habit of the dark glasses was older than his acquaintance with Hassan. The dark glasses dated from the day he had bought them in Palma where the ship had called on their journey out to India. He had had a headache and had attributed it to the sun in his eyes. Later, on the ship, sitting in a deck-chair, he had studied Lila through them without her knowing. He had studied everybody on the ship through them without their knowing, and had not been studied in return. The thing had been a game and yet he had come to rely on them, to live behind the dark glasses. Irritated now with all the possible meanings in the forgotten dark glasses he looked sternly at the boy and said, "Do you know who I am?"

"No, *huzoor*." The boy shook his bowl at him. Unknow-

ingly Prabhu was walking slowly along the road again with
the boy trotting beside him and holding the bowl in front of
Prabhu's face.

" I don't know who you are, *huzoor*. Perhaps you are
generous."

" Can't you see by my clothes that I am not rich ? I am
an ordinary man. Go and beg from the rich. What did you
mean when you said I must give while there is still time ? "
He stopped and waited for the answer, bending, and eyeing
the boy as if he expected a confession.

" Many rich people are going about now, *huzoor*, in
Gandhiji's poor man's homespun," the old man called to
him in a shaking voice. " Forgive the boy's impudence,
huzoor. You have a rich man's face. Otherwise the boy
would not have bothered you. Pardon, *huzoor*. Soon we will
not be allowed to beg. Unless the Maharajah banishes Hassan.
I am too sick to work. They are saying that we are all to be
driven into a labour force."

A rich man's face. Pity for all men enmeshed in the world-
wide money hunt, in the battle not to go down in starvation
and defeat, took over Prabhu's whole heart.

" You mean I look rich ? " he asked the old man. The
old man was laughing silently, toothlessly, looking senile
and pitiable but for the sharp, knowing light in his faded
milky eyes.

" One cannot mistake the rich, *huzoor*, even when they
are clothed from head to foot in a shroud," the old man
replied. " There is no mistaking the face of the man who is
rich."

It must be a confident look of well-being, a look of a man
who has no worry about where the next five thousand meals
are coming from, and whose personality is released for higher
things, or lower things, and is secure in every single moment
flowing through his body towards the painless past.

He gave the man a rupee. No, it was worth a lot more than

that. He gave him five rupees. That was not enough. Why stop at five? The man had given him enough to think about for a month. He gave him ten. Now he knew he was ruining the beggar, spoiling everything for those who would be begged from after him, and once again he had shown no discretion. Furious, he told the man and the boy to go away now. And when they went he was sorry. There was no way in this world of squaring oneself with the poor. If you gave too little they sneered quietly and shuffled off cursing. If you gave too much they knew you were mad, and you knew you had marred something. If you gave nothing it nagged you all day like an ache down deep in the spirit.

He called them back. He shouted loud for the old man and he saw him turn and look back, frightened, and then the old man fled with the little boy racing after him.

" He thought I wanted the bloody, filthy money back," Prabhu moaned. He felt sick now, all the contentment of his victory over Hassan dissipated. All the way to the hotel he thought of the sick, ugly baby with its stick-legs and its big, sore head, and how the old man had nursed it tenderly with the habit of his body while his mind had been clutching outwards at the money he might get. A dark misery filled him as he made his way through the crowds. He saw the militia with their rifles looking importantly at people and sauntering up and down in soldierly idleness in the throngs. A bloody lot of good they were going to do Hassan now they had come out at last with their armbands. Even so that old man with his sick child and his few words had drawn a sharp line under certain thoughts about Tolstoyan poverty, the goodness and the uselessness of it, the sheer luxury of it. That heavy-shouldered, dark, sweaty, Jew would have given Tolstoy (" and me, I suppose ") a punch under the jaw, preferably in some temple or other. He wondered. The old man, too, had pointed to Hassan with his quavering voice. Was Hassan right? Had it not been a dirty trick to pull the spiritual trump out of the bag and hold that parade and snare the people away from the man of soil, Hassan?

Hari Lal had been genuine and sincere about the parade, sincere about the spiritual way and about his hatred of quarrel and violence, and yet Prabhu *knew* he was being clever, and had wanted to defeat Hassan. Was that spiritual? Wasn't he himself the same as Hari Lal, delighted with the whole thing? He had glowed with happiness when Hari Lal had described the big meeting by the river, about how he had preached about the new pool of lands, " The Surrender Fund," which would be more powerful than any government-forced land reform. But he had been sincere, just as he was sincere at this moment. The people had loved it.

He saw the adventure before himself and Hari Lal. He was going to make Hari Lal a sort of *Diwan* who would administer the great spiritual drive to shame the rich. Despite everything, though, he, Prabhu, knew that the spiritual way was only *technically* the best, and would never wring the loot out of the rich. Out of some of them, who could be shamed, yes, but not out of all of them. The thing would limp along, like all religion, which man would pay for but did not want to be bothered by. And Hassan seemed to know that. The communists knew it too; men were never going to be voluntarily good. They had to be made to be good if the poor were going to eat twice a day instead of once, or instead of not at all. He was desolated with petty intellectual grief as he considered the impossibility of the heaven on earth. If you flogged and beat the haves into giving to the have-nots, that was not paradise. That was brute force. And if you preached the spiritual thing you were only making yourself happy while the hard-hearted, cynical rich looked on and discussed their investments. The simple days of sword-conquest seemed to be over, and man faced his problems for the first time and did not know how to cope.

" I've got to believe," he muttered. " I've got to believe.

I've got to get a grip and go on and believe. Otherwise I'll peel all the skins off my philosophical onion one by one and find nothing inside. Nothing."

He ran lightly up the steps of The Moghul Hotel. He could never walk up stairs. They were there to be run up, a barrier hiding the next scene. He was not in the right mood now to meet Clegg-Bray, this person he had known about for so long and had never feared or disliked once he had discovered the pathos of the whole thing. The right mood, he had thought, would be cold, insulting contempt wrapped in a masterly indignation which never raised its voice. He had even worked out the opening line. " I'm terribly sorry to butt in on you like this, old chap, but I'm the husband. I just wanted to ask if you'd mind not seeing my wife again. We've both had enough." The " old chap " bit had thrilled him when it had found its way into the sentence during rehearsals. It had *everything*, insult, chilly friendliness, dramatic falsity, irony.

He sent a bearer up to Clegg-Bray's room to say that a gentleman would like to see him. In five minutes the bearer came down to say that the Colonel Sahib had said to bring the gentleman up, providing he was not a salesman for enamel-work or anything like that.

" Do I look like a salesman ? " Prabhu demanded of the bearer. " Do you know who I am ? "

" No, *huzoor*."

" Show me up to the Colonel Sahib's room." Prabhu was angry already and he forgot to remember to control himself. He began to pass the boy on the stairs, rehearsing new lines, eager to face this impudent, bald-headed war hero who had sat in so many churches in London with Lila for hours at a time.

He opened the door of Clegg-Bray's room and came upon him, sitting at a desk, looking up at his visitor, unperturbed, calm, a fountain pen in his hand, and stacks of hand-written

manuscript all over the table at which he sat. He was wearing
an old khaki army shirt and slightly frayed khaki shorts, his
pink, bald head shining in the sunlight pouring into the
room. Prabhu watched the bony, red knees crossed under
the table. Clegg-Bray looked absorbed, disturbed, almost impatient, as if anxious to go on with the writing with which he
was so obviously engaged.

" I have a distinct impression that it's the Maharajah himself," he said, as if not speaking to his visitor but to somebody
beyond, somebody invisible. He seemed to be at grips with
himself, as if he would forget Prabhu at any moment. He
began to stare hard at the wall behind Prabhu, then said,
" Now it's happening, it seems quite unreal. Quite unreal."
He pointed to an arm-chair and waved his hand at it. " Do,"
he said, " please do. Do." He was silent for a time, scrutinis-
ing Prabhu with suspicious, frowning eyes. " You look as
you look in your photographs," he added. " A very disturbed
personality indeed. A man like myself. A weakling."

He continued to study his visitor with alert, darting eyes,
dreams in them while they gave extraordinary discomfort to
Prabhu, who had forgotten his opening lines, his devastating
and disturbing opening lines. Prabhu settled into the arm-
chair and devoted himself to looking at ease, meeting the
strange, blue eyes which were fixed on his face.

" What's this nonsense about ? " Prabhu heard himself say.
" What have you come out here _for_ ? " He began to recover
possession of his exterior person, his masks, his defences.
" I've read your letter, the one you wrote to my wife. It's
hardly the letter of a war hero, is it ? "

" Hardly," Clegg-Bray agreed, shaking his head. " Hardly.
But who is there who always writes the right kind of letter
in a crisis, a letter he wouldn't mind strangers reading ? Who
is there ? You have the position, though, in my letter. Disgrace for us all. And all because of you. It's your fault, all
of it. What a swine you've been to that marvellous woman,

your wife. I want to marry her. Why not hand her over and have done with it ? Or is your pride involved ? " He asked these questions so matter-of-factly, so *knowingly*, it seemed to Prabhu, that his visitor had to say the first thing that came into his mind.

" Did you have a good trip out ? " he asked Clegg-Bray. " How British have I become ? " Prabhu asked himself as he heard his own question. " Did you have a good trip out ? What do I care what kind of trip out he had ? But he's a cool one, by God. Cool." Clegg-Bray said he had had a delightful trip out. Engine trouble at Cairo. He had gone for a drink at the old Gezira. Had Prabhu served in the Middle East during the war ? Burma ? Ah, yes, Lila had mentioned Burma. " She said you won the Military Cross in Burma. You don't look like a Military Cross type to me. You look as if you must have been very surprised to get it. Were you surprised ? "

" Shall we talk about the basic issue ? " Prabhu said, angry now.

" Basic issue." Clegg-Bray's face assumed a look of distaste, an expression of controlled disgust, just enough disgust showing to show his visitor what he thought. " That's an interesting expression to cover a disaster like yours, a disaster like your marriage to the marvellous woman you've treated so badly." Clegg-Bray then shouted at Prabhu, his blue eyes sparkling with indignation. " You've no right to such a woman. None." He broke into Urdu, Urdu so good that Prabhu could not understand it. Clegg-Bray finished his Urdu with a question, raising his golden eyebrows after asking the question and adding in English, " You think not ? "

Prabhu was incensed, not knowing what had been said, not certain that Clegg-Bray had deliberately used a language while knowing his visitor did not understand it, trying to humiliate him, to be more Indian than him, to show him up for what he was, a brown Briton who did not know his own language.

" Well ? Do you or don't you ? " Clegg-Bray asked again in English. Prabhu sat there glowering, tapping his fingers together, saying, " You have a bloody nerve coming out here like this. You'd better get out of Jashimpur before midday to-morrow—or else."

" I've asked you a question," Clegg-Bray said bluntly. " Answer it." Prabhu suspected that Clegg-Bray knew that he could not be given an answer to his question because it had not been understood. It was the most humiliating moment of his life, being asked what seemed to be an important question in his language, which he did not understand, by an Englishman who handled it with mellifluous ease and baffling grammatical correctness.

" Get out of my State," Prabhu said, and then shouted it again. " Get out of my State."

" Answer the question." The fellow was quite obviously not going to desist until he had been given an answer, or, more likely, had established that his visitor did not know what he had been asked in his own language. Prabhu was brought to a stop. He knew the other knew he could not answer the question.

" Let's have it in English," Prabhu said, gay with embarrassed carelessness, his eyes smouldering. " Let's have it again." And Clegg-Bray asked the question again, in Urdu again, and that was too much for Prabhu. He jumped out of the chair and brought his clenched fist down on the table amongst the manuscripts with a force that bounced Clegg-Bray's fountain pen into the air.

" I want to know what this is all about ? " he cried. " What have you come here for ? "

" I've told you,"said Clegg-Bray in English. " And I asked you a question, and you won't answer it." He repeated the question in Urdu.

Prabhu would not now admit he did not know what he was being asked. Things had gone too far. He was too angry. Even though he was sure the Englishman was torturing him into admittance of his ignorance of his own language, he had decided to brazen it out, to admit nothing. He was already being put in a losing position. He could not put up with it any longer.

"The question is very important," Clegg-Bray said. His gravity and his solemn and unperturbed manner was so disconcerting that Prabhu weakened and said, " Why not ask it in English ? What's wrong with English ? Why ask a question in Urdu and then bluster in English ? What the hell's this all about, may I ask ? "

" I cannot discuss such a subject in English," Clegg-Bray told him with an air of almost forbidding reminder, reminder of what must be propriety. Was it about *that* ? There was no question that *that* was involved, Prabhu was quite certain. What was it then, this question in Urdu ?

" Let's have it again, then," Prabhu said. He listened intently, like a bird with his head cocked on one side while Clegg-Bray asked his question in the same classical Urdu. Despite all his worried attention, Prabhu could make nothing of the words, only knowing them to be excellent Urdu quite beyond his knowledge. He had recognised only one word, *Kya*, which was no help at all. He was furious with curiosity and boiling with frustrated anger. He did not know what to be angry about, Clegg-Bray's torment of him, or his own ignorance.

" Well ? " The tall man's eyes were fixed on him, his big, red hands on his narrow hips. Clegg-Bray stood towering above Prabhu as if it were Prabhu who must explain himself, and Prabhu had accepted and given life to this impression.

" There's no clear -cut answer to a question like that," Prabhu said, giving an appearance of conviction to what he said by the direct and challenging look he gave his tormentor.

" And anyway, the question's nonsense. I'm not here to be questioned. I'm here to tell you to get out of this State by to-morrow morning." He had made his guess about the question, watching Clegg-Bray while he tried to bluff him. But the tall man was too cute for that. He smiled and scratched his chin.

" You haven't the vaguest idea what I've asked you, have you ? " he said. " Or have you ? You haven't, have you ? "

Prabhu would not admit it. He was in great mental pain with his own ignorance, his own denationalisation so brightly mocked by Clegg-Bray, whom he did not resent, but whom he envied for his good nature. He liked the fellow already, why, he had no idea. Perhaps it was Clegg-Bray's open, trusting manner, his disarming honesty. Prabhu did not fear him. He feared what Lila liked in him, though, and he guessed it to be Clegg-Bray's uninhibited and catching charm. He had great charm, even now as he put his hand on Prabhu's shoulder and said, " Don't feel so badly about it. *I'm* Indian enough to know how you feel. You *should* know your own language. That's why I'm here. I want to make Lila an Indian. You can't do that. You know nothing about India. I'm an Indian in many ways. I love this country."

" That's ridiculous," Prabhu snapped at him.

" I asked you," Clegg-Bray said, " in Urdu, if you——" but he hesitated and broke into Urdu again. Whatever it was he was asking he could not say the words in English.

" This thing has got to be kept out of the papers," Prabhu said hotly, ignoring the question in Urdu, though consumed with curiosity about it. " I can't afford any kind of scandal just now. What exactly have you come here for ? "

" For Lila, of course. What else ? "

" Just like that ? For Lila. The coolness of it. For Lila ! " Prabhu was quiet now, his voice edged with threat. " Isn't one woman enough for you ? Your wife ? Lila's had enough of this nonsense, and so have I. You must leave this State to-morrow morning. I know there's been nothing—nothing —nothing——"

" Nothing carnal."

" Nothing carnal between you." When he had used the word given to him Prabhu's eyes flashed angrily, but he went on. " In fact, I think it's pitiful that it's come to this—you coming out here like this with your bloody mess with your wife."

" Listen to me," the other pleaded. " Listen to me. You don't know what's the matter with me. I mean you don't understand. The war, I suppose. Can't sleep properly. Can't relax. Four wives don't make you the sweetest person in the world——" It was as if he were talking to himself, looking into himself, Prabhu forgotten. Some mania, some compulsive inner monologue.

" *Four* wives ? " Prabhu stared at him.

" You can't just stay the same person after that, and the war and so on. The war. The war. Yes. I can't believe it's over. A grenade, you know. Smashed hip. They threw me out in nineteen forty-five. Three D.S.O.s, two Military Crosses, a bagful of French and American gongs. A colonel, at my age. Psychology's no use to me. What's the use of psychology to a fellow like me ? Four wives, and the last one of them planning to drag me through the muck in the Press, and Lila too. And why ? Because I did what every one of them wanted. I married them. I mean I let them marry me. I never wanted to marry. Ask anyone who knew me. They'll tell you. I never ran after a woman in my life. My heaven's in deserts and jungles and on mountains, alone, utterly alone. Nobody knows what I've gone through. Nobody. When Lila came into my life I found someone I could talk to. I'm a shy person, a retiring person. I can't talk about things to many people. With Lila I was so happy that I didn't mind being a civilian. I could face life again. I loved war and soldiering. What else is there for a man left in this hell of a world? I found myself through Lila, that gentleness and understanding. Her unhappiness is like mine, the same exactly. She helped me with my book. Until you came back from Burma and wrecked everything she was typing the manuscript for me. *Man and Bird Through the Centuries*. There it is on the desk, there in front of you. It's more important than you and your piddling little State and your socialism. My God, when I think of all we did for people like you, civilising you and printing books for you, and all you can do is yap about fair shares for all, and you can't even speak your own language. I used to take Lila bird-watching on the river—what a wonderful person, what an observant person, what a delight to be with her." He came out of his trance and walked across to Prabhu. " You've got to give her to me," he said gruffly. " I can't go on without her." He had filled the room with his tremendous ego, with his useless energy and his quiet, frantic madness.

" Bird-watching," Prabhu was murmuring. " Bird-watching. It's not possible." He looked up into Clegg-Bray's mad eyes. " You know, of course, that she hasn't the slightest interest in birds. Or in religion. Or in you? She likes you. You're quite a nice chap, even though you're cracked, I suppose. But you've got to get the bird-watching bit out of your head. She's beautiful, Lila, and if she'd been ugly you wouldn't have looked at her. She's an actress. You're an actor. I was watching you just now. No woman could stand that kind of thing for long. Why don't you have a course of treatment? Get properly demobilised. Go back to one of your wives and settle down. *Four* wives, my God! *Four*. You're not pulling my leg, are you? "

" Unfortunately no," Clegg-Bray said in a whisper, looking out of the window. " Sometimes I can't believe it's all happened. Why must you go on bullying and crushing Lila? Give her to me and have done with it."

" I'm sorry," Prabhu said coldly. " I can't do it. This is

x

one wife you can't have. Go back to your most recent wife."

An expression of pain came into Clegg-Bray's eyes. There was such a look of loneliness on him then that Prabhu thought he saw everything—charm and innocence permanent in the tall, rangy, lonely-looking body; many women would want to look after it all, to understand it and have it and control it and love it, but it would have none of it. Nobody would ever own this person, this pale-eyed bird-watcher who carried his mass of manuscript round the world. The war. Clegg-Bray must have been one of those types to be found in every regiment. They played with captured enemy shells, undid grenades, read Lawrence of Arabia, wanted to go in disguise to Lhasa one day, climb Everest backwards with no oxygen, lead long patrols into dangerous territory, had no fear at all, were not asked out on mess parties or drink sessions. They stared out of windows and dreamed about tactics and about parachuting down into Hitler's headquarters, a grenade in each hand. They were in every army. In peacetime, saturated with achievement and with the perfection of their bravery and their egotistical experience become medals, they spun in their unwantedness and became ill with sorrow for the lost patrol, the finished importance, the spent career. Some drank. Some disappeared. Some switched off the war like a light and showed a greater bravery. Some, like Clegg-Bray here, were not to be understood, even by themselves. Somebody had thrown a shillingsworth of metal made by some unknown fraulein and his hip had got in the way, and he was given his bowler hat. But for that piece of metal he would now be in Palestine playing with Arab head-dresses and new maps, and reading the Old Testament to find out what it was not about. The Clegg-Brays lived their marvellous lives and deserved them, the Marco Polos who rediscovered the fabulous lands of fear, other people's fear, and never discussed them save as adventures in the name of glory. Prabhu was jealous of him.

" I know damn' well it's over," ruminated Clegg-Bray as if

he had not heard. "That it's as if it never happened. And yet Lila used to understand me and talk to me. We exchanged a million thoughts. I wonder if we were being children, rehearsing things that never happened and should have happened? She had no brothers and sisters, neither had I. Utter loneliness, perhaps. And ground to powder by narrow religion. Could it be that? I wonder. I just packed a case and got on a plane and landed in Delhi, then drove up here, and here I am sitting talking to you. I used to think the same kind of thing during the war when I reached the front line. I used to say to myself, 'It's queer. You just travel and travel and you get to the war, shells bursting and men shitting themselves with fright. Just an ordinary sort of journey in trucks and on foot and so on. Anybody could go,' I used to think, 'if they put on a uniform. Travelling to a war, just like that, an actual place where men were doing each other in.' You don't know what I'm talking about, do you? No, of course not. Fair shares for all and unemployment insurance from the age of fourteen." He gave a shout so loud and frantic then that Prabhu recoiled in shock. "What do you do it for? Why don't you enjoy your silly life and let your wife be of some use to you?" He quietened again, speaking in a lower voice than usual. "That's pure tension. Nerves. Forgive me. The shouting, I mean, not the wisdom. Christ, I wonder what's the meaning of this mess I'm in? I can't live without Lila. Don't ask me why. I can't. That's all. I can't."

"You'll bloody well have to, chum," Prabhu said. "You need a long lie up in a rest home or something. I remember reading about you during the war. That time you killed a couple of hundred poor bastards somewhere in Greece or Italy. We all envied you like hell. I still do, as a matter of fact. Queer, isn't it? I'd like to have killed a couple of hundred poor bastards and to have finished up with a breastful of fruit salad. What a shocking thing to admit, yet it's a fact.

Does that kind of thing prey on your mind? All that killing you did. Is that what's eating you?"

"Prey on my mind?" The biting scorn in Clegg-Bray's voice was a surprise, an unexpected force to have come from behind those holy, visionary's eyes with their gaze fixed on something beyond, no matter what they appeared to be regarding close at hand. "Prey on my mind? What are you talking about? I loved every minute of it, and I'd do it all again to-morrow if I had the chance. War's the only adventure there is, the only one that's simple, and has point and meaning. Everything else is a mess and a jigsaw puzzle. That's why men like war. It's simple. To kill the other clot, and to do it well, and feel satisfied afterwards about the way you did it. And then planning the next show. All that cock about how terrible it all was. It's just mush. Mush! Every time I think of the little weasel-faced bastard that threw that grenade at me and got me a bowler hat, just outside of Caen in Normandy, I could weep with bloody rage. And he got away. The last of his squad. I'd finished the rest of them. I went after the little bastard but he got away because I couldn't run. A little shifty, back-street face he had. I'll forgive him one day, I expect, when I've discovered humility. Prey on my mind! My God, how I hate claptrap."

"I don't know how to apologise, Colonel," Prabhu said bitterly, wounded by the other's merciless scorn. "I've only killed three people, in a bunker with a grenade—a mere Military Cross, and yet even I find myself at times thinking about their wives or mothers or something in Japan. Mush, of course."

"Yes, mush. Pure, bloody mush," Clegg-Bray said vindictively. "And you know it. Prey on my mind, indeed. My God, it's enough to make one sick. That's what kills Lila, you know. Your shocking vanity and your phoney social bunkum about raising the standard of dying and so on. She's not meant for that. She's meant to live happily and with someone like me, a wreck like herself. I was mad to come here. Shall we bring this chatter to a halt now ? "

" You get out of here in the morning. I've nothing against your nonsense with Lila. You're round the bloody bend, that's obvious. Bomb-happy or something. That's not my pigeon, as we used to say. If you want to help Lila, then go back to your wife, the most recent wife—the one who says she's going to drag you through the mud, and keep yourself and Lila out of the papers. If there's any mention of Lila in any paper, anything to do with you, do you know what I'll do ? "

" You'll shoot me," said Clegg-Bray satirically.

" Correct," Prabhu said, but Clegg-Bray had spoiled it, made it ridiculous. The nerve in Prabhu that had not been reached for some time, the Jashimpuri sense of the ridiculous, was touched acutely and suddenly, and he threw his head back and broke into hysterical laughter. Even Clegg-Bray smirked sadly, watching him, too unhappy to meet him half-way in that laughter, yet knowing well why Prabhu was laughing. The ridiculous posture of human indignation had to be laughed at when satire, the satire of a look, of a dry voice, had torn its bright, dramatic clothes off and left it shivering with its hands joined across its middle in terrible shyness. " You'll shoot me," Clegg-Bray murmured to himself, catching the gone moment again, and laughing softly and dejectedly himself.

Prabhu went out of the room and down the stairs, laughing, and thinking, " The nicest madman I ever met. Mad as a bloody hatter."

An earth tremor went through the floor like the creaking of a ship in a storm, and Prabhu staggered with it, his mind knocked off its platform as the ripple came back and the mind could get no sense from his limbs. Then it was over. He leaned against the wall, panting, trying to get his mood of righteousness back. People were yelling in the street, congratulating each other that it had only been a tremor. It was some time before Prabhu recalled that he was the Maharajah dressed in peasant homespun, the leader of the new spiritual way of reform, being stared at by the people with admiring eyes as he went up the road. He was half-way home before he realised that he and Hari Lal now had a real mission before them. " Work. Work. Work. That's the thing. Work," he exulted as he neared the palace. And yet it was all somehow finished for him. He felt spent.

As he climbed the flight of steps leading up to the palace, the incidents of the past forty-eight hours began to go off inside him like time-bombs. He was in that state of nervous exhaustion when the will, despite whatever victories it has achieved, has collapsed, so that the personality is naked to the many cold winds of doubt. He had won. He had defeated Hassan after his deep humiliation following the weird razor incident. He had, while the maniac, Clegg-Bray, had orated out of his massive, indestructible ego, seen all his own mean-ness with Lila. He had seen how necessary it was that Lila feel free with somebody, with a wreck like poor Clegg-Bray. More than anything he had seen that he was not meant to live in and to rule Jashimpur. He was no longer interested in the place, only in the *idea* of it. And his body knew that winter was coming, the first cool tingle of autumn already announcing the snow and the ice that lay beyond in the moun-tains, waiting for time to unleash them. He remembered how he had disliked the Jashimpur winter in boyhood. Silence, cold, a frozen world of isolation.

He had begun to plan his going, and he knew he could not find the real reason for it. He knew, though, that he must talk about it with Lila. She did not want to stay here and he knew now that he wanted to give her what she wanted most. And he knew it would be to depart from Jashimpur. Was he using her (as usual) as his excuse for going from here? He did not know. He did not care so much this evening about

Jashimpur's future as he had cared yesterday. From the top of the palace steps he looked down towards the city and knew, with a tired wonder at his own lack of any real convictions, that he did not care about it. Hassan did. Hassan loved it and wanted everyone to be ready to die for it. Standing in that first crisp breath of autumn, Prabhu wished he had not met Clegg-Bray, who had poured the greyness of failure into his ready being. He knew he was turning now to the impossible, the effort to solve a human relationship, and Lila was waiting.

Chapter Thirty

Nasrullah Beg in his police office had known all along why the people would not rescue Hassan, would not come out into the streets with clubs in their hands to do what Hassan knew was their will, his will, peasantry's grudging, bloody will to have an end to things. The news from India, which Hindus and Muslims in Jashimpur sought not to discuss with each other, had gradually burdened them all with the fear and the threat of that terror in the Punjab which had become ferocity. All glory, all war, Nasrullah Beg knew as well as the next man, was done out of fear. Bravery and ferocity were fear in a uniform, or in bloody rags behind some slogan or other about the menace to the race, the religion, the family, and there was no escaping it. For it was true. Men could not leave each other alone. Was it boredom which made men long to kill and destroy? Yet he knew that even his own heart cried for revenge as he listened to the radio. And some of his Hindu friends wanted revenge too. But they could not speak of it to each other. But they felt the load of their religions, their religio-politics which had never caught on in Jashimpur. It was very frightening.

Like everyone else, he had had enough now of this piece of modern *Panchatantra*, this degrading public comedy between the Maharajah and Hassan, even while he had known what a safety valve it had proved to be. Their public performances had entertained the people and, as much as the bloody tidings daily from India, had helped to bring atrophy into the dangerous emotions he knew to be awake in the people. That frenzied outburst against the soldiers, that wilful and thought-less burning of the stacked files of dead administrations, had now expended the remaining sullen rage of the people. He always thought of " the people " with amused contempt and suspicion, and was never sentimental about them. Why should he be ? Only for luck he might have been out in the streets during these hours, been punctilious and unswerving in duty, and become a corpse, *katm*, murdered and flung aside by a desperate herd of peasants. Well, it was over now, and it was very interesting to go over the reports from the city —everywhere remorse and guilt. " We are no better than those madmen in the Punjab," they were saying. " Who are we to boast now, or to condemn ? The files, yes. Burn all the files if possible. But to kill the brainless soldiers, no. That was a sin." It had always been the same in Jashimpur. Remorse and regret for the sudden storm of fury, uncertainty, doubt, a longing for forgiveness. There were no real hardened criminals in Jashimpur. They all wanted to confess in the end. It was due to broken, tender hearts, and to vanity. They all had it. He had it himself. He had noticed it. History and isolation and undying love for tradition, the curse of an ancient and indestructible race which would sooner be Jashimpuri and in rags, than something else and rich.

What about these mysterious Christians who were said to have come down from Kangla to take that withered old Miss Sahib at the palace back with them ? If all reports were true, those three had set off the waiting explosive in the people, by preaching religion in an eating-house near The Poet's Bridge.

He was having them watched while he collected all the stories of their doings since their arrival in the city. The *Kotwal* was working as smoothly as usual, the police investiga-tions as steady and smooth as always. While there was an unvoiced agreement, as it were, among the police officers, not to get involved in shooting or mob incidents until the Maharajah and Hassan came to some sort of terms, the spies and the informers kept adding to the heaps of information. The three curious converts were being followed about, and a servant up at the palace had come on to the police pay roll again as an observer, waiting for when the converts met their prophet, the old Miss Sahib, who was teaching the two brown English boys how to live in their country.

How very simple the official world had been only a few years ago. He put all Asia's troubles down to the year nineteen hundred and five, which added up to the sinister number of the unknown, seven (anyway, if you called it nineteen hundred and six when the evils had been achieved). It was in nineteen hundred and five that the Japanese had opened a secret door in Asia by showing that non-whites could defeat a white power. They had broken Russia with their undreamed-of fanaticism, and bravery. And nineteen hundred and five was the year the British had disturbed Bengal with their stupid wayward political theories, which had to be made to work for the sake of face in the end. They knew they should not have done it. When they had finished the gunmen and the devoted martyrs were everywhere, trying to kill a Viceroy, something too non-Indian for that world to imagine possible. Then Gandhiji and the new cow-worship as Jinnah saw it, and then Jinnah, the man who was set on hacking a piece of Mother India into a country called Pakistan in which it would be safe for non-Hindus to live, as Gandhiji saw it. As everyone was seeing it now, though, the wisdom of India was only less than Europe's, whose peoples had murdered each other for centuries, but always sound business reasons for it.

There would be no communal slaying in Jashimpur now. The mob had had enough of itself. Jashimpuris had never been sincere and lasting in mob formation. Nasrullah Beg lit a cigarette and looked out across the wide river to the open country and the mountains where he had begun life as the son of a forest ranger. His father had been shot by the old Maharajah at forty yards during a bear hunt. The old Maharajah had lost his spectacles, and rather than miss a shot had fired at the dark form which had appeared before him. From that time Nasrullah Beg's life had gone straight and unwaveringly, from service in the police ranks (very hard to get into, the safest job in Jashimpur even now) right through to to-day, when he knew that no man can know the misfortune that can give him fortune.

The telephone went off like an alarm clock, breaking his reverie, and he picked it up and said, " Well ? " It was his number-one man in the city, an ex-student, a post office clerk who did spying in his spare time, for pleasure and for the few rupees it brought him. He was too smart for Nasrullah Beg's liking, too full of unasked advice and opinions. But he was thorough and incurably suspicious. Here he was at it again, not merely reporting, but interpreting, clarifying, interfering with his detective-novel reader's mind, his film addict's childishness. He was a sly, over-dressed young man who lived for the cinema and who was writing a film script called *Death in the Taj Mahal.* Part of the script lay on Nasrullah Beg's desk now, unread, unasked for, unwanted.

He spoke in English, good, student's English oiled by years of the cinema and from talking interminably with European and American tourists about his plans for his life.

" Mighty events are in train," he said, not too dramatically, yet imparting to his voice a certain amount of his own dark, conspiratorial love for himself in his role as police spy in the small political department. " As I have often forecast to you and to others, the spiritual awakening of the people is taking place at last. Our race has not lost its feeling for the spiritual force which Gandhiji has worked all his life to bring back into India, into the souls of all of us. To what am I referring ? What mighty events have I seen ? You may well ask———" (Nasrullah Beg had not spoken. He was breathing hard at the other end of the telephone.) " To-day, half an hour ago, I saw with my own eyes the downfall of the materialism which

Hassan and his Party have threatened us with. I saw with my own eyes the crowds I telephoned you about earlier with their ropes and clay round their necks—I saw them turn away from Hassan while he was shouting at them from his balcony, and I saw them follow Hari Lal, his father and many *mahants* and *fakirs* into the new way, the way of atonement and restitution. I have decided not to draw my pay for this particular piece of work to-day. It shall be sent to the Atonement Fund set up by Hari Lal. One tenth of my pay is going to that fund in the future. I wept. I wept as I watched it. So did others. This is the message we have for the world. This is the meaning of India, and here in Jashimpur we can show India how it is to be achieved. People can sneer at me if they like. What do I care ? I have seen a miracle worked. The scales fell from my eyes. I was like the man who was in darkness. I knew this awakening was possible but I did not believe. Hassan is finished here. All he can do now is become more spiritual, less worldly, less communistic and violent. Are you laughing at me ? " As he said this last sentence the spy's voice was sharp with wounded sentiment, his exalted mood suddenly marred.

Nasrullah Beg, who was bending over his desk with his hand pressed to his mouth, had been unable to stifle all his laughter. But he denied it in an immediate and dignified reproof, even remembering to insult his spy for having the impudence to ask such a question. A deeply religious man himself, Nasrullah Beg had no time for woolly emotionalism about the spirit. He knew that India was one of the most materialistic countries on the face of the earth and he knew that she had never denied it. It was her penitents who denied it. It offended him whenever a fellow-Indian tried to weave some more of the fiction about Indian spirituality which the romantic West had invented for Asia. As a policeman he knew that starving peasants threw flower petals in front of gods in order to get something or to have something forgotten, or to abolish some uncontrollable fear. He knew that he, too, prayed harder and more fervently when he was frightened. None of that cancelled the depth of the essential Indian tenderness and yearning for God. But this emotional syrup smeared all over everything by a mere spy who would live in the cinema if he could afford it brought out his laughter, and disturbed the warning contradictions in his own heart, whisky versus goat's milk, sincere belief in soul-force instead of air-bombing, while knowing that air-bombing had always won, and wanting India to be a power, the whole seething, whirlpool of a race come into its own again and looking for a direction. He had thought a good deal about these things while reading the news and thinking about the new India, which was not new, only old, and decayed, but as vital and fecund behind the decay as ever she had been.

When he had got the full story out of his spy by rude, abrupt questioning, he too had to agree that it was amazing news, this incident in which the people had followed Hari Lal. He refused to sound amazed, knowing the vanity of his spy who would boast about it in the police station. He ordered him to organise a watch on the Englishman called Clegg-Bray staying at The Moghul Hotel, and to see to it that all his conversations with anybody at all were overheard. Yes, that was all. The spy wanted praise. He gave him a small, begrudged morsel of it.

"You speak very well on the telephone," he said. "Very clearly," and rang off.

The spy came on again the next day at the same time. This time he reported that the Maharajah had walked down to The Moghul Hotel from the palace wearing peasant dress, and without his dark glasses. He sounded shocked about the peasant dress and was of the opinion that it was a disguise.

"People are saying the Maharajah is about to follow Hari Lal's father into a hermitage. That is impossible——"

"Kindly be silent for a moment while I ask you some

questions," Nasrullah Beg said icily. " Did he meet the Englishman ? He did ? What was said ? Were they in the hotel ? "

" No one could hear what was said," the spy reported. " The Maharajah is very cunning. He closed all doors of the Englishman's room. Once or twice they shouted. That's all I can tell you."

" You are discharged," Nasrullah Beg said with savage and cutting emphasis. " You are finished." He slammed the telephone down. When he was twenty-five and a young detective he had once climbed into a room and hidden under a man's bed while the man had been reading a newspaper. He had no time for talkative fools who failed when the great opportunity came to them. He cursed his spy, all spies, all police work. He had so much wanted to know what this Englishman and the Maharajah would say to each other, though he had hoped that the Maharani herself would some-how contrive a night visit to the Englishman and perhaps shame him and humiliate him for his shocking act in following her to Jashimpur. Nasrullah Beg was a family man with a small, tight, dry moral code. He had never been unfaithful to his wife, never been drunk, had never stolen, or been caught in some sin or other. His only vice was a crippling inability to believe in the innocence and goodness of any human being. That was why he had to fight not to despise the Maharani. Where there was smoke there was fire, especially if there was a woman behind the smoke, but his loyalty to Prabhu's family was unshakable and he went back to dreaming of ways to help him get rid of this Englishman.

He was upset and querulous because of it when his spy came into his office that night holding a swollen, blue-black right eye. The eye was completely closed and swollen to the size of an egg. The spy explained that after his dismissal he had gone back to The Moghul Hotel to try and get into the Englishman's room, to have a try at clearing his name and getting back his job as a spy. The Englishman had caught him hiding in the lavatory, had closed the door, seized him, and then struck him hard with his fist in the eye, saying, " Go now. Return once more and I will punch the other one. *Khuda Hafiz*."

" His Urdu is beautiful," the spy moaned. " I put him down as a gentleman when I first saw him. But when he hit me he looked like a criminal. He had the face of a murderer. You will not sack me ? You will give me another chance ? I love my work. I will work for nothing for a month."

" Go back to The Moghul Hotel and keep watch on it," said Nasrullah Beg. " With your other eye. I want full reports on the Englishman's doings. The usual expense account. Ten annas to a servant for every report. Put in your expense sheet at the office as usual. I'm sorry for your eye. You tried. *Khuda Hafiz*." He dismissed him with a thin smile.

" *Bahut mehr bani se*," the spy said, forgetting himself and making as if to go down and take Nasrullah Beg's feet, but he remembered who he was and what year it was and gave a short bow instead.

Nasrullah Beg thought well of the Englishman for closing the door of a lavatory and striking a spy inside it, quietly and efficiently, privately. That was discreet and any spy deserved it. It was very interesting this studying of men. A man blacks a man's eye and wittily dismisses him with a religious good wish. It was truly a world full of interest.

His nerves then noticed that a strange, eerie silence had come over the world, a kind of thick hush. His heart, knowing before his mind what this silence portended, went into a heavy, thudding rhythm. Sweat broke out all over him. As his mind took the situation in he started with fear. All this in one or two seconds. It was nearly midnight.

Chapter Thirty-One

There was no explaining to himself the cold, desolate feeling which soaked Hari Lal even while he wept with happiness on his way home from the great meeting by the river. He had tasted God in his mouth and in his heart, and yet there was no God. He had the kind of mind which knew it wanted God because there was none, and if there *was* one his mind and heart were too dry, too deflowered of trust and innocence to accept such a thing, even were God to produce his proofs. He would have to go on with the pensive wondering and the snap and click of cool reasoning, and use God for what He was for, taming men whose final brutal answer to dilemma was to kill somebody or other and burn down cities for love of justice.

It was Hari Lal who brought the three converts along to Miss Bullen. Before he took them to the palace he gave them tea, and even drank tea with them, to the amazed but discreet disgust of the man who owned the wayside teashop. Hari Lal had broken all his caste rules, which he thought of nowadays as class-rules, year by year, but this was the first time he had ever drunk tea with peasants. He learned a great deal, the most important lesson being that men were quite transfigured by a newly discovered belief in God, and although he found their garbled faith distasteful and embarrassing, he knew he must respect it. He must respect all sincerity when it was trying to move towards goodness. He kept this respect even when Shadrach, without meaning to be impudent, said to him, " I feel sorrow for people like you who are lost in the darkness we lived in until we found our faith." He knew they might go back to Islam one day, but only to be better Muslims. He shook off all the questions which began to beset his mind. He was too pleased for Miss Bullen's sake to give in to the temptation in his heart, the temptation to question their new faith into the small, broken pieces he was sure he could make of it. Was that his Western half urging him ? His Hindu half was happy for them. And he envied them their almost childish and rapt enthusiasm, and approved their love of the old woman they spoke of as " Mother." In the storm of this world who could not be moved by being with three simple men who were made happy by a love for God, in whom they said they trusted completely ? He told them to finish their tea quickly and he would take them to the palace.

Although Prabhu had asked him twice to start wearing peasant dress, Hari Lal had refused. " It wouldn't be *me*," he said. " I can't do it. I haven't the courage." He had laughed himself to sleep thinking of Prabhu in his peasant dress, friendship and love in the laughter. Prabhu would never rid himself of that aristocratic *right* to eccentricity, the thing that made Maharajahs safe even when they were wealthy socialists by emotional conviction.

Hari Lal had planned the wonderfully successful procession and led it as a last gesture against Hassan, and he had had faith in it, a feeling of certainty that it would succeed. He had both believed in the spiritual power of his father's surrender of lands, and had used it as well, coldly and efficiently. He was never surprised by himself, never lied to himself or caught himself with a mask on. He could wear a mask, in an emergency, but he always put it on himself, and always chose the mask. No matter what he had done, or why he had done it, he had killed Hassan's " Workers' and Peasants' State " as he always thought of Hassan's future Jashimpur.

From now on the way was open for the countless achievements of men's consciences, and for their mistakes.

"Here, Miss Sahib, is a deputation from Kangla to see you," he told Miss Bullen when they reached the palace. The old woman was teaching Narendra Nath and Roshan Lal how to make various kinds of knots and how to plait string in the village way. They were sitting in the garden under a tall *chenar* tree. The boys had begun to speak Urdu with Miss Bullen and from time to time she made them follow her in the chanting of nouns, pointing out blades of grass, birds, her fingers, their clothes. Hali Lal was chilled by her cold ("British") reception of Mishak, Shadrach and Abednego, who looked as ridiculous as their names when they stood before her with their hanging heads and announced that now, at last, they were genuine Christians and had brought a message from Kangla.

"Indeed?" she said, folding up the string and tying it in two neat bundles. She told the boys to go and play with their cricket gear for a while. She invited Hari Lal to sit down. The three converts stood where they were, silent, with bowed heads, contrite yet hopeful, certain of their eventual acceptance as genuine religious men who had been sent to bring the Miss Sahib back to Kangla. They knew how to wait. They had been waiting all their lives. They said nothing while she asked questions about Kangla and answered them herself, one after the other, the whole series being a sharp-tongued attack on the habits and customs of the people of Kangla. She ended with, "And does the place still smell? Of course it does. Why shouldn't it? It's only dirt after all. Have you had some tea, you three religious men from Kangla?"

Yes, they had had tea, thank you, Miss Sahib, thanks to the kindness of this gentleman whom they had been advised in the town to see before coming to the palace.

Miss Bullen looked at Hari Lal and smiled dryly. "Your

fame and influence are growing, young man," she said. " And I'm glad. I think you have a good influence."

" I have the greatest faith in the Maharajah," Hari Lal said with a modesty which the old woman found very fetching. One thing she liked in young men was a modesty counterbalancing that brashness and vanity which marred their gifts until the shadows of experience brought longer and longer silences in their monologues. Hari Lal was never brash. She always imagined his brain as a shining, oiled machine. She knew Hari Lal was subtle, honest, and scheming almost without knowing it to have complete influence over the Maharajah. She could think of no one she would prefer more than Hari Lal to have influence over Lila's erratic and wayward husband. Hari Lal was a gentleman.

While she looked up at the three silent converts Prem approached. He looked very ill, wan and large-eyed, like a good-natured, ailing panda. He was wearing old grey flannels and a khaki army shirt. He nodded to Hari Lal, some friendly mockery in his eyes.

" You did Hassan in the eye all right, I'll say that for you," he said. " But is God going to like it ? I mean, is God going to fall for your spiritual revival ? I'll lay you fifty rupees, Hari Lal, that you have about as much belief in God as that tree over there. No offence meant, of course. While I'm delighted with the way you blackened Hassan's face with that soul parade you laid on, I don't believe you did it for spiritual reasons. You're too like me, you know, except for the drinking I do. You're one of these empty jobs, a hell of a long way now from Krishna fluting, and adrift on a copy of *The Golden Bough*. Have you read it ? " He looked at Miss Bullen now. " Have you read it, *Mataji* ? I finished it last night with a bottle of whisky. Always read shattering books with a bottle of whisky from now on, that's my motto. Read it. It stripped the remains of my Hinduism bare, and most of my second-hand Christianity as well. To-day I'm very low, very empty, very sad again. We're all a very long way from Krishna fluting. How I loved him as a boy. How I wanted to have a blue throat like Krishna. I'm poisoned, like Krishna, but no one knows."

Hari Lal was smiling indulgently while Prem delivered his bright, despairing prattle. Hari Lal agreed with some of his friends that Prem would be found dead in bed one morning. For Hari Lal each day of life was another splendid and unexpected gift from The Great I Am, as one of his school professors had called God.

"I must read *The Golden Bough*," he said to Prem. "As for my belief in God, that's God's business. I am an evolving being, evolving every minute. For that I thank every form of God there is. I was born to be happy."

"Neat," Prem said, nodding approvingly. "Quite neat. Who are these blithe-looking sons of the soil?" He pointed at the three grave, respectful converts who, while not looking directly at him, had managed to study Prem by flickering their lowered eyes.

"Three of my boys from Kangla, Prem," Miss Bullen told him. "They've accepted Christianity. I didn't try to convert them. They say they became Christians on their own."

"That's the reason for those long faces and that gloom, is it, *Mataji*?" Prem smiled at her wistfully. "D'you think they'll dislike me for drinking?"

"You can be very naughty, Prem. Very naughty," she said, not without some asperity to go with her bright, smiling grey eyes. She knew Prem would never accept the Christ he so admired and had seen working in doomed men in his prison jungles. He would never be able to look at God through the blazing spectacle of Christ, unless some miracle happened. She had hoped so much for his conversion but she found from their many talks that Prem analysed everything until all that was left was a small heap of broken words and crippled meanings. He was like his brother in that, a man who feared capture. For Prem, this universe was essentially a chaos never to be understood, totally without meaning, and yet he had the heart of a believer. He *knew* there was God and that Christ as understood by the West was going to make the future world. She had tried to tell him how one day all our present ideas would be seen as mere clues.

" These Kangla men want to give you the message from your old home," Hari Lal said to her, breaking in on her small gloom about Prem. By the way Prem had lit another cigarette and was now smoking two, one in each hand, she knew he was drunk. He seemed so very sensible when he was drunk.

It was Mishak who gave the message. He had practised it for many days, word by word, cadence and rhythm, and the soft weapon of his appealing voice showed its edge now and again when he reminded her of her duty to Kangla—" Which God put upon you." He gave her no opportunity for indignation even though he described in harrowing detail how they were all lost now up at Kangla without her at the mission. Even when he told of a baby who had died—who would not have died had the Miss Sahib been at Kangla to treat it—he did it in a way which praised her. He praised her in such a way that all her forty years' experience of good-natured flattery could not prevent the blush of pleasure which mantled her face, spreading from her neck like a pink smoke through her skin. He brought the tears he was working for. They came unwillingly and hung in her eyelashes, like tiny, sparkling icicles on thorns.

Prem and Hari Lal, who were listening to this piece of heartfelt oratory, saw its skill but were both moved by its sincerity. They got a look into the seldom thought of relationship between a lonely missionary and the people among whom she lived in a backwater of a remote and isolated State. While neither approved of proselytising, Prem could not find it in him to deny anyone's right to exhibit whatever secret they had about this permanent mystery, God. Hari Lal, who was fond of the old woman, and somewhat contemptuous of the three simple men who were voluntarily complicating their lives with something they would never understand, was moved most of all by that burdensome pity men feel when they witness what they suspect to be futility. He knew they were happy but there was drabness in it for him now. Mishak was telling how the three of them had known that they were true Christians not long after the Miss Sahib had left Kangla. They apologised, all three of them, through Mishak, for their early falsity. They had done it in obedience to the elders who had agreed that the Miss Sahib should at last have three apparent Christians to comfort her after her bitter years. Example, happiness, learning with her, had all contributed to a wish to serve her as Christians and to worship God as Christians for evermore. And the elder had ordered them not to come back without her. Without her they could not go back.

"And what about the others?" She asked them when Mishak had finished. "Are there others who want to be Christians too?"

"None, Miss Sahib. No others will ever come forward. The *Mullahs* have now begun to teach religion regularly. There will be no more Christians at Kangla—unless God decides to make a change in men's hearts. Everyone is now thinking about religion at Kangla. That is what we have done by our coming across to Christ."

"Well, that's something, *Mataji*," Prem said with a smile, happy for her. He was rather proud of her, notwithstanding what she had done to Lila with the pledge. "At least you've done that. You've got three Christians and everyone else thinking about religion up there. God, if only one could be a simple man, or a child again."

"Yes," Hari Lal agreed. "Anything that makes men good is good. Even these three woodenheads here mean it when

they say they're Christians. I believe they mean it." His eyes
as he looked at them revealed his renewed pleasure in their
pride of faith. He was very near laughing at them. They
saddened him so. "So what will you do, Miss Sahib? Will
you go back to Kangla? They seem to love you there very
much."

The earth began to move under them and all six of them
became sharp-eyed and intense as the disturbance of the never
noticed, always reliable, steady rhythm of the world occurred
in a slow, sliding, quivering looseness underfoot. It broke
in on the old darknesses of their beings like deadly magic.
The tremor began to come back, the other way, Mishak
crying, "It's sideways." Then it was calm again, as if a monster
inside the earth had been placated. There were still many
in Jashimpur who knew there was a giant mole burrowing
far down in the world, and that he made this disturbance.
They let out their breaths and Miss Bullen, who had been in
one earthquake in her youth, said, "I never like it. I never
get used to it."

"It's only a tremor," said Prem. He was breathing fast.
He was quite pale.

Ignoring the tremor's effect on them all, Hari Lal asked
Miss Bullen again what she would do, stay here or return to
Kangla.

"I'm taking the twins down to school at Delhi next week,
Mataji, remember," Prem reminded her. "You'll be free
then. But I hope you're going to stay with us. Think of all
the nice days we've had together talking and arguing. Don't
go. You've done your stuff in the Lord's army. You're
demobilised now. Stay with us. I might even give up drinking
if you do. We'll compose a pledge together."

"Yes, stay," Hari Lal said. "The Maharani won't let you
go anyway."

"Even though you've made her sign that paper, *Mataji*,"
Prem was laughing. "She loves you too much to let you go."

He was not as amused as he pretended about Lila's signing of the pledge. Lila was walking about like a ghost inside the palace, like a ghost with a bomb hidden in the middle. She was fighting hard to stand by her signature and was undergoing the suffering of moment by moment temptation. Prem had been angry when he first heard about it and saw Lila shivering, staring at the wall in mute resentment while she played cards with the two boys. But Lila had assured him that she wanted to give up drinking, and was going to fight until she won. He knew she was not going to last out and he had told her so. Like all heavy drinkers he suffered if he saw another drinker giving it up. Like a homosexual, who has to be a missionary for his group so as to decrease the loneliness and the feeling of persecution, Prem maintained that every human being was a repressed drinker. His case was well put and the temptation to tempt Lila into having a whisky was on him all day. Since her signing of the pledge he had shown some querulousness and had nagged Miss Bullen about the marriage feast of Cana. There was booze at that wedding, once Christ had arranged it. What then was wrong in drinking ? Christ had had nothing against drinking. Miss Bullen would not be drawn.

" I don't know what I'll do," she told Prem and Hari Lal after she had sent the three converts to the servants' quarters where they would wait until she called them. She had given them five rupees each as a present. They had refused it and she had made them take the money. She was flustered now they had gone. Her mind had been totally absorbed by Lila until now. Lila had told her about Prabhu having gone to see this Englishman. Imagine it, a Maharajah going to talk with a man who was trying to steal his wife. There was something so degraded and *modern* and cold-blooded about that. What would they talk about ? Would there be violence ? Lila was lying in her room, looking like a mouse, her spirit shrunk. There was a bottle of whisky on the table by her bed, a siphon and glasses. She wanted the temptation always beside her. She could defy it better, knowing it was there if she wanted it. " And my God, you know how I want it," she had said cuttingly to Miss Bullen. " I'll show you if I have a will or not. I'll show you what I can do when I want to. And if I change my mind I'll get drunk." Her eyes had been resentful, her voice shrewish and accusing as she told this to Miss Bullen. Things were very strained just now.

The two boys and Miss Bullen went in to tea with Hari Lal and Prem. Hari Lal gave them all a brilliant description of the procession again, Prem asking dozens of questions, about Hassan's speech, Hassan's face, the people's response to the speeches by the river. Once again, he thought, the Jashimpuris had shown their mysterious hand, this time holding a torch for the way that had not been allowed of old, Gandhiji's difficult way.

" Hassan's Party can be useful in the State," Hari Lal told them. " But as a force it's finished. I'm quite proud of that. I loathe demagoguery, and from the moment Hassan did that thing with the razor I made up my mind. My father, by the way, has sent his blessings to everybody here in the palace. He's walking all the way to Hariwar. When he gets there he's finished with the world. Just think of it, a man who's had everything the world could offer, giving it up."

" You browbeat him into it, didn't you ? " Prem remarked. " I know he wanted to do it, but he'd never have done it if you hadn't worked on him for years. It's like *Mataji* here with the Maharani. She'd never have given up drinking if it hadn't been for *Mataji*. I only hope you're both right, you and *Mataji*. It's quite a responsibility."

" Prem, I don't want to discuss the matter, if you don't mind," Miss Bullen said disapprovingly. She did not like Lila's weakness being bandied about in front of Hari Lal, who after all was an employee *not* living in the palace with the family. She was an employee, too, but there was a difference. Family was family, and she felt one of it now, and her loyalty was aroused. She did not approve of any of them but that was her right, not Hari Lal's.

"Don't let's worry about Hari Lal. He never gossips," said Prem, slapping Hari Lal on the back. "This is the shrewdest member of the twice-born we've ever had in the palace."

"You're very kind. Very kind," Hari Lal said with a gentle irony curling his shapely lips. "I keep forgetting I'm a Brahmin and you're a warrior."

After tea Miss Bullen went to have one of her exciting talks with Doctor Kholi. She gave him his medicine after listening to an hour-long talk about the psychological factors involved for both mother and child in the act of suckling, and its importance for the human race, indeed for the destiny of men in general. He was never disgusting or embarrassing now. She pitied him. He looked so worn and pathetic, like a small mannikin who has forgotten his role. Hassan kept telephoning the palace and asking to speak to him, but the doctor always refused, saying, "I'm too ill to face anything. I'm unable to talk. Tell him I'm dying." He was grieving over his desertion of Hassan.

The twins were looking forward to their new school near Delhi. It had been a school for Maharajahs' sons. There was to be plenty of sport, cricket being the main game. "They should be sent to Moscow for education," Kholi told Miss Bullen. "The only decent conservative education left is to be got there now."

When the twins had gone to bed Miss Bullen saw Prabhu, so dreadful-looking in his peasant dress, going into Lila's room. He did not look angry, or as if he had fought with the English colonel. Rather he looked sad and resigned, so sad that the old woman wondered if the Englishman had given him some terrible news, news about *that*. It was impossible, unthinkable. She hurried away to join Hari Lal and Prem in a game of cards.

Before she reached them she had come to a decision about Kangla. She would go back. God was sending her back. She knew that when she was alone in her room, relaxed in her bed, she would see all the meanings of the mysterious journey of her three converts. That they were true Christians she did not doubt. Strange that God should send them to her after she had turned her back on Kangla. Oh, how to know God's will ?

She played cards badly, prayers and plans trickling through her mind while the two young men joked with each other about her poor manner of play. Prem said that it was obvious to anybody that God did not want missionaries to play cards.

" He plays cards with us humans," he added. " I've always felt rather like a useless bridge-hand myself."

" Yes," she thought. " Perhaps He does," but without conviction. Being with people like these was very bad for her. It was so exciting, so very corrosive to the soul's long, carefully preserved intactness.

Chapter Thirty-Two

Lila had made up her mind by the time she heard Prabhu's step outside their bedroom. She was trembling and tired, standing by the window where she had been staring at the far mountains unseeingly for over an hour. She must say good-bye to Clegg-Bray, dismiss him softly in person, and not evade what needed no evading. She had nothing to be ashamed of, to fear discussing with the Englishman. She had tried hard to turn against him and to find fault with him, but being without alcohol had confused her mind and she could not see with her usual inebriated clarity. She now thought that she had written a letter insulting him, a letter dismissing him with the curtness she had tried to evoke to please Prabhu. She had written the short letter so often in her skull, and had scrawled so many versions of it on a writing-pad earlier in the afternoon that she thought she had sent it. Frantic for a drink, she was hallucinated enough to imagine she had been tricked by Miss Bullen and Prabhu, that they had combined while pretending separateness, in an effort to break her will. For some days she had been wondering if Prabhu and Miss Bullen talked about her when she was absent. She remembered imagining their sudden silences when she had come into a room where they were talking. Her head was aching and the craving for a whisky was enough to keep her on the edge of bitter tears.

" I'm going down to the hotel to see him myself," she said as soon as Prabhu appeared in the doorway of their bedroom.

She was wearing a blue silk sari sprinkled with tiny silver birds perched on small mango designs. Her hair was perfumed, brushed to lustrous darkness; her eyes ringed with blue-black *surma*, her small feet in white doeskin sandals with little gold clasps winking on them. She had her white handbag held tightly in her tremulous hands. She looked so pathetic that Prabhu sighed and threw out his arms and said, "For God Almighty's sake will you be sensible and have a drink? Let me get you a drink. Sit down."

She obeyed, sitting on the edge of the big bed, the battle-field of their incoherent and tangled selves, where they talked all night, plundered each other, slept in undreaming blisses.

"I've got to see him," she said. "I'll tell him he must never write to me or see me again, but I must do it myself. I shouldn't have sent that letter with you. It was too cruel, too horrible. I've nothing to be ashamed of. Did you quarrel with him? Did you lose your temper?"

"What letter? You didn't send any letter with me." He narrowed his eyes and searched for signs of madness, of hysteria. "Are you feeling all right, Lila?" he asked her, showing his concern for her in his eyes.

"There's no need to treat me like a child," she said. "You know what letter I mean. I'm ashamed of it. I shouldn't have let you browbeat me. I'll see him and finish it properly. You've made me a coward so often, but I can't be a coward in this. Did you give him my letter?"

"Lila, darling, there was no letter. What letter are you talking about?"

"Prem can drive me down," she said, convinced now that Prabhu was deceiving her. She could not remember very well what had been going on during the last day or two, yet she was full of suspicions that she was being handled, dealt with, discussed as some kind of case.

"He took it very well," Prabhu said. "I must say, although he's balmy, I liked him. He's everything I'm not, isn't he;

weak, soft, cracked, kind, easy to mould. Ego? Don't ever talk to me about ego again, Lila. He talked me to a standstill. Tell me, darling, just for interest. What was it you liked about him?"

She did not answer for some time, regarding him with the meekness of tired will and exhausted senses.

"I *am* in love with him," she said. "What's the use of denying it? What's the sense of pretending it's not true. I *am* in love with him. Harmlessly. It's silly, I know it is. But there it is. I'm so terribly tired, Prabhu. How can I be in love with him when I love you?"

"You mean, 'Where's it all going to end?'"

She was too preoccupied with her own anxieties to be stung by the affectionate mockery of his question. In fact, he was reproached enough by his own remorse for what he had said when he considered her useless pathos as she sat watching him with her dark, meek eyes.

"Why is it you're not jealous of him?" she said. "You said last night that you'd had us watched in London. You were proud of it. Why have you never been jealous about it? Aren't I worth being jealous of? Is that it? Doesn't it mean anything to you that I'm in love with him?"

"No," he said, shaking his head. "It doesn't. There's no harm in it. You're round the bend too, you know, like he is. *I* don't understand it. As a matter of fact, I'm tired of it. I came away just now from that character with a better understanding of you and your feather-bed of a mind. Desert me, if you want to. Go on. Go to him. In the state I'm in just now it doesn't matter any more. I'm beaten. I admit it. Hassan won. As for the religious nonsense dreamed up by Hari Lal, I couldn't care less. I'm sick of you all. I've had nothing but people pouring their trash down my ear—nobody listens to me. Nobody wants to hear how *I* feel about anything. I feel ill, as a matter of fact. I feel quite sick of the whole thing. Why didn't you tell me he'd had all these wives?

Did you think there was something a little unusual about that, four wives ? "

" All I want to do is say good-bye to him, face him, and not hurt him too much. You'd no right to make me write that letter. It was typical of you."

Prabhu came forward and brought his hands down with a loud slap on the small writing-table near the bed. " There *was* no bloody letter," he shouted. " Do you hear ? Have you gone mad ? "

" Don't you start shouting at me like that again," she said proudly. " I'm not going to put up with that in my state just now when I'm going through hell. I think you ought to know what it is I hate most about you, Prabhu. It's your——"

" What you hate about me is me," he said, covering her voice with his. " That's all it is. Me. And all I've got to offer is me. The same old me. You want to go and see your lover now ? "

" He's *not* my lover."

Prabhu pressed his clenched fists against his temples. " Go then," he said. " And when you come back shall we call it a day ? Do you want me to take up bird-watching, then ? "

" You callous brute. You sneer at everything, don't you. Well, you won't master me ever again. I'll handle my own affairs in my own way."

The telephone by the bed shrilled, sudden and harsh. Prabhu went and picked it up. " Hallo," he said.

It was Nasrullah Beg to inform the Maharaj Sahib that an English visitor had just committed suicide in The Moghul Hotel. He was speaking in a low, velvet, conspirator's voice, as if he had got himself actually inside the mouthpiece.

" And you thought I ought to know. You thought you ought to inform me. Is that it ? " Prabhu had to sit down as he spoke, his knees weak, his heart wrenched as he thought of those lonely blue eyes in the bony bald head of the tall monomaniac whom he had already begun to think of with amused affection. It seemed impossible that such a man should be a suicide, but on the other hand there was that coldness, that deep devotion to self, that record of fierce and chivalrous bravery. As for the love for Lila, he did not believe in it. He did not believe in such love, in such all or nothingness. It did not make sense, that kind of stuff—" If I can't have her then I can't live." Yet here it was, coming through the small, careful voice of Nasrullah Beg. His face burning with embarrassment as he thought over the excellent police work Nasrullah Beg did in watching his own Maharajah, Prabhu asked careful questions, one eye on the apathetic Lila, who was looking hard at her handbag.

" I've taken every paper in the Englishman's room, Maharaj Sahib. All he has on him now is his passport. Only the manager of the hotel and one of the servants knows about the incident. Both have been warned to say nothing. I've taken the liberty of threatening them both with expulsion from the State if they open their mouths. Maharaj Sahib, I have a suggestion to make. There is a guest-house, as you know, a mile over the State border. It is unoccupied at present. I could move the body there with his belongings to-night, myself. It could be found there to-morrow some time. A foreign visitor, a suicide, and so on. The buses pass there to Delhi. He could have got off one of them. Or would you prefer I left the matter as it is ? "

They were talking about a man who had come out here from England to see the Maharajah's wife, and Prabhu knew it, and knew Nasrullah Beg knew it. His admiration for the policeman's speed and tact, and his own sense of outraged privacy sought to scatter his thoughts as he tried to come to a decision.

Already Clegg-Bray had become a body, a dead body overshadowing the fantastic conversation he had with him. A decision was wanted and he came to it in a rush. He used words which neutralised all hint of the tragedy for Lila's ear.

"It would be best not to leave it as it is," he said. "The other idea is a good one. But I'd like it to be much farther away than the place you mention. Can you manage that?"

"The guest-house over the border, Maharaj Sahib? You mean you'd like the body outside the State?"

"Yes."

"I can assure you, Maharaj Sahib, that this matter will have no consequences in the State. I shall arrange everything."

"Thank you." The click at the other end did not cut all his connections with the man called Clegg-Bray, who had now become a shadow, a large shadow of a person who had committed suicide because he could not have Lila. Because it was ridiculous, it was frightening.

"He's gone," he said dully to Lila. "He's left the State. He's gone back to his wife. Were you listening?" If she found out Clegg-Bray had made this suicide over her, which he had not—he had made it over a million other things all centred in his own curious person—he would live for good between them, a monument to pain and to the ravelled errors of which human beings knitted their insoluble personalities. Clearly he saw how each day of living obscured further the original motives for this or that aspiration, this or that direction. It was impossible to shut out accident and complication.

"Is that what the phone call said?" she asked him, her big eyes judging him, not doubt in them, but readiness to doubt.

"Yes."

"What's the matter with you, Prabhu?" She got up and came close to him. "You look terrible. You look ill. What's happened?" She was alarmed now. "Tell me. What's happened?" Did people sometimes breathe fear from each other, disaster? As she spoke he felt ill, sad and despairing. He sat down on the edge of the bed. Should he tell her?

z

Why not? The truth was easy. Lies were things that had to go on and on for years. Why should he worry himself any more?

"I told you I didn't feel well," he said. "My head's aching." He began to act, hands, eyes, bending down, sighing and so on.

"Gone back to his wife?" she said, incredulous.

"Don't nag me, Lila darling. Get me some aspirin. They're in the cupboard over there."

"I'm going to have a drink," she said resentfully, a hint of tears in her voice. "Why should I suffer like this for nothing? I can't believe it. Gone back to his wife. He hates her. He hates her."

"Pour two whiskies," he commanded her. When she hesitated he said it again, louder. He lay down on the bed, feeling faint.

"No. I'll go on with it. I'll show you all what I'm made of. I know you've planned this with Miss Bullen, Prabhu. But I'll show you." She went to the cupboard where there was whisky and poured him one. She handed it to him with two aspirin tablets.

He sat up, pale and sick-looking. "I'm sorry, Lila," he said. "I quite liked him. I don't mind you being in love with a clot like that. What's the harm. I'm not jealous of you about something harmless like that. God, I feel fed up and done in."

"He's dead, isn't he? Something's happened to him. Is he dead?" Her voice was small. It was strange, but he thought of it suddenly as a little, white, terrified voice.

"Yes," he said, "he's dead. How did you know?"

"He always wanted to commit suicide," she replied. "That's all I did for him, not let him, make him sensible. That's all it was about. He used to make me frightened."

"You mean he'd threatened to do it before? Did you know he was mad?"

" He never threatened. He just used to say he wanted to do it. He wasn't mad."

" Why did he want to do it ? Why ? Did he tell you ? "

" I can't remember if he did or not. He just used to talk about it, like you'd talk about reading a book or going for a walk. He wasn't a usual kind of person. I knew he'd do it some day. He did it because he was terrified of it, terrified of dying. That's why."

Prabhu looked up at her and caught her hand. " How do you know that ? " he asked, believing her, knowing her right because of how she had said it, but wanting to argue about it.

" He used to talk for hours about everything and I can't remember what he said. Oh, don't start being angry because I can't remember. But I know he did it because he wanted to see if he could do it. My letter must have hurt him."

" There was no letter," Prabhu growled at her, raising his voice to say it again and again. " No letter. Do you hear me ? No letter."

" Are you sure ? "

" Yes, quite sure. No letter. I'm not having a *thing* made out of this. I've got enough on my mind as it is. I'm sorry about it. He was round the bend."

" Poor Derek. What a waste. What a waste. I learned one thing from him anyway."

" Oh, did you ? And what was that ? "

" That it's wonderful to feel needed, to know you can help somebody. But you can't stop somebody who wants to die, can you ? "

" I don't know," he said. " I've never wanted to die. Give me another whisky." He let her talk about Clegg-Bray while he sipped three whiskies one after the other. He had suspected her of meddling in Clegg-Bray's disordered personality, of interfering stupidly with its violently shaken works, but he could see as she talked that she had kept him alive for a time, been an ear for all the streams of thoughts she could not now remember. It was soothing to him to see how detachedly she viewed the irreparable wreckage of that person, the frantic areas beneath the kindness and gentleness she praised in him. Her practical, almost cold, view of his final act, so often discussed in churches and restaurants, was repugnant to Prabhu, who liked her to act, even though her acting always angered him, because it was never perfect. But he remembered how a woman could ignore enormities and all sorts of horror in a man she had decided to love or support, especially when the failings were placed on the altar of trust, admitted. His jealousy of those shared secrets, those hours of revelations and probably excited mutual discoveries, shared fears and enthusiasms, was something he could file away like an extracted tooth, a souvenir of pain, which he could take out and polish if he wanted it. Once more, as he listened, and watched her beautiful face in profile, he wondered at her curious little wisdoms, so surprising, so unbelievable when he considered her stupidity about dates, history, everyday happenings in the world, names of prime ministers, geographic locations, the meaning of a Stock Exchange, a political occurrence, the general *feel* of the actual world. It was the strange way she said, " How do we know there isn't a God who causes people to meet like that, so as to teach us something, so as to make us help each other ? " Which made him feel again his enormous difference from her. Irritation claimed him again as she developed this thought. She had not cried about Clegg-Bray. She had not fainted. She had not blamed herself. *He* was blaming himself, though. He was thinking already—" If I hadn't said or done so-and-so to-day when I was with him, would he be alive now ? Have I caused his death ? " He was the complicated one, and he knew it. Clegg-Bray was already a great shadow across his love of life and his belief in everyone's right to happiness.

" Lila," he said, one of the day's time-bombs going off in his deeper memory. " Do I have a rich face ? Do I look rich ?

I mean, if I were naked, would you know by my face that I was rich?"

"What, darling?" she said, frowning, annoyed by this sudden tread across her stream of thoughts.

He saw the wall opposite, the cream-coloured wall with the pictures hanging on it, splitting open, showering grey dust into the room as the floor began to heave and come upwards under his feet, the building swaying and emitting grinding, cracking noises. A servant in the garden was screaming. He was screaming, "It's up and down. It's up and down."

Lila cried, "The children. The children," and ran from him as he was about to catch her. It was like being in an aircraft in the monsoon over Burma as the forces of wild storm forced the aircraft up as if to drive the human legs up through the belly into the neck. He remembered the sensation of airborne fear as the wall exploded and the rumbling and thundering from the earth deafened him. He went through the door of the room as tons of masonry poured down behind him.

Chapter Thirty-Three

Hassan had led the prayers that evening at the mosque as he did each week. Thousands were present, the well-off hidden among the poor, no special places for them in the oneness and classlessness of Islamic prayer. Even a king could claim no special place in the ranks of those at prayer. In Islam even the slave could rise to king, even the negro command the pale ones, and Hassan thought of that with numb gladness as he looked out over the thousands when he made his speech after the prayers.

He had described for them his sensations when the people had come to punish him and to salute him earlier in the day (with their clay and their straw ropes and their bent heads, and their slavery). " Be honest," his heart had warned him. " Tell everything."

" I see you all want another way than the one I wanted you to follow," he had told them after the prayers. " Another way from the way the Maharajah wanted it." (His intuition told him that had Prabhu been in that procession of Hari Lal's he would not have spoken thus to the people after prayers. Prabhu's absence had freed him from some of pride's chains.) " You want to try and make the rich give up their loot and power by example, by religion. I wish you well." They could all detect some bitterness in those last words. The tone of those words made them all even more attentive. " I will go on," he added, " in my political struggle to unite men as brothers in the fight for justice, to make trade unions, to increase political awareness. I honour the religious way—

why should I not honour it ? But I will no longer try and make you fight for what is rightfully yours. If the holiest of men support the religious method as they showed to-day they do, then I accept the message I was given to-day "— this was the hardest part for him, not to go on and say—" by the slaves who believe rich men's hearts will be moved by calls to religion." But he resisted it and said, " I accept the message I was given to-day when the people followed another kind of call than mine."

The storm of applause that went up in praise of this courageous and manly admittance almost broke his heart. He had to stand and accept it. It was a worse moment than he had gone through on that balcony when they had all deserted him. He thought of Doctor Kholi who would not come to the telephone to answer him, who was hiding at the palace, a guest of the Maharajah. Self-pity, pride's friend, came to his aid, and he turned away, still in control of himself, though near to burning tears of indignation and defeat. He knew he had done well. He knew he had made his mark in their hearts by that honest declaration of his acceptance of their soft, human, sentimental will, but their fervid applause drove him away from them and sent him back to his office, where he hoped to think out an idea about where he might be going from here on.

He had been thinking about God all day, and about the meanings of the Prophet's wisdoms concerning men and their doings with and to each other. He had never doubted the correctness of that teaching about justice (though he had endured mental struggles about the laws concerning women, who got such justice in Islam but who were caught in fine traps made into customs by men) but he was sure that a time had come in the world when those who had everything must be forced to disgorge their enormous collections of natural riches of every kind, which no legal documents could rightfully make theirs. Oil, coal, water, land, beasts, and men.

They had had men yoked to fear of money's power for too many centuries. His head was aching with his pain when he got to his office. Dokra Singh and Nabha and half a dozen of the other stalwarts were there. He noticed their meek, quiet attitude to him, a kind of condolence for his lost battles, and he was too weary to snap at them for this instinctive expression of their devotion to him. They all looked uncertain, in need of a new goal. They depressed him. He sent them all away once they had given him their reports for the day. He needed to be quite alone, to grieve and to look ahead.

Thoughts about leaving it all and becoming a labourer, a forest worker with an axe, a ploughman, were with him. They were alluring, for he was sick of man to-day, and sicker of man's folly, and at the same time he was impressed by the way the slaves had followed the religious men. His heart was a battlefield in which the Prophet spoke against this and that, and the voice of this and that, called politics, denied everything, and without complete conviction.

Had he a wife now, some intelligent, loving, understanding woman, he could have discussed everything with her. He had always cherished a dream of some woman who would have a fine politically educated brain but who would have lost none of the magnificent femininity and sensuality, so vital, while learning the world. He had only ever been in love with one woman, a landlord's wife half a day's walk north of Kangla. There was—there had been—— He shut that memory out and took out his diary in which he recorded his thoughts about each day's mishappenings.

The building was swaying. He looked up at the black wooden ceiling and saw the circle of the light moving on it, and he heard the creak of wood. It was just on midnight. He got up, remembering he was two floors up in a three-story building which was a mass of cut sandstone and plaster. His soul was well tuned to these uncontrollable convulsions of the world's heart, a heart no one had ever seen, a boiling heart of black metal. The tremendous load of the Himalayas lay on the earth's breast and he believed that this groaning weight was sometimes too much for the spirit inside the earth to bear. Perhaps the colossal range of mountains had been slowly settling for millions of years. Wild, geological fantasies gave quick performances in his brain as the sway came back the other way and the building shuddered. Then it was quiet and still again. He noticed his fast breath, his thudding blood, his suspicious nerves bidding him think twice about sitting down again. But he sat down and went on writing, calming his fears. He was no village peasant now, fretting about the mood of the giant mole burrowing down through the world's heart. He was a leader who had made several mistakes and he wanted to explain them to himself on pieces of paper.

He, too, caught the menace of the deep silence, and it was as if the heat of the night had increased to stifling thickness and discomfort. He tore open the collar of his white silk shirt after loosening his blue tie. He wrote in complete absorption. " The Maharajah has had enough. A good-hearted phoney—I liked him. I even respected some of him. It is Hari Lal and his breast-beating apostles whom I will have to fight from now on. There was always a way out for the people, an escape from my policy which required courage, and Hari Lal found it. But we must work on. We must destroy the landowners and the moneylenders, one by one if necessary——"

On the other side of the town, not even thinking of sleep, Clegg-Bray paced up and down his spacious room at The Moghul. Had he done right? Had he said the right things to that twisted character who had owned Lila for so long, who had held her prisoner within herself all these years? Oh, if only he could speak to her for a few minutes, he would have her back as his again, who understood him and calmed him always.

He had written a long letter to his wife, forty-six pages of it. He always wrote long letters to his women when he had trouble with them, but this was the longest he had ever written. He had read it over and he was thrilled with admiration for the power of it, for the way he had caught exactly the meaning of his estrangement from his last wife ; well, soon to be the last of his four. He had resorted to a threat at the end of his letter which made him ashamed, but it was necessary in order to protect Lila whom his wife had sworn to " flay alive in the Press." He had written that he would give all her letters to a Sunday paper for printing if she brought her case. " Think of the juice and the smacking of lips if that happens," he had written. " You remember the letters you used to write to me when you were lonely in London and I was fighting for what you called ' the American way of life,' in Italy in nineteen forty-three ? I'll do it if you don't promise to leave us alone. You know I love you as much as I ever did. I've never been unfaithful to you. Think it over." Pages and pages of it. His arm was tired. And he could not relax. He walked up and down between one corner of the big room and another. Would he shoot himself now Lila had not come to him ? Did he care for her that much ? Could he not live without her ? He thought not. He thought he might be able to shoot himself. He was not interested in life without her now. He was not quite sure, though.

He had always known what was the matter with him. He missed the army too much. He was lost without it. His disability caused by grenade fragments in his thigh, some pieces of metal as big as pinheads, had changed the direction of his life. He had tried administration—they gave him a job back in London in a chair—but he fought with everybody because he was unhappy and he had resigned after six months of it.

Driving down to Registry Offices every few years in a taxi, taken there in fact by each woman, and driving to lawyers' offices between each marriage, had taken a lot out of him. He had never asked one of the women to marry him. They had all married him with his consent. He had never taken any of it very seriously. After all, there was plenty of him to go round, but he had had enough strife now. His nerves were frayed through. This last wife had got him right down on the floor and made him beg for mercy, and he knew he was not going to get any. The world was out of joint, four times. The gentleness, the beauty, the good sense, the complete perfection of Lila had won him. He had never known a woman like her.

In America together he and Lila could start what people called " a new life." He knew there was no new life, he had had four tries at it, and there was only the old life with an extra woman thrown in each time to fight with. He lived in a sick age, et cetera. His heart was sore with war, woman-war. He badly wanted to die, and to live.

He suddenly stopped and looked up at the ceiling and said, " Eventually You will believe in me fully, as I believed in You in one or two tricky situations with metal flying about. I die. Therefore I have existed." His face darkened, a look of wild rage coming into his eyes. " Useless," he growled as he started to pace again. " Cowardly, hopeless, and yet I go on doing it. The trick-cyclists can't help me. Only a good lawyer and Lila, and about two million miles away from it all can solve me. I'm tired. I can't go on like this. What am I going to do ? Was I mad to come all the way out here ? Probably. Yes, probably I'm mad. I wonder if I'm mad." He took a pistol from his air-bag.

" Twenty-five Stafford Place, God," he whispered inanely as he fell bleeding to the floor of the room, some address which had meant something, some time ago, for some reason or other.

Chapter Thirty-Four

"It's up and down," people screamed to each other in the streets, to the sky, to themselves, as the earth split open and gulped down houses, trees, people. People ran blindly for space, for sanctuary. The river rose like a shining curtain of steel, held still in the moonlight for a second, and then with the roar of its surging joined itself to the deafening noise of the earthquake, the continuous rumble and thunder which drowned cries and screams as the city came apart. The wall of water swept people away as the wave travelled across and through falling buildings to dash itself somewhere.

Hassan found himself down two flights of stairs, blinded with sweat, before he knew he had moved. He knew he was too late. He gripped his head in his arms as the explosion of the walls about him struck his ears and put out the light of his senses. He felt the building take him as it fell and some prayers shot up out of the recesses of his memory and found stuttering tongue before the many knives of pain entered him.

The palace took it well at the start, and it was as if the forces in the earth knew they had to fight, for the building stood and shook and shook again until the small weaknesses deep in the ancient structure were found, weaknesses only an earthquake of unusual power could find. Prabhu saw the wall open across the bedroom and then fly apart, its noise joining all the other noises which added to the pandemonium of screams and yells. Lila was running, screaming the children's names. He went after her, lurching and staggering on the surging floor.

Terrific snapping and grinding sounds preceded a deep groaning and crushing within the huge building, and then he heard the gathering thunder of its surrender. He got Lila out of a door into the corridor. He saw through dust and showering plaster Miss Bullen with the two children running like soundless ghosts into a mist of white dust. The roof took a long time to fall in an avalanche of beams and mortar. It came down in a thunderous cascade. He saw the stars for a moment. He was deaf. He was screaming. He was unable to move now because of the waves of earth movement which buckled his knees and tore his reason away from his flesh. More of the roof was falling. He heard it, like the noise of artillery in a valley, its sound cutting through his deafness and his confused terror. Lila was wrapped about him, stripped of sense, trying to protect him.

In the living-room Prem turned over on the couch and lay where he was, face down, holding a case of jazz records over his head, and saying, "I knew some bloody thing would happen to me. I knew it." He had a couple of pints of whisky inside him, anyway, and he shut himself up like a clam as he heard the roof coming down. "I knew it. I knew it. I knew it," he recited as he waited to be crushed.

Hari Lal went through the door on to the veranda like an arrow, realised what he was doing, and then rushed back for Prem. One of the royal family must live—he could not think that Prabhu would escape in the catastrophe of the deafening collapse he had seen occurring from the side of his eye in his flight. Hari Lal still had a hand of cards in his clenched fist. He had been winning. The old woman had not spoken when the floor lifted and opened, spraying polished wooden blocks all over the bright room. She had gone straight for the children's room. The fearful and continuous noise robbed the mind of its last feeble muscles. Hari Lal seized Prem. He uttered implorations in Jashimpuri while the building swayed and struggled against the titanic unrest being forced into it from the rolling, increasing upward push from the earth's heart.

In the city buildings were falling, piling up on each other. People just ran about screaming for their children, or to God, or stood paralysed some distance off, safe, wondering what they were doing there while they watched the buildings swaying, opening, falling in the bright light of the moon towards which enormous clouds and veils of dust were rising. A red glare flickered and pulsed among the buildings as flames took hold of timber. In this upheaval, with its overpowering noise, with its assault upon the quailing, shrinking mind, nothing could be done except to try and exist, and to grapple with wonder and elemental fear.

Soon the darkness of dust clouds covered it all, and the fires sought to reach above the dust. They pulsated like glowing red blossoms in the midst of the dust-fog.

As the crumbled palace hid itself in its own dust, Miss Bullen told the two trembling boys to kneel down on the swaying lawn and pray for their parents' safety. "And don't move from there," she said with unusual, shrill sternness. She was quaking as the earth quaked under her. The two boys in their pyjamas knelt down and did what they were told, what they found they wanted to do. They said whatever came first in the way of prayer, a supplication, a begging, the first prayers they had ever said to the unknown grown-up mystery called God. They were praying to fear. Miss Bullen had run back into the shifting mountain of wreckage in which she had been playing cards a few minutes before.

The police, as usual, and after the usual delay, were efficient, Nasrullah Beg directing operations from a small hut at the end of The Moghul Hotel gardens. Flames licked at the drifting dust-clouds about the mounds of rubble. In an hour's time Nasrullah Beg had a telephone set up by signal troops sent under Brigadier Kapra Singh's orders. The Party organisation joined the police, two squads toiling to find Hassan in the ruins of the Party house. As never before—there had not been an earthquake within the memory of anyone under seventy—the Jashimpuris slowly became one under the ruthless goodwill of Nasrullah Beg. Kapra Singh had survived the cataclysm in blue pyjamas and long black cigarette-holder. He borrowed a battle dress, with medals on it, from one of his majors, and organised soup kitchens. He broke open the rice-godowns, issuing chits to the wailing owners who were driving about in big cars looking for relatives. It seemed certain that hundreds were dead. The town and the country surrounding it looked as if it had been carpet-bombed.

Just after eight o'clock a fighter of the Indian Air Force flew over at about a thousand feet. About midday three Dakotas came and dropped medical supplies. At four, doctors with a team of Indian army helpers parachuted down across the river.

A squad digging at the palace found Lila alive and Prabhu dead. Prem lay under hundreds of tons of wreckage. Hari Lal, his right arm broken and his face masked with blood from a deep head wound, had failed to rescue Prem but had managed to drag Doctor Kholi out. The doctor joined the army team in the city. Miss Bullen, the two boys and the three converts moved into Hari Lal's house in the town. From there the old woman began to organise a dressing station and a kitchen. Enormous cauldrons, once used by the forced labour units on the frontier, were brought out of storage, and in these the old woman cooked rice for the shaken survivors who came in dumb, shivering lines.

Hassan appeared out of a sewer just before dusk. He was exhausted, having levered his way through rubble with an iron bar he had found in the ruins of a wall. A cheering crowd carried him to Miss Bullen's emergency kitchen, where she fed him and then cleaned his wounds. Within an hour of eating the *dhal bat*, heavily chillied lentils on rice, he was giving orders to Kapra Singh, who took them quietly. Hassan commandeered an army jeep and toured the broken town. He made his headquarters at Hari Lal's house, after some sentimental and emotional words between them. Hari Lal agreed with him that in a time like this it hardly mattered any more about who was boss, but Hari Lal was boss. He took an office in the small secretariat building and drafted all Party militia troops into the State forces under Kapra Singh. He informed Hassan of this when it was done, and Hassan took it well. Hassan wept over Prabhu's death when the news came to him. He was heard to say that although he had never liked the Maharajah, he had loved certain things about him, particularly his sincerity about the plight of the Jashimpur people. Not even the cynics in the town had anything clever to say when that was passed to them. Everyone was too innocently thankful to be alive. Narendra Nath, who was the eldest of the two boys by ten minutes, lit Prabhu's funeral pyre. Miss Bullen held their hands after the ceremony and watched the oily flames devour the piled wood on which Prabhu lay. All over the burning ghats beyond the river the funeral pyres smoked. The Muslim dead in their thin shrouds were borne in lines to the cemetery near Hussein Beg's Leap, the precipice where the famous slave had jumped with his tired master so long ago. Grief lay on everybody, like part of the smoke and dust masks they wore. Hassan drove the emergency squads in their rescue digging, and people were glad to slave late into the night. They slaved, and ate rice at Miss Bullen's kitchen from the rows of cauldrons, and then slept in heaps all over the place. A Red Cross unit arrived from India, bringing the reporters and the photographers. Within three days Hassan had control of Jashimpur, and Hari Lal had control of Hassan. The secretariat worked like a clock under Hari Lal's direction. He forced the landowners to offer large donations of money to the Disaster Fund, and taught them to vie with one another over who shamed who in the amount they gave.

Doctor Kholi's wife arrived four days after the earthquake, bringing with her her astrologer, her *ved*, a practitioner in ancient Indian medicine, a monkey which could deal cards and could print its name when a bell was rung, and a library of five hundred books on *yoga* and tantric religion. She was a tall, beautiful, blonde Scandinavian-American, with a large bust and a small waist, and two great cold green eyes, wearing a black sari and a load of golden bangles on each white wrist. She carried her own foods, raisins, nuts, apples, in a large string-bag swinging on her arm.

She moved in with Miss Bullen, put on coarse *khaddar* cotton trousers and tunic, and worked as a cook. She would not approach Doctor Kholi, who was working in the ruins of the town. He must come to her, she told Miss Bullen. The astrologer, one Ganga Lal, set up a gramophone in the emergency kitchen and played records of Saigal all day. In this nightmarish atmosphere Miss Bullen knew at last that working for people during a time of disaster, working until hardly able to crawl to a bed, was the greatest drug for doubt and quarrel with God. She did not even quarrel with Pryamvidda, Kholi's wife, when the strange woman blessed the rice each morning and intoned a *mantra* over it.

" You have the makings of a great saint," Pryamvidda told her one night in the middle of frantic rice serving. " Your aura is yellow and blue. You radiate willpower."

" I'm so glad, dear," Miss Bullen replied grimly. " There are times when one needs to know things like that."

Late one night when a great crowd had been fed, and Miss Bullen was alone and thinking of Lila silent in her room upstairs, Hari Lal and Hassan visited her and asked for cardamom tea. She handed them a samovar and cups. They sat with her and chatted, these two enemies who had to value each other now in disaster.

In a silence they heard the voice of an old man singing in lament outside the window where sleepers were huddled

2A

under a tarpaulin. They all listened together to that ancient voice coming out of prayer and sorrow. Miss Bullen could not catch the slurred words which were bent to the craft of the music and wound like sighs into the microtonic skills of the singer. Hari Lal, solemn, but smiling in apology for himself, spoke the words as they came, Miss Bullen drinking in their pious, innocent message.

" I bow down before you, Mother, you who are cleansed by the great rivers, by the rains, and lapped by the oceans. The crops and fruits come up out of your breast in the love of the waters and the sun. Millions nourished on your breast kneel and give thanks to the everlasting God in gratitude, and to you, Mother. Ten-handed mighty Mother, raise your weapons to shelter your children. Is it because we have forgotten our devotion to you that you have punished us, oh Mother ? "

" Amen," said Miss Bullen, her tired eyes fond as she looked at the two young men.

" Ah women ! Ah Mother ! " said Hari Lal, smiling, offering his cup to her again. They all laughed tiredly, each one of them affected by the gravity of the prayer to India, sung among the ruins beyond the window by a poor man.

Chapter Thirty-Five

The winter came in with dry, powdery snowfalls, thin, piercing winds tearing the fine white skin off the Himalayas on the journey from Central Asia. The first white hush of the winter covered some of the earthquake wounds. In the still valleys axes rang on the iron-sounding wood of the forests, and the river was like a sheet of black steel, snowflakes hissing in it. The woodmen came down from the mountains like trudging oxen under their loads of firewood, the pad of their straw sandals soundless on the thick snow.

They exchanged news with the townsmen about the new courts set up in the countryside and in Jashimpur City, copied it was said from a plan talked about in Kashmir. The courts were open to all, and often were held on a piece of village green. The moneylenders were called and asked to give an open declaraton of what was owed them, and by whom, and for how long, and at what interest. They were called popularly " Hassan's Courts," though everyone knew that the ubiquitous, all-seeing, all-hearing, *chalak* personality of Hari Lal had given subtle and powerful life to Hassan's raw plan. Poor men were free to creep uncertainly forward and face the money-lender and then give details about which ancestor had borrowed how much and at what interest, and what had been sold, or not enjoyed ever since, so that the interest should be paid. As peasant and townsmen agreed, it was an amazing thing to see a moneylender bow his head in shame before the silent crowds as the tale of his profits was enfolded. It was curious too to hear the clapping for that rare person, the soft-hearted moneylender who had not squeezed the victims too desperately. Hundreds of creditors and debtors were being sent aside by the judges after all had been heard, so that they could come to an agreement, a washing of the stain, a finish to enchainment, for once the case was heard moneylender and victim had to come to final solution so that the public could hear it. Although Hassan's plan to take the lands from the landlords was not spoken of now, at least he had tamed the moneylenders. There was much quotation of an old prophecy which had told how God would show His anger about Jashimpur one day and tumble buildings and kill people as a sign of disgust with rich and poor alike. " The rich because they despise us, and we, the poor, because we deserve it," a story-teller put it, and an angry young man who had lost all his family in the earthquake had pulled the old man's beard and added, " And the story-tellers because they never have anything new to say."

Hundreds of men were engaged on public works. Every village must have a school before another year had passed, Hassan had ordered, and Hari Lal had confirmed. It did not matter what the building was made of, or who paid for it, or who built it, but small boys and girls must be in some kind of a school before the next year's winter began. Old men in far villages were learning to write and to read. One old man had been brought into Jashimpur town to show how he, who had never held a pen, could now write on a piece of blackboard with a quill dipped in white paste, " I, Ahmed Salah of Nanpur, am sixty-eight years old and am well." Crowds followed him, even in the snow, to see one more exhibition of the old man's childish happiness in his discovery of who he was, for as he told the people, " Now I know who I am."

The country was in a fever of self-expression and argumentative frenzy about three times seven, and with the magic of Persian and Devanagri script.

The great procession which had followed the Maharajah's body to the burning ghat as the first chill winds had swept over the smoking city, had come back to the town in a grieving mood and had held a public meeting. Hassan had addressed it, and Hari Lal had confirmed all he had said to the crowds. In death Prabhu had become the symbol of liberation, a man who had had them all in his heart. Hassan spoke his remorse for having kept the Maharajah out of the Party. "I did it for my bitterness," he said. "I did it for my hatred of past oppressions, and I am sorry for it. I am sorry for meaning so well so meanly." All sucked the juices of that phrase in their mouths over the stoves that night as the first snow began to fall. To be sorry for meaning so well so meanly. "It is worth being wrong to have the pleasure of saying that," the older story-tellers agreed.

Blizzards came down in screaming clouds of snow, the "ghost winds" of the old poets, and the stoves were stoked until they glowed cherry red.

Doctor Kholi had been given an empty palace to make into a hospital. The place had not been lived in for fifty years. It was as solid as a prison, and volunteer groups of young men toiled on the alterations to its structure. The joke of Kholi's mystical white wife had taken its place in the ever-gathering folklore of the bazaar and the village. Men were pleased at the way she brought in ancient methods of diagnosis for illness, and everyone laughed at Doctor Kholi's furies with his wife's magic. People who were not sick went to the new hospital to be entertained and to enjoy the curiosity of the marriage which had shown the celibate doctor to be truly one of themselves, an acrobat of the uncertain and tricky heart, an unwilling and unhappy liar. As people said, "Your right hand is stealing your own money while you preach against theft." The doctor, though, was not happy with his wife and spent a lot of his time cursing ancient superstitions to which she was giving fresh life in a country cursed with the past. How patient was his calm, beautiful wife with her green eyes piercing through people's hearts. It was said, and all agreed, that she would win Kholi.

Miss Bullen, with Lila and the three converts reached Kangla a week before the first snowfall. She was expected. Lila, who had not spoken a word since the day of the earthquake, had a nurse with her, a young Indian woman from Delhi. It was said that Lila's mind had gone, but Miss Bullen knew better than that and forecast a recovery. God was good. She had her own doubts, though, and she cried a good deal at night after a day with the stunned, pale Lila, who never spoke, but who understood everything that was going on around her and had no interest in it. The twins had gone to their school near Delhi, which was the best thing that could have happened just then.

Before they left the city Hassan had called on Miss Bullen and had embraced her and called her " Mother," and had said, " Why must you go, Mother, when I need you here in the city ? If you want to do good, do it here. You've broken yourself against Kangla, like I broke myself on the Maharajah." He had become upset and tearful. He was like everyone else after the earthquake, quivering inside and bruised all over the mind, and he grieved over Prabhu, his friend and enemy. It was hard for the old woman to speak to him, for she could not forgive him several things and she lectured him about his ruthlessness, and he listened and even agreed. He won her over with his humility. He consoled her for Prem's death, telling her that it was better to be killed by an earthquake than by a bottle of whisky in the end.

Miss Bullen and Lila left a ruined city behind them, the silent people working like ants on the heaps of rubble. She felt no regret in leaving it. She wanted to withdraw finally into herself, to grieve at Kangla and to sieve out her heart again. A long course of prayer and fasting was planned while the trucks in which she and Lila travelled crawled up the mountains towards Kangla.

The whole village was out to meet them, and the Garris, a mountain tribe, had come down to put on a dance and a singing festival for her. Her heart was sinking as the truck stopped in the middle of the cheering people. She regretted having come back here, for it was home, better cherished in exile, but the thing was done now and the people claimed her through the welcoming speeches of the headmen and elders. There they all were, in a line, dressed in their best, the men who had defeated her for forty years, the men who loved her for what she was, not for what she had promised them they could become if they only accepted The Word. She could not love them, even though they loved her, and this was further proof to her of her own smallness of heart. But she had to face it. She could not deny what was true. She sniffled a little, though, throughout the generosity and warmth of the welcoming speeches. The heart was not to be understood, even if lived with carefully for a lifetime. The mind was quite another thing, something she had never feared. Her hardness was her own, never to be swallowed up in India's warm fatalistic forgiveness.

Lila sat like a dead queen throughout the welcome spoken by the elders, her large eyes open, looking past everything, a shut person, someone at melancholy anchor on black, uncharted waters.

The Garris had set up their long drums in rows on the village *maidan*, which each year they had flattened into yellow hardness under their dancing feet. They were one of the last free peoples left in the whole world, a tribe who had come to almost perfect compromise with man's two demons, the need to wander, and the need to have a settlement all their own to sigh for and to die on. They hardly ever used money, they never used matches—each man carrying steel and flint in his girdle, and they traded horses, repaired utensils, grazed sheep,

exchanged a few spices for a little tea and salt. They wandered
freely through the mountain ranges. They had lost none of
the artless innocence of the tribal world, but they could drive
a hard bargain with resourceful cunning in hard times. They
looked like Europeans, fresh of skin and ruddy cheeked,
light-eyed often enough, and like other tribes in the Himalayas, mistakenly thought that Alexander the Great, *Sikander*,
had fathered their ancestors, and were proud and happy in
the mistake. They gave homage to rivers and trees, sun and
moon, and even had a Celtic god called Donn. A few books
had been written about them, frail fingers tugging at far mists
which covered ancient origins.

Miss Bullen had never got herself to approve of them,
seeing in their artlessness the father of their shiftlessness, and
she was repulsed by their casual regard for death, and for the
journey to it. The excited greetings they gave her, though,
got through to her heart and caused her to feel that indecision
between compassion and gratitude for shown love, which
might be love itself. She could not possibly pretend that she
did not want them gathered in, civilised, tamed by taxes and
laws, but when they danced before her and Lila she knew a
twinge of regret for the harness that was going to come to
them sooner than later. The slowly rising river of Western
civilisation had taken centuries to seep outwards from the
burst banks, and the Garris were dancing in a village which
Hassan had promised, as his own village home, would have
a secondary school and an electric light plant within a year.
This might be the last time the Garris were allowed to dance
to their thudding drums in the centre of Hassan's village,
which Miss Bullen had dragged up out of a dark sleep of
decay. As the drums throbbed she sniffed the air, and sniffed
it again, and could not detect that shaming, angering smell of
fecklessly cast ordure. My God, was it possible that they had
taken their grudging hands to the *kurpas*, the little trowels
she had handed round so often, and had begun the war on

dirt, the struggle to learn revulsion for some of the body's grosser savageries? Was it possible? She called the headman and asked him. He was vain enough, and humble enough, to claim the honour of having begun punishment for carelessness with "that habit we have," and to praise her for her patient lessons.

"When you had gone," he said, "we had time for shame." And there was no ironic glitter in that large, black Jashimpuri eye. She had been pleased with the way he had come with an old cushion, a gold coin on it, as a gesture of *nazar* (dead Prabhu's honour, really) to the Maharani, silent, gracious Lila, and Lila had touched it following Miss Bullen's clever hidden whisper to her.

A Garri tribesman in grey homespun woollen jerkin and tight jodhpur trousers of the same coarse wool, and bright, jaunty turban, stood in front of each drum and beat it with clever hands, spun, twitched, whirled between tattoos, and jerked his head with bared white teeth glistening, all of them beginning to forget where they were as the terrific, surging rhythms took hold of their surrendered minds. Daggers shone in their girdles, daggers hundreds of years old, handed down from father to son, blades which had drunk a fill in happier, wilder times. They beat their hands on the daggers and sang love songs to them, praising them and asking them forgiveness for their long rest during the new century of the forbidding government orders.

The hammering drums, with their insistent call to the sealed groves in the heart, seemed to get through Lila's silence and her cheeks grew warm. The happiness of the Garris could not be watched and not felt, not enjoyed, not awaken love for men, and for the women who were putting on burnished pans of curry under striped shelters of cloths, the nomadic *shamianas* of the tribesmen. Their women were lovely, overdressed in bright colours, jealous, watchful, shrewish with each other about how to cook and when to mix and where to serve food.

Sitting close beside Lila, Miss Bullen heard with alarm the sound of a surge of breath in Lila's throat, that unmistakable signal that the heart is opening to release its struggling guest, bitter sorrow, or even a deeper mystery, the phantom of the lost freedom, the buried pagan joy of the ancient world of which these Garris were doomed relics. In the museum of themselves they went mad with happiness before their drums, spinning and yelling while the rhythm increased its pace and throb.

There was a young man who looked like Prabhu and Lila was staring at him, a Prabhu on whom the shadow of the cement wall and the sheet of statistics had never fallen, some Prabhu who had never heard of Marx, Ford, and the long-distance patrols of the soul-engineers. But it was not about him that Lila cried. It was because she felt love for the first time for people, and while she knew it was emotion driven at flood pace by the drummers, she let it take her over, feeling some overpowering pride in the splendour of the tribesmen, and aching with a nostalgia for their joy in themselves. Miss Bullen was patting her hand and whispering, "Would you like to go, dear? Is it upsetting you?" Lila shook her head faintly so that the tears would not fall from her eyes. She wanted to speak, but knew that what she had to say was unspeakable. Had she opened her mouth all that would have come out would have been a wild screaming, and a moment after that she would have rushed out among the Garris and danced with them, danced until she died of exhaustion. Had Prabhu been there, and had she expressed such a thought, he would have said, "How corny can you get, Lila darling?" But nothing was so corny as life itself, and she had never been able to tell him that. Now he was dead she knew everything she had wanted to say to him, and all the words, all the explanations, lay about her heart, hurting like sharp stones.

She would never forgive him for dying, and never forgive herself for living. The tenderness and care of the old woman was almost too much for her.

" Try and pray. Try and forgive God, my dear," Miss Bullen had said earlier in the week. The words echoed in the sullen cavities of her torn-up spirit. How fine to have God to set up as a wall to wail against. She wanted to wail. She wanted to kneel down and wail for ever, but she did not know whether she would wail for herself, or for everybody alive, and for everybody who was going to be born and to suffer, and to be unable to explain anything to anybody.

Like a bombardment which goes on too long and to which the shaken become accustomed, the drums broke themselves on her and the emotional eruption thinned out into a weariness. It depressed her that the ecstasy did not last in her, and that the joy was gone along with the bayonet of pain which had transfixed her for a time.

Men brought shining brass bowls of curry and set them down on two silver *tals*, huge silver trays heaped with rice and surrounded by tiny pots containing varied arrows of pleasure to fire into the palate, spices of every kind. Lila ate hungrily and neatly, all the women watching her slyly and admiringly. They had impressed on the films of their minds, her breasts, her waist, her eyes, her modern cut hair, her dignity. They mourned for her dead man, the young king who had been crushed in his palace by the madness of the giant mole in the earth.

When the long festival with the jugglers, the acrobats, the comedians and the whirling swordsmen, had ended in trickles of clapping and shouts for more, Miss Bullen and Lila withdrew to the courtyard surrounding her old house.

The old woman came to a standstill before the door and stared up at a large picture of Gandhi beside a larger picture of Jesus holding his impaled sacred heart (a Papist bauble), and then shifted her outraged eyes to another picture beside that of Christ, a large oleograph portrait of Subhas Chandra Bhose, who had loved Gandhiji, admired Christ, and detested British rule, even dying in a Japanese bomber to prove it. His big bland face in its spectacles seemed to challenge her.

" My God ! " Miss Bullen exclaimed in a shocked breath.

Once upon a time she had taken such things as carefully studied insults, and sometimes they were, Jashimpuri jests meant to upset smugness or self-righteousness after a lecture on morals or evil. But she knew that the putting of Christ beside Gandhiji was to please her, was to show their oneness with her about the innocence and strength of all holiness. And she knew that Subhas Chandra Bhose was a hero, one who might not really be dead, one who might have gone into some strange *samadhi*, some yogic sleep, and who might return with his tireless strength to help his beloved mother, his broken India. Gandhi had not hated his adversaries, had not wanted to raise an army to smite them, and had never wearied of conferences and talk and correspondence with them, but had exhausted those who had loved all three, and had won. He had talked them all on to the ship, prayed for them, praised them, called them " My Dear Friend " and had tipped up the Viceroy's thrones with his rude staff. He had been mighty, and unhateable, almost lovable, thought Miss Bullen, her nostrils quivering as she stared from Gandhiji to her Master, Christ, in a Papist role, the Man who was to baffle all men, and confuse His own race, for all time. Love for Him drowned her rage with Bhose in his big horn-rimmed spectacles and Rangoon-made uniform, until she met again that quiet gaze of the bespectacled ex-Mayor of Calcutta, the one who had endured great risks so as to raise an army against her beloved empire, Netaji, whose portrait was appearing all over India in little badges. No, she could not take Bhose, who had dared to call openly for revolt and had raised an army in Burma to conquer British India. Giving in to her ineradicable patriotic pride, she went forward to take Bhose's picture down, and Lila spoke for the first time since the earthquake.

" Leave it where it is, Bella," she said. " If I have to fight whisky and try and love God, you must try and let others love what you don't love. Love even your enemies. They had to love *your* people."

Gladness and surprise in hearing that soft voice again, even in reproof, took away from Miss Bullen's smoking anger with the Bengali who had not behaved like the Babu he looked to be.

" Lila, my child," she said, clasping Lila in her arms, one of her waves of emotion overcoming her. " You've spoken at last. I thought you'd never say anything to me again."

It took a few moments for those curious words, " *your* people " to make their small bruise on Miss Bullen's heart. It was as if Lila had thrown up a sudden wall between them, Lila who had never spoken of *your* people or *my* people. Fearfully, the old woman apologised, adding, " You can't expect me to like Bhose, dear. I can't. But I'll leave him there if you want him."

It was a great surrender of one of those small points for which men slay each other by the million every so often, the bloody manure of patriotism which is called fanatical nationalism in the opponent. Miss Bullen's ancestral hatred of fearless rebels who could not be bought or knighted was much greater than that known to some other people, and she recognised it as she swallowed and looked up at Bhose and clutched Lila's warm arm.

" Will you say a prayer with me in my room, Lila ? Just one. A prayer for understanding and guidance. Just one. So that we can help each other and get over everything." Miss Bullen kept her eyes on Christ, hoping Lila would reply and would not withdraw again into that terrible silence.

"Not now. I hate God's ways of doing things just now, Bella. But I'll sit there while you pray." Lila's eyes were shadowed over again with her new companion, dull, unearned pain, as yet unvalued, unsieved for its horrific gold. She knew the old woman was lucky to have God to wail to, to trust, to accept punishment from with the same willingness as she accepted the gift of breathing. But beautiful people suffered more than others, she remembered an old servant telling her father years ago. They got everything more easily. They loved themselves more willingly, were fatal more quickly to others. They ran before they walked. She had thought about it the other day in front of a mirror, watching herself weep, tears like pale distilled blood coming up out of her heart.

She sat on the chair in the corner of the scrubbed room with its flashing unpainted timber walls, its cosy imprint of a careful and methodical personality slightly hostile to her, a man on a horse waving a sword in the only picture in the room, the smasher of ancient Papist Ireland. She could read the title of the picture with her sharp eyes, *King William of Orange, of Glorious Memory*. A sort of Bhose for some people in the world, probably. Everyone had their Bhose. Aching, sodden right through with grief, Lila was sorry she had spoken. Locked in her silence she had enjoyed the numbness of acceptance, savoured with cold pleasure the assessment of all the shattering blows dealt her for some reason or other by Miss Bullen's terrible and magnificent God. Having spoken she was involved again, and got down from her crag and entered the area of all those traps, people and their visions of themselves, and their readiness to involve others in their dilemma, in their enchantment with their doings and their plans.

To-morrow she was starting work with Miss Bullen in teaching the village girls to sew, and to darn, and to cook, and to scrub, and to feed babies properly. She had offered to do it as soon as Prabhu had disappeared from the earth in that bed of Hindu fire. And she had not spoken from that moment to this. Depressed by the thought of the work to come, she watched the old woman praying in silence, the withered, strong hands clasped, the eyes closed, and she felt no embarrassment in watching this most intimate and sorrowful act of innocence. She did not know why she loved the old woman. She knew why she resented her, but it was a small thing lost inside the love she felt.

She pulled down a shutter over the earthquake zone in her memory—it was an actual place, like a quaking battlefield of noise of screaming, and when that was done she spoke again. The old woman was rising from her knees.

" Bella," she said. " Did God invent race, and coloured skins, and divisions between people, and hate, or did man ? What are they for ? "

" If we couldn't hate we could never know sorrow, dear," Miss Bullen said after considering it, and after lighting a cigarette, an open vice with her now. " And if we didn't know sorrow, how could we grow up ? How could we die ? How could we deserve pity ? "

" Is that your own, Bella ? Did you think that out for yourself ? "

" It took me forty years to learn that, my dear, and a few more to understand it. And I may be right after all. Shall I make you some *misi ki roti* for supper ? " Lila was fond of this country dish.

" I hate God, Bella." Lila said it with quiet but heartfelt bitterness. It was a measure of how far their friendship had travelled that the old woman was not shocked. She accepted Lila's almost childish savagery by now.

" That's a start, my dear," she said, ringing the little bronze bell for a servant. " That's better than indifference. I'm not too fond of Him myself at times."

After that it grew dark and they went to the kitchen to make *misi ki roti* on the big clay *chula*, which was Kangla's form of stove. It began to snow, the flakes pouring and drifting down silently outside the black, shining window of the warm kitchen. The two women worked in silence, comfortable silence, one of them old and beginning to die, and the other dead, for a while.